THE DEVIL'S PRAYER

LUKE GRACIAS

The Devil's Prayer by Luke Gracias
First Published by Australian eBook Publisher
© Luke Gracias

1st Edition 2016, pbk.

Cover design, editing and typesetting: Sharnai James-McGovern, Australian eBook Publisher
Front cover photograph: "Semana Santa Zamora 2014", Manuel Ballesteros.
Back cover photograph: "The empty streets of Zamora", Luke Gracias
Illustrations: Jeff Phillips

Publishing Facilitation: AuthorsUpFront

The Write Place
A Publishing Initiative by Crossword Bookstores Ltd.
Umang Tower, 2nd Floor, Mindspace, Off Link Road,
Malad West, Mumbai 400064, India.

Web: www.TheWritePlace.in
Facebook: TheWritePlace.in
Twitter: @WritePlacePub
Instagram: @WritePlacePub

The Devil's Prayer

CONTENTS

PROLOGUE

According to a thirteenth century legend, a young Benedictine monk known as Herman the Recluse, from the Podlažice monastery in today's Czech Republic, was sentenced to be walled-up alive for breaking his monastic vows.

In an attempt to escape this slow death, he promised to create, in a single night, a book filled with all human knowledge that would glorify the monastery forever. The monks agreed to let him try, knowing that the task would be impossible.

As the deadline loomed, Herman realised he would never finish the task alone. According to the legend, he made a special prayer to the fallen angel Lucifer, asking him to finish the book in exchange for his soul. Lucifer—the Devil—agreed, and completed the *Codex Gigas* that very night. Herman then added the Devil's picture in the book out of gratitude for his aid.

This book soon became known as the Devil's Bible.

In the winter of 1222, the Benedictine monks of Podlažice wrote to Pope Honorius III for a donation to save their precious monastery. It wasn't until the August of 1223, that their prayers were answered in person, by the Papal Legate himself, Arnaud Amalric.

It soon became apparent that Amalric would only help

the Podlažice monks if he could claim the *Codex Gigas* or Devil's Bible held by the monastery for his own.

The monks refused to sell the book. Amalric then offered to lend the Benedictines a thousand crowns to help pay off their debts, but only if he could hold the Devil's Bible as collateral.

The monks reluctantly agreed and offered Amalric the key to the chest containing the book, a form of security for the loan until it was repaid.

The chest containing the monks' beloved script was transferred to the Cistercian monastery in Sedlec, neutral territory, close to their own monastery in Podlažice.

Over seventy years passed before the Benedictines managed to reclaim the chest from Sedlec. However, the key was nowhere to be found. When they finally pried open the box, they found the Bible inside, its ornate metal and leather cover slightly worn with age. When the book was opened, they discovered twelve pages were missing.

PART ONE:
UNFINISHED BUSINESS

CHAPTER 1

"ELI, ELI, LAMA SABACHTHANI"

17TH APRIL 2014

Perched high on a steep granite outcrop, outside the small town of Granja de Moreruela, some thirty-five kilometres north of Zamora, Spain, lay the ancient Convent of Santa Teresa. Isolated and inaccessible, its steep incline was covered with a dense forest. The convent was not built as a residence, and consequently had no kitchen, nor access to water. It had no occupants at its time of completion. With no trade routes nearby, it was not built to shelter weary traders or travellers.

According to folklore, the granite outcrop, on which the convent stands, is cored through the centre by a bottomless pit. From this pit once emerged a creature that was half-man and half-beast—a centaur. It was said that black-winged creatures would fly around the centaur as it roamed the surrounding forest.

The convent chapel was built of solid rock over the top of the hole, not as a place of worship, but to seal the bottomless pit, which was thought to be the 'Gateway to Hell'.

Enormous granite steps have been hewn into the hill, leading through crumbling stone porticos to the chapel at its peak. Every so often, beside the sharply inclining steps, is a small platform, carved with a humble candlelit grotto.

There are fourteen platforms in all, for each of the fourteen Stations of the Cross. The dense forest shrouds a secret ritual that has taken place every year during the *Semana Santa* (Easter Week) since the thirteenth century.

The Brotherhood, dressed in black robes with black pointed hats, held torches aloft and dragged cat-o'-nine-tail whips behind them as they trudged up the steep incline. The *Semana Santa* procession was led by a penitent dragging a large wooden cross; he was flanked either side by two others holding gold crosiers.

Drummers accompanying the parade played an eight beat. *Tut-tup, tut-tup, tut tut-tup BOOM.* The kettledrum was followed by the loud whip crack of penitents indulging in the ancient ritual of self-flagellation. The hypnotic drumbeat repeated itself as others with chained and shackled feet moved in unison up the hill.

The Maundy Thursday full moon silhouetted the high walls and chapel of the convent above the tree line. Hidden within its dark walls, Sister Benedictine kneeled on the carved rock floor of her room. Her habit was bunched around her waist and revealed a naked back, so crisscrossed in welts it was almost devoid of skin.

Mesmerised by the repetitious drumbeats drifting in through her tiny window, she whirled the cat-o'-nine-tails above her head and lashed her back, timing each strike in sync with the rhythmic whip cracks of the Brotherhood. Women's screams travelled down the corridor to her room from deep within the bowels of the convent, but Sister Benedictine remained silent, save the deep breath she took each time her whip carved out more flesh from her back.

Her stone-walled room was threadbare except for a simple bed, desk and chair. Atop the desk lay a well-thumbed Bible. The walls were bare, save for a nondescript wooden cross and a solitary line of graffiti chalked in coal that read, "*Eli, Eli, lama sabachthani?*"—Christ's words in his last hour, as he hung from the cross—*My God, My God, why hast thou forsaken me?*

Over the relentless drumming, distant trumpets blared the funeral march, and heralded the start of the next procession. Sister Benedictine lowered her whip and stood. She lifted the black nun's habit to cover her back and put her coif over her head. She tightened the white cord around her waist and looked out the hewn rock window down the sheer walls of the convent.

The torchlights carried by the black-clothed monks snaked up the hill and coiled into a circle at the candlelit grotto of the Eleventh Station of the Cross.

A male voice boomed in Spanish, "*La Undécima Estación: Jesús es clavado en la cruz.*"—'The Eleventh Station: Jesus is nailed to the Cross.'

The drumbeat was replaced by sounds of nails being hammered into wood and muffled cries. More trumpets blared, drowning out the sounds of the hammers and cries. At the base of the hill, a sea of torches held by monks dressed in red habits followed the trumpeters on their journey to the First Station of the Cross.

Sister Benedictine scurried tentatively out of her room and into a long corridor lined with arched doorways. The dancing firelight of the sconces painted long shadows on the granite walls and on the sister as she slithered past. The sound of women's screams grew louder as she reached an opening to a small spiral stone staircase. Ignoring the cries, she continued on. The passage rose upwards with a few rough steps and led to a heavy wooden door.

Sister Benedictine heaved the door open and entered the modest convent chapel.

The room was empty, dimly lit by two sconces and a candle chandelier. Painted on the walls of the ancient chapel were murals, now old and faded, depicting a vile monster, witches, and black bat-winged creatures with contorted human faces.

Adeptly, the sister moved behind the altar and reached a pale hand below to extract an old kerosene lamp and a box of matches. She propped herself up with the lamp on a ledge by one of the tall windows adjacent to the mural of the archangel Michael pinning the fallen angel Lucifer. Her fingers worked quickly to release the latch. The window swung open to reveal a cliff on the opposite side of the hill, away from the noisy procession. Shielded by the thick walls, the sounds of the trumpets and the procession were barely audible.

A cold breeze swept across the sister's face as she looked out at the land, which fell away steeply before it was covered by the dense moonlit forest below. In the distance she saw the lights of the city Zamora, obscured from sight, but recognisable by the hazy glow in the outlying sky.

Sister Benedictine gingerly climbed out of the window, wincing as the frame brushed against her raw back, and perched precariously on a thin rock ledge below. She gripped the lamp and matches tightly as she pulled the chapel window shut behind her. Moving with care, she lowered herself down the steep incline into the encompassing cloak of the forest. She rushed down the slope through the trees to the base of the hill till she arrived at a clearing. There she saw the ruins of the old Moreruela Cistercian Abbey.

Lit only by the moonlight, she skirted the edges of the ruin, along the broken-down passageways, through the hall of the monks, and past tourist signs leading to the abbot's residence. She hurriedly entered a large dilapidated room, the hem of her habit picking up dirt along the way. Among the carvings on the walls was a circular depiction of the Devil, lying sideways, head cocked by his right hand. From the Devil's mouth, a small fountain of water flowed into a concealed drain below. With her left hand, she blocked the current of water. Then, with her right, she gripped one of the Devil's horns and swiftly turned the carving sideways. The carving spun all the way around, halting the flow of water.

There was a groan of stone in the opposite corner as a slab of granite disappeared behind the wall, creating an opening in the ground just large enough for one person to squeeze through. Sister Benedictine lowered herself into the recess. In the dark space, she fumbled with the matches briefly before lighting the lamp. The firelight shone out and illuminated an underground tunnel.

The entrance to the tunnel was paved with large slabs of sandstone. A few metres ahead was a large pool. Sister Benedictine walked carefully to the edge and stood on a large, nondescript slab. It slowly sank under her weight until she was knee-deep below ground level. She watched patiently as the pool of liquid ahead of her started to drain, revealing a recess three metres deep. As the last drop disappeared, the entrance in the ceiling groaned shut.

Sister Benedictine stepped out of the small hole she now stood in. With her kerosene lamp lighting the inky darkness, she climbed down the notches in the side of the recess.

She ignored the few human skeletons that lay scattered at the bottom. The liquid that had been there had stripped the unfortunate intruders to the bone.

She walked past the skeletons, and then at the far side

of the recess, she climbed back up again. She followed the tunnel another twenty metres until she reached a dead end, where she found large iron studs embedded in the wall. She placed her lamp on the floor. Then, with practised precision, she picked two studs and turned one clockwise and the other counter-clockwise. The adjacent rock wall slid open, allowing Sister Benedictine to squeeze through the opening and into a scriptorium beyond.

The domed scriptorium was untouched by time, and not a single mote of dust hung in the air. The walls were lined with ancient texts and the room still held numerous desks complete with inkwells and quills. She glanced briefly at the enormous painting on the wall of the abbot Arnaud Amalric dressed resplendently in red, paying a thousand gold crowns to the Benedictines of Podlažice. In the foreground of the painting was an open ornate palanquin with four posts to carry it, the Devil's Bible could just be seen within. Sister Benedictine pushed forwards until she reached the far side of the room and the abbot's intricately carved desk.

Sister Benedictine placed her lamp on the abbot's desk and brought a match to the two large candles that sat there. She crossed to the corner, where stood a beautiful life-sized bronze statue of Saint Peter holding the key to the kingdom of heaven. Deftly, she relieved him of his key and inserted it into the keyhole of the palanquin box in the large painting. Turning the key, she pulled hard at the left side of the frame. With great effort, it swung open to reveal a vault. With both hands, the sister lifted out a large, heavy book. A thick, linked chain connected to it came reeling out like an uncoiling snake. She placed the book on the abbot's desk, carefully so that the chain did not clatter. She delicately turned the pages, each encased in glass. After turning to the sixth and last page, she pulled out a folded piece of paper and a pen from her habit. She unfolded and smoothed the paper, which was the same size as the pages in the book. The sister took a deep breath and began to copy the detailed drawings and text from the page.

She worked scrupulously by the dim light of the kerosene lamp, and did not look up as the two candles burned down to pools of molten wax. Each stroke of her pen was painstakingly precise.

There was a loud crash as the heavy, time-worn doors flew open and three monks, wearing scarlet robes and wielding torches, burst into the room. The sudden gust of air blew the loose papers from the abbot's desk, and Sister Benedictine yanked the lamp out of the way.

The monks rushed towards her, the first hissing in Spanish, "The scripture is sacred, you are defiling it!" his words hitting like knives. The other two monks drew swords from their sides as they advanced. "Nobody is allowed in here," said the first monk, his teeth hitting the consonants sharply. Sister Benedictine edged towards her secret exit as the monks recognised her habit. "She is from the Convento de Santa Teresa," one of the sword-wielding monks exclaimed, lowering his weapon.

"It does not matter—she cannot leave here alive," the third monk said with ice in his voice, as he moved towards Sister Benedictine.

She threw the lamp at the third monk. He leaped out of the way and it shattered, exploding on the bookshelf beside the outraged monk. The ancient texts were ablaze within seconds and the monk screamed as the flames scorched him.

"Save the texts!" shouted the first monk, his eyes not wavering from Sister Benedictine.

The sister heaved the large book above her head. "Take one more step and I shall let the sacred book fall," she threatened in broken Spanish, "The glass will shatter and destroy it forever."

Closing in on Sister Benedictine, the two monks halted their advance as the third monk continued to battle the flames consuming the books.

She took another step back, edging her way closer towards the opening of the secret passage, the book's chain clanking as it unravelled. The first monk put his left hand up in an attempt to pacify her and took a step towards the sister, the second monk close by his side. Threateningly, she lifted the text again, and the first monk held the other back.

Her retreat was halted when the chain refused to give anymore. Desperately, she glanced back to find it was fully extended.

The third monk turned to join his comrades, the destructive flames finally subdued.

Cornered, and out of options, Sister Benedictine threw the heavy tome up in the air and ran. The monks dropped their torches and weapons and dived to save the book. The nimble-fingered second monk managed to save the book from destruction by mere centimetres. By the time the monks recovered, they could only watch as the massive stone walls came together.

On the other side of the wall, Sister Benedictine turned the iron studs, sealing the passage entrance, then retraced her steps back to the convent as quickly as her feet and aching back would allow.

Ignoring the commotion in the lower levels of the convent, she rushed to her room and shut the door behind her firmly. Turning to her bed she grabbed at the closest bedpost, dragging it away to reveal the floor below. The sister bent down to remove a loose tile and extracted a key from underneath.

She grabbed her Bible from the desk and cautiously cracked open her door, to peer out. Scarlet-robed monks were in heated discussion with the nuns in the long corridor. She saw that the nuns were furious at the intrusion, but the monks were determined and muscled their way past them in order to search the rooms.

Sister Benedictine quietly pulled her door shut. She strode quickly over to the window and looked out. Below were granite steps that led to safety, but it was at least a ten-metre drop.

The sky had begun to lighten, with the night in retreat under the pursuit of dawn. She ripped her bed sheet in two and fashioned a rope. Tying one end to her bedpost, she tested that it would not come undone. The other end she threw outside. She dragged the bed to the window, tipping it so it leaned against the wall. The light frame wedged itself against the window as she climbed out, the thin sheet barely holding her weight. She lowered herself as far as the sheet would allow, only half the distance to the ground. The flimsy sheet tore and she fell down into the thicket beside the steps. She tested her limbs quickly; uninjured, she stood and then ran towards the forest.

As the sister disappeared into the forest, she glanced behind to see red monks gesticulating frantically at her from the window, but she did not falter. Clutching tightly at the key and the Bible, she ignored their angry shouts as she raced into the shadow of the trees.

During the day that followed, Sister Benedictine made her way through forests and riparian vegetation to Zamora. In the shadows of dusk, she left the forest and crossed the train tracks to blend with the crowd pouring into the city from Zamora's ancient train station.

During the *Semana Santa*, Zamora—a small city that lies on a rocky hill on the banks of the Douro River, in the northwest of Spain—holds the oldest of all penance processions, dating back to 1179. The Holy Week in Zamora is well known for its funereal and solemn nature. At this time each year, the city swells with at least a quarter of a million penitents and visitors, who have either come to take part in or watch the processions.

The brotherhoods walk the streets in their ancient penitential robes with conical hats, or *caperuzos*, used to conceal the face of the wearer. The robes have been used since medieval times for *nazarenos,* or penitents, to demonstrate their penance while still masking their identity.

As evening faded, the yellow sodium lights accentuated the sandstone citadel walls and the Moorish dome of Zamora Cathedral. People lined the streets leading to the main square and watched the exquisite statues and floats, which accompanied the sombre parade of *nazarenos*. The roads from all directions filled with cars moving slowly, trying to find a parking space as close to the city centre as they could manage.

As the darkness of night enveloped Zamora, the crowd migrated towards the city square. *Nazarenos* dressed in purple, blue, white, brown and black; small children in *nazareno* outfits; band members; and women in black veils congregated from every direction. As part of the tide of people flowing into the city centre, the sister occasionally lifted her head to glance at the red monks searching from the roofs of the buildings and every street corner. She shuddered and moved along with the multitude, clutching her Bible.

She reached the police station, which overlooks Plaza Mayor, the square in the heart of Zamora. The lower balcony of the police station was filled with members of the public using the elevated ground to get a better view. They watched the *Semana Santa* parade climb the slopes along *Calle Riena* before it spilled into Plaza Mayor.

Sister Benedictine edged through the back of the crowd, bunched closely along the railings of the police station balcony, momentarily moving to the front and perching on the top rail. She nervously eyed the *Iglesia de San Juan Batista* which occupied the centre of the square.

A row of security guards and police cordoned off the spectators, allowing the parade to move uninterrupted on the road between the police station and the church.

Barefoot penitents dressed in purple carried processional candles and home-made wooden crosses and walked slowly ahead of a magnificent *paso,* or float, showing the Sorrows of the Virgin Mary. The Virgin's eyes filled with tears depicting her grief for the torture and killing of her Son. The sculpture was three metres tall, carved and painted with the Virgin dressed in black. The float itself was elaborately decorated with fabric, hundreds of white roses and candles.

The crowd gathered in Plaza Mayor had their eyes transfixed on the spectacular *paso*, which had started to slow down as it negotiated the corner out of the square. Sister Benedictine watched the head of the purple *nazarenos'* parade start to disband after it turned the corner. In the distance, she saw the next parade with the white penitents heading up the hill towards the police station. She knew that once they reached Plaza Mayor, it would be another half hour before she could cross. She had to move back to the street.

The parade of the purple *nazarenos* came to an end, and a small group of people hurriedly crossed the road to the restaurants and cafés on the other side of the square. By the time Sister Benedictine reached the crossing point, the marshals had sealed it off. She cursed under her breath. Moments later, another group broke through and the sister joined them. As they headed towards the cafés, she darted away towards the Church of *San Juan Batista*. She did not stay in the open long, and quickly blended in with the crowds perched on the church steps and walls.

The white *nazarenos'* parade had now entered the square and Sister Benedictine looked along its periphery. Perched on each balcony and roof, surrounding the square, were red monks staring into the crowds. Two monks scrutinised the spectators from the police station upper balcony and two more crept through the masses gathered near the church, studying each face.

The sister peeled off from the throng and slipped through the back door into the church. She shut the door gently behind her, blocking the noise from the parade outside. Inside, a few nuns kneeled in the front pews, singing in prayer.

Sister Benedictine genuflected briefly before sitting in a pew at the back. She observed a middle-aged priest move silently along the side of the church and enter the confessional. Clutching her Bible, she rose and entered the side to address her confessor.

A few minutes passed before she retreated and returned to her pew. The priest hurried away towards the sacristy and disappeared beyond the sister's line of sight.

The nuns started to sing *Confiteor*—"I confess"—in Latin. There was a loud creak and the door at the back of the church opened. As fervent male voices echoed in the background, a few nuns glanced around but did not halt their song.

Sister Benedictine sang fervently with her eyes shut, her palms joined in prayer and her head tilted to the heavens. The approaching footsteps stopped, and two people settled at either end of Sister Benedictine's pew. She glanced slyly to the left and saw a red monk kneeling. She looked to her right and saw another monk kneeling at the other end. She twisted her head around and spotted two more red monks at the chapel door. She nodded her head solemnly, a silent signal to the monk on her right that she would follow him peacefully. The monk stood and stalked towards the door, leading her out. The monk on her left followed behind, staying close.

As she reached the aisle, she paused to genuflect towards the altar before turning her back. The monk behind her halted his progress as she bowed her head towards the crucifix above the altar. He too then paused to genuflect. In that split second of distraction, Sister Benedictine broke away. She rushed to a wooden staircase and hastily climbed to an inner balcony. She raced along the short timber corridor and up a flight of stairs, burst through the door and latched it behind her.

Sister Benedictine turned. She was on the exterior stairs connecting the exposed rooftop to the bell tower of the Church of *San Juan Batista*. The parade below her was in full flow, and the sounds of trumpets playing the *Mater Mea* filled the air.

The sister did not stop to enjoy the spectacle. The door behind her was already shifting as the monks on the other side attempted to smash it down. She took the steps two at a time. The small latch and feeble hinges protecting her would soon give way.

At the top of the stairs, she swung open the bell tower door. She stared down and saw more agitated monks gathered in the crowds pointing towards the tower. There was nowhere left for her to hide. Eyes closed, she tilted her head to the heavens and sighed—a sigh of resignation. She looked back at the red monks in the crowd and folded her hands, making the sign of peace. She smiled.

The door at the bottom of the stairs burst open and two red monks spilled through. They ran up the stairs but it was too late, Sister Benedictine shut the second door in their faces. The monks pummelled and the old wood trembled. The church bells rang loudly drowning out the trumpets and the drums.

The entire parade froze as the eighty thousand people in Plaza Mayor gasped.

Sister Benedictine dangled from the end of a thick rope attached to the church bells, a makeshift noose around her neck. Her body shuddered as life escaped her. Swinging like a pendulum against the sandstone walls of the bell tower, her lifeless body rang the church bells in haunting percussion.

CHAPTER 2
THE MEMORIAL SERVICE

MAY 2014, CURRUMBIN VALLEY, AUSTRALIA

Siobhan Russo kneeled on the worn wooden floorboards in the lounge of the old Queenslander house. She looked through her tears at photographs scattered on the coffee table. At only twenty-three, Siobhan had grown old too young.

In the corner, her Nanna Edith silently swayed back and forth in her rocking chair, tears streaming down her wrinkled cheeks. The old woman's lips moved silently as her withered fingers stroked the beads of her rosary.

Jess, Siobhan's precocious seventeen-year-old sister, stood with her arms folded, her hip propping up her athletic frame uneasily against the old piano. While Siobhan was soft and pleasant in appearance, Jess was hard and striking, her dark brown hair neatly cut to accentuate her chiselled features and piercing black eyes.

Siobhan peered through her tears at the crestfallen face of Inspector Mick Jones. Over the last six years, she had visited or called his office once a week religiously, searching for her mother who had mysteriously disappeared without a trace. She lowered her eyes as he approached her. Jones reached out and gently took her hand in his and squeezed it compassionately.

Siobhan wiped her tears away with her sleeve. "Did she

leave a note?" she asked, pleadingly. Inspector Jones shook his head. "Nothing. Nobody knew who she was. They buried her two weeks ago."

Jess paced the floor impatiently, clearly agitated. She glared at Siobhan and then broke her silence. "If she wanted to contact us, Siobhan, she would have. She had more than six years to do it."

Siobhan pleaded with her sister, "Please, Jess. Mum brought us up with everything she had."

"You bloody brought me up Siobhan, not *her*," said Jess, coldly. "You had to drop out of uni because she left."

Edith cleared her throat. "Jess, darling, your mother loved you both more than anything else in the world. Everything she ever did, she did for you."

Jess turned sharply. "Nanna! She was not a hostage; she ran away and joined a convent. A convent in *Spain*! That's about as far away on earth as you could possibly get from here."

Siobhan looked up at her sister, green eyes meeting black. "Jess, you don't mean it. There must have been a reason. There has to be."

Jess shook her head and threw her hands up in exasperation. "Can't you see it, Siobhan? She abandoned us." She paused, then added softly, "I was only eleven."

Jess stormed out of the lounge and slammed her bedroom door.

Siobhan sighed as she watched her sister disappear. Inspector Jones excused himself and she walked him to the door, thanking him as he left.

That next afternoon, Edith, Jess and Siobhan, all dressed in black, stood quietly at the gate of an old bluestone church.

A painted white cross adorned the top of the modest bell tower, which in turn sat atop a slanted wooden roof. A dozen seniors milled about inside the church compound, also dressed in black.

Edith was crying and Siobhan was barely holding it together, but Jess was still agitated.

"This is so hypocritical. I don't remember *ever* going to church!" she blurted unsolicited.

"Shut up, Jess. You'll just upset Nanna." Siobhan snapped. "It's just one hour. We can talk about it later at home."

Jess scowled. "You do your thing. I don't want any part of this," she said, turned heel and stormed off.

"Jess. Jess!" Siobhan shouted after her, but she didn't turn back.

Siobhan went to go after her, but Edith reached out and held her back. "Let her go darling, she is grieving in her own way," she said calmly.

After a very emotional service, one by one, people paid their respects and left. Siobhan, with Edith next to her, stood beside a beautiful picture of her mother. The portrait of Denise Russo was from the year before she'd disappeared. Her green eyes were soft, like Siobhan's, but her expression was hard. Siobhan sighed. She knew where Jess got her stubbornness. The picture had been placed in a large frame with silver engravings and now rested to the side of the altar. Blooming lilies were scattered around it artfully, their fragrance filling the air.

When the crowd had dwindled to just a few stragglers, Inspector Jones approached and took Siobhan's hand in his. At the inspector's soft touch, Siobhan, who had held her composure all through the service, broke down sobbing.

Jones put his arms around her, offering wordless comfort. Siobhan was grateful for it. With Jess being so antipathetic, she had barely time to reconcile with her own grief.

Once Jones left, Siobhan saw a middle-aged priest dressed in black vestments rise and make his way towards her. She didn't recognise the man, but he had been praying during the service in one of the back rows. She looked over to Edith, but she was engaged with the last mourners, an elderly couple.

"Siobhan?" the priest asked, standing before her. The way he said her name, as a question, seemed to be as though he was confirming someone he once knew. She looked at the stranger, trying hard to place him, but nothing stuck.

"Yes," she replied. "I'm really sorry. I'm not sure we've met."

The priest had a thick eastern-European accent. "You do not know me," he said. "I am Father Jakub. I knew your mother."

Siobhan smiled. "Thank you for coming."

Jakub continued as if Siobhan hadn't said anything. "May I have a word with you in private?" Siobhan looked up at him curiously. The priest added, "I knew your mother as Sister Benedictine."

Siobhan turned to see Edith, still engrossed with her friends, then nodded to the priest.

He led her towards the back of the church where he handed her the Bible he had been holding onto. "This was your mother's Bible. She asked me to give it to you."

Siobhan's eyes widened. "When?" she asked the priest, her voice coming out louder than expected.

Father Jakub signalled Siobhan to keep her voice down. "It was her last wish that you tell nobody," he said. He pointed to her bag and she tucked the Bible inside. As the priest turned to leave, Siobhan tugged on his sleeve. "Father, please! My mother disappeared for six years. We never knew anything about why she left or what happened. We *need* to know."

Jakub's expression softened. "I don't know either. Six years ago, Reverend Zachary asked me to drive Sister Benedictine from Prague to Zamora. Your mother had taken a vow of silence. She never spoke to me during that entire trip.

"Each year after that day, we met at midnight on Good Friday in the confessional of the Church of Saint John the Baptist, in Zamora. I slid open the confessional window and I would hand her a sealed envelope from Zachary and in exchange, she would give me one to deliver back to him. He made me swear on my life that whatever I was given would never be delivered to or shared with anyone else."

Siobhan's eyebrows crinkled, her curiosity written plain on her face. "What was in the notes?"

The priest responded blankly, "I don't know. I never opened them."

She persisted. "Where can I find Reverend Zachary?"

The priest shook his head sadly, and his voice came thick, "He died last year. There was a fire in his study." He wiped away tears from his eyes. His voice wavered off emotionally, "I am sorry, he was like a father to me. I was an orphan and he raised me."

"I'm so sorry," Siobhan said instinctively. Then, clutching at straws she added, "So my mother said nothing to you?"

Emotions in check, Jakub answered her. "On Good Friday, I went to tell her about Reverend Zachary. As soon as she entered the confessional, she handed me the Bible and a note with your name and address. She then broke her vow of silence to say, 'Please give my Bible to my daughter Siobhan. This is our last meeting, you must leave now, it is not safe here.'"

Siobhan's mouth opened to ask a question, but Jakub continued, "I started to say something about Zachary, but she cut me off, saying she already knew. Then she hissed at me, 'You must leave!' and then added, 'Now, please!'" Father Jakub looked at Siobhan, eyes apologetic. "She was clearly desperate, so I did as she bid. When I looked behind me as I left the church, I saw she had gone back to praying at the back of the church."

"Did my mother commit suicide?" Siobhan asked. "Or did someone kill her?" This was her deepest fear.

Father Jakub shook his head. "The door to the bell tower was locked from the inside. People from the parade saw her enter alone."

The silence between them stretched on. Eventually, the priest looked to the heavens and shook his head. "Sisters of God do not commit suicide. And not in front of eighty thousand people."

As Father Jakub noticed Edith approaching, her friends having all left the church; he raised his voice. "Read the Holy Bible my child, it has all the answers."

Edith hurried over and pulled Siobhan away from the seemingly overzealous priest. "Not today, Father. Not today."

CHAPTER 3

SILENCE SAYS MORE THAN WORDS

It was dusk when Siobhan and Edith returned home from Denise's memorial service. Jess sat in the lounge with the lights off, staring blankly at the wall. Siobhan sighed.

Kicking off her shoes, Edith spoke of the beautiful service and Jess nodded sadly. Rising from her seat on the couch, Jess went to her sister and embraced her. "I'm sorry, I know it means a lot to you, but I need time." Siobhan smiled weakly as she hugged her sister briefly but tightly, then let her go.

Edith held her arms out and Jess snuggled up to her nanna. Siobhan glanced over as the older woman ran a hand over Jess' hair. "I know you are hurting, darling," she said, and kissed Jess on the forehead. Siobhan smiled and excused herself. It had been a long day.

Siobhan's room was untidy. On the floor was a mixture of papers and clothes, and her doona was awkwardly flung at the end of the bed. Even though she was twenty-three, she had never invited a friend to her bedroom. And so there had never been a good reason to tidy it. As an intern journalist, she worked long hours, and the rare spare time she had was consumed in taking care of Jess.

She locked her bedroom door and retrieved her mother's Bible from her bag. It was well worn, the pages dog-eared.

She opened the front cover and found a small inscription in the top left corner: *Sister Benedictine.* Stamped just below the name was *Convento de Santa Teresa, Moreruela.*

In the centre of the front page was a short note in handwriting that Siobhan recognised as her mother's:

Siobhan

There is something you need to know. Come to Zamora—tell nobody.

Mum

Siobhan leafed through the Bible, hoping there was more to it. Surely after six years, her mother would have had more to say? She rapidly scanned through the book, looking for lines or words that may have been highlighted, or for another note hidden between the pages. Nothing.

Disappointed, she pulled at the ribbon bookmark tucked in the spine and realised it was loose. She pulled harder, surprised at the weight of it. It came free, and hanging from it was a small iron key, worn with what looked like centuries of age. The key had a coat of arms she could just make out with the words *El silencio es una respuesta* engraved on it. Siobhan pulled out her laptop and translated the engraving from Spanish: *Silence is an answer.* Etched on the back of the key was a set of strange characters in a script she didn't recognise.

Siobhan read the note again. It had been more than six years, but there was no term of endearment, no darling, no dear and no love. There was also no apology or explanation as to why she had left them. Why had she become a nun and taken a vow of silence? Why Spain? Was Jess right? Had their mother abandoned them?

Siobhan shut the Bible and placed it under her mattress. The last thing she needed was Edith or Jess finding it. She lay back on the bed, shoes still on and closed her eyes, knowing it would be a restless night. They do say less is more, and the few words Denise Russo had written left more questions than answers.

It is the prerogative of night, when thoughts, like relentless waves, break on the impressionable sands of the mind. Questions, theories and suppositions come crashing ashore, and just like waves, they disappear into the grains of the mind without a trace. In this sea of uncertainty, stormed by nocturnal nightmares, the mind slips in and out of consciousness. It is the melting pot where logic and fantasy combine until supposition becomes hypothesis, and hypothesis morphs into unsubstantiated fact.

The words of Father Jakub anchored Siobhan's uncertainty. *Sisters of God don't commit suicide. And not in front of eighty thousand people.*

Each thread of connection she made had numerous frayed ends of doubts. Who was Father Jakub? Why had he come all the way from Prague to deliver this Bible in person? What were the notes her mother exchanged with him each year on Good Friday? And who was Reverend Zachary? Did he really die in an accident or was he murdered? Had all the exchanged notes been burned in the fire?

Finally, as weak dawn filtered through her bedroom window, Siobhan knew what she had to do.

At the breakfast table, she broached the topic with her nanna and sister. "I need to visit the convent where Mum lived."

Edith was shocked and tried to placate her, but Siobhan

was adamant. "I need to know why she went to Spain. I need to know why she did not call." As her voice trembled into tears, she cried, "I need to know why, Nanna. Why Mum died so alone."

Edith put her arm around Siobhan consoling her and tried to reason with her. Jess remained silent and distant. She stared discouragingly at her nanna and sister, each time either looked to her for support.

Siobhan had made up her mind and would not be swayed. The longer she waited, the colder the trail would be and the harder it would be to find answers. These questions, if left unattended, would haunt her forever. She had to go.

Jess stood up and went quietly to her room. Siobhan thought for a moment that she had upset her, but a minute later Jess came back with a couple of hundred dollars in cash.

"Here," Jess said, and gave the wad of cash to her. Siobhan knew it was money Jess had saved from her job at the supermarket. Jess had been planning on using it to buy a dress for her school formal that was coming up in a few weeks. "Jess, I can't take this."

"You raised me after Mum left," Jess said. "I don't know if I can forgive her yet, but I know you need closure."

Siobhan knew it had taken a lot for her sister to be able to say that. She squeezed Jess tightly with bleary eyes.

Jess tugged at her shoulders. "Come on, that's enough." But they were laughing. As they came apart, Siobhan saw Edith tear up at the scene.

A few days later, Siobhan was on an aeroplane to Madrid.

The trip to Moreruela turned out to be a lot more difficult than she imagined. With limited resources,

Siobhan had trudged with her luggage from Madrid airport onto the local train lines and then to Madrid Chamartín station, where she got the last train to Zamora.

The train pulled into Zamora at around 1 am. Siobhan, seriously jetlagged and exhausted, was the only passenger left in her compartment, and the only person on the desolate platform. A solitary fluorescent light flickered intermittently, illuminating the silent eighteenth-century railway station.

She wandered onto the street, a backpack slung over her right shoulder, dragging her suitcase and a hand luggage bag behind her. The sound of her shoes crunching loudly on the loose gravel and the scraping wheels of her bags echoed off the old buildings in the darkness. There were no taxis, no cars and no street lights. She shuddered at the emptiness of the town. She looked back at the station. The white woodwork of the railway office windows looked eerily like large crucifixes in the wavering light.

As she dragged her bags along the empty streets, Siobhan could just see the Romanesque silhouette of Zamora Cathedral in the distance. Passing an empty square, lined by skeletal, twisted sycamore trees, she noticed a shadow move from behind the trees towards her. She heard another set of footsteps echoing in the deserted street behind her.

Siobhan saw a dim light in the distance ahead and hastened her pace, almost breaking into a run. Whoever was following her hurried their gait in response. Terrified, she raced ahead, her bags bouncing along the cobblestone road behind her. As she came out of the shadows and into the lit area, a man stepped out in front of her. Siobhan jumped back in fright.

A policeman stood there, face full of concern. Relieved, Siobhan dug out a piece of paper with the name of her hotel written on it and showed it to him. She looked around, and spotted the police station to her left.

In front of her was the Church of Saint John the Baptist. She trembled as she looked up at the lonely staircase leading to the dimly lit bell tower. A tidal wave of grief gripped her as she looked upon the place her mother had died. It took all her resolve not to break out in tears.

She snapped back to reality when the policeman pointed to a fluorescent sign at the end of the street that said, *Hotel Zamora*.

A monk dressed in a red habit appeared out of the dark street behind her. He pointed to Siobhan and hissed venomously in a thick accent, "Go home."

The policeman escorted Siobhan to the door of her hotel and opened it for her. "Pay your respects and go home. You are not safe here," he said quietly in English and held open the door.

"Nobody knew I was coming," she replied, shocked.

The policeman shook his head and turned to the empty city centre square. "Everybody knows." He looked her in the eye again. "Outside the *Semana Santa*, nobody visits."

CHAPTER 4

THREE RED ROSES

Siobhan surfaced from her jetlagged slumber around noon. Not wanting to waste the day, she went to reception to find out the best way to get to the convent.

The hotel receptionist handed her a pamphlet that referred her to a minibus, which ran twice daily to the ruins of the old Cistercian Monasterio de Santa Maria de Moreruela, some four kilometres from the rural village of Granja de Moreruela. Siobhan read in the pamphlet that the origins of the Monasterio de Santa Maria de Moreruela were obscure. The original Benedictine monastery had been built around the ninth century before being handed over to the Cistercians around 1160 A.D. By the early thirteenth century, it was considered the grandest and richest monastery in Spain.

Siobhan hopped off the minibus at the monastery, and glanced at the edifice briefly, noting its ruined beauty. She quickly set off on foot, headed from the sandstone plains on the banks of the Esla up towards the forested hills in the distance. She could see her destination by the chapel spire that peeked above the forest line.

Half an hour later, Siobhan found herself at the base of a hill with large granite steps ahead of her. She hitched her backpack higher on her shoulders and began to climb. Soon she passed between the time-ravaged castellated walls and through the dilapidated gates, but it was another twenty minutes before she reached the chapel at the top of the hill.

Undaunted by the fact that the chapel was built on the 'Gateway to Hell', Siobhan knocked confidently on the solid wooden doors in front of her.

A few minutes went by and Siobhan began to wonder if anyone would answer. The sound of wood sliding on wood alerted her that she was not alone. A grated peephole on the ancient wooden door opened and Siobhan saw an old nun peering through, looking curiously up and down at her. It was obvious that it was not often that a young girl dressed in blue jeans and a white t-shirt arrived at the Convento de Santa Teresa.

"My name is Siobhan Russo. I am here to—"

The nun raised a hand to silence her, then signalled Siobhan to wait. The peephole slid shut. While Siobhan waited impatiently, she looked up and saw that above the archway was engraved a coat of arms and, underneath it, the motto *El silencio es una respuesta*. The same coat of arms and words engraved on her mother's key. She was in the right place.

A few minutes later, the door opened and a young nun dressed in a black habit with a peculiar white cord tied around her waist appeared.

The young nun queried, "How can I help you?"

Siobhan explained. "My mother, Denise Russo, was Sister Benedictine. I would like to visit her grave."

The sister nodded sadly and introduced herself as Sister Catherine. She led Siobhan back down the steps to just outside the main gate. There, in a bleak patch covered with fallen leaves, was an unmarked grave.

Siobhan sighed heavily as she gazed at the final resting place of her mother. She looked in askance at the sister.

"Mother Superior would not allow us to bury her within the walls of the convent. Suicide is unforgivable."

"Are you sure it was suicide?" Siobhan probed carefully.

Sister Catherine looked at Siobhan, pity in her eyes. "The police had to break down the ancient door to the bell tower to get her down. It was locked from the inside—she was in the tower alone."

"Did she say anything to anyone?" Siobhan pleaded, tears pricking at the corners of her eyes.

Sister Catherine shook her head. "Sister Benedictine took a vow of silence. Not once did I hear or see her speak to anyone."

The tears that had threatened to fall now rolled down Siobhan's cheeks. Ignoring them, she took off her backpack and kneeled next to her mother's grave. She pulled out a cylindrical box, and from it took out three long-stemmed red roses. She placed the first rose on the mound and said softly, "This one is from Jess." Her voice hitched as she placed the second next to the first. "And this one is from Nanna." Sister Catherine placed a hand on Siobhan's shoulder as she lowered the third and last rose to the dirt. The sobs were impossible to keep at bay. "And this one, Mum, is from me."

The young sister kneeled down beside Siobhan and put her arm around her. Siobhan couldn't stop sobbing; she was inconsolable. Sister Catherine waited patiently.

Eventually, Siobhan took a slow, deep breath and wiped the wetness from her face, attempting to pull herself together. She briefly grasped Sister Catherine's hand, acknowledging her support, before she nodded and stood.

Siobhan looked at the nun. "Is it possible to see my mother's room?"

Catherine nodded. "Of course."

For one last moment, Siobhan turned and looked upon her mother's grave before she followed Sister Catherine back up the steps and through the ancient chapel. The corridors were lit only by the fading twilight that streamed through the unadorned glass windows. The chapel was unlike anything Siobhan had seen before. It had no statues, and the ancient murals were so faded they were hard to decipher. There were images of winged creatures, witches, and the angel Michael holding down Lucifer. There were also murals of Saint Christopher cradling baby Jesus. The chapel altar, illuminated by the gentle light falling through a window behind it, had no cross. Siobhan found this strange, but said nothing.

Sister Catherine opened a heavy wooden door to the convent and they entered a gloomy tunnel lit by torches. The tunnel descended lower and lower, following the slope of the steep granite outcrop. Eventually they entered a long corridor and passed numerous rooms; some doors were shut while others were open, revealing either nuns in prayer or nothing other than sparse furniture. Sister Catherine finally ushered Siobhan into an empty room at the end of the long corridor.

In the corner was a single bed with a thin uncovered mattress, a nun's habit folded neatly on top. Next to it lay a cat-o'-nine-tails whip. Siobhan thought to ask what the whip was for but elected to stay silent, preferring not to know. The wooden chair and writing desk sat dusty and unused in the other corner by the window. Siobhan took in the sparsely furnished room, barely able to believe that her mother lived like this.

"Did she have a cupboard? A box where she kept her things?" Siobhan asked the nun.

"No. We are not allowed any worldly possessions," Catherine replied simply.

Siobhan fished around in her bag and pulled out her mother's Bible. She gently pulled at the ribbon bookmark, revealing the key attached to it. "My mother sent me this before she died. Do you know what this is?"

The sister took a small step back, clearly surprised. She folded her hands in front of her lips and rocked her head, thinking.

Siobhan pressed further, using the same tone she used with reticent interviewees. "It must belong here. The words on the key are the same as the ones above the main door. I saw them."

Sister Catherine remained silent for a moment. "Come with me," she said and left the room. Siobhan scrambled to catch up.

In stark contrast to the impoverished section of the nuns' dormitory, they entered the grandiose quarters of the Mother Superior. Sister Catherine told Siobhan to wait behind while she carried on through a gate of barred iron. Through the bars, Siobhan saw Sister Catherine approach the Mother Superior, who was studying an old tome while seated in a wing-back chair behind an intricately carved desk. Siobhan was momentarily beguiled by the opulence.

Mother Superior was deeply wrinkled with a kind face. She clasped Sister Catherine's hands and spoke to her in Spanish.

From the body language, Siobhan could tell it was not going well. The older woman was shaking her head. Then fervently she said, "*Absolutamente no!*"

Sister Catherine pleaded in English. "She has come all the way from Australia. Sister Benedictine was her mother."

Mother Superior broke into English too. "No. She cannot go there."

Sister Catherine tried one more time. "Sister Benedictine could have chosen numerous ways to commit suicide within these walls. She sent her daughter the key. She must have had some unfinished business."

But the senior nun was adamant. "The Vault of Confessions is out of bounds, as is the Room of Repentance. *Absolutamente no!*"

While Siobhan wondered about the 'Vault of Confessions' and the 'Room of Repentance', Sister Catherine bowed her head, conceding to the wishes of the Mother Superior.

Both nuns finally came to the gate. The Mother Superior looked at Siobhan and spoke softly. "I am sorry that you must mourn your mother. We are stewards, not owners, of the life God has entrusted to us. It is not ours to dispose of. Your mother has brought negative attention to our order with her very public suicide."

Siobhan realised her request was being denied by the Mother Superior. She looked pleadingly into the woman's eyes, hoping she would yield.

The old nun remained stoic, her soft eyes now devoid of compassion. She escorted Siobhan up the long corridor leading to the chapel and the exit. "You must leave."

Sister Catherine pointed to the now dark landscape visible outside the window. "Sister Margaret, she is only a young girl. It is not safe for her to go down the hill alone. She will not reach the last bus before it leaves."

Mother Superior Margaret grudgingly conceded. "You may stay the night, but at first light you must leave."

Siobhan muttered a thank you and followed Sister Catherine back to the nuns' quarters.

Sister Catherine left Siobhan in her mother's room while she went to fetch a fresh set of sheets and a towel. When Catherine returned with the threadbare linen, Siobhan asked her if she would visit the Vault of Confessions on her behalf.

"Even if you have the key, it is forbidden to open someone else's Vault of Confessions without instructions in the nun's last will and testimony."

Siobhan desperately tried to convince Catherine that perhaps she *had* been instructed to do that, and as she could not go, it would be perfectly appropriate for Catherine to do it at her behest. The sister shook her head sombrely. "I cannot."

As Catherine made to leave, Siobhan was able to ask one last question: "Can you please tell me where the Vault of Confessions is?"

Seeming to ignore her question, Sister Catherine lifted Denise's habit from the bed and placed it in Siobhan's hands. "Nobody from the outside world is allowed in there. Tonight, you will hear the sounds from the Room of Repentance. The vault lies beyond. You must leave at sunrise." She paused, then imparted a warning, slowly and deliberately, "You *must* then leave Zamora." She paused. "Please."

CHAPTER 5

THE VAULT OF CONFESSIONS

As night fell, Siobhan looked out of the window to see a dark, moonless sky. Over the forest canopy there was only darkness, except for faint lights from the small town of Granja de Moreruela.

Siobhan looked skywards; it was as though the heavens had opened up. The clear night, so distant from any light pollution, had summoned every star in the sky to shine. Siobhan believed that there was a camera in her mind that took snapshots of discreet, unconnected moments to haunt her. The image of the night, of billions of stars glowing, would forever be etched in her memory. Baring its soul, the night in all its magnificence was a grim reminder of herself. A soul obscured by the light pollution of the daily grind in suburbia. Six years ago, her mother had left. As the years passed, she, like a threatened tortoise, had retreated into her shell, too scared to love. Too scared to feel the incomparable pain of loss. The pain of losing her, of missing her, had been impossible to bear. For six years, Siobhan's heart lifted each time she saw her mother's resemblance in a stranger. She looked wistfully at her mother's folded habit. "I will no longer search the crowd to see if that stranger is you," she said, her voice breaking.

The night air was still, and the silence of the forest was

deafening, devoid of any sounds of nocturnal wildlife. In that silence, Siobhan realised how impossible it was to listen to her own soul above the noise of her daily life. She was twenty-three, and she had never loved. Love had passed her by. Infatuations never materialised to even a fleeting romance, each disappointment drawing her further into her familiar tortoise shell of work. The pain of her mother's loss was fresh once more, the silver scars ripped open to reveal the raw grief underneath.

As she listened to the silence and absorbed the brilliant night sky, her thoughts drifted to her mother and the enigma over her disappearance and death. Had her mother come here to listen to her own soul? Had she somehow dragged Siobhan here to do the same now?

A scream shocked Siobhan from her reverie. The horrible sound was laced with inhuman pain. The cry came again, emerging from within the bowels of the convent. She rushed to the doorway and strode down the corridor. The nuns she passed were deep in prayer in their rooms, unconcerned.

Siobhan quickly realised that these were the sounds Sister Catherine had spoken of. The ones from the Room of Repentance. Swiftly she turned back to her mother's room, changed into her mother's habit, removed the key from her mother's Bible, and quietly crept along the edge of the long torch lit corridor, head down.

Reaching the end of the corridor, Siobhan found the screams emanated from a low, dark opening. She crouched and entered a small tunnel that descended to a narrow spiral staircase. With each downward step, her heart raced faster as she knew she was trespassing. From below, Siobhan could see the glow of a reddish light and hear whip cracks.

A woman's voice shouted, "*Veinte uno.*" The temperature progressively increased as she made her way down. She was sweating now. The sound of a whip cracking came again and was followed by another scream. A woman's voice echoed, "*Veintidós.*"

Siobhan reached the bottom of the stairs, which then opened into a long bluestone corridor with open chambers. The stairs and the room were both lit by a pit of red hot coals to the right of the centre path. Another woman, dressed in a sack cloth, which extended just below her waist, screamed in agony and, Siobhan thought, ecstasy, as she walked over burning coals. Sweat dripped down her face as she chanted the Act of Contrition loudly in Spanish: *My God, I am sorry for my sins with all my heart. In choosing to do wrong and failing to do good.*

Quickly, she breathed in and out, and refocused her mind—a technique she'd learned to numb her emotions while investigating—then pressed on. She passed by the second chamber, illuminated by a solitary burning torch. The whip crack came again and Siobhan braced herself for the scream that followed. Within this chamber, a woman with her hands shackled to the wall was shaking, her naked back covered in welts and her habit tied loosely around her hips. Another woman, who was whipping her, counted, "*Veintitrés.*"

Siobhan raised her hand to her lips, stifling her horror as she realised the function of the whip she saw in her mother's room.

Siobhan could hear whispers in the next chamber. As she passed it she saw a woman, wearing a sack cloth, hanging from an X-shaped cross. "*Mea culpa, mea culpa, mea maxima culpa,*" the woman murmured fervently.

In the fourth chamber, the walls were lined with an assortment of grizzly iron tools of torture. A small coal fire burned and in it a couple of irons were turning red hot. Three women kneeled on the floor around it, each whirling a cat-o'-nine-tails above their heads and whipping themselves. "*Mea culpa,*" they chanted softly. As Siobhan tiptoed past, the three cat-o'-nine-tails whirled again, landing in sync on the naked back of each woman.

Beyond her horror and shock, Siobhan realised she was in an ancient dungeon. Judging by the state of some of the torture tools and techniques, it dated well back to the times of the Spanish Inquisition.

Siobhan looked inside the fifth chamber. It was empty, but housed a large rack and pinion. Overwhelmed by anxiety and uncertainty, she hid within the room, needing a moment to calm herself. Her pulse racing as she tried hard to slow her heavy breathing for fear of being discovered. She looked down at the key she held in her hand and knew it would be her one and only chance to discover what her mother had bequeathed to her. With one last careful breath, she straightened her back and exited from the shadows. She walked apprehensively towards the sixth and last chamber.

The chamber had an assortment of spikes, claws, and a chair with nails pointing up from the seat, back and arms along the far wall. As she passed the entrance, she saw the Mother Superior was in the last chamber, dressed in her habit with her back to Siobhan. She was verbally chastising a nun, who had her head down, cowering in submission. Siobhan moved past silently and opened the door at the end of the passage. The opening was only a metre high, and Siobhan had to crouch again to enter.

She went into the hallway beyond and shut the door

behind her. Suddenly she was engulfed by darkness. Quickly, Siobhan returned to the corridor, scurried into the empty fifth chamber and stole a torch. She headed back towards the corridor. As she was about to exit, she noticed Sister Catherine leaving the sixth chamber. The young sister spotted her, and signalled frantically. Siobhan fell back into the fifth chamber and stood with her back to the wall. She watched anxiously as Catherine walked past, just centimetres away from her, Mother Superior following closely behind. Siobhan tried hard not to breathe but her pounding heart made that impossible. Fortunately, they walked straight past her, as she had slid along the wall farther back into the room and out of their line of sight.

A moment later, she stuck her head into the corridor and checked that it was empty. Seeing that it was, she strode back to the door at the end of the corridor. Now lit by firelight, she could see a short passage leading to a tightly wound spiral staircase. She walked quickly to the stairs and descended. She counted forty steps before finding herself in front of another heavy wooden door, adorned with outward-facing spikes.

She tried to push the door open, but it would not budge. She pulled, and it creaked open loudly. Entering hesitantly, she looked around, then shut the cumbersome door behind her.

The room was about five metres long and extended nearly twenty metres either side of the door. The ceiling and the floor were solid granite rock. The walls were lined with numerous catacomb-style vaults, each with a small metal door housing a keyhole. Each door was adorned with a number of symbols. Siobhan looked at the symbols on the back of the key and started to match them with those in front of her.

Moving halfway along the left wall, she heard footsteps coming rapidly down the staircase. Siobhan panicked, and quickened her search for the matching vault. The door creaked open behind her. She pressed her torch flush with the floor, till she smothered out the flame and then hid in a dark corner.

The old nun entered the Vault of Confessions, carrying a torch of her own. She briefly looked around and then walked towards the end of the room where Siobhan was concealed. But then, just a few feet away from Siobhan, she stopped, clearly looking for a certain vault. Siobhan did not dare to breathe. Mother Superior pulled at the small handle on the door to one of the vaults. The vault was stuck shut, and the old nun huffed to herself, apparently satisfied that it was locked. Without hesitation, Margaret turned heel and left. Siobhan was left alone in complete darkness. In desperation, she walked blindly towards the vaults where she had seen the old nun checking. Using her hands she felt for a keyhole and then slid the key in. It didn't turn. She felt her way to the next vault down and inserted her key in the lock. She tried this a few times without luck and was becoming more frantic, until finally the key turned. Siobhan pulled on the door handle and the vault door opened.

She thrust her hand inside and removed what seemed like a thick leather-bound book. Feeling along the rest of the vault, she touched a piece of stiff paper. Plucking it out, she put it into the book, which she tucked into one of the large pockets of her mother's habit. She checked once more, but there was nothing else. Shutting the vault, she locked it and removed the key.

Carefully, she felt her way out of the darkness, through the wooden door, and up the staircase.

Once she got back to her mother's room, she tied the key back onto the ribbon bookmark of her mother's Bible. That done, she took the book out of her pocket and before tucking it away in her backpack, she looked at it closely. It was a diary. The faded yellow cover was titled in black *The Confession.*

She took off her mother's habit, folded it carefully and lifted it to her face, breathing in. She sniffed it hoping for a faint scent reminiscent of her mother. There was nothing. Siobhan kissed it, smiled sadly and placed it on the table. She turned to see Mother Superior standing in the doorway. Siobhan flushed, unsure how long the old nun had been watching her.

"May I come in?" Margaret asked politely. Siobhan sat on the bed, in front of her backpack, and offered Mother Superior the chair.

She declined and chose to remain standing, holding the back of the chair for support. "Please accept my condolences."

Siobhan nodded in acceptance. The nun then added, "I was asked by Reverend Zachary, who was a very holy man, to give your mother a home and to respect her vow of silence. I did not know Sister Benedictine. I never spoke with her, but I do know this my child: your mother was the most tortured soul I have ever known." Siobhan remained silent, her eyes locked with Margaret's, unsure whether the Mother Superior had knowledge of her recent acquisition. She steadied herself, realising that even if Margaret had seen her holding her mother's book, she could have no knowledge that it had been removed from her mother's vault.

Margaret continued, "Guilt is the currency of the Catholic faith. Guilt is the mortgage on our souls, held by the faith. We pay for it in repentance, abnegation, altruism, and charity until the day we die. Our penance is a journey, and, as we travel down its road, we are given a sense that we are being forgiven or healed. It is some sort of cosmic wheel that we choose to believe in, to help us shut out the devils of our past." As Mother Superior spoke, Siobhan remained quiet, understanding that silence was the only appropriate response to her words.

"The past slowly blurs into a permanent scar, which visits us without warning in the darkest hours before the dawn. In time, we all heal and dedicate our lives to doing good." Margaret paused. "That is a pattern I have seen with every nun who has visited and lived here—except for your mother. She lived without hope, believing that whatever she had done was beyond redemption. Never before have I met anyone so bereft of hope.

"In all my years, I have never known anyone to inflict so much pain on themselves without a whisper of complaint. Yet, I know she did not believe in redemption."

Margaret read the graffiti on the wall aloud. "*Eli, Eli, lama sabachthani.*" *My God, my God, why hast thou forsaken me?* The only words of Christ on the cross noted in two of the four gospels.

Siobhan remained silent.

Margaret looked straight into Siobhan's eyes. "My dear child, you must know by now that one cannot give what one does not have." The old woman took Siobhan's hands in hers and pressed tightly. She smiled. "Whatever was in your mother's confessional vault brought her only suffering. It was sealed in anguish, and all it can give you is the same."

Margaret lifted Denise's folded habit from the table and handed it to Siobhan. She smiled again gently and said, "This belonged to your mother, and the choice to take what she left behind is yours alone." Siobhan tucked the habit into her backpack. Mother Superior Margaret nodded her head, eyes unwavering, and left. Siobhan mulled over Margaret's parting words. She had left her with the choice to take what belonged to her mother accompanied by a warning that it may bring her nothing but sorrow. She wondered if the Mother Superior had by her last actions just granted her access to the Vault of Confessions, or if she knew of her breach already. Perhaps she had simply been justifying her decision to deny Siobhan access. Uncertain, she decided not to risk reading her mother's confession for fear of being discovered and relieved of it. She decided it could wait till she was in a place that was safe and secure.

Siobhan barely slept, clutching her backpack tightly as she used it as a hard pillow. At first light, Siobhan made her way back down the hill to the Moreruela Abbey, knowing she could read the book once she got back to her hotel room.

An hour later, the bus arrived. It was almost mid-morning when an exhausted Siobhan arrived at the reception of the Hotel Zamora. She opened the door, ready to collapse, and found her room turned upside down. Her suitcase was open with the contents spilled on the floor. The inner lining of her suitcase had been slit open. The contents of her wallet and passport were strewn on the side table along with her money.

The warnings of the Zamora police officer and Sister Catherine rang in her ears. *Pay your respects and go home. You are not safe here... You* must *leave Zamora.*

Siobhan tucked *The Confession* away in her mother's habit. Then, with her passport, tickets and money in her hand luggage, she went to report the intrusion to reception. The hotel manager phoned the police and told her to wait in the lobby.

For ten minutes, Siobhan rocked backwards and forwards on her heels as she waited for the police. When the bell rang over the door announcing their arrival, it turned out to be the same policeman who had escorted Siobhan to the hotel the night she arrived. He asked her to confirm that nothing was missing from her luggage and insisted she should leave Zamora for her own safety.

Siobhan checked out of the hotel and the policeman escorted her to the train station. There he put her on the next train out to Madrid.

In the late afternoon, Siobhan finally checked into a room in a budget hotel near Madrid Chamartín station. The meagre third floor room had a tiny balcony that overlooked the noisy railway tracks of the second largest train station in the city. Her initial jetlagged night, followed by the events in Convento de Santa Teresa, had taken its toll, but Siobhan knew she had to open the book.

She locked the outer French doors to the balcony, then sat at the desk. She opened her mother's confession and began to read.

My darling daughter Siobhan;

The soul has only one mirror and that is love. The search for this reflection is the journey of life.

Without love, the soul cannot see its beauty. You must know that I have always loved you more than life itself. Your love was my soul's mirror and this book contains the reason I chose not to bathe in its reflection, the source of my life's greatest joy.

Your walk of life is yours alone, others may walk it with you, but nobody can walk it for you. This is my story and the reason I chose to walk my last years alone.

In the western world we believe our destiny is ours to make. You make your own luck. In the eastern world, the arrangements are decided and all you can do is attend to the detail. Your destiny is written for you.

My destiny, I would learn, was written for someone else altogether.

This is my confession and my legacy. It is for you and you alone. It will be hard enough for you to come to terms with my ordeal—hard enough for you to believe—that being cryptic would only confuse you further. There are many things I did that I wanted to take to my grave. As your loving mother, this is not the way I would have wished you to remember me. Yet I have included every detail, no matter how uncomfortable it was for me to write you, or how trivial it may seem. This is because you need to know and it may just be something that could save you in the future. They say the Devil is in the detail and it is this detail that will allow you to verify my story.

At the end of this book is a sealed section containing pages from The Devil's Prayer. I beg that you do not open it until you have read my confession in its entirety.

With all my love,

Mum

PART TWO:
LIKE A BULL TO THE SLAUGHTER

CHAPTER 6

HIDE AND SEEK

OCTOBER 1994

Currumbin Valley was a sleepy suburb in 1994. Located south-west of the surfing beaches of Burleigh Heads, it was only about seven kilometres away from the busy Gold Coast highway—which made it easy for me to get to work. It was the kind of place where everyone had large front yards and a pool in the backyard—a family neighbourhood. Often you would see young men leaning on the trays of their utes joking around. Everyone knew everyone and we all looked out for each other. Perfect for us.

Our Queenslander was nestled in a quiet cul-de-sac among other modest houses. Children played in the yards and rode their bicycles up and down our quiet leafy street. The plots on our side of the road backed onto the dense forest of the Nicoll Scrub National Park.

It all started one October evening, when you, my beautiful three-year-old girl, who I loved with all my heart, asked your nanna if you could play hide and seek. I will always remember the way she described it.

As she counted with her eyes shut, you squealed, running around looking for a place to hide. "Nanna, not yet! Nanna, Nanna don't cheat. Shut your eyes!" As she counted past twelve, the pitter-patter of your little feet faded away.

After counting to twenty, Nanna started to look for you.

She briefly looked in the lounge, then walked through the large corridor, deliberately stomping her feet on the old wooden floorboards expecting to hear your giggles, which, of course, she would ignore. She slowly and purposefully opened the small cupboards calling as she always did. "Siobhan, are you inside the cupboard?" ... "Siobhan, are you under the bed?" She then announced her arrival as she entered each bedroom. After she searched unsuccessfully in the four bedrooms, Nanna came back to the lounge, a little flustered.

She looked around behind the curtains just in case, and then back under the dining table. "Siobhan, darling? Where are you?" She then walked into the adjoining kitchen, thinking you might have hidden in the pantry.

Unbeknownst to your nanna at the time, you had followed our golden retriever, Kami, outside through the dog door and onto the pool deck.

In the dying light of dusk, our neighbour, Simon Carter, my childhood sweetheart, stood, waiting on his balcony. As a country boy from Wandoan, his family had moved here when he was just six years old so he could get a better schooling. Once the kids grew up, his parents moved back to Wandoan and his siblings migrated to the bright city lights of Brisbane and Sydney. Simon got a job at the local council and stayed behind. The family farm was in the endless negotiations of being sold to a multinational coal company. Simon, however, wanted nothing to do with the constant family feud that had ensued over the unrealistic expectations of his siblings. It had been four years since I met your father and broke Simon's heart. Although he had been dating Samantha for a few months now, I somehow still felt he had not yet moved on. Every evening, without fail, he would stand in his balcony and wait to say a little hello.

He watched you crouch behind Kami, looking unwaveringly towards the kitchen window. In the silence of our leafy suburban street, Simon could hear Edith's voice. "Siobhan, where are you hiding, darling?" He assumed that Edith was out on the pool deck with you.

It was then that the cacophony of my little Holden Gemini, with Cold Chisel's *Khe Sanh* on full blast, came down the street. It was spring, and the beautiful jacarandas were in full purple bloom, and the orange birds of paradise, which dotted every garden, proudly pranced in the evening breeze.

Simon waved to me and I honked, as I did each day, and, as always, he smiled back shyly.

Simon turned his attention to me. I think that you were trying so hard to stay out of your nanna's sight that, step by step, you inched backwards, unknowingly getting closer and closer towards the edge of the swimming pool.

As I drove my car into the driveway, Kami came running with her tail wagging. I could barely hear her barking over my loud music. Still in the driver's seat, I slowly collected my things, singing along to the music. I switched the car off and opened the door to an excited Kami, who was barking furiously. I crouched down to pat her when I heard Simon scream, "Denise! Denise!"

I ducked my head out from under the carport and looked up at Simon on his balcony. He was pointing furiously at the back of the house. "Siobhan is in the pool!"

I heard nothing else.

I dropped everything I had and ran to the back of the house. It was dusk and in the dim light of evening, you were there in the pool, face down. You looked lifeless. I jumped in, heels and all, and dragged you back to the edge. By this time Simon had run down from his balcony and helped me hoist you onto the pool deck.

Nanna came out a blubbering mess, trying to explain what happened. I never heard a word she said. I was trying CPR, pumping away at your little chest. Simon bolted into the house to call an ambulance.

I don't know how long it was, but the sounds of sirens finally came. The flash of the reflecting red and blue lights could be seen even in the backyard. Two paramedics pulled me off you and set about to try and revive you. They were asking me questions, but I couldn't understand a word. My mind was numbed into a blur. A small crowd of neighbours had gathered around by this time.

To babysit your grandchild is perhaps the oldest foundation stone of the pillars of intergenerational family love. Your nanna was beside herself, praying fervently.

The paramedics took out an automated external defibrillator and gave you a shock. You didn't respond. They pumped again on your chest, this time a bit harder and more desperately.

I prayed like I had never prayed before. They stopped pumping and set up the AED for a second shock. Your little body jolted from the ground with the shock, but still you didn't respond.

Then one paramedic looked up at the other and shook his head. The collective gasp of sinking hearts created a vacuum, sucking the last traces of hope from the air. Nanna fainted.

My world was plunging into a black abyss, and I could feel my will to live being plucked right out of me. I tugged at the sleeve of the paramedic. "No, no. Don't give up," I begged. I could sense that they had resigned, yet to appease me, they started half-heartedly to pump your chest again. I prayed aloud—or silently, I do not know—and I cried. "God, please help me. Someone, *anyone*, please help!"

A nondescript man, about forty years old, wearing a grey fedora, stepped out of the crowd. I had never seen him before. He handed the paramedics a larger set of AEDs. "Give the child the adult dose," he said. They shook their heads in disagreement. The stranger commanded softly in a compelling rasp, almost in a whisper, "Do it. You have nothing to lose."

As though compelled, the paramedics did as they were told. They hooked it up and gave you a perfunctory third shock to appease the persistent man. To their disbelief, you spluttered back to life. They pumped away furiously as you coughed up the water from your lungs, reviving slowly.

As I watched you breathe, I knew I had been given another chance. The paramedics started to pack up. I remember clutching your little hands and kissing them incessantly. It was only then that I thought to thank the man who saved your life. I looked around, but he was nowhere to be seen. He must have slipped into the night.

The next morning, I found our beautiful Kami dead in the pool.

Currumbin Valley used to be a peaceful country suburb. Somehow I always felt that day was the day it lost its innocence.

After two sleepless nights, Siobhan, overcome by jet lag, shut the book and drifted off into a deep sleep.

Her dreams re-enacted the evening her mother had written about.

Siobhan was a three-year-old, running squealing after Kami, the big sedate golden retriever. The dog, wanting nothing more than peace and quiet, squeezed out through the dog door, but Siobhan had gleefully pursued her. Out on the pool deck, she watched Edith's silhouette walk past the kitchen windows. Not wanting to be seen by her nanna, Siobhan retreated backwards, step by step. Just then, Kami barked and ran. She took another step backwards, and suddenly there was nothing but air and then water as she fell in the deep end of the pool.

She thrashed around, gasping for air, and then quickly sank to the bottom as she inhaled more and more water. She slipped into blackness; she was moving down a pitch dark tunnel, gravitating towards a white distant light. As she moved towards the light, a man grabbed her little hand and led her away from the white brightness.

Siobhan woke from her dream, still sitting at the desk in her room, cold sweat making her clothes stick to her skin. Sunlight filtered through the French doors. She checked her watch. It was just after 9 am. She had slept for nearly twelve hours. Hungry, she hurried down to the local shops near the station to get a snack. As she strolled, she wondered why her mother had excluded even Jess and her nanna from her confession. She realised Jess was only eleven when their mother left them and perhaps her mother still remembered her as a precocious child. As for her nanna, Siobhan smiled with the realisation that her darling grandmother could not fight her way out of a paper bag. After a quick bite, she returned to her room, settled back at her desk, opened *The Confession* and continued reading.

CHAPTER 7
THE LUCK OF THE DEVIL

My luck had changed and I sensed it. Everything started to click. My career as a newsreader started to skyrocket. I had been signed from the local Gold Coast channel to anchor the evening state news on one of the major channels.

Less than a month later, I went with Simon and Samantha for the opening of his friend Matt's restaurant.

Matt Chambers had finished his stint in the Australian Football League with Saint Kilda and had moved to Currumbin to start a restaurant near Elephant Rock, out on the beach. Simon and Matt were friends who had played footy for the same team in Nerang for a season. It was a strange friendship between the extroverted Matt and the introverted Simon.

Simon often struggled to make ends meet on his meagre wage as a Gold Coast City Council worker. Although he had numerous chances to take bribes to push permits through, Simon was as straight as they came. As always with him, it was his heart that ruled his head. There were rumours circulating in the local parish that he had bent the rules for the first time when he approved the permit applications for his buddy Matt.

For me, it was love at first sight. It was a few days until

Matt became my best friend; he was a bloke's bloke, but he melted me with his charm. After a whirlwind eight months of romance, Matt proposed and I had no hesitation in saying yes.

The diamond in my life was you, shining more brightly each day. Perhaps your joust with death made me appreciate each and every second I had with you.

8TH AUGUST 1995

It was the day I turned twenty-eight. Life could not have been better. My friends organised a party to celebrate my birthday at Matt's restaurant.

At around six in the evening, I was having a quiet glass of wine on the front deck with Edith, to celebrate my birthday. You were playing on the deck with your dolls when I heard a familiar whistle.

Simon popped his head over the fence, and your eyes lit up. He waved you over and you ran to him, abandoning your dolls. He reached over and handed you a small wrapped gift.

I chided him, "Hey! It's not *her* birthday." He just smiled his shy smile and nodded to me. "You ready to go, birthday girl?"

Minutes later, I was in Simon's beat-up, maroon coloured Magna driving to Matt's restaurant. Simon honked his car as we left and I waved to you and Edith standing out on the front porch.

Matt's restaurant was on Currumbin beach, on the north-facing side of Elephant Rock, so named for its suggestion of a mammoth in its shape. The ocean often lapped at the base of the rock when the tide was in. The restaurant overlooked the beautiful Pacific Ocean to the east, Burleigh Heads and Surfers Paradise to the north, and the seaside town of Coolangatta to the south.

The restaurant was quiet, but that was to be expected for a Tuesday night. It was winter, so the sun had set early, and the beautiful sea views blended into a dull blackness.

A corner table had been set aside for us, overlooking the lights of Currumbin. My best friend, Carine Sanderson, came running. If I ever pictured someone as a cheerleader or prom queen in an American movie, it was always Carine. She gave me a bear hug. "Happy birthday, gorgeous girl. Hope your day has been filled with sunshine, sparkles and love!"

It never struck me then, but over the years that followed when I relived this night a million times over, I realised that our friendship was just as improbable as Simon and Matt's. Here was someone glamorous, vivacious and extroverted, associating with me, a single mother focused on the reality of bringing up a daughter and juggling a hectic life with a job in the media. Deep down I was slightly jealous of how Carine seemed so much more fitting for Matt than me. Matt sensed it and he always made light of it, assuring me that glamour went hand in hand with high maintenance and trouble. That's what I loved about Matt; he just knew those little things that got me worried and intuitively dispensed with them and let me fly.

Carine handed me a wrapped present. "This is from me and Vince." I walked towards Vince, who was standing at the table, and pecked him on the cheek to say thank you.

Vince Batista was a wannabe gangster. He worked hard at the gym and always dressed sharp. He wore black, trimmed his hair in a crew cut like a boxer, wore large gold chains and had a few tattoos. It was this bad boy stereotype that Carine was perpetually drawn to, like a moth to a flame.

Much too often, like *Groundhog Day*, her teary voice vowing never to go down this path again. Within a few days it would all be forgotten, a new beau on the scene, a carbon copy of the one departed or with the same rap sheet, written in another language. However, in Vince's defence, he was neither in a disastrous relationship nor married. And for a change, Carine was not the other woman.

Ironic as it all was, Carine worked as a legal secretary in one of Brisbane's leading law firms. The sharp lawyers and professionals of Queen Street doted on her, chased her, sent her flowers and put up with her numerous late starts. She flirted with their rich clients, but deep down they were all just boring to her. Carine always wanted what she could not have.

Vince introduced me to Dev (or "Davo" as everyone called him), an Indian friend who had joined his garage as a business partner and was currently sharing his house till he found a place of his own.

Davo was scrawny, wiry and probably in his early forties. When I welcomed him, he seemed overtly grateful just to be out with people. He timidly extended his hand to wish me a happy birthday, and I squeezed it warmly. As he came close, I discovered that he reeked of an expensive male perfume, just that little too much. I smiled and said, "Oh, you smell nice, what are you wearing?"

"It's Issey Miyaki," he announced proudly. I turned, trying hard not to cover my nose, and smiled on seeing the big banner strung from the window behind our table: "Happy Birthday Denise." Matt, as always, had gone out of his way to make it my day.

A few seconds later, Simon's girlfriend, Samantha, came out of the restaurant kitchen. Six months pregnant with their first child, she was working at Matt's restaurant to supplement their income. She gave Simon a perfunctory kiss.

On her own, Samantha was charming, but I hated what she had done to Simon. She never let him forget that—in her mind—she had 'settled' for him. She was a try-hard, and I was always wary that, beneath her superficial smile, she never really liked me. Perhaps Simon's continued kindness and thoughtfulness to me had something to do with it.

She turned to me and handed me a wrapped gift. "It's a little something for you," she said, then looked daggers at Simon and added unnecessarily, "It's not much, but Simon's wage doesn't help."

Simon turned red, and the rest of the group looked away pretending not to hear. I screwed up my face and made a funny, mock-angry face at Simon. It was all I could do to defuse the situation.

Finally, Matt came out of the kitchen, wearing a chef's apron. I jumped up and ran to him. He lifted me off the ground and kissed me. He pulled a slim black case out of his back pocket. "Close your eyes and hold out your hand," he told me.

When I opened my eyes, I had the most beautiful silver diamante watch on my wrist. It sparkled in the restaurant lights. I was speechless. The engagement ring just two weeks ago and now this.

"To the best times I've had, and to the future," said Matt. He winked at my agape expression. "You can make it up to me tonight."

Everyone chuckled, and out of the corner of my eye, I noticed Carine's face take on a jealous hue. I was momentarily taken aback, but I guess I would have been jealous if Matt had been her fiancé.

Before Samantha went back to the kitchen, she verbally stabbed Simon one more time. She pointed to her own watch. "Watch and learn," she hissed. Simon looked at the floor, shaking his head.

After a few moments of awkward silence, Simon tried to move on. "So mate, how did you get such an ocker name like Davo?" he asked Vince's Indian friend. Davo smiled inanely; he seemed to have that expression permanently fixed on his face. "My surname is Dev."

"Like that cricketer?" I chirped in.

Davo beamed. "Yes, just like Kapil Dev. You follow cricket?"

I quickly backed out. "No, not really."

Slowly our not so quiet table got going as alcohol flowed and the food came out. The restaurant was empty except for three other tables, and soon enough we drowned out the others with our boisterous celebrations. When the birthday cake came out, Simon led the chorus of shouting. "Make a wish! Make a wish!"

I blew out the candles.

"So Denise, what did you wish for?" Davo asked.

"I am so happy here with all my friends and my fiancé. I wish this night would never end."

"You know in India they say, 'be careful what you wish for,'" said Davo, to everyone's embarrassment. I shrugged and smiled politely while Vince glared at his friend.

In time the cake was gone, and the food was finished. Simon, slightly drunk, put his arms around Samantha's waist. "Darling, can you get me another beer?"

Samantha squirmed out of his hold and placed a glass of water in front of him. "We can't afford it." Simon turned a bright red as the rest of the group pretended again to ignore it.

Simon followed her to the kitchen, and once out of earshot from the table, he gently tugged at her elbow. She turned around and hissed into his ear. I couldn't hear what she said, but Simon was ashen faced when he came back to the table.

He sat down and pushed his chair back, his elbows on his knees. He cupped his face, looking straight down at the ground between his feet. Vince tried to comfort him by putting his arm around Simon. "She's pregnant, mate. They get very hormonal."

Simon lifted his head and looked blankly at the ceiling, shaking his head for a while. He got up, placed a fifty-dollar note on the table and looked at me. "I'm sorry, Denise. I have to go." He turned and walked to the door.

I ran after him and caught him just as he opened the door. Simon ignored my tugging at his shirt until we were both on the outdoor deck alone.

He turned and looked at me and I saw tears in his eyes. He said nothing. I put my arms out to hug him, but he just smiled meekly. I knew I had to let him leave. I watched him walk down to the car park and drive off. To the west, the houses perched on Currumbin hill beyond had now lit up as the tail lights of his car disappeared into the dark night.

The table settled uneasily for a few minutes and Matt, as always, had the answer. He borrowed Carine's camera and coaxed one of the few remaining patrons to take a photograph of our group. I sat in the centre with Matt at my side and we took the shot.

Siobhan, I left a photograph in the vault—face down. It is the only photograph I have of him. Throughout all these years in Moreruela, I could never look at it again. The same man who saved your life. He was there that night, peering through the window.

Siobhan remembered the card she had pulled from the dark vault and had placed inside the diary. She fanned through the pages and removed it.

It was a photograph of her mother surrounded by her friends, looking lovingly into Matt's eyes, who obviously adored her. Siobhan recognised Carine Sanderson as the beautiful blonde standing next to her mother, her arm around a tattooed, good looking, muscled man she assumed was Vince. Standing next to Vince was the scrawny tanned Davo, and standing on the other side of Matt was the pregnant Samantha. Their glasses were raised. It was a happy snap. In the corner behind Samantha, through the window, was the face of a nondescript man wearing a fedora, smiling strangely at the group.

Siobhan looked at the clock, it was close to noon. The sun would have just set in Australia. She called home and spoke to Edith and Jess. Siobhan described the unmarked grave, but thought it best not to alarm them about her running away to Madrid.

"Did she leave a note or anything?" Jess asked, but Siobhan stayed silent, not sure what to say. Jess read the silence as disappointment. She knew how badly her sister needed closure. "I had hoped she had for your sake," she said. Siobhan knew that for Jess it confirmed what she'd always known: their mother had abandoned them.

CHAPTER 8

WHEN YOUR NUMBERS DROP

August 1995

We had just taken the first photograph and were settling for a second one, when the sounds of three Harley Davidsons, in quick succession, roared into the car park below. "Fuck. Not now!" Matt muttered to Samantha, and quickly headed towards the restaurant door.

Before he reached it, the door was flung open ferociously. Three heavily tattooed bikies, in full leather gear, prowled inside, their faces furious.

Matt approached the leader of the pack. "C'mon Charlie. It's my fiancée's birthday. Can't this wait until tomorrow?"

Charlie smiled wickedly at his two mates. "Boys, we must have forgot our invite."

A short, stocky bikie came out from behind the other two and smiled strangely, pointing to Vince. "Oh lookie who's here… it's our mate Vincey."

He strutted deliberately towards Vince, who cowered in fear. It was a strange sight to see. "Rod, I was coming to see you. I swear," he squeaked.

Rod leered back. "Of course you were." He pulled on the back of Vince's shirt and yanked him up, relieved Vince of his wallet and emptied the contents on the table. He took all the notes and flung the wallet back into Vince's face. "Looks like Barbie and you have been sampling the merchandise. You'd better have it all when you come to see me tomorrow."

The third bikie turned to Carine and lewdly grabbed his crotch. "My favourite girl." He winked at her and pulled her up by the arm. "C'mon Barbie. Let's go party."

Carine, embarrassed, tried hard to wriggle out. "Not today, Steve."

Steve looked disdainful. "Not asking, bitch," he said. Without having much of a choice, Carine reluctantly allowed him to drag her towards the restrooms.

I stood up and objected, "Leave her alone!" Matt stepped in between the bikies and me and signalled me to calm down.

At the same time, Vince tugged at my arm and whispered, "Don't. It's fine." Confused, I backed down.

A bespectacled patron dining with his wife watched the bikies curiously from another table. Rod saw him and flew across the room. "What the fuck are you looking at, dickhead?" The man quickly lowered his eyes. Rod snatched the man's spectacles and smashed them under his boot. He turned to the other two occupied tables and the patrons were staring down at the tablecloths in front of them.

Steve came out from the restrooms with Carine closely behind. She sniffed loudly, her eyes were wide. She readjusted her bra and skirt as she walked, seemingly oblivious of anyone else in the room. I rushed over to her. "Are you okay?" I asked anxiously as she sniffed again and rubbed her nose.

Carine waved it off, a bit manic. "Yeah, I'm good! I'm fan-fucking-tastic!" I had lived a very sheltered life; it never even crossed my mind that Carine had gone with the bikie to snort a line of cocaine. Always the last to know, Carine fed her habit in cash or kind from whoever would supply it.

By now Charlie and Steve had dragged Matt by his collar to the door. Charlie snarled, "I don't like being dicked around. Don't fuck with me."

Matt meekly replied, "Charlie, the winter is never a good time for a beach restaurant, give me a month or two and we will be back on track."

"We don't give a fuck what season it is. Rent is due, you have one week." Charlie pointed at me. "You fuck with us and we know where to find her. Got it?" He pushed Matt away, hard. Matt stumbled back towards us.

On their way out, Rod upended a table, sending glasses and plates shattering to the floor.

As soon as I heard the bikes roar away, Matt began to calm the patrons. He offered to waive their bills for the night. Finally, he settled back down at our table. "What the hell was that all about? What is going on?" I demanded. Matt shrugged it off. "Not now, darling. I'll explain everything when we get home." He turned to the group and announced, "Let's not spoil this special evening. Drinks anyone?"

Carine and Vince loudly cheered and walked with Matt to the bar. I approached Carine. "What is going on?" She just smiled brilliantly and said, "Denise darling, it's your night." Matt turned from the bar, scrunched his face at me, and sternly added, "Let it go, honey."

I am not sure what I could have done differently, but it was then I realised there were things I did not know about my closest and dearest friends. I thought perhaps my birthday celebration was not the best time or place to air this dirty laundry.

Shortly after the bikies left, the restaurant emptied out,

except for our group. The alcohol flowed freely and Davo was visibly drunk and gawking at Carine.

Matt teased Carine. "Looks like you have a fan." She light-heartedly winked back at Matt. "At least he has good taste." Davo blushed, knowing he was busted, and as he raised his hand to cover his face, he knocked over his beer. "Shit yaar!" he exclaimed. It was the first time his Indian accent came out. I was a bit tipsy and laughed at him. "That's so quaint, you hardly have an Indian accent except for that."

Davo recovered quickly and laughed. "Well, I have been in Australia for ten years, Denise."

I looked at my wrist, admiring my new diamante watch and realised it was 8:30 pm. I grabbed the remote and changed the channel on the TV above the bar. Matt and Vince had been following the footy and immediately reacted. I pleaded, it was just for a few minutes. I wanted to see the lotto results. Vince conceded. "Only because it's your birthday." Samantha came out of the kitchen holding her ticket too and we both stood side by side.

I watched intently as the announcer on TV called out the numbers. "The fifth number tonight is thirty-seven." Matt tapped me on the shoulder and said light-heartedly, "Darling?"

I put my hand up. "Just a sec, Matt." The next number rolled out. The announcer excitedly added, "The sixth number tonight is eight." Matt teased, "Hey, that's your birthdate... you must have it." My heart was pumping wildly and I gasped barely audibly. "I have all six so far... come on number three." Samantha huffed and tore her ticket in disgust.

The TV announcer boomed, "Fifteen million dollars tonight! It's a big one for sure!" My eyes were glued to the screen. My heart stopped when a yellow number rolled out of the barrel. I knew now it was a small single digit number.

I strained hard to read the number as it rolled along the tube and as it slowed down I was almost certain it was the number three. The number stopped rolling and came to a stop. The TV announcer's voice came out over a dead silent room and confirmed it. "Tonight's last number is three."

I heard a collective gasp. I double-checked and triple-checked the numbers. I put the ticket away, in a state of shock. I was not going to let it into anyone else's hands.

Suddenly, Matt broke the silence with a scream, and there were high fives and cheers and everyone was congratulating me. Carine asked to see the ticket and I held it tightly, never letting it leave my hands and then quickly hid it away again. My hands were shaking.

Matt popped a bottle of champagne to celebrate. "Fifteen million! You could fly to Paris and buy a whole new wardrobe," Carine said, wistfully.

Samantha added dryly, "Wardrobe! With fifteen million, she could buy a mansion—or three."

I remember Matt lifting me off my feet and kissing me. I had one arm around his neck and the other hand in my jeans, clutching tightly on to my winning ticket. I knew then that my life would never be the same. Had I won the fifteen million alone, or were there others who'd had the winning numbers as well? Even with five winners it was still a lot of money.

Once everyone had calmed down from the excitement, we started relaxing and having fun. Davo had only got drunker and was openly staring at Carine. He smiled at her, and she nudged Vince to attention.

Vince tried to be polite. "Davo, mate. It's really late. It's getting to be a time for close friends only." Davo beamed brightly and nodded his head. "Oh Vince, thanks!" he said, and settled back into his seat.

Carine looked up in exasperation and dragged Samantha onto the outdoor deck for a cigarette.

I fell back into my own world. I was thinking of who I would share my win with, what I could get Edith and my friends. Perhaps buy a house, a car, take a trip with Edith, Matt and you to Europe and even donate some to the poor. People talked around me and I could barely concentrate on what they were saying. My mind was racing at a thousand miles an hour.

I remember Samantha and Carine being out in the balcony for a while. Carine briefly popped her head back in and caught Vince's attention. She signalled for Vince to join them on the outdoor deck and he did. I was happy to be with Matt while Davo looked wistfully at the balcony door, contemplating whether to join the party outside.

When the three returned, Carine and Samantha pulled Matt away from me. They headed into the kitchen and were gone for a while. I was sure they were planning a birthday surprise. Left with Vince and Davo, I pretended to watch the footy game on TV, to avoid making pleasant chit chat.

It was a while later that Matt came out with a bottle of Moët. There were six filled glasses on the tray, and one had a ribbon tied to it—a special decoration for mine.

With everyone around the table, Matt raised a toast and shouted, "Bottoms up!" I downed the glass. He poured out another round and we sculled our drinks again.

I sat down feeling very content and then the champagne

hit me. I suddenly started to feel very groggy and drunk, and lost the ability to focus. When I came back to, I noticed Carine watching me intently. When she saw me looking at her, she bit her lip nervously as she smiled gently. Davo still had his eyes transfixed on her. Samantha was busy, laying the tables for the next day. Matt was deep in conversation with Vince as they both watched the footy.

Carine excused herself from the table and walked towards the toilet, swaying her hips very deliberately. When she reached the bathroom hallway, she looked back straight at Davo and winked at him. Then, curling her finger, she summoned him. Davo looked over at Matt and Vince who were completely engrossed in the game, and then excused himself and followed Carine. I could not believe my eyes, but I was finding it extremely hard to focus or to concentrate as thoughts and images drifted in and out. I had a feeling that something horrible was going to happen. I didn't know what was wrong with my friends, but my insecurities had kicked in. I was feeling more drunk than normal, and perhaps a little paranoid. I pulled my lottery ticket from my pocket and hid it within the waistband of my underwear.

I must have dozed off, because I woke to a huge argument, which had erupted between Vince and Carine. Vince was dragging Davo along the floor by his collar. Carine was pleading. Vince was screaming at her. "Fuck off! I can't believe you were fucking this loser!"

Vince turned his attention to Davo, threatening to beat him up, when Matt intervened and asked Vince to take it outside. Vince kept smacking Davo on his head as he dragged him out of the restaurant. Carine followed them out crying.

I staggered to the window and opened it to get some

fresh air. With my head hanging out, I could hear the argument between Vince, Davo and Carine and see them in the shadows in the car park below.

Suddenly the argument stopped and I heard a car drive into the car park. Simon entered the restaurant, and he waved to me before heading into the kitchen where Samantha and Matt were noisily cleaning up. I drifted off again.

I awoke to the sound of raised voices coming from the kitchen. Simon stomped out, fuming. He cursed, shaking his head. "Fuck this for a joke." As he headed towards the door, Matt called out. "Hey mate, could you take Denise home, she's not feeling well."

Simon turned to me and forced a smile. "Hey birthday girl, c'mon it's time to go home."

I tried to get up, but my head was spinning. Simon rushed over and caught me, and I slumped with one arm over his shoulder. I slowly made my way out with him. Simon laughed. "Haven't seen you this drunk since high school."

My childhood sweetheart, he had a heart of gold. He was always there for me. Once in the car, I felt more at ease. We drove away from the beach and soon crossed the Gold Coast highway into the hinterland.

Simon began to curse. He was shaking his head, clenching his fists on the steering wheel. His driving was growing aggressive as he complained bitterly about how hard he tried, but could never please Samantha.

We were driving through the forested area in the hinterland, and the trees drifted past my vision as green blurs. Simon tried to talk to me, or maybe he was just venting. "Denise, I swear. If it wasn't for the baby, I would leave her." I was struggling to stay awake.

I could see a car approaching through one of the side

mirrors. It made to overtake us. As it came alongside, the driver swerved heavily and rammed our car.

I was jolted and, sensing danger, became more alert. Simon tried regaining control, as the car temporarily kicked up dust off the side of the road. He just managed to bring it back up on the road again when the other car reappeared and deliberately barged our car again. This time we ran off the road. Simon hit the brakes, but it was too late; the car slammed into a tree.

I saw Simon was slumped over the wheel.

"Simon. You okay, Simon?" I shook him in panic as I called out to him to wake up, but he was out cold. I had to get him out of the car and get some help. I managed to pull myself together. I groggily staggered around the car to the driver's side to drag Simon out. I heard footsteps on the gravel behind me; I turned, and only had time to briefly glimpse a man in a makeshift balaclava before a thick cloth bag was yanked over my head. I screamed. I heard another man running and a large hand stifled my scream. Someone grabbed both my hands and started tying them together. I tried to kick and get away but I was sandwiched close between the two men and had no leverage to move. I bit the hand that was muffling me and it momentarily left my mouth.

"Help——!" I managed to scream, before a fist crunched into the side of my head. It felt like my skull had exploded. My legs gave way and I blacked out.

CHAPTER 9

BE CAREFUL WHAT YOU WISH FOR

When I came to, everything was completely black. I was lying sideways and I could feel the bag tied tightly over my head. My mouth was gagged with what tasted like someone's dirty gym socks, and my hands were tied behind my back with a zip tie. I could hear the road under me and, after a few bounces, I realised I was in the boot of a car. A short while later, the ride got bumpier and noisier as smooth bitumen was replaced by rocky dirt. My body was pressed against the rear of the boot as the car climbed a hill for quite a while and then it stopped.

The boot popped open and I was roughly lifted out. I struggled, trying to shake off my abductors by kicking out at them. Someone very strong was holding my tightly bound hands behind my back and had lifted them up uncomfortably behind me so I was forced to crouch over. I could no longer kick. I was manhandled towards the front of the idling car.

Through the thick cloth bag on my head, I could just see blurred shapes silhouetted by the headlights of the car. Someone was holding me tightly—I could feel the bruises forming under calloused fingers. Another person reached towards my belt and quickly undid the fastening. I wriggled away, but the hands holding my arms yanked and I whimpered. My belt made a dull sound as the buckle hit the ground below. Soon my jeans were undone as well.

My captor released my arms momentarily, but it was only so they could grasp me under my armpits. I was hoisted above the ground with such ease that I knew my captor must be incredibly strong—a man. I wished I could scream, but the bundle of socks had been shoved in too tightly for me to spit them out.

Rough hands pulled at my feet until my legs were almost perpendicular to my body. I winced as my knees jolted in their sockets. Forcefully my sneakers and socks were yanked off. My legs fell back down awkwardly. I heard my shoes land in the distance, first one then the other. Someone grabbed me by the ankles, and tugged at my jeans. I felt the waistband slip further down until, with a soft crumpled sound, they came off entirely. The cold night air enveloped my bare legs and I shivered.

I'd heard that when one of your senses is deadened, every other one is heightened. And, at this moment, I discovered this to be true. Without my eyes to guide me, my hearing became sharper. About a metre or two away, I could hear the sound of fabric being turned inside out.

While the sounds were stronger, so was my sense of touch. I felt my captor lower me to the ground with fingers that pressed hard into my shoulders. I had the sudden sensation of cold dirt on my bare feet. There was a rock under my left heel, but I had bigger problems than the discomfort it offered. Those prodding fingers pushed me round until I was facing the man. I could tell by the angle of his hands that he was much taller than me.

My blouse, a gift from your nanna for my birthday, was ripped sharply apart, fragile buttons twanging in the night.

The man yanked the shirt past my shoulders and down, but stopped when he realised it couldn't pass over the zip tie that held my hands captive. There was the sound of ripping fabric and my blouse came away in, what I imagined was, tatters. A piece of sleeve got caught in the new watch Matt had given me. The watch was removed from my wrist and thrown in the same direction as my jeans. I heard someone catch it.

A gentle breeze—the only gentle thing about my trip home so far—brushed at my stomach and I realised uncomfortably that I was standing in the middle of who-knows-where, with who-knows-who, in only my underwear. I whimpered through my gag.

My bra came off next. I let out a cry through my gag. It was beyond humiliating. I was trembling in embarrassment and fear. The delicate fabric I'd picked out for my fiancé was ripped carelessly off my body. I could imagine it lying there on the ground, the white fabric smeared with dirt, the intricate lace ripped from seam to seam so that I could be divested of it.

I had only my panties left, and then soon they were gone too. I heard rather than felt the fluttering of my lotto ticket disappearing in the wind.

I took comfort that at least they couldn't have that. I heard one of them run after the paper to grab it while the other held me with one hand. I tried to break away, but my strength could not match his.

I knew at that moment that whoever had abducted me was after the lottery ticket. What else could it be? The true betrayal was in the knowledge that the person responsible had to have been in my group of friends that night.

I learned that day that premonitions were real and had

substance—although they were not set in stone. If you did enough to get out of the situation where the worst could happen, or if the perpetrators could sense their actions would have consequences beyond the reward, and abort, then you might just be safe.

A new set of hands was holding me. These were thinner, and I could hear the heavy footsteps of my previous captor move away from me in diminuendo till they faded out completely.

I could smell a familiar male perfume—Issey Miyaki. It was the cologne that Davo was stinking of at my party. Although blindfolded, I could feel his lecherous eyes study my naked body.

Davo held me with his left hand and used his right, to grope my naked body from behind. I kicked hard backwards and threw him off balance. He blurted, "Shit yaar!" as he fell away from me.

I ran blindly into the forest. My balance was off with my hands still tied. As I ran, I grazed a few branches and trees but I just kept going. I managed to get away some twenty, maybe thirty, metres before I tripped and fell forward at full stretch. With my hands tied, I could not get up quickly enough. I managed to kneel up again and tried desperately to move away from Davo's fast-approaching footsteps. I tried walking on my knees as fast as I could, but in seconds Davo tackled me and held me down.

I had a bag over my head, I was gagged, my hands were tied behind my back, and, to top it off, now I was pinned flat on my stomach. Davo sat atop my back, holding my neck down in the dirt with one hand. His other hand started to work its way between my legs. I tried to keep my legs together, but he pressed on my neck, forcing my face hard against the rocky ground. I didn't even feel the sharp stones cut my face. I tried to scream, but the muffled sounds that escaped me wouldn't have been audible from more than a couple of metres away.

Helpless and alone, I had no options left. Knowing who it was made it all the worse. As my body was violated, I felt defiled. Tears of humiliation streamed down my face.

Davo's wandering hand was prying deep inside me when I heard heavy footsteps approaching. Davo stopped his pawing, and now I could hear him breathing deeply. He didn't move, but continued to sit on my back and hold my neck hard against the ground.

I heard the zipping sound of the newcomer's fly being undone and my heart sank. Davo got off my back, yet he kept his hand firmly pressing my neck into the dirt. Two large hands grabbed my waist and lifted my hips upwards. My knees were kicked inwards under me so I was kneeling, my face pushed into the ground. I could not have been more vulnerable.

I have thought long and hard before writing the sordid details a mother would never want her daughter to know. I fear, should I leave something out, anything out, in an attempt to save my dignity and your opinion of me, it could well be at the cost of your safety.

The bigger man then proceeded to push my legs apart and rape me.

My only recourse during this was to focus my mind elsewhere and pretend that it was happening to a stranger. The accident and abduction had started to make some sense. Davo was a stranger to me, and he had seen an opportunity to change his life by stealing what could be fifteen million dollars. While Davo's molestation was fuelled by ungratified sexual energy, the actions of the second person made no sense, it was not about sex, but it was as though he was taking out his frustration with life by humiliating me.

When the bigger man finished with me, he moved around and firmly grabbed my neck and pressed down. I felt Davo's weight come off my shoulders and realised it was now his turn. Resigned to my fate, I was helpless as Davo fumbled his way into me. My wish that this night would never end had come back to haunt me.

Davo's grunts were growing more animated when I heard the rumblings of a car approaching. The heavy pressure on my neck released and I heard the big man start to run.

Davo, still engrossed in finishing, seemed oblivious. Without the bigger man holding me down, I attempted to wriggle away. The sound of the car approaching was now much louder.

"Shit," Davo muttered, and he pulled out of me and stumbled away.

I heard him run fast in the direction of his accomplice; soon they were both out of earshot. The approaching car stopped, its headlights beaming on me. With the bag over my head, all I could see was a blur. I realised that my gag had come loose in the struggle and I spat it out. "Help! Help me please!" I cried. My voice was feeble, broken and croaky.

I kneeled on the uneven ground. The scent of blood—my blood—was in the air, and I had begun to feel the sting of scrapes and cuts, not to mention the agonising pain below. The car simply idled with its headlights on me. I could see a blurred silhouette of a man standing in front of the car. I walked on my knees towards him.

The man remained unmoved.

I tried to stand, but I stumbled and fell flat. I tried hard to kneel again as I pleaded louder, "Help me please!" A sense of rage and repugnance at being so unfairly abused, pillaged and raped overwhelmed me. I turned and attempted to look to where I thought Davo and his friend had run. I shuddered in revulsion, wishing to shed my skin and could not stop myself from hissing venomously, "Davo."

I saw shadows move behind the blur of my obscured vision. The silhouette walked away. I heard the door of the car open and shut. The car continued to idle and I could make out the sound of whispers over the hum of the engine, though I couldn't make out the words.

I shuffled on my knees towards the car. I had nearly reached it when I heard one of the car's doors open. Shortly after, I heard footsteps retreating and then another door opened—or perhaps it was the car boot. Then another door opened and I heard heavier footsteps approach me and then pass me. The footsteps stopped. I sensed there was someone standing behind me, away from the light. As I turned my head towards the darkness, a fiery pain shot up the length of my back. The pain was like none I'd known before. It was like ice and fire had got together and created something so excruciating, I could practically taste it. I could no longer kneel as my torso collapsed and my body crumpled forward. My voice was hoarse from my screams. I didn't think I would ever stop. The pain went on and on. I was aware time was passing, but still I screamed.

Slowly, through the pain I realised my body was limp, and I couldn't actually hear my voice. Even though my body was lost to me, my mind was awake.

I was alert enough to know that I was being lifted and carried. Each movement was like a lancet into my spine. I had been thrown over the man's shoulder, my head hanging downwards, my legs over his front, and my arms still tied behind my back. I was aware of the source of my pain, which had sharpened into a point. There was something embedded in my back, but though the pain was unending, I could not scream anymore.

Through the fiery haze of agony, I felt the person throw me forwards. I expected to hit the ground suddenly, but there was nothing. I fell through the air until I could no longer stay conscious. Then there was darkness.

Hot tears fell onto the pages and Siobhan shut the book. Her horror mixed with rage and denial. It couldn't be true. Had this really happened or had her mother lost her mind?

She studied the loose photograph again. It was proof of her mother's memories. Was the second man her mother described, with the big hands, the unnamed person wearing the fedora? Siobhan struggled hard to jog her memory, but she was only four at the time when this happened.

She couldn't help but reopen the book.

CHAPTER 10
OF FRIENDS AND ALIBIS

AUGUST 1995

As I fell into the blackness, my last thoughts were of you. I saw your beautiful smile and somehow in my darkest hour, it made me wistful. I thought of all the things I wished I could have and should have done.

I saw from afar my own shattered body lying on a rocky ledge, near the bottom of a cliff. I saw my blood run red and my skin glow white, the dark bruises littering it a stark contrast that mocked the paleness. A tunnel of light beckoned me, but I did not want to leave. It was all so unfair; it was all so unjust.

I looked down on my own body, battered on the rocks and then back at the tunnel calling to me and drawing me in. A white light lay ahead, but I was frozen. I could not move towards it. I just watched over my body from above.

Later I learned that two mountain climbers attempting to scale a steep face of Mount Tomewin had found my naked body smashed against the rocks at dawn. A rescue helicopter had then air-lifted me to a hospital.

I was lost in a world of nothingness. I was sliding downhill into a blizzard at breakneck speed and I had no control. Everything around me was a perfect white.

Voices and screams faded in and out. I was helpless, the blizzard was the coma I was trapped in. I was gaining momentum as I travelled downwards, faster and faster. I was being sucked away. I grabbed at the white behind me, trying to stop. I tried to use my feet to slow me down. Nothing worked. Suddenly I realised I was holding on to a man's wrist. Gripping it so tight I thought the tendons in my hand would snap. I tried to dig my feet harder to stop, then noticed the white gave way to a thick mist. In the distance, there were shapeless forms. I heard Edith's sobs and prayers and a constant stream of footsteps.

The voices became more distinct. Edith was wailing, "She was drugged and raped and then some sick person impaled her with a crowbar. The doctors say her spinal cord was almost severed."

"Has she said anything?" That was Carine, her voice full of concern. Edith sobbed and said no, I might never wake up.

"It must have been those bikies." That voice was Matt's. I wanted to shout no, but I had no voice, no strength.

Edith said the police had thought that too, but the bikies in question had spent the night at a strip club in Surfers Paradise.

The sounds came and went and I could feel time slipping by.

This time Edith's voice was arguing bitterly that Simon should never had taken me home if he was drunk. Matt interjected that Simon had taken me home a million times before. The voices sometimes completely faded out as the blurred figures disappeared in the haze.

Eventually the mist cleared and I could hear the sounds of the hospital clearly. There was the beeping of machines, the clattering of wheels on linoleum, nurses rushing to and fro and the hushed breathing of someone beside me. There were smells too; I could smell the disinfectant in the air, trying to cover the stench of infection and death. I could smell my mother's perfume sharply in my nostrils, and I inhaled its comforting scent.

I knew I could open my eyes if I tried. My eyelashes were gritty and the movement of my eyes was sluggish, but, still, I opened them. The first thing I saw was a sunbeam overhead and I realised it must be daytime. I moved my eyes to my left and saw Edith sitting in an uncomfortable looking blue chair next to my bed. Her eyes were closed and her breathing was soft. I kept staring at her, comforted knowing my mother was watching over me, her rosary in her hands.

I called to her, but to my horror, no sound came out. I realised I could not move my tongue. I tried to lift my hands, but I could not feel them. My neck wouldn't move either. I lowered my eyes, trying to scan my body. I could not see my nose, just white plaster.

Edith must have sensed me, because she shifted in her chair and opened her eyes, glancing over at me. When she saw that my eyes were open staring at her, she gasped and rushed to me.

She was struggling to form words in her excitement. She raced out into the hallway. "Come quickly. She's awake! My Denise is awake," she called out, her voice thick. She rushed back in to me and covered me with kisses. "Oh Denise, my darling, I'm so glad you're awake." Though I could feel my mother's kisses on the small sections of my face not covered in plaster, and the stroking of my hair, I could not feel anything else.

"I didn't know if..." Edith babbled, "Well, it doesn't matter now." Her smile was watery as she looked up towards the heavens. "Oh God, thank you. Thank you for answering my prayers."

"Mrs Russo, please move aside," said a man dressed as a doctor. Edith seemed not to hear him, because she kept showering me in kisses and telling me how glad she was that I was awake. "Mrs Russo?" called another voice. "Please move. We need to examine your daughter." Still my mother didn't listen. Eventually the doctors had to pull her off to get to me.

After that, it was a constant stream of doctors and nurses, but Edith was always there. I found out that I had been in a coma for twelve days. Twelve days since I had been found on a ledge some one hundred feet below a cliff face at Mount Tomewin.

They told me that the basal area of my brain, the frontal lobe, the right and left eye sockets, and the left zygoma—where the cheekbones join the skull—were all broken and depressed. There were four holes in the dura mater—the protective outer membrane between the brain and my skull. A branch had pierced my throat up into the roof of my mouth, and another had pierced my left lower thorax. Both my shoulders were dislocated and fractured. Both wrists were shattered and I had four ribs broken on the left and two on the right. I had a fractured left elbow and humerus, a comminuted fracture through the spine of the left scapula, and compression fractures of the seventh and the eighth dorsal vertebrae.

All the while the doctors tended and Edith fretted, I worried about you and waited to see you.

On the third evening of being awake, I heard the pitter patter of little feet and your angelic voice. "Nanny, which room is Mummy in?"

"She's down here, sweetheart," said Edith at the door. My heart lifted when you entered and saw me. Your eyes scanned my plaster-covered broken body. I saw you tremble just before you screamed your lungs out. Your feet twisted and you bolted out of the room. Edith smiled at me apologetically and rushed after you.

How frightening and grotesque I must have seemed to a four-year-old, wrapped up as I was with only two holes for eyes and a small section open near my mouth and cheeks. It was then I learnt that though I was paralysed everywhere, I could still cry. At that moment, I stopped believing in karma.

There was nothing I could have done to deserve this.

Siobhan's memories of her life at the age of four were all a blur, but there was one that had haunted her. It was her recurring nightmare: a white plaster-covered face with two eyes that pierced her darkest nights. Now she knew why.

There was so much that she hadn't known. She realised that both her grandmother and her mother had deliberately chosen never to speak to her about this. Siobhan knew she had to go on and reopened *The Confession*.

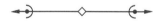

SEPTEMBER 1995

One evening, just before the end of visiting hours, about a week after I'd awoken, I was alone with Edith when Inspector Jones and a detective from the crime squad visited. They tried to communicate with me through blinking only to realise I had an uncontrollable twitch which set me off blinking erratically.

As the detectives left, my eyes flicked to the door when I heard the familiar beat of Matt's footsteps. I had been through so much, and I was thankful for the little blessings I would normally have taken for granted. My spirits lifted in the knowledge that my fiancé was still standing beside me.

"Evening, Edith," he greeted before his eyes turned to me. "How are you, honey?" I blinked slowly and then the involuntary twitching set in. He sighed.

"Edith, can I have a word?" She nodded and Matt led her out of the small cubicle and behind the green curtains that partitioned the room. I expected that they had perhaps found some leads about Davo and his accomplice and he didn't want to upset me. I could hear the deep rhythm of Matt's voice as he spoke, but, over the sounds of the television, I couldn't make out the words.

Edith suddenly raised her voice. "No, Matthew! Euthanasia is against our beliefs, which you should know full well. She has progressed so much."

"Edith, I know you don't want to hear this," Matt said louder, trying to drown out her huffing, "but Denise and I always said that if either of us were ever to become a vegetable, we wouldn't want to be kept alive on life support."

"This conversation is over," Edith said. "She is young. She has a daughter, for goodness sake." With that, Edith came back through the curtains. Her face was flushed and her brow was furrowed as she looked at me.

Matt, as always, was charming and caring, vowing revenge on whoever had done this to me. The bell rang and it was time for visitors to leave. Edith, perhaps in response to her altercation with Matt, decided to walk him out. Behind the curtains she stopped and I could see the two shadows clearly. Edith gently held onto his elbow. "Matt, the hospital bills have been very steep. Denise's health insurance doesn't cover all of it. Can you help out?"

Matt walked away and his answer was indistinct. After a while, Edith returned and started pacing up and down. Without warning she blurted, "Overextended on his restaurant? I don't believe this." She shook her head and spat with venom, "His restaurant! Not one cent towards the recovery of his fiancée."

I did not have much, but I did have time—all the time in the world to think, re-think, and overthink.

I had joked with Matt once over a bottle of wine that I would never want to live as a vegetable, but who would? If my spinal cord was so badly damaged and I had no sensations anywhere below my neck, was it really worth continuing to fight and live like this?

I'd heard before that the only honest mirror you ever have is the eyes of a child. And you had been so terrified of what had become of me that you ran. Was Matt being cruel to be kind? Maybe he just couldn't bear to see me like this.

I tried to reason out Matt's actions. Maybe he was scared that he, as my fiancé, would have to carry me for the rest of his life, and I was all but completely broken.

My mind flitted to his excuse to Edith about being overextended on his restaurant. I remembered the visit from the bikies. It was evident that he owed people money. He had kept me in the dark that the restaurant was not returning enough for him to service these debts.

All my life I'd believed the best in people. Some called it naïveté, but it was the way I was brought up. A part of me wanted to let go and give up—surrender to death—but there was another part of me that needed to live, even if it was just to prevent the perpetrators getting away with attempted murder and benefiting from what they had done to me.

When I discovered I'd won the lottery, the restaurant had been empty except for my group of friends and me. Back in 1995, mobile phones were a novelty and I didn't have one. I hadn't told anyone else, not even Edith. After my abduction, surely someone would have told her about it? Yet when Edith asked Matt for money, she seemed oblivious to the money I had won.

I realised that if the ticket had fallen into the hands of a stranger, it was unregistered and would be the finder's to claim. I also considered that perhaps Edith was told about it, but who would have suspected someone at my birthday party capable of such a heinous deed?

If they believed it was a random rape and attempted murder, the ticket could have been lost in the forest, fluttered away in the breeze, its value unknown to my abductors. It was possible that neither Matt nor Edith could bank on the ticket ever being found.

My mind weighed up other possibilities. Surely someone who was there that night must have mentioned my lottery win to the police? Even if there were multiple winners, it would be possible to trace my winning ticket as it was highly unlikely there would be more than one winner from the Currumbin area. Of course, my lotto ticket may not have been cashed in as yet. Maybe the police were keeping the win a secret, waiting for the perpetrator to cash it in. Perhaps Davo and his accomplice were waiting for me to die before cashing in the ticket.

I knew I had to get better, even if it was just so I could talk. If I could speak, I could say the ticket, though unmarked, had my numbers. The forensic evidence they got from me would be enough proof to nail Davo for the rape. He would squeal on his accomplice. Then the lottery money could go towards making sure your future was secure.

Resolve is a wonderful thing. It makes pain seem irrelevant. I had found a reason to get better and it started to show.

After another fortnight, my wounds were healed enough that I could be discharged and placed in my bed at home.

It had now been six weeks since that fateful night. The plaster around much of my body had been removed, but I still had no movement from my neck down. I could not even move my head. My tongue had started to loosen and I could swallow without assistance now, albeit with great difficulty, yet that in itself was a huge achievement.

I had only one goal: that I would be able to speak again.

I was disappointed that Matt had not visited me at home since that day at the hospital when he and Edith had argued. Perhaps he could not bear to see me like this, or perhaps he really was struggling for money and could not face Edith.

Simon on the other hand had never shown up at all. I had really wished to see him. I knew Edith blamed him for what happened that night and, knowing Simon, he probably blamed himself too.

Of course, as the bandages were removed and my swollen face subsided, you, my darling daughter, came and held my hand each day. I could now feel your little hands pressing my skin, but my brain had no control over any motor functions and I could not reciprocate.

Edith did her best to get me onto a wheelchair each day and take me out for a stroll. Part of me wanted to be out and about to break the monotony, but I also didn't want the world to see me like this. It was a terrible time, dreading people's reaction on the street, yet wanting to get out from my prison of a bedroom.

After six weeks at home, the swelling had significantly subsided. Much of the surgery on my face had gone well, but my body from my neck down had no mobility and I still could not speak.

One evening, nearly two months after that fateful night, Carine and Vince visited. Carine fussed over me effusively like a peacock. She chastised herself to Edith. "I wish I had never left her that night," she said. Edith clutched Carine's wrist and comforted her, saying she should not hold herself responsible for this. Carine asked if I had started to speak. Edith replied that I had now managed to move my tongue and was able to make some sounds. She told them about how the detective from the crime squad had returned, but as yet he could not make any sense of my attempts to communicate. Edith was confident, "It's only a matter of time."

Edith asked Vince and Carine to help put me in the wheelchair, as she needed to go to the chemist and would like to take me for a walk. Vince generously offered, lifted me up and set me down in the wheelchair.

The walk to the chemist was uneventful. Carine was genuinely concerned about my health and asked Edith questions all the way. To me it was a mountain I had climbed, but all I had achieved was to get a few sounds out of my throat like a clogged drain trying to empty.

We reached the pharmacy at the top of the hill. Edith opened her purse and realised she was short on cash. She asked Carine if she could spare some money. It tore me apart to see this, as I knew how proud Edith was, but it seemed she was struggling more than I realised. Carine searched through her bag and couldn't find her wallet. I noticed her nervously biting her lip as she apologised profusely. Vince dug into his back pocket and revealed a fifty-dollar note, which he handed to Edith. She thanked him warmly and went inside.

I was left with Carine and Vince, both standing behind my wheelchair. As soon as the pharmacy door shut behind Edith, I heard Carine hiss at Vince, "You idiot."

Then she came around to face me. She seemed distracted as she fussed over me, tucking my blanket around my legs. I saw her walk towards the pharmacy entrance. She glared past me at Vince before slamming the glass door shut behind her.

I could tell something was wrong almost instantly. My wheelchair had started to roll towards the slope of the hill. Vince was somewhere behind me, but I could not hear his footsteps or concern. It was as though he was preoccupied. My wheelchair slowly gained momentum on its downhill run. My hair started whipping around me, and the rushing air made my eyes, wide open with fear, water.

Ahead of me, at the bottom of the hill, I could see the T-junction connecting to the main road. Cars hurtled across the intersection at eighty kilometres per hour. My wheelchair was gaining speed. I wished I could move to throw myself out of the chair as the consequences of falling on the hill were certainly less dire than those that awaited me at the busy intersection.

I must have travelled at least halfway downhill when I heard Vince shout out. He had finally realised that my wheelchair—with me in it—was heading towards the T-junction. I heard his feet rushing to catch up with me. In the distance, Edith and Carine were screaming at him to run faster. Vince was close when I heard his foot scuff the path and stumble. He fell forwards catching at the edge of my chair. His grip didn't hold, and only resulted in pushing me away even faster.

I was now just metres away from entering the intersection when a motorbike roared and a siren wailed behind me. I glimpsed a reflection of red and blue lights in the side windows of the traffic speeding on the main road ahead of me. My wheelchair entered the intersection but, miraculously, the oncoming traffic in the first lane had slowed perhaps to give way to the emergency siren. I heard the bike's brakes screech. As the wheelchair came to a stop, my body swung forwards but was held back to the chair from one side. My body was now perpendicular to the wheelchair and I was facing the police motorcycle and, beyond it, the oncoming traffic in the second lane of the busy road. The brakes of a passenger car in the second lane screeched loudly and the car skidded towards the police officer on the motorbike shielding my wheelchair. Millimetres from impact with the motorcycle, the car came to a stop. It was Inspector Jones who got off his motorbike and wheeled me back to the top of the hill.

Jones took out his pad and started to take statements. The incident was suspicious in his mind. Carine was belligerent and defended Vince, saying he would have saved me had he not tripped.

Jones was not convinced. "Someone raped and tried to kill this woman just two months ago."

Edith was a mess. One moment she was sure she had put the brake on the wheelchair, the next moment she turned to Carine asking if she remembered seeing her doing it. Carine lifted her hands up and shook her head, indicating she wasn't sure. Vince explained that he hadn't noticed right away because he was watching Carine and Edith in the shop. He did say that he had seen someone in the reflection run away in the opposite direction.

Because my range of motion was so limited, I couldn't tell exactly what had happened either. In any event, I could not convey anything to the police, even if I had seen it.

There wasn't much Jones could do, but he made it clear that he was going to investigate further. Jones then insisted on putting me under police protection.

That night, Edith came by after tucking you into bed. As always, she said the rosary and then tucked me in too. She pulled the curtains together and left.

I couldn't sleep. My mind replayed each sensation I had experienced that day—each word and sound. I relived it over and over again in my mind; I studied their actions and body language and each facial expression, looking for something that would absolve Carine of being party to such a heinous betrayal. She had always bitten her lip when nervous. Did she do it because she could not find her money or was it because Edith had told her it was only a matter of time before I could speak?

Carine was my best friend, and Vince had even given Edith some money for my medicine. I glanced over at my wheelchair in the corner and stared at the brake. Had Carine accidentally released the brake when she tucked me in before she went into the shop? Or had Edith in her desperation to ask for money forgotten to lock the wheel? Even she was unsure of her actions. Had that glare which Carine gave Vince before she went into the pharmacy meant something? Had Vince deliberately pushed the chair, was there someone else or was it just a freak breeze?

After the incident, the police would drop in to check in with Edith daily. I learned from their visits that patrols drove by the house at random intervals. A couple of uneventful weeks later, the patrols were discontinued and the visits stopped.

CHAPTER 11

SILENCE SPEAKS LOUDER THAN WORDS

Six months passed by, and my health had neither deteriorated nor improved. The visits from my friends had petered out after the altercation with Carine and Vince, and were now merely two minute pop-ins. Perhaps they were too scared to be around me in case something might happen again.

It was the April you turned five. I remember Edith bringing you in to see me. There had been no new dress and she had not been able to find the will or money to throw even a small birthday celebration for you.

I realised then that I was costing you your childhood. Everything Edith had was being thrown in to keep me alive.

A week later, you threw a tantrum. You didn't want to go to kindergarten. Edith had moved you from the private school kindergarten I'd fought so hard to enrol you at and into a less expensive state one.

All she could say was, "We can't afford it, darling. We need the money to get your mummy well again." You stopped crying, jumped on my bed and gave me a big hug. "Mummy, get better soon please."

Edith guided me in the wheelchair to your pre-school as you walked alongside. As we approached the front gate, a couple of the older kids made faces at you. One of the older students, probably around ten years old, even walked crouching by, pretending to be a cripple.

You stopped walking. "Nanny, can I go from here please? The older kids tease me and make fun of Mummy." Edith paused her step, bent down and held her arms out. You rushed in to hug her and then you came to hug me too, before rushing off. We stayed behind, watching as you took the last twenty metres into the front gate.

Children can be terribly cruel, and it tore my soul that my little girl was ashamed to have me as her mother.

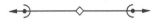

Siobhan put the book down. Tears rolled down her cheeks and she shamefully buried her face in her hands. "Mum, I was only five."

APRIL 1996

Once we came back to the house, Edith put me back into bed. Rather than hurry away to get the house chores done, she collapsed heavily into the chair beside me. I could only watch as sobs racked her frame. She seemed to weep for an eternity without ever saying a word.

I appreciated that she had always battled on through everything life had thrown before her. But in all the storms she had faced in life, this was the first time I had seen her broken.

That night after Edith tucked me in, I stared at the ceiling watching the shadows of the fan as it turned slowly in the night breeze. I started to pray. It was a habit I had cultivated since the attack.

I prayed that I could talk again so I could get some justice. As doubts crept in, I prayed that I would not falsely cast aspersions on people who may have been innocent. I prayed that Edith, who had sacrificed all her pride in her attempt to save me, would have the strength to go on. But most of all, in this, my darkest impotent moment, when I could not protect myself from harm, I prayed for you. I prayed that God would grant you His protection, which as your mother, I could no longer provide.

As I finished my prayer and shut my eyes, I heard a male voice whisper. "He's not listening."

I was startled. It was an unmistakable compelling rasp that I had heard before. I looked to the source of the voice and saw, sitting on my window ledge, a man wearing a fedora. The man spoke slowly, softly and deliberately, "Your prayers, Denise—He's not listening. God has abandoned you." The brim of the fedora had cast his face into shadow, but now he raised his face into the moonlight. I recognised him instantly. "You're the man who saved Siobhan."

The man smiled and continued, ignoring my acknowledgement. "Oh maybe He was listening after all... You were praying that you could speak again."

I jolted back in shock as I realised I had just spoken for the first time since the attack. I cast the miracle aside as the man turned to leave. I called after him, "Wait, who are you?"

He tipped his hat at me. "You know exactly who I am."

I shuddered and turned away in fear. I realised then that I *did* know.

The Devil looked at me and mocked, "Well, look at you

now. You can turn your head away too. Go on Denise, why don't you get up and walk?"

My toes wiggled under the blankets, and, though I was apprehensive, I was compelled to try. Satan urged me impatiently, "Go on. You can do it." I swung my legs to the side of the bed and stood up. It was as though I had never been injured at all.

The Devil propped himself against the windowsill and patted the ledge next to him. I walked gingerly over, expecting my legs to fail at any moment. They didn't. I reached the ledge, and hoisted myself up to sit beside him.

A car drove down the street and into Simon's driveway. It was a Ferrari. In the darkness I saw a man get out of the driver's seat. It could only be Simon. Then Satan added, "The very *broke* Simon. Wasn't that a beat-up Magna he drove into a tree that night?"

I had not seen Simon since the day of the crash. The Devil grandiosely articulated, "At least he has not been two-faced like the rest of your 'friends.'"

I winced and shivered in the night air. Satan reached to my clothes rack and draped a scarf around my neck. I looked down at my feet, unsure what to say. When I looked up again, he was gone. I was back in my bed as a mute quadriplegic.

The next morning, a very confused Edith removed the scarf from around my neck.

13TH MAY 1996

It was a month later that Samantha visited for the first time. She'd had her baby and now exuded wealth. Her clothes were designer labelled, her shoes were brand new, and her jewellery was worn to be seen.

There are two kinds of rich people. Those who naturally look rich, and those who wear expensive clothes to prove to the world they have money. Samantha fell into the latter category.

Edith took the opportunity to leave me with Samantha to pick you up from pre-school. I felt like a little puppy left with a cruel kid in a room. As soon the front door shut behind Edith, Samantha pulled out a cigarette case from her purse. Of course, it was diamond-encrusted. She opened it and selected one. Her red-painted nails glinted as she placed it between her lips. In a slow, deliberate movement she closed the case and took out a lighter. Holding the flame to the end of the cigarette she inhaled, her cheeks squeezing inwards. The end of the smoke glowed brighter as she sucked in. She pulled the cigarette away and exhaled towards me. The smoke filtered over to me and into my nostrils. I made a gargled cough. Samantha smirked and eyed me up and down.

She pulled down the sheet covering me and studied me. "You used to be such a diva. So perfect. Look at you now."

I stared blankly at her.

Samantha set her cigarette down on the side table and doubled my body over so my face was now near my knees. I could not see what she was doing, but I saw my hospital gown come loose at the edge of my vision; I realised she had undone the ties. Her hands dropped to her sides and I pictured her examining my ruined back. She re-fastened the gown and pushed me into a seated position, propped up by a large pillow.

Samantha lifted my hospital gown high and uncovered my legs completely before spreading them. She then retrieved her cigarette, flicked the ash out the window and turned back to me. Placing the glowing ember against my inner thigh, she watched my face intently. I realised she was looking for a reaction.

As her cigarette burned into my skin, I could smell my burning flesh, but fortunately my nerves in the area were dead. The pain would have been intense. I did my best not to let my face show any emotion.

Samantha took another drag. "You really are a vegetable."

She then sat on the side of the bed and pinched my nostrils shut. I breathed heavily with my mouth open. Samantha held her cigarette between her lips and put her spare hand over my mouth.

I could not breathe and I could not struggle.

My eyes opened wide, and Samantha just continued to watch me intently with the cigarette hanging out the side of her mouth. Apparently satisfied, she let go and I breathed deeply, trying to catch up on the air I had missed.

"You really should give up. Your life is worthless."

I heard the front door open and Samantha quickly got off my bed, rearranged my body to as it was when Edith left and hurriedly adjusted the covers. When Edith returned, with you in tow, Samantha was seated nonchalantly in the chair beside me, her cigarette gone.

Seeing you, Samantha made a big show of affection, speaking in a baby voice and squeezing your cheeks. I smirked inwardly when you frowned.

"Thanks so much for minding Denise, Samantha. It just makes the trip so much longer when we have to get the wheelchair out."

"No problem at all, Edith."

Edith smiled. "Your dress is beautiful, where did you get it from?" Samantha pirouetted proudly and went on to describe her Chanel dress, her Gucci bag, her Cartier watch, her Dolce & Gabbana shoes...

"Oh lovely," Edith said. I could hear the impatience in her voice. "I'm sorry to ask, but is there any chance you could spare some money? Just till Denise gets better."

Samantha quickly retracted, "I've just had a baby, Edith. I really can't help." She looked at her Cartier watch and said, "I am really late; I have to fly." Then she strutted out.

That night as Edith bathed me, she was mystified by the burn on my inner thigh. "Hmm, must be a bed sore," she said to herself, "I'll keep an eye on it." It was frustrating that Edith did not even contemplate that Samantha could have done this to me. Then again, would I have suspected one of her friends had I been minding her?

I lay wide-awake thinking. When you over-think something, your mind is like a needle stuck on a vinyl record playing the same lines again and again and again. I knew it couldn't have been a pregnant woman who had impaled my back with a crowbar, carried me over her shoulder and thrown me over a cliff. Yet Samantha had looked at my back, the same way a miser checks his money is still where he hid it. The expensive clothes and watch were signs that she had received some of the proceeds of the lottery ticket, like Simon's Ferrari.

My thoughts drifted to Simon. Had he pretended to pass out in the accident and then come back to stab me with the crowbar? Simon, my childhood sweetheart, the person who never fell out of love with me? No way.

In the dark, I heard the sound of a liquid spraying into the air just behind my left ear. The room filled with the unmistakable scent of Issey Miyaki and a hand waved a delicate glass bottle in front of my eyes.

A voice rang out, "Shit yaar."

"Davo," I hissed, responding with guttural hatred.

Satan came out from behind me. "Yes I agree. His accent is 'so quaint.'"

I was in shock. "You were there?"

He ignored me and continued, "There was a second person who raped you that night. When Carine visited with that same someone, he heard Edith say that it would only be 'a matter of time' before you would be able to speak. That same someone then gave your wheelchair a gentle nudge down a hill."

The Devil knew that I had already guessed this. It could only have been Vince. The body type, the connection with Davo... It all added up.

Satan added, "You know, your poor mother would have died believing she had not secured the brake on your wheelchair."

I bit my lip and held my tongue, not wanting to encourage him.

He probed further. "Edith comforted Carine by saying she shouldn't blame herself for leaving your party early that night. Do you remember who Carine left with?" My heart fell further as realisation sunk in.

"No. It can't be." The words came out involuntarily.

Satan looked at me and shrugged. "If you say so. Don't you remember her going to the restroom that night in front of everyone with a drug dealing bikie? Nobody stepped in. Wide-eyed and fan-fucking-tastic, your best friend came back from a walk on a white line of cocaine."

I was not buying this and I didn't want to. I protested, "I would have shared it with Matt."

Satan smiled. "That may be so." He then paused deliberately and added, "Euthanasia? Does that ring a bell?"

I looked away, out of the window. I knew he was right. Again I could see the red Ferrari pulling out of Simon's driveway. He chided me, "That is such a nice car."

I contested vehemently. "Not Simon."

He looked at me straight in the eye. "They couldn't rob you and leave you for dead in the restaurant now, could they? Somebody had to get you out of there. Who better to take you home than the person who had done it a million times before?"

I wasn't convinced. "Simon is the softest and sweetest guy I've ever met. I was his first love."

He interjected, "The operative word is 'was'. You were engaged to Matt. Simon was never going to be with you. You shut the door on him."

"This was an act of hate. Simon could never hate."

Satan squeezed my hand. "You are right, it is impossible to hate someone." He paused and added, "That is, unless you loved them once."

I was silenced into thought and doubt. The Devil prodded me further, "Remind me again, what was Samantha's problem with their relationship?"

My eyes blazed as I glared in anger. "She didn't love him."

He laughed. "Love? Love had nothing to do with it. She thought Simon couldn't afford her."

It was the second time I relapsed into a voice of hatred as I spewed out her name. Satan put his arm around my shoulders.

"Oh Denise, don't be so hard on her. In the words of the doubting Thomas, 'Except I shall see in his hands the print of the nails, and put my finger into the print of the nails, and thrust my hand into his side, I will not believe.' Samantha needed to know for sure that you couldn't take back the wonderful life you have given her."

I was silent. The evidence was overwhelming.

The Devil, sensing victory, closed in. "History has numerous examples of ordinary people doing terrible things as a mob. People have killed for a lot less than fifteen million dollars."

My mind went into overdrive. Satan sat silently on the sill and let me stew. There were only six other people there that night who knew about my lottery ticket. I had searched long and hard through every incident of that fateful night and studied the actions, the facial expressions of each and every one who visited.

I was certain Davo was one of the rapists. It was the first time we'd met and he had seen an opportunity to change his life by stealing my win. It did not condone the theft or the rape, but he didn't know me. As for Vince, he only barely knew me. From the comment made by the bikies about 'Barbie' and him 'sampling the merchandise', I deduced that he must have been a part-time drug dealer. The bikies were insinuating that both Carine and he had consumed some of the drugs he was meant to sell and he owed them money.

Samantha's visit confirmed my suspicions that deep down she hated me. She was willing me to die, checking on my scars like a doubting Thomas, and her new-found wealth all corroborated the Devil's hypothesis. It was not a good enough reason to leave me for dead, but there was no friendship there in the first place.

It was true, history had numerous examples of ordinary people banding together to commit heinous acts. People had killed family and friends for a lot less.

Although Davo, Vince and Samantha did not owe me any allegiance, Matt was my fiancé, Carine my closest friend and Simon my childhood sweetheart. Looking back, the visit from the bikies indicated that Matt had financial issues and Carine had a drug problem. Had Carine's jealousy driven her to such depths?

As for Matt, I would have shared the win with him and all his financial problems could have easily been forgiven. Surely he would be worse off sharing it with five others. It baffled me as to why he would turn on me... yet he did. His actions spoke louder than words.

It is true Simon loved me and I had shut the door on his heart, but was he capable of hate? Had I been so blind to not notice the change in his demeanour?

I had never realised Carine had a drug problem and was oblivious to Matt's financial crisis. Had I missed other tell-tale signs in my naïve belief that my friends would be there for me forever? Had I inadvertently done something to conjure such jealousy and betrayal?

The Devil patiently waited me out as I paced up and down the room in indecision, searching desperately to find a flaw in his argument.

These were my closest friends, the people I trusted the most in the world; my entire faith in the human race was on the line. It was no longer a debate. "It can't be. I have known Carine nearly all my life, I was going to marry Matt, and Simon couldn't hurt a fly."

The Devil nodded and said nothing. I waited for his answer and when none was forthcoming, I began to believe I had finally stumped him.

Then Satan spoke deliberately, "Money talks, but more is said by staying silent."

I was beaten.

Money talks. Samantha had come in reeking of money. Seeing Simon's car only confirmed my fears that my lottery ticket had been cashed in. What I heard and what I saw was all I had.

It was when I shut out the noise of the events of the day that their silence on one matter spoke louder than any words or actions ever could. Inspector Jones had yet to find a motive for my abduction, rape and attempted murder. Had nobody spoken to the police about my winning lottery ticket?

Their silence condemned each and every one of them.

Beaten, I gave in. "Okay, what do you want?" I asked the Devil.

"Exactly what you want."

"Justice," I replied.

He laughed. "You can call it what you like. Justice, karma, revenge. You want your life back. Give me their souls and I will give you your life back." Truly he was the Prince of Darkness.

I shook my head in disagreement and refused. "I can't do it. I am not a killer." I turned to face him, but he was gone. I was back in my bed, a quadriplegic once more.

CHAPTER 12

OR FOREVER HOLD YOUR PEACE

30TH MAY 1996

It was two weeks later that Matt and Carine visited. They stood facing Edith's chair with their backs to me. The expensive new clothes, shoes and accessories they wore filled the room with the smell of new money. Carine slipped her hand in Matt's back pocket, leaving her ring finger out to flaunt its new diamond adornment. She kept moving her finger up and down, as if to make sure I saw it.

Matt spoke to Edith, "I hope you understand, I have to move on." Perhaps Matt didn't think it important to address me directly with his future plans as he thought I had no comprehension of what was going on around me. Carine snuggled up closer, slid her arm around Matt's waist and then passionately kissed him.

Edith was upset, but spoke firmly, "This is incredibly insensitive of both of you to come here like this. Please leave."

Carine questioned Edith about the kind of life she was forcing me to live. She added, "She has nothing to live for. You should really let her go." Matt shook his head to Carine and reinforced her views, "It's no use. I've already told her. Denise would never want to live like a vegetable."

I was indignant. I was not a vegetable, I was right there in the room with them.

Edith raised her voice. "Denise has a daughter and her whole life ahead of her."

Carine threw her final punch. "Edith, her medical bills are crippling any chance Siobhan has to get a good education."

Edith had enough. She screamed at them—something she never did. "Get out!"

Cometh the night, they say. Cometh the night when the confidence of the day abandons you, and deep, dark insecurities rule your mind. Was my stubborn resolve to hang onto life ruining your future? Would my family be better off if I just let go?

I lay awake that night and watched the windowsill. I realised that in ten months I had only spoken to the Devil, and this night I wanted to talk to him more than anyone else. It made me realise why some people stay in relationships they never want to be in, out of the fear of loneliness.

The more I relived the events of the last months, the more I realised that there was a fine line between justice and revenge. Any doubts I had that Matt and Carine were not complicit in the crime were erased beyond doubt by their visit that morning. The reasons for their betrayal I did not know, but now I was certain they had been a party to it and had profited from it. They had stolen my life and now they were blaming me for stealing yours, Siobhan.

Perhaps with Simon, his allegiances with his girlfriend Samantha and his best buddy Matt were in conflict with his allegiance to me. Yet he chose to remain silent and the Ferrari was proof that he had profited as well. Much as I wanted to believe that money itself was not enough motivation, the acts including that of deliberate silence of all my friends pointed to their complicit guilt.

My mind went back to the deal the Devil offered and I wondered if I should have agreed. With impeccable timing, Satan appeared. I tried to turn my head and I could. There, standing against the wall, was the Prince of Darkness. He was staring straight at me.

I said nothing. I had waited all night to see him, but I did not know how to cross the threshold.

He reminded me of what I already knew. "Two men raped you. You know for certain that one was Davo, and Vince pushed you down the hill.

"After they ran away, someone left you for dead. Matt wanted you euthanised, Sam tried to make you feel worthless, and, when all else failed, Matt and Carine tried today to break your heart so you would give up and die."

I corrected him, "That's five. You want six." He smiled wickedly, "Forgive me, you are not the type of girl who wets herself over a Ferrari."

For the first time, I spelled it out. "Six: Davo, Vince, Carine, Matt, Samantha and Simon."

Satan nodded his assent, "Those six, nobody else. You give me their six souls in six nights and you will have your life back."

I looked at him and then gestured to the bed I was still lying in. "Six nights. And how am I supposed to do it like this?"

"During the day you will be crippled, but during the night, while your mother and daughter sleep soundly, you will be as you are right now: whole."

"And?" I sensed a catch.

The Devil smiled, acknowledging my caution. "If you agree to the deal, you have to see it to the end, or I will take your daughter's soul as payment."

"No way." I refused to gamble with your soul.

Satan played another card. He pointed to the threadbare room. "There is nothing left to sell. Have you not noticed your mother has sold her wedding ring? You know she will run out of people to beg from and then you will die."

I was already dead; this wasn't going anywhere.

He continued, "She will be heartbroken and perhaps then she will die too, but in any event she is too old to give Siobhan the life you dreamed for her. If your mother dies, your daughter will go to a state-run home. The world will be her oyster... alcoholic, drug addict, prostitute—" The Devil cut himself off and smirked. He was pushing my buttons, but I refused to respond. "Oh, forgive me Denise," he said in mock seriousness, "I misspoke—your sadistic alcoholic father would become her legal guardian, not the state." I shuddered. He added, "Is Siobhan not the same age as you were when you started to have those horrible, horrible nightmares?"

My body shook, repulsed. I knew I had no choice but to take the deal.

"What if I fail?" I said, considering.

Satan looked at me with utter disdain. "How can you possibly fail? Just imagine one of them telling the police, 'A quadriplegic visited me and tried to kill me.'" His tone was imperious and mocking. "You have the perfect alibi."

I needed reassurance and asked him bluntly, "What if you don't deliver?"

He turned his lip up, disgusted with my lack of faith. "The last time you prayed, your daughter had drowned. I delivered then with nothing to gain. Why should I fail you now?"

The Devil had played his hand perfectly, withdrawing into silence each time I refused him.

He took a step towards me and said, "Are you in?" He held out a hand and then pulled it back slowly. "Or forever hold your peace."

I gave in and grasped desperately at his retracting hand. I looked him straight in the eyes and shook on it.

Like most people, I prayed hardest in my time of need. My prayers were heard by the Devil.

Siobhan pushed her back against the back of her chair and closed her eyes. Was her mother insane? Could any of this be true? And if it was, did the Devil own her soul or had her mother delivered on the deal?

Siobhan shut the book and put it in her backpack. She looked up at the clock on the wall. It was eight in the evening.

She entered the bathroom and started to brush her teeth. Reflected in the mirror, through the open bathroom door behind her, she could see the lights of Madrid shining from across the railway tracks.

The view was interrupted as a monk dressed in red climbed up onto her balcony.

CHAPTER 13
TO A DESTINATION UNKNOWN

Siobhan screamed. The monk smashed a window of the French door with his fist. He pushed his bleeding hand through the shattered glass and attempted to undo the lock.

Siobhan grabbed her backpack, flung open the door and ran out into the corridor. Standing at the end of it was another red monk. She turned towards the fire escape and ran down the stairs. The red monk chased after her. She came to an exit that opened onto the busy Avenida de Pio XII. The street was buzzing with people and traffic. Ducking and weaving, she ran in the direction of the railway station, turning briefly to see the two red monks in pursuit.

As Siobhan approached the Madrid Chamartín railway station, she saw a small police station and ran towards it. The monks stopped at the gate as she entered. The police station was busy. Travellers and locals sat in rows of benches, waiting patiently while staring at the red numbers on the electronic display.

She took a ticket with trembling hands and sat on a bench closest to the police booths. Siobhan looked towards the door, her feet tapping uncontrollably. The two monks were waiting outside, guarding the only exit.

With one eye on the door, Siobhan picked up the local newspaper from a side table and browsed intermittently through the pages while she waited for her number to be called. On the third page was an article mentioning the Convento de Santa Teresa. There was a small photo of Sister Catherine inset in the corner of a larger image. In the bigger picture, the nun lay on the ground in an area cordoned off by police tape, her head bleeding against large granite steps. In the picture, next to the spot where Catherine died, was Denise's grave. Siobhan could see the red roses she had left there, though now wilted. Siobhan knew instantly that Sister Catherine had been murdered for helping her.

Who were these red monks? Why were they chasing her? She figured that they thought she had something they wanted—her mother's confession? With the way they guarded the door, she sensed that they would stop at nothing to get it. Her mind cast back to her first night in Zamora when a red monk, undeterred by the fact that she was talking to a police officer, hissed at her to 'Go home.'

Even the police seemed reticent to take any action against them, encouraging her to leave as well. She sensed that it would be no different here in Madrid. She considered alerting her sister and nanna of her plight, but it would mean telling them about *The Confession*. That would be a betrayal of her late mother's final wish and she decided against it.

She got up and walked casually to the ladies restroom at the end of the waiting area. Once inside a cubicle, she checked the contents of her backpack. She had her mother's confession, Bible, nun's hood and habit, and her own wallet. She put all the contents back inside except for the habit.

She loaded the backpack on her shoulders. Then she put

on her mum's hood and habit, effectively concealing her face and the backpack completely.

She exited the cubicle and checked her appearance in the mirror. Not too bad. She stooped a little, so the backpack appeared like a hump.

With a shuffling gait, she left the restroom. Luckily, the police station was full enough that no-one noticed a twenty-something girl had gone in and a hunchbacked nun had come out. Keeping her head low, she walked behind a small group of tourists, mingling in their number. When she passed by the two red monks, her heart was hammering so fast she was afraid they'd hear it.

Siobhan stayed close to the chattering tourists and walked with them into the Madrid Chamartín station. The last train for the night was about to leave the platform, headed for Barcelona. Without a backward glance, Siobhan boarded the train.

She settled quietly into a carriage with only a few people in it and impatiently counted down the seconds until the train pulled out of the station. Once it was on its way, she went to the toilet and locked it. She took off the habit and backpack. She paused for a moment, looking at the habit on the ground and considered her situation. She decided to put the nun's disguise on again.

Once everything was back in place she unlocked the toilet, now carrying her backback. When she passed an empty cabin, she entered, shut the door and took the seat closest to the window. Now certain she was alone, she pulled out *The Confession*.

31ST MAY 1996

My soul was sold that day I shook the Devil's hand.
I had never hurt anyone in my life and now I had promised to kill six people. In my heart, it was justifiable homicide; they stole my life and now they were stealing yours. The Devil had answered my prayer, and it was your soul I had gambled with. To me, the consequences of not completing my end of the bargain far outweighed the consequences of being found guilty of murdering six people.

As dawn broke, I started to form a plan. How would I get to them? What would I wear? Who would be first? Where would I find them? How would I kill them?

As I thought about it, I felt colder inside, more detached. I decided that I had to start by choosing the first victim, but that presented a dilemma. I worked backwards and made a mental list, starting with who I would find the hardest to kill. Instantly I knew that killing Simon, although he lived next door, would be the most difficult for me. He was my first love and I needed time to come to terms with his betrayal. I wondered briefly if he and Samantha were still together. A Ferrari did not a family car make.

That brought me to Samantha. She had a small baby and that weighed heavily on my heart. Then there was Matt, who was once the love of my life. I hated him, but not as much as I hated Carine.

Carine must have known that Vince had raped me, yet she'd come with him to visit. Despite the betrayal, killing her would be hard. She was after all, once upon a time, my best friend.

Vince would be a challenge, simply for his bulk and strength.

Then there was Davo. He would be first. He was the only one I was absolutely sure had been there that night. Thinking back, whoever had slammed the crowbar in my back had done it because I'd uttered Davo's name. They must have feared that Davo, if arrested, would implicate them.

I remembered him explaining to Simon that the reason he had an Aussie name was because his surname was Dev. I didn't even know his first name.

Making Davo my priority, I moved to the next task of how I would get around. This was a family-friendly suburb with no wild night life. Public transport ceased at midnight, and being an ex-news reporter didn't really help when you wanted to travel incognito.

For ten months, the hatred in my heart had grown. Even before the Devil had come to me, I had imagined my attackers suffering and dying in a multitude of horrible ways. That wasn't too abnormal; I was sure that people who have been attacked have had these kinds of thoughts. The difference was that I now had to act on my murderous imaginings.

The next step was to find a weapon. I knew there were knives in the kitchen, and the medicine cabinet had numerous prescription drugs—my staple diet. I had every possible cocktail available and enough drugs to put a large dinosaur to sleep.

I decided I would dress in something dark to help with concealment; something to cover my face and disguise my appearance; and something comfortable so I could run. The thought amused me, running after being bedridden for months would be such a treat.

I'm sure it will be impossible for you to imagine being

crippled and helpless as I was then, seeing injustice thrive at my expense, and then being given an opportunity to make things right. The closest analogy I can think of is someone in a loveless and abusive relationship who, one day, is pushed over the tipping point and decides to break free. Be it out of love for a child or partner, or from the fear of rejection or loneliness, allowing yourself to succumb to emotional blackmail was quadriplegia of the heart. Some people live it slowly and painfully through a relationship or marriage and then reach a point of no forgiveness. Like them, deep down inside, I felt a part of my life was robbed from me. Forgiveness was not an option. The time had come for the blood-letting to start.

As night descended, I waited patiently for Edith to pull my curtains and kiss me goodnight. As she fluttered around her room and I heard you toss and turn, I willed you both to sleep.

Soon silence descended on the house, and I wondered for a few minutes if it was all a bad prank, as I still couldn't move. Then suddenly, I could. First I moved my legs and hands and knew it was real.

I jumped out of bed, whipped opened my wardrobe and dressed in a pair of black track pants and a top to blend into the night. I picked a scarf, a pair of sunglasses and my handbag and tiptoed to the kitchen. I took a large knife from the block on the bench, and then quietly rummaged through the bottom drawer to find a meat cleaver and a rusted old icepick. I took all three, then headed to raid the medicine chest.

The medicine chest could put a small hospital to shame. Painkillers, local anaesthetic, sleeping pills, syringes, anything that could relieve me of my pain. Armed with my weapons and drugs, I slipped out the front door to the carport under the stretched wing of our Queenslander. It was empty except for my old Holden Gemini.

The car was unlocked. I pulled down the sun visor on the driver's side and the key fell to the floor. Normally, I would have been worried about Edith leaving the car unlocked, but no-one in their right mind would steal this junk on wheels.

I put my handbag containing my weapons on the passenger side and turned the ignition, hoping it would start. It choked and shuddered. I waited a minute or two, then tried again. It spluttered at first, but then the engine fired.

I drove the car out on to the street. The fuel tank was almost completely empty. Reaching under the driver's seat, I searched for my small change box and, luckily, it was still there. I opened it, but all it had was two fifty-cent coins.

At the nearest petrol station on the highway, I filled the tank and drove off without paying. If I were going to kill someone, stealing was really the least of my problems.

It was 1996 and the old Telecom phone booths still dotted the Gold Coast highway. After about fifteen minutes, I stopped near a brightly lit one in Mermaid Beach. As I looked him up in the phone book, I hoped Davo still lived on the Coast. It would be just my luck if he'd moved overseas.

The Gold Coast was just like a big country town, and there were only three people with the surname Dev. I called the first and got a very irate woman on the line, angry that I'd woken her up. I checked my watch, it was only 10:30 pm. I shrugged, having clearly dialled the wrong number. I put my second and last fifty-cent coin into the phone and looked at the remaining two numbers. Fifty-fifty. I made the second call. The phone rang and then a voice came on the line. "Davo speaking."

I was silent. My body shuddered on hearing his voice. He spoke again. "Hello? Who's there?"

I hung up and looked at the address. Davo lived in one of the swanky apartments overlooking the Pacific Ocean and the Broadwater in Surfers Paradise. I pulled out the local street directory and found it.

"Surfers", the heart of the tourist and glitter strip, was a good fifteen minutes away from where I was. I hopped in the car and drove.

Beach Tower was a large imposing building in the heart of the Surfers Esplanade, facing the beach. There must have been some kind of event on, because the streets were packed with teenagers screaming and shouting and running amok. I parked by the beach and walked into the building foyer. The building was still busy with young party goers, shouting from one of the higher floors, broadcasting their night plans to the whole world. Out the front was a name board. Davo lived on the twenty-first floor.

I got in the lift and, as I ascended, I planned what I would do to get in. The lift opened to a stylish foyer and I saw there were just two apartments to each floor.

I tried Davo's door and, to my surprise, found it was unlocked. I gently pushed it open, and there I was, in his apartment without breaking a sweat.

I was closer and closer to committing murder, and with each step came a quiet confidence. Perhaps it was easier when the consequence was worse than the predicament you were already in. I realised then that by entering the pact with the Devil, I had divested myself of guilt—the first tenet of my Catholic faith.

CHAPTER 14

DAVO'S BLIND DATE

The door opened into a small entranceway with a large abstract painting covering the wall in front of me. To the left, a short passage opened up to the dining room. I could see that Davo hadn't shied away from spending my winnings. The huge travertine marble dining table stank of opulence and there was a bar bench stocked with top-shelf liquor to the side.

From the entranceway, I observed quietly, making note of the position of everything. Beyond the dining room was a sunken living room with large bay windows that overlooked the Pacific Ocean. A crescent moon shone outside, and the lights from Surfers lit up the foreshore. In the living room, sat Davo, watching TV with two women. One a brunette and the other a bleached blonde, both were snuggled up to him.

I slid away in the opposite direction, to the right-hand passage, towards a modest study, which then opened out into two bedrooms with attached ensuites. It was clear to see which was the master bedroom, because one was fully decked out and the other was spartan to say the least.

Davo had opted for the older style oak wood king bed with four solid bedposts. On either side of the bed were matching polished bedside tables, and on each sat a large fossil stone lamp. Against the wall was a large chest of drawers, the bottom two of which were not fully shut. Once had some socks in it, while the other had cheap ties peeking out from within. I removed a few of the better ties and a pair of sports socks. There were still a few unpacked boxes in the spare second bedroom—his move must have been recent. In this room I discovered a pair of scissors, some duct tape and rope used for packing boxes. I smiled as I added these to my armoury.

When I heard Davo's amorous advances progressing into a financial negotiation, it confirmed what I suspected. Davo—a balding forty-year-old with a slight paunch—did not seem to be the person who could entice two pretty young girls to spend an evening with him.

I contemplated my attack. I needed to kill him slowly. I had waited ten bedridden months for this day and I needed information. I contemplated my next step: isolating him. I had to get him alone and away from his female companions.

Davo got up and went to get another round of drinks for the girls. He was now alone by the bar but he was only a few metres from the two women in his lounge, well within earshot if there was a struggle. Now armed with two drinks, Davo returned to his seat between his two house guests to continue negotiations. Perhaps I would have to wait a few hours for his guests to complete their sojourn before I could get him alone. I was starting to panic.

Davo suddenly got up and staggered past the guest bedroom door I was hiding behind and headed to his master bedroom. A light came on and I could hear Davo relieving himself.

He must have been holding it a while, because I had enough time to loosen my scarf and tiptoe into the master ensuite behind him. I covered his eyes with my hands, in a playful, 'guess who' kind of way. Davo jumped.

"What the—"

"Don't spoil it honey," I giggled, disguising my voice in a higher pitch. I pressed my body tight to his from behind. Davo guffawed excitedly and moved his free hand behind him to feel me; I just pressed in closer.

"Close your eyes," I whispered in his ear. I secured my scarf over his eyes—tight. Then, blindfolded with his pants still unzipped, I led Davo away into the adjoining bedroom. He continued to paw me clumsily. No matter how repulsive I found him, I kept reminding myself of my purpose. I encouraged him with fake moans and caresses, dodging his wandering hands as best I could, yet I led him on. "Easy, tiger." This was my best chance to get him exactly where I wanted him.

I laid him on the bed and put my finger to his mouth, indicating for him to stay quiet. I took one of the ties and used it to fasten his right wrist against one of the bedposts.

"What are you—"

I nuzzled his ear and whispered, "Shhh... You are ruining it." He calmed down and I fastened his other wrist.

I could hear the tapping heels of the two girls getting restless in the lounge, so I extricated myself from Davo, brushing his body flirtatiously to keep his mind occupied. I strode swiftly to the door and locked it.

Back by the bed, I removed his shoes and socks as swiftly as I could while remaining 'seductive'. Sitting on his chest, I rolled up one of his socks into a ball, and shoved it into his mouth, sealing it shut with the tape I'd stolen before.

Davo was now secure, blindfolded and gagged. All traces of my seductress act were gone, and he could tell something was drastically wrong. But it was too late. He tried to scream through the sock, and thrashed his legs about, but my weight held him down.

Perhaps his thrashing had attracted the attention of his house guests, or maybe they had just run out of patience. Stilettos clicked their way across the tiles to his bedroom door. I knew all would be lost if his visitors raised an alarm. Without hesitation, I took out the icepick from my bag and plunged it sharply down, impaling Davo's meaty thigh. I felt the muscles underneath contract instantly around the foreign object. His scream would have been ear-piercing if left unmuffled.

"Shut up, stay absolutely still or I will do it again," I hissed. There was some whimpering and shivering, but he stopped struggling.

The girls tried to open the bedroom door and failing that, they knocked loudly. "Hey? Hey, what's going on? Open up!"

Davo started thrashing again, trying to call for help. "*Mrphmf!*"

I ignored them and set about securing each of Davo's legs with the rope. The girls, hearing the movement on the bed, knocked louder. "Hey, what the hell are you doing?"

I had to get rid of them. I dug into Davo's pocket, pulled out his wallet, took out all the cash—about five hundred dollars—and shoved it under the door. "Go away," I said in my bitchiest voice. "He's mine."

One of the girls shouted back, "What the fuck, bitch?" Then she added, "It's two hundred short!" Then the other girl piped in, "Yeah! The clock started from when we came here, okay!"

I rummaged around in Davo's drawers, found a few hundred dollar notes stashed away, and pushed a couple under the door. I heard shuffling sounds as they counted the money. "Fucking weirdo," said one. Finally, I heard the clicking of their stilettos leaving and sighed in relief.

Over the last ten months, I had learned that there were two types of fear: the fear of the known, and the fear of the unknown. The latter brought out your deepest and darkest insecurities as you searched for answers without clues to blinker your rambling mind. It was the fear I faced the night I was abducted, raped and left for dead. I did not know the perpetrators. Not in my wildest nightmares would I have considered a betrayal of any magnitude from my closest and dearest friends. The fear of the unknown left every possibility of confession open and brought every anxiety to the surface.

The fear of the known is heightened because you know the nature of the beast. This was the fear I knew after Vince pushed my wheelchair down the hill. I knew then that people wanted me dead. Of course, I had no means to fight it. It was the fear I knew when I was left in the care of the sadistic Samantha.

Now, alone with Davo, I wanted him, no *needed* him, to know the fear of the unknown. I perched myself back on his chest and then ripped the tape off his one-day-old stubble and removed the sock from his mouth. He screamed for help.

A few girls from another building screamed in response, and then some others joined in the chorus shouting from a building further along. Suddenly it was a Mexican wave of screams as drunken teenagers celebrated in Surfers Paradise.

I removed the pick that had been embedded in his thigh, and was surprised at the spurt of blood that accompanied its extraction. I drove it hard into his other leg. He howled louder.

"Shut up or I will give you something to really scream about," I said malevolently.

Davo's mouth slammed shut. He was sweating profusely and shaking. The pent-up hatred in me had finally found a vent. I was sure his wounds were hurting and I was enjoying seeing him writhe in pain. Looking back, I was shocked that I felt no remorse in exacting revenge.

"What are you going to do?" he asked quietly, fear staining his voice.

"What did you do the last time you had someone bound and gagged?"

He was silent. I withdrew the icepick and plunged it down again. Davo screamed again.

He pleaded. "I swear I don't know what you are talking about. Please stop. I really don't know why you are doing this." Angered by his denial, I wiggled the icepick, like I was shifting gears, and warned him again. Davo implored beseechingly this time. "If it's money you want, I will give it to you. You must have the wrong person."

An element of doubt crept into my mind. I wondered if I'd got it wrong. I had based my entire supposition on Davo's distinctive cologne and his accent when he'd spoken. I removed his blindfold.

Davo's face drained of colour. "Shit. It can't be... It can't be." He started shivering and shaking furiously as though he had seen a ghost. "You were there that night," I said, slowly and deliberately.

Davo pleaded his case, "I swear I never wanted to have anything to do with it. I was dragged into it."

Outraged, I hissed at him, "Dragged into abducting, raping and attempting to murder? Talk—I'm all ears!"

Davo was silent. I extracted the knife from my bag,

laid its point on the tip of his nose and watched his eyes go narrow, focused on the blade. I pressed down slightly, breaking the skin, and he whimpered.

"Okay, okay! I'll talk." I prodded at him to go on, leaning back to deliberately twist the icepick. Suddenly the words began to pour out. Davo confessed that he was infatuated with Carine the night of my birthday. Sometime late that night, she'd invited him to join her in the restroom. Shortly after that, Vince busted them and dragged Davo out into the car park by his collar, an apologetic Carine trailing behind. I remembered that strange incident.

It was in the car park that they insisted that Davo leave. Being around eleven-ish, it would have been almost impossible to get a taxi unless he walked all the way to the Gold Coast Highway, at least four kilometres away.

Just then, Simon's car drove into the car park. Davo had continued to apologise to Vince and said he would ask Simon for a lift to the nearest taxi rank, and that's when it all changed. Apparently Simon had arrived too early. He was supposed to come after Davo had left. Davo was never supposed to have been part of the scheme.

Carine had taken charge of the situation and ordered both Vince and Davo to get into Vince's car. They got in with Vince at the wheel and Carine in the back, and drove off.

They pulled over at the stretch near the neighbouring Currumbin National Park and waited in the darkness. Vince ran to the back of the car and opened the boot. He'd dug out a beanie, an old t-shirt, a black cloth bag, a couple of zip ties and some gym socks. He grabbed the beanie and ripped two holes in it, then pulled it over his head. Vince threw the old t-shirt at Davo, telling him to make some holes for eyes and put it over his head.

Davo questioned Vince as to exactly what was going on and was told that Simon would drive Denise home and they would run his car off the road and make it look like a robbery during which the winning lottery ticket would be lost in the forest. In a few days, they would encourage me to offer a finder's reward and then one of them would find the ticket. They thought I'd be so grateful that I would share the money or at least pay a significant reward.

I was not buying it. "That's a ridiculous plan." I pulled out the knife and lowered it to within millimetres of his left eye. He shut his eyes and pleaded, insisting that he was telling the truth.

Davo concurred that drunk as he was, he thought it would not work. Carine, however, would not be swayed. "It's an unregistered ticket. It's finders keepers, she will definitely give us a reward."

I paused for a moment, realising he was telling the truth. Carine had many a time accompanied me to the newsagent and knew I meticulously filled out my lotto numbers each time I bought my ticket.

Davo continued. "Vince said they'd roofied you. You weren't supposed to wake up or remember anything." Davo tried to make it clear he was stuck in a situation with Vince, a wannabe gangster with debts, who he feared would kill him. I drew the knife back and Davo exhaled.

"Whatever you do, don't say a word," they'd told him. Davo was to put the black bag over my head and Vince was to take care of Simon.

"Was Simon not part of it?" I asked in a rush.

"He must have been, because Carine and Vince said that Simon had come too early. They were definitely expecting him."

It was a shock for me to get confirmation on Simon's involvement.

It seems that while they had waited, Vince had reached inside his glove box and taken out a couple of small plastic packets. He emptied the contents of one into his mouth, handed Davo the other and encouraged him to take it. "Speed mate, it will wake you up."

Davo said he'd looked at Vince blankly and Vince had scoffed at him. "Just put it under your tongue and let it melt away."

Carine was growing increasingly anxious and asked Vince if he had something to steady her nerves. He reluctantly reached under his car seat and pulled out another packet. He laid out two lines of white powder on the box cover between the driver and passenger seats. Both Carine and he snorted it in. Davo believed it was cocaine.

Simon's car, with me drugged in the passenger seat, passed them. They followed us westwards through the sleepy hamlet of Currumbin Waters and all the way to a remote forest section between Currumbin Waters and Currumbin Valley. It was here that Vince bumped Simon's car off the road. Davo said they'd expected me to be out for the count, but when I staggered from the car, he'd got the bag around my head while Vince tied my hands. As I was screaming, Vince crunched his fist into the side of my head to silence me. Out for the count, they secured my hands with a zip tie and shoved a sock under the bag into my mouth. They then secured the gag with rope before bundling me into the boot.

I gestured for Davo to hurry up. I knew this bit.

Vince pointed to the driver's side of the car and Davo took the wheel while Vince went back to Simon's car. Vince returned shortly and tossed my bag into the back to Carine. He pointed to Davo to drive away.

Carine went through my bag and discovered that the ticket wasn't in it. Vince directed Davo to take the left turn at Tomewin Mountain Road.

Davo drove up Mount Tomewin for about five minutes before Carine tapped Davo on the shoulder and signed him to turn off into a concealed gravel driveway. The climb got steeper for a while and it led to a deserted car park. They continued to drive on a tree-lined track that led to a small clearing in the forest. This is where Carine checked each item of clothing as they were removed one by one. Davo added it was Carine who signalled for my underwear to be removed. When the ticket flew away Vince ran to follow it, leaving Davo to guard me.

I was mortified that my best friend had been there, and that she had not just watched it, but was the one who gave the signal to strip me and leave me naked and defenceless.

My heart shattered.

Hearing that Simon was involved left a large crack in my heart, but his absence gave me some solace that he had remorse. Carine's actions destroyed my faith in humanity.

I got off Davo's chest and he silently watched me pace the floor. There was nothing he could do, he was completely immobile, but I could tell he was beginning to hope. I felt a sense of malevolent reparation, knowing his irredeemable hope would fuel his desire to confess.

Standing beside his bed, I said menacingly, "Continue."

He struggled to find words, wary of my response. I knew why: this was the part where he'd started to molest me.

I placed the tip of the knife on his genitals.

"No, no. *Please*," he begged.

I lifted the knife away, and loosened the bindings slightly on both his legs. I slid his arms up the bedposts, so his back was now inclined at about a sixty-degree angle. I propped him up with pillows, so he was spreadeagled and then tightly secured each of his bindings again. Now I was certain he would be able to see his own genitals.

Davo was wide-eyed when I put the knife to his manhood again. He pleaded, "I'm sorry! I was fucked up on drugs with a naked girl who was tied up. I'm ashamed of what I did, but I couldn't stop myself."

"Who was the other man who raped me?"

"Vince," he confirmed without hesitating.

"Was it Vince who stuck the crowbar in my back?"

"No, it couldn't have been. We ran back to the car together. You were alive when we left you. I have no idea who did that, it was never the plan to kill you."

I was stumped; if Vince hadn't done it, then who did? The man who lifted me after I was impaled was solid and strong, not scrawny. It couldn't have been Davo.

I threatened him, pressing the tip of the knife harder against his skin, "It makes no sense; if Carine intended to steal my money, why did she leave me naked with you?"

Davo looked blankly at me. "I don't know. Carine was off her face. She was supposed to come back to Vince's with us. Once she had your ticket, everything changed. She and Vince went for a walk together and Vince came back alone."

"Carine didn't have a car. Who did she go back with?" I asked, suspicious.

Davo answered sweating, his eyes fixed on my hand with the knife, "I swear I don't know. I was staying with Vince at the time. We went back to his place."

I was not convinced. I looked at him threateningly, contemplating whether to stab him again.

Davo continued, "We washed up and threw all the clothes we wore into the fire at Vince's. We were about to take the car to the panel shop and fix the dints when someone knocked on the door. Vince sent me to bed, thinking it was the police. Our story was gonna be that we came home together.

"It wasn't the police though. I heard an agitated woman's voice through the walls of the bedroom. About ten minutes of this animated conversation went on before Vince knocked on my door and I came out. He was with Carine. She looked like she'd seen a ghost.

"The drugs had worn off and she was petrified that we'd get caught. Vince told her though that the roofie would make sure you wouldn't remember anything. But Carine didn't trust it. She said we should all say we came back together from the party and had spent the night here. It was the original plan, we agreed. Vince threatened to kill me if I ever spoke about that night to anyone."

I raised an eyebrow. "You told the police *that* and they believed you?" Davo shrugged. "Carine and I had never been in trouble before and Vince had no prior convictions. We all went to the panel shop at the crack of dawn and sorted out the dints in the car well before the police came around. There was no motive for us to lie and nobody doubted the story."

"What about the money?"

Apparently they'd waited about nine months before they'd cashed the ticket in for the full fifteen million. When Davo asked for his share, Vince told him they were the only two who would fry as their semen was irrefutable proof they had been there that night. For his silence, Davo received half a million dollars.

I still needed more information, "And where can I find Vince?"

Davo feigned ignorance. "I don't know. We used to meet at his panel beating workshop on Industrial Drive, but he's rarely there."

I stabbed Davo's upper thigh this time to extort an answer. He cried out. "He'll be at Showgirls—h-he's there every night." This was a strip club just a few blocks away on the Esplanade.

I shoved the sock back in Davo's mouth and replaced the tape. He started to shake uncontrollably. His eyes opened wide when I took out the meat cleaver and he tried to speak through the gag, sobbing.

I swung.

I'll spare you the worst of the details, Siobhan. But know this, I may be good with a knife, but swinging from a height with a cleaver requires a different kind of skill. My aim was off. It took me a few tries to castrate him completely, but I got there in the end. It wasn't clean.

Afterwards, I went to the bathroom, got in the shower and washed the blood from my skin.

When I returned the sheets were soaked with his blood. I removed the gag from his mouth and the icepick, which was embedded in his leg. Davo howled and I just watched him, listening to his cries become weaker. I didn't want to leave until he was dead, but I didn't have the luxury of time to waste. I went to his kitchen, found some rubber gloves under the sink and put them on. I removed two carving knives from a stand near the fridge.

Davo was nearing unconsciousness when I returned to the bedroom, but I slapped him a couple of times to make sure he would feel what came next. I pushed one knife through his right eye—he screamed—then embedded the other in his throat. Then I watched his life drain away.

I emptied the drawer where I had found the money to pay the prostitutes. There was another two thousand dollars in it. Next time I would be able to pay for my fuel.

I checked my outfit in the mirror. Davo's blood had blended into the black track pants and top I chose to wear that night. I washed, packed up my assortment of weapons and took another shower. I then meticulously sprayed and scrubbed the shower floor with all the cleaning products Davo owned. I deadlocked his front door and left the building.

I went home. It was only half past one in the morning. I changed out of my tracksuit into something more appropriate for a night out to a strip club. I packed the blood-stained clothes in a garbage bag and dropped it off in a rubbish bin down the road before I went to stalk Vince.

CHAPTER 15
IN GREED WE TRUST

1ST JUNE 1996

Showgirls had a ten-dollar cover charge and I used my new-found wealth to enter the club. It took a while for my eyes to adjust to the dim lighting. I was in a large room with two well-lit stages; on one, a scantily dressed brunette was baiting two young patrons to join her; and on the second, a blonde was dancing for one of the guests. The first room led to the main room of the club. The performers on the three stages in this room were busy entertaining patrons seated in the chairs surrounding the tables. There were a few ornate chairs along the periphery of the room, some occupied by a couple of other—also attractive—girls lap dancing in the background, entertaining their clients.

A large bar spanned the far wall. Next to the bar, sitting at a corner table, I spotted Vince drinking with a beautiful young dancer. I realised that, if Vince recognised me, it would all be over. I looked away and headed for the ladies. I stood there for a while, staring at myself in the mirror, wondering what to do. I noticed a fleck of Davo's blood under my chin I'd missed, and scrubbed it off.

A blonde-haired dancer entered and started to powder her face in the mirror next to me. She took off her wig and placed it on the sink. She had short brown hair underneath.

I smiled at her. "Busy night?"

"Not too bad, had a couple of buck's nights in earlier."

"I'm thinking of getting a job here actually, but I wouldn't want anyone I know to recognise me."

"That's why I've got my wig, and makeup works wonders."

"Reckon I could try it on?"

She laughed and said, "Sure."

She showed me how to put the wig on properly to hide my hair. "Not bad," I said to myself as I looked in the mirror. I turned to her. "Think I could buy it off you? And the makeup kit too?"

She laughed and looked at me like I was a complete weirdo. "Wha-what?"

Then she realised I was serious and emphatically said, "No." She continued to stare in the mirror plucking her already-thin eyebrows.

I slowly and deliberately laid out five hundred dollars on the edge of her sink. I asked again, "Would you at least consider it?"

She hesitated and looked at me strangely. She was thinking about it. I laid out another five hundred. She smiled and took the money. A few minutes later, I walked out as a thickly made-up blonde with dark eye shadow and crimson lips.

I sauntered to the bar next to the table where Vince was sitting. The young dancer kissed him gently on his cheek as she stood up. Vince's eyes followed her as she walked seductively to a table nearby and jumped up onto it. She winked and waved to him. I chose my moment; I walked past his table and bumped it, spilling his drink. He swore as his glass fell straight on his lap. I rushed over.

"I'm so sorry," I apologised, "Let me help you with that." I picked a napkin off the table and wiped off his wet jeans, intentionally rubbing his crotch. Vince's face said he clearly liked what was happening. "Can I buy you a drink?" I asked.

Vince smiled flirtatiously and said, "Only if you have one with me."

I went over to the bar and bought Vince a rum and coke and got myself a coke. Protected by the dim lighting in the club, I emptied the contents of a Valium capsule into his drink and gave it a quick stir before returning to the table.

Vince's charming opening line was, "What's a nice girl like you—"

"Doing in a place like this?" I finished coquettishly. He nodded, smirking. "It's a long story," I admitted.

"I've got nothing but time for you, love." I grimaced inwardly.

"Well..." I started, and fed him the tale of a young mother who had an abusive, junkie boyfriend who left her pregnant with a little girl she had to care for.

It was easy to tell a compelling story, particularly as this one was true.

I told him that I really wanted to spend time with my little girl during the day. Without an education, I had few options that would pay enough to feed two mouths and give my child a future.

A damsel in distress was the perfect bait, and Vince soon forgot his charming dancer, now marooned on her dance table. He lunged forward and gently squeezed my hand. Jokingly he said, "You know, I could be your sugar daddy."

I giggled, "You're way too young and handsome to be one."

I knew the clock was ticking. His dancer friend was

staring daggers at me and would soon be back to relieve Vince of some more of my money. I encouraged him to drink up, and sculled my own drink.

"Well, it's late," I began, but Vince waved over a waitress as I pretended to get up to leave.

When the waitress arrived, he ordered a second round of drinks. "The same again, thanks."

As we continued drinking, I snuggled close to him and was now whispering in his ear. It gave me a chance to slip a second dose of Valium into his drink.

I saw the dancer growing impatient as she waited to finish her set. Another customer joined her and tipped her. She busied herself with her show for her new patron. I had a little more time.

Vince's speech began to slur. I suggested that we should drink up and go back to his place. Vince gulped down the remnants of his drink and shakily got up. I had to prop him as he staggered out of the club with me.

A few minutes later, I had him seated in my car and we headed off towards the panel shop Davo had mentioned. Vince was out cold in the passenger seat. Thankfully, I'd dropped Carine off here once before and already knew about this place.

I stopped outside the garage and rifled through his pockets to find his keys. Eventually I found the right one and opened the garage door. I drove in and shut the roller door.

I tried to pull Vince out of the passenger seat. He was so sedated that he didn't react. I pulled with all my might and he toppled sideways and flopped on the floor. I searched the place and found exactly what I was looking for.

I rolled the console table on its castors to where Vince had passed out. I tried to lift him, but he was way too heavy. I noticed the garage had a chain block. I found two slings and managed to get them under his waist. I then hoisted him up and rolled the console table under him. When it was in the right position I lowered Vince onto it, his arms and legs hanging off the sides. I found some nylon rope that I cut and used to secure his limbs to each of the table's solid steel legs. I tried to wake him up, but he was out for the count. I drew out the gaffer tape and used it to gag him. I found a tarpaulin and covered him up, effectively blinding him. Lastly, I pushed the table to a corner and locked the castors—he wasn't going anywhere. I checked the clock on the wall. It was 4:15 am. I would have to come back the next night. Killing Vince in this state was a gift he did not deserve; I wanted him wide awake.

I drove out of Vince's garage and locked it. The sky was growing lighter, and the pre-dawn rays of sun peeked through rain clouds. With a sigh, I hopped back in the driver's seat and drove home.

Once back in the carport in Currumbin Valley, I put the blonde wig in the boot of the car. Just as I entered the house, the heavens opened up, washing every trace of tyre tracks into the monsoon gutters. I cleaned the knife, cleaver and icepick again, then put them back where I found them. I scrubbed my face and slipped into bed around five. Blackness enveloped me as I sank uncontrollably into an abyss, and, just like that, I was back in quadriplegia. I had taken one down and the second was strapped and bound on death row.

As a child I remember not wanting to go to sleep, too excited about the wonders of the next day. This day in my bed, although exhausted, incapacitated and unable to move, was the same. Sleep was a weapon; I knew I needed it and was determined to get all I could. Strangely, with one murder and abduction, the only thing that I felt guilty about was the petrol I hadn't paid for.

The day passed slowly, and I wondered if they would find Davo, or worse, find Vince before I had finished with him. The whole day I dreaded Edith bursting in and telling me she'd heard on the news that they had found Vince tied up in his garage. But the day passed uneventfully and my fears set with the sun at dusk.

Edith usually went to bed early, but this night she pottered around much later than she normally did. I waited and waited, getting more and more frustrated and anxious. The longer it took me to get to Vince, the more chance he had of escaping. Finally, at 11:00 pm, Edith came in, sat by my bed and, late as it was, prayed the rosary. After ten minutes that seemed to drag on for years, she drew my curtains shut, kissed my forehead and left. I shut my eyes for what I thought could only have been two seconds, but I woke up with a start just after midnight. I rushed out of bed, repacked my arsenal and drove out to see Vince.

When I arrived at Vince's panel shop, the surrounding industrial estate was deserted. I was grateful for that—the last thing I needed was to be spotted. I unlocked the large roller door, drove in, and locked it behind me.

I flipped a switch and was startled for a moment at the dazzling lights. The cyclical hum of a large fan kicked in as well. It cast an alternating shadow, like a strobe, as it slowly spun in front of the large ceiling tube lights. I put the wig back on and a pair of dark glasses.

I wheeled the table out of the corner to the centre of the room and pulled off the tarpaulin. The acrid smell of stale urine filled the room. Vince had spent an uncomfortable twenty-odd hours here, but he was now awake. And, with no toilet access, he had wet his pants. I smirked at the dark stain on his jeans.

He had heard the footsteps, and muffled cries escaped his gagged mouth.

I removed his gag and he launched into a tirade of threats: "What the fuck is this?" ... "You have no idea who you're fucking with!" and so on.

I ignored him.

"Untie me, bitch!" he demanded.

I opened his tool cupboard and found an angle grinder. I plugged it in, squeezed the throttle and it sprung to life, the remorseless whirl of steel screaming like a banshee. I held it up for Vince to see. Then I found a pair of earmuffs and put them on. The muted sounds of Vince's shouts over the dampened whirr of the grinder had become more panicked as his eyes opened wide and he started wriggling, his bravado quickly dissipating. I brought the grinder from behind so it was now whirring close to his left ear. He tried moving his head away, but his neck could only stretch so far, and I took a chunk from his steroid-filled shoulder muscles. Blood squirted onto his ear and across the side of his face. I moved one side of the earmuffs away to hear his horrifying yells. It was fruitless, the panel-beating garage was heavily clad to muffle the screeching of grinders and saws. There was no-one on the empty streets outside to hear his screams, and he knew it. Vince's resolve had been broken and he morphed into a sobbing mess.

I undid the lock on the trolley console to which Vince was tied, and pushed it towards the two steps leading down to a sunken portion of the garage. I let the end with his feet drop down and put the wheel lock back on. Vince was now on an incline and could see his lower body. Looking down, he could now see a linear saw—strategically placed between his spread legs, less than half a metre below his crotch.

I turned it on and looked at Vince. He was watching the sharpened steel whirr as it inched closer to his crotch. I could see his mouth moving so I pulled the earmuffs off altogether, letting them sit around my neck.

He started to beg. He hadn't recognised me, and why would he? To the world it could not possibly be me. The last time he'd seen me, I had been bedridden, with no hope ever of recovery.

I stopped the saw, now just centimetres away from his groin.

"Confess," I urged him, knowing full well that this opened up every possibility of other women who could have held a grudge against him.

"I haven't got anything to confess," Vince pleaded, "I've never hurt a woman in my life, but if I've hurt you I'm sorry. This is all a misunderstanding. Let me go and we can talk it over."

I took off my glasses and wig. His pupils dilated and he gasped.

"Before I hacked your mate Davo's balls off, he said, and I quote, 'Vince said they'd roofied you. You weren't supposed to wake up or remember anything,'" I told him, my voice mocking. "Now I want you to remember what happened that night for me."

Vince's lips didn't move.

I shrugged, and turned the linear saw back on. It continued its determined crawl towards him.

Vince broke immediately. "No. Wait. Stop. I'll tell you, Denise. Please stop it. Please."

I stopped the saw to hear him out. "I was dragged into it." I rolled my eyes, the blame had been passed up the tree again.

Vince explained that Carine and Samantha were out in the balcony chatting while he was watching the footy game. Carine came inside, dragged him out and asked him for a roofie. He knew something was up and that's when he got roped into their plan.

I remembered Samantha going out with Carine for a cigarette and Carine asking Vince to join them, but it never crossed my mind that they were plotting there.

The plan was for them to steal the ticket and then leave me there in the forest. Simon was to be tied up and gagged so he wouldn't raise an alarm. Eventually, he would be discovered, and shortly thereafter a search party arranged, which would have found me.

In hope, I asked again, "And Simon agreed to this?"

Vince confirmed, "For sure. Out on the balcony, Sam said the plan was that she would call Simon and he would take you home."

I had a sick feeling in my stomach. I started to wonder if Simon had pretended to be out cold when he crashed his car.

Vince claimed that he wasn't convinced and asked about Matt. Samantha and Carine had been confident that Matt would play ball.

I was shocked. "Why? It makes no sense. I would have shared it with Matt. With your plan he would've had to share it with the rest of you, rather than just me."

Vince raised his eyebrows as he responded. "I don't know. The girls were sure Matt would be in."

Vince gave the roofie to Carine. It was Matt who'd brought out the tray with the champagne glasses, including the one given to me with a bow tied to it, to celebrate my birthday and, sardonically, my lottery win.

As Vince recounted his version of that fateful night, it seemed that Davo had told me the truth. They were trying to get rid of him when Simon came early.

Vince said that the night went horribly wrong. All they planned to do was steal my ticket. But when they hadn't been able to find it in my bag or pockets, Carine had upped the ante and told them to strip me naked. Hearing his attempts to deflect the blame angered me.

I started the saw again. Vince screamed.

"I'm not looking for excuses. I need answers," I said.

He said that once they found the ticket, Carine started to walk away with it.

Greed is a terrible plague, and it infects the mind with mistrust and perceived fortuity. With a ticket potentially worth fifteen million dollars in her hands, everything changed.

Carine hadn't trusted Vince, and he hadn't trusted her. He told me that while Davo watched me, Carine had led him to the nearby car park where a solitary car flashed its lights, waiting for them.

Matt had stepped out of the car. He wasn't going to let his share out of his sight.

A heated standoff ensued and Matt reminded Vince that he needed an alibi more than anybody else, since it was his car that would have all the dents on it. Matt suggested he better go. He assured Vince that they would pay him for his silence.

With the winning ticket in their hands, everyone's expectation of their individual payout rose significantly. Their sense of entitlement was no longer based on a finder's fee being shared by many, but on the value of the ticket itself. For the role he played, Vince expected far more than what the others were planning to give him. Further, the others expected Vince to compensate Davo from his share. Vince was concerned he'd be short-changed.

"I told Matt *exactly* what would happen if he cheated me out of my share," said Vince, his voice dark. With Davo and Vince's stories, I was seeing a different side to my ex-fiancé. I would have sworn black and blue that he loved me, but could someone who loves you really do this? I was beginning to realise just how broken my friendships were to have got this far and how much greed had overtaken them.

Vince continued. "Sam popped her head out from the front passenger window and shouted at us. 'Hurry up! Someone will find Simon in his car soon, and we all need alibis.'"

With the saw still threatening, Vince revealed that Carine started having second thoughts, and wanted to distance herself from the crime. Yet, she was not going to put the ticket in anybody else's hands. Nobody trusted anybody. There were two cars, one ticket and I was still alive. And everyone now had a higher expectation of their share in the booty.

With time running out, Vince folded and went to collect Davo. "I always thought Carine and Matt were cheating on us, and that was proof."

I could tell that he was trying again to divert my anger to Carine.

"Tell me about Carine. Why did she change her mind and come back to your house later that night?"

"Carine was hysterical when she arrived. Matt and Sam

dropped her off and they left in a hurry. She just kept saying, 'We're fucked. We're fucked.'

"I asked why but she wouldn't say."

Carine's request to say they all came home together from the party gave Vince and Davo the alibi they needed and so they gladly agreed.

"Where is she these days?" I asked, feigning nonchalance. I was sure he could see right through it.

Eager to divert my rage, he confessed. "Carine must have taken the lion's share. She's living in a bungalow called 'Hacienda' on Albatross Avenue. It overlooks Mermaid Beach."

I whistled in disbelief. "On Millionaire's Row?" Vince nodded, keen to cooperate. Using his hope against him, I continued with my interrogation. "How did my wheelchair roll down that hill?"

"I really don't know." Vince was all innocence.

I started the grinder and took out a large chunk of his right knee. I was growing numb to the sounds of screaming. I went for his left knee. "Wrong answer. You are about to lose the ability to walk."

"Stop! Stop! It was Carine."

I answered disdainfully, "Carine was inside the pharmacy with my mother when it happened." I threatened him by edging the grinder close to his right knee.

Vince quickly added, "Your old lady was saying it was only a matter of time before you'd be able to speak. Carine panicked. She was terrified that if you spoke again, we would all go to jail. She undid the brakes while she pretended to fix up your blanket. She slammed the door behind her after she entered the shop, then glared through the glass doors and waved at me to push the chair downhill."

It could have been true, and it could have been his attempt to wriggle out of further torture. Little did he know there was no way out. It was all a waiting game. I had to ask to be certain. "Why did she say 'You idiot!'?"

Vince looked momentarily perplexed, like he wasn't sure, but then, "She was mad at me for lending Edith the fifty."

It was as I suspected. When Vince contributed to my medication, Carine believed he was jeopardising their future. She was fearful that if I recovered, I'd get them sent to jail.

Hope was the only carrot I offered in order to elicit confessions. I patiently extracted the information I needed and in the process, exorcised months and months of built-up hatred. A quick death was not an option.

Of course, the best was left for last. "Tell me what happened when you left the group in the car park that night and came back to me."

He was silent.

I turned the grinder on, but he still refused to speak. I shrugged and lunged forwards. I hacked his left knee and his screams rang out, pleading and begging with all he had.

Over the sound of the blade spinning, Vince sobbed that he was certain Carine was going to sleep with Matt that night. Even if he did get something for his efforts, he knew he would get ripped off.

When he came to find us and saw we were missing, he followed the noises to find Davo already on top of me. I was there, tied, gagged and naked.

"I was high on speed," said Vince, "and had chased it with cocaine. The drugs made me angrier. You wouldn't know what it's like, but it's as if your muscles are full of fire and you just have to get it out. I took my frustrations out on you. I'm sorry for what I did. I was very angry and——" Vince stopped, clearly realising that telling me any more would just incriminate himself further.

"Well," I said, completing the story for him, "After you'd finished raping me, you held me down so Davo could have a turn." I spat out the words, my glare icy.

Vince said nothing. Just then, his mobile phone beeped. I took it out of his pocket for him. It was 1996, and mobile phones had just become more accessible to everyone. He had one of the top-end Nokia phones. I decided to keep it.

"Who stabbed me with the crowbar?"

He corroborated Davo's story. They had run away and left me alive.

I asked him if the others, apart from Davo, knew what he had done to me. He admitted he never spoke of the rape to the others.

That didn't match with what Davo had said. He'd said that he'd only been given five hundred thousand because he and Vince were in no position to bargain.

"The truth. Now," I said, gesturing that I would hack him again with the grinder.

Vince said he had been bargained down to two million by the others, who said he could have been placed at the scene of the crime because of his car. He was supposed to split it with Davo. He made up that bit about the rape and the evidence to Davo so he didn't have to give him as much.

The depraved depths of friendships sealed in my blood had reached a new low.

I started up the linear saw again and let it run. The squealing of the teeth tore through the air, rebounded off the walls and made the floor throb. The atmosphere was alive with impending death.

Vince screamed and begged, as it crawled its way up the bench to cut through his jeans. I pulled the earmuffs from my neck and put them on.

Like a bicycle wheel splashes water as it rides through a rain-drenched road, the linear saw lifted a red splatter across the white walls and ceiling. After the saw had completely mangled his genitals, I stopped it. I let him bleed.

Vince's workshop was full of weird and interesting contraptions used for panel beating. I relieved him of a crowbar, a small can of liquefied butane, his Zippo cigarette lighter, a can of petrol, some rope, and an assortment of other tools, which I packed along with my own stuff into the trunk.

I checked my face and clothes in the Gemini's side mirror. I was covered in blood and nothing was going to change that. I turned back and started the linear saw again. Detached, I watched it split Vince from bottom to top. Two down.

It was 4:00 am when I drove home.

The night had confirmed my worst fears that everyone was guilty. However, if Matt had left with Carine and Samantha, then who had driven the car that spooked Vince and Davo, and who attacked me with the crowbar?

Soaked in blood, I took a quiet road home and found myself passing by Currumbin Beach Road, past Matt's restaurant. Out the front of the restaurant was a large "For Sale" sign with a mobile phone number for interested parties to call.

At 4:30 it was still dark. I whipped out Vince's phone and tried the number on the board. An irate real estate agent answered. I posed as an American buyer looking for a unique restaurant and ignored his disgruntled comments at being woken up so early. The agent's greed soon got the better of his irritation though. A short while later, I had arranged with the agent for Matt to show me around the restaurant the following night with the aim of a quick settlement before I left the country.

Once home, my bloody clothes went into a plastic bag and into one of the garbage bins left out on the street for collection. Birds had started chirping, and the black of the night was changing to the dark blue hue of pre-dawn. I had run out of time. I risked a quick shower and realised I had nothing to fear. The Devil wanted me to succeed, so he kept both Edith and you asleep. I realised then that winning a lottery was one of the worst things that could happen to someone. The large pot of money was stirred by greed and spiced with mistrust. Everything good about the humans I'd once called friends had drained into a snake pit of lies and deceit.

Back in bed, blackness enveloped me and I went into a deep slumber.

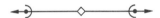

Siobhan shut *The Confession*. This was not the way she wanted to remember her soft-spoken, loving mother. This was a woman possessed by rage. Yet through the haze of confusion and disappointment, she knew she had to get through her mother's disturbing memoir. Siobhan's soul had been gambled with the Devil, and she needed to know the outcome of the wager.

She looked out of the window; the train was now snaking its way through a sleepy city. Dawn was breaking and the train slowed. The PA system crackled to life, heralding the imminent arrival into Barcelona Sants.

Moments later, the train pulled into the station. Siobhan picked up her backpack and disembarked.

CHAPTER 16

THE PRICE OF JEALOUSY

Siobhan checked into a small hotel near the Barcelona Sants station. After climbing up a narrow staircase to her room, she called the hotel in Madrid. She let them know she had left and asked them to keep her bags and passport safe.

Siobhan had barely settled into a hot shower when the phone rang. Thinking it would be reception wanting more details, she grabbed a towel, went into the room and picked up the phone.

"Hello?"

"Siobhan, this is Father Jakub." He was the priest who had given her the Bible and key after her mother's memorial service.

"How did you know I was here?" she asked incredulously, but he brushed her question aside.

His message was curt and urgent. "Siobhan, I found you, it is only a matter of time before they do. Take the 10:20 train to Gare de l'Est Paris. I will meet you there."

"Who will find—"

Jakub cut her off. "10:20 to Gare de l'Est. You must leave now!"

The phone went dead.

She didn't hesitate. She dressed and donned the habit she had arrived in, packed her backpack and hurried out, leaving a surprised hotel manager with an apology. As she made her way to the station, she saw two red-clothed monks running towards her hotel. Siobhan melted into the busy crowds heading towards the station. She boarded the high-speed 10:20 TGV heading to Paris. As the train pulled away from Barcelona Sants, Siobhan opened *The Confession*.

2ND JUNE 1996

It was early evening when Edith ushered in an unexpected visitor. Inspector Jones had brought the news that Davo was found late that morning by his cleaner. Barely had the sleepy city of the Gold Coast come to terms with his murder when Davo's friend, Vince Batista, was found sawn in half in his panel beating shop in Nerang.

Vince was last seen leaving a strip club with a blonde-haired woman. A dancer at the club claimed a woman who looked like the TV presenter, Denise Russo, had bought a wig from her in the toilets.

Jones also said there was an incident about a woman with a similar description, who had driven off with a full tank of fuel without paying for it.

I was lucky. Back in 1996, closed circuit TV cameras had not been installed at all petrol stations.

Edith listened to Inspector Jones and nodded her head, smiling mischievously. She was clearly amused and decided to let him say his piece uninterrupted.

"Inspector, my daughter is a quadriplegic. She can't move nor speak. I have to feed her, clothe her, and empty her bedpan, for goodness sake. Though it would give me no greater pleasure than knowing my Denise could drive a car, steal petrol and go to a strip club to pick up men. I don't really see that happening. Do you?"

They looked at me. I blinked in response.

Jones was visibly perturbed. He'd clearly known it would be a long shot, but it was the only lead he had.

Jones was convinced from visiting the murder scenes that these were sexually motivated murders. He was on his way to visit Carine Sanderson to see if she could shed some light on who may have had an axe to grind with her ex-boyfriend, Vince. Oh, I'd thought then, if only I could be a fly on the wall when Jones asked Carine for her opinion.

As night fell, my impatience was like a junkie awaiting my next fix. My active mind was imprisoned by my immovable body, unshackled only when you and Edith were whisked away into a deep sleep.

The large glass doors of Carine's lounge were open, extending it out to a beautiful wooden deck, overlooking the ocean. She sat with Matt out on the porch, their eyes transfixed on the large TV inside, watching the nightly news. I'd found a quiet corner in the darkness of the garden from where I could keep an eye on both of them. Headlining the news was the double murder of Vince and Davo.

Carine was seeking reassurance from Matt, who brushed it off nonchalantly. He said that Vince and Davo had probably done what they did to me before, or had done it again after. It was now apparent that Matt and Carine knew what Davo and Vince had done to me that night. Yet my fiancé and best friend—or at least I'd thought at the time— had chosen to stay silent.

Once the news broadcast ended, Matt readied to leave for his appointment to sell his restaurant, the one I'd set up the night before. Carine had a bad feeling and tried to talk him out of going so late, but he promised he would be back soon. She walked with Matt to his car, and I used the opportunity to climb onto the deck and hide in the kitchen.

I had known Carine all my life. From the sleepovers as a child, I knew she was afraid of the dark and when alone, always slept with the lights on. Only in my company did she brave her nyctophobia and let me switch the lights off as she shivered and huddled close to fall asleep. I was terribly fond of her, and, perhaps ironically, she was the first person who looked to me for protection from the unknown.

The sleepovers continued into our adulthood, more often occurring when she was heartbroken from yet another failed relationship.

Her fear of the dark had followed her into her adult years, triggering disfigured perceptions of what would or could emerge from the dark unknown. It made me wonder if our fears were a premonition.

Carine returned to the house and, when inside, she shut and locked the door to the deck. I watched as she double-checked the other doors, turning every light on as she went, and then anxiously climbed the stairs to the bathroom and got into the shower. I listened to the water start before I ascended the stairs.

Carine's shower was disturbed when the bathroom light went out. I pictured her cautiously stepping out of the shower, dripping into the dark. She would grope around for the light switch. Then her shaking fingers would find their target. I saw the flicker as the bathroom light came back on.

I heard a thump upstairs as Carine must have jumped in

the shower. And no wonder. The sound of loud music and chattering voices had suddenly filled the air. Carine came down the stairs covered in only her towel, trembling. The doors to the deck outside were wide open and swinging in the wind. On the outdoor table was her portable radio, blaring at full blast. From my hiding place, I watched her peek into the lounge and then rush to lock the swinging doors, leaving the radio still going outside.

With the remote, I switched the TV on behind her and she screamed. She bolted up the stairs, dropping her towel behind her. I could hear her furiously getting dressed and trying to phone out.

I dialled her number from Vince's mobile. I could hear the phone ring and ring, but Carine didn't pick it up. A few minutes later, she came charging down the stairs and into the garage. She started up her new BMW and drove away, the still-opening automatic garage door clearing her car's roof by millimetres.

At the first set of traffic lights, she pulled out a business card and dialled the number. She spoke to Inspector Jones and told him about receiving a call from Vince's mobile number. She was heading to the police station now. Inspector Jones assured her he would put a tap on Vince's phone.

After waiting another minute or two, Carine picked up her mobile and cursed while dialling a number. "Fuck you—the police will know exactly where you are."

Vince's phone rang, and lit up the back seat of her car. I watched her silently from behind the driver's seat. She turned to look at the phone in the rear passenger side seat, froze, then looked up in her rear-view mirror. Our eyes met.

She would have seen my face, lit up in a ghostly hue by the phone, staring back at her. She started to scream, but nothing came out. She slumped forward on the steering wheel, seeming to lose consciousness. I was sure she had fainted with shock. The car ran off the road and into the unrelenting bulk of a large camphor laurel tree.

Carine was still out for the count. I quickly gagged her, secured her arms and legs, and then dragged her over to the passenger side. Although damaged, miraculously the car was still drivable.

I reversed back onto the road, but chose not to drive Carine back to her place, lest Matt return. I knew of an abandoned home nearby, that I had covered in a story just prior to my accident, so I decided to take her there. The house, tucked away on the edge of the Currumbin Sanctuary, about fifteen minutes northeast of our place, had been tied up in litigation for years. Our legal system had ensured the house was still empty.

I drove onto the dirt road leading to the back of the house, which fronted with the forest. I parked it in the bushes and pulled Carine through a break in the hedge into the small backyard. I kicked the old granny flat door open and dragged her inside.

Once inside, I laid her on a creaky old flea-ridden mattress, then lit a small fire in the grate. I removed her gag and then sat behind her on a rusty stool and watched.

Eventually Carine woke. She wriggled her torso, but she could not move her arms or legs. I watched as she turned her head slowly towards me, as though sensing my penetrating glare.

"Denise?" she asked, dazed and confused. Then more urgently, "Why can't I feel my arms or my legs?"

"You can speak and turn your head. That's more than I could do," I hissed.

All my life, I had been protective of Carine, and could never remember a moment I had been cold to her; I doubted she could either.

She pleaded, "Denise, take me to the hospital please!"

"Hospital? You left me naked in the forest with your boyfriend and Davo to rape me."

Fully awake now, Carine protested her innocence. "That was never meant to happen."

I was furious. "You left me bound and naked with those two animals. What did you expect? Tell me Carine, what *was* meant to happen?"

Carine was silent.

I walked to the fire and dampened it until it dimmed to a pit of glowing embers. The dilapidated granny flat had one tiny window and it was almost pitch dark. Carine, sensing she would be left in the dark, screamed hysterically. "Denise, please don't leave me!"

With my back to her, I said, "Perhaps you will die of thirst, or perhaps some animal from the forest will find you. Perhaps someone will discover you, and, depending on your luck, they may save you or take advantage of your helpless state."

I turned and faced her, one eyebrow cocked. Carine confessed. "Denise, please. I was on cocaine and owed a lot of money. That night just fuelled itself and the stakes just got higher and higher."

"Higher? From stealing, to gang rape, to attempted murder? What happened, Carine? You were my best friend!"

Carine sobbed as she spilled her sordid tale. She told me that Samantha was with her in the balcony, bitching about how lucky I was, when in a moment of jealousy she told Samantha that the ticket was unregistered and I marked my numbers out each time.

"Sam said it was 'finders keepers'," cried Carine. I could just picture Samantha's wicked smile.

It was here that the plot was hatched to 'borrow' the ticket. They now knew that if anyone else found the lost winning ticket, it would be theirs to cash in, and I would have no recourse to claim it.

Samantha figured it would be very easy to convince me to stay silent on it, while they embarked on a massive treasure hunt in the forest with me. Of course, when it was found, I would give them a large reward for helping me find it. This story was consistent with what both Davo and Vince had said. I now believed it to be true.

Carine had asked Vince for a roofie and he'd known immediately that they were up to something. It wasn't long before he was recruited.

I remembered that when Carine and Samantha returned with Vince from the balcony, they dragged Matt away, leaving me with Vince and Davo.

"So how did you convince Matt?" I asked.

She said nothing.

I walked to the fire and started to put it out. Carine started to sob. "Don't, please don't. It was Sam."

Finally, I thought. The room was now lit by the reddish glow of the embers. "Go on," I said.

"Sam threatened Matt that she would tell you about all his affairs—"

"Were you one of those women, Carine?"

She looked away and immediately said, "No!" But I knew she was lying. I laughed bitterly. She knew that I knew. "There just never was the right moment to tell you," she began, defending herself.

"When, Carine, is the right moment to tell your 'best

friend'"—I pulled my fingers into air quotes—"that you are sleeping with her fiancé?"

Carine didn't answer.

"So Matt decided to join you both because Samantha threatened to tell me that you were sleeping with him?" I was disgusted.

"No, he said no at first." But then Samantha had pulled Matt aside into the cool room, leaving Carine in the kitchen. "When they came back, Matt had changed his mind."

"What happened in the cool room?"

"I honestly don't know," she said, her voice laced with fear.

"What happened after Vince left you with Matt in the car park?"

Carine told me that just before they left the forest with the ticket, Matt had said he wanted to see that I was all right. Inwardly, for a fleeting moment, it crossed my mind that maybe I hadn't been wrong, perhaps Matt had loved me.

Carine directed them back to the clearing where she had left me and saw that Vince's car was still there. They drove further, to where the noise was coming from.

"As we got closer and stopped the car, we saw Davo on top of you. He stopped and ran into the forest as well."

Matt got out of the car and approached.

"You'd come crawling, naked, begging for help, with blood dripping down your arms and legs. We freaked out and didn't know what to do. We'd realised that the night had reached the point of no return. And then you'd said Davo's name and if you knew that it was Davo who'd raped you, we were all going down for it."

"What happened next?" I asked coldly.

Carine went on to explain that they'd sat in the car and whispered about their options. They were certain that Davo and Vince would rope them all in. It was Samantha who got out of the car, opened the boot and handed the crowbar to Matt.

Carine claimed she had been distraught and couldn't bear to watch.

After my run-ins with Vince and Davo and having heard their stories, I'd figured that it had to be Matt who'd struck the paralysing blow. Still, I reeled when Carine confirmed it. Matt had been my fiancé, the man I loved with all my heart.

And he had gored me with a crowbar.

I summed it up shaking my head in disgust, "So you decided to go back to Vince's because you figured out that if the shit hit the fan, that was the safest place for you to be. Even if Vince and Davo were convicted, you could plead ignorance to the rape and it did not make you an accomplice to attempted murder."

I rifled through Carine's pockets and found a set of keys. It was on a key ring that I had once given Matt, a plastic snow globe of the Gold Coast shoreline.

"What do these keys open?"

"They're to Matt's new place," she said without hesitation. She was clearly too scared to keep anyone's secrets.

"Where?"

"Coomera. It's a farmhouse." Coomera was only a little over half an hour north.

"How could you possibly hook up with Matt after all this?" I asked her. Carine lowered her eyes and said nothing.

Through her silence, the rhetoric was answered. The biggest and greatest threat in any friendship is jealousy. Sure you love them with all your heart, but what happens if your friend gets what you have always wanted? My perfect life and boyfriend were bad enough in Carine's eyes, and then I had to go and win enough money to buy the lifestyle she always dreamed of. In my mind, we had never been competing, but I guess in hers we were.

"You stole my money and my fiancé. You stole my life, Carine. Isn't it ironic that you now get to experience my quadriplegia?"

I needed to be alone and turned heel.

"Please. Please," she pleaded through ugly tears. "Don't leave me like this."

Just before I got to the door, I turned back. "It's only local anaesthetic. It'll wear off in a couple of hours. You should be glad. I've been in a worse state than this for *months.*" My words sparked hope in Carine's eyes.

"I'm sorry, Denise. Please let me fix this. I-I'll give you the money back. I'll make it up to you. I promise."

"My money, Carine? I thought that the cost of keeping me alive was ruining Siobhan's future."

I left the room and came back with a can of petrol. I doused Carine and the mattress with it. She started screaming.

I roughly forced the small can of liquified butane I had taken from Vince's workshop into her mouth. Such was the strength I used that I heard the crunch of breaking teeth as the can lodged firmly with its nozzle down her throat. I secured it with tape.

I lit a match and watched Carine for a moment. She was dripping in sweat and trying to scream with the can in her mouth.

I threw the match and watched her burn. The flames licked at her clothes, catching on the synthetic fabric. Her attempts to cry out were muffled by the butane can and the tape. With her eyes wide in terror, she watched as her clothes curled and melted into her skin and then her silky blonde hair caught alight. I stood back as the flames reached the butane can.

It exploded, with a loud popping, rushing noise. Instantly it blew out Carine's once-beautiful face. Her brain-matter and skin slicked the dilapidated walls behind. For one last moment, the anaesthetic seeming to have worn off, Carine sat straight up, then fell back onto the flaming mattress.

I quietly left the granny flat and slid into the dark shadows of the forest. As I looked back, the side of the house was dimly glowing with the flames of the flat. Fire engine sirens wailed through the night air as red and blue lights flickered intermittently on the orange walls of the abandoned house.

It was a twenty-minute jog from the house, along the beach-side path and back to where I had left my car. I was glad I'd worn track pants. As I ran, each footstep pounded on the pavement and reminded me of the paralysis I had momentarily escaped. My thoughts turned cold. Unlike Davo and Vince, I'd grown up with Carine; we had shared many memories together. I expected to feel remorse, but instead I felt none.

It was then I understood the prophetic words of the Devil: "You cannot hate someone if you have never loved them."

I had learned to hate.

CHAPTER 17

LOVE TO ASHES AND DUST TO DUST

3RD JUNE 1996

For months I had thought about who had done this to me. Without a voice, without a working body, I hadn't been able to discuss it or search for evidence. All I had were my thoughts, which travelled in circles, around and around. I had been brought up to see the best in people. Now, I knew better.

Perhaps it was a series of events that had progressively escalated beyond my friends' imagination or control, but the events *did* occur, and at no point did the mob turn around and stop their devastation of my life. I didn't know what it was, but deep down I knew there was something I had missed.

Davo, I believed, had been dragged into it to some degree, and then in a drug-fuelled haze, he'd acted purely out of lust. In Vince's case, it was drugs and greed and then perhaps a sadistic sense of venting his anger for being dumped.

As for Carine, she was drugged up and jealous, so she stole my fiancé and my money. Then she decided to steal my life.

The thing I could not understand, though, was why Matt would do it. It made no sense. I would have shared the money with him—surely he'd have known that—and he had definitely ended up worse financially from having to split his share with five others.

I am not sure I would have believed Carine if Matt

denied they'd had a relationship. It would have been his word against hers. Were there others? What did Samantha say to Matt in the cool room that got him to cross the threshold?

As for Simon, I struggled to believe he was capable of hate, yet the others had counted on him to deliver me to my ambush.

That night, when you and Edith were put to sleep by the Devil's spell, I drove to Matt's property in the Gemini. His farmhouse was a large sprawling place, with a tree-lined drive, nestled away from prying neighbours on a five-acre lot.

I let myself in with Carine's keys. I tiptoed through the house slowly, only to realise it was empty. The interior had yet to be fully furnished, but the lounge had already been decorated with Matt's football trophies. The open plan dining and lounge area was separated from the kitchen by a large granite-topped island bench. Polished red gum sleepers formed a modern stairway leading up to the mezzanine floor. Matt was never one to under-spend.

I waited and waited and was about to leave when, at 2:00 am, a car's headlights shone in through the lounge window. I hid myself in a small wall closet, among the coats and spare electrical appliances.

Matt entered the house, locked the doors and then put on the safety chains. He double-checked that all the windows were locked before he sat down in front of his large TV and poured himself a stiff scotch from the decanter on the coffee table. He was obviously on edge.

After a while, he loosened up and was engrossed in watching a late night show. Once he was relaxed, I slid out of the closet and tiptoed across the dining floor towards him. I steadied a large crowbar above my head. I aimed at his right elbow and came down with all my might. Matt must have seen my reflection in the television, because he moved his arm at the last second. I pierced the couch, but not his skin.

In a flash, Matt, using his football skills, tackled me. The crowbar went flying, crashing into the glass display case behind me. As I fell, I felt my head brush something. I looked up and saw I had narrowly missed hitting my head on the edge of the glass coffee table. Desperately, I pushed up at the table. It flipped and the glass shattered on the floor next to me. I seized a large shard and speared his shoulder. Matt screamed and let go of me. As I crawled away, he recovered quickly and grabbed my ankle, his grip firm. I lunged forward desperately and snatched a marble statuette of a lady from a side table. I smashed it down on Matt's arm and his hold loosened.

Again I tried to escape, but Matt rose to a crouch and dived towards me. I dodged, but he caught my shirt. I pulled away, and the shirt ripped from my body, leaving only torn remnants in his hands.

I no longer had the element of surprise, and Matt was decidedly stronger than me.

I ran to the kitchen, leaping over the island. I opened the first cupboard I saw—full of dinnerware—and started to throw its contents at Matt. I went for everything I could lay my hands on: utensils, bottles, glasses, cutlery.

Matt dodged a few, but not all. One of the bottles smashed into the TV screen and blew it out. Around the kitchen island we danced as Matt tried to lunge at me. With my right hand I jabbed at him with a large carving knife, and threw whatever I could find with my left. Matt was determined and just kept coming at me.

He launched up onto the kitchen island and dropped down on me in a tackle. We slammed down on the kitchen tiles, hard. I bit, scratched, punched and stabbed at him. He pulled back, relenting, and I managed to get up and continued punching and stabbing.

In the tussle, my track pants had loosened and had slipped down to my knees. I wasn't embarrassed, but they did prevent me from moving freely. In a few short seconds, Matt had me trapped. One arm was pinned behind my back and he had pushed my neck down so that my face was pressed flush with the granite.

Using his body weight to keep my arm pinned, he let go and reached for the kitchen phone. "I knew it," he said. "You killed Carine, Vince and Davo. Let's see what good ol' Inspector Jones makes of this."

I cautioned him against it. "I wouldn't make that call Matt; I can also tell him what happened on my birthday."

Matt kept my neck and face pressed sideways against the stone top. He pinned both my hands behind my back before securing both my wrists with his right hand. Now with his free hand, he grabbed my neck and pushed down until my face was pressed down sideways, flush against the stone bench top. He moved around and lowered his face close to mine. I kicked off the track pants to regain mobility and tried to kick him. He avoided my legs easily and pushed my neck harder into the stone.

Matt smiled, it was a smile I had never seen before: the corners of his lips curved up, showing too many gleaming white teeth, and the expression in his eyes glinted with a promise of violence. He whispered, "I'm just going to have to finish what I started at Mount Tomewin."

I looked for a way out. "The police will find my car parked outside," I warned him. "They will come looking here for me. How will you explain this mess?"

Matt was not swayed. "It's my house to mess up, and it's insured to burn down. And thanks; they won't find you or your car here."

What happened next was completely unexpected. Matt left one hand pinning my neck flat against the bench top and slid back over my body as it was bent over the kitchen island. He was now close behind me so my legs had no leverage again. He let go of my hands. I tried to fight him off from around my back but it was nearly impossible, as the pressure on my neck only increased as I reached out.

Matt used his other hand to rip away my underwear. I knew immediately what was to follow. The sound of a zipper. Forced penetration.

The rape was brutal, and I fought against him with all that I had, but he was too strong, too determined.

I had to think of something. Matt always spoke of his prowess as a lover. I knew his vanity would be his weakness and he may believe I was actually getting into the sex. Gradually, I stopped struggling. I feigned arousal and moaned. I used my free arms to touch him gently and try to hold him. I rubbed my chin against the hand that held my neck, trying to kiss it. Matt released the pressure on my neck, still holding it, but I could move it. I kissed his hand and turned my head to look at him as lovingly as I could. With the pressure off my neck, I managed to move my hands above my head and play with his arms. With his loosening grip, I started to buck wildly. I breathed heavily and sighed, "Oh, Matt!"

His groans indicated he was close to climax. I whimpered, "Not yet. Turn me over." Matt hastily obliged and turned me around on my back, but held both my hands pinned under his. I responded by arching my face towards his. He leaned forwards and kissed me. I gingerly pulled one hand out of his grip and moved it behind his head, drawing him more passionately into the kiss.

I started to buck more furiously, wrapping my legs around him, simulating an orgasm. He released my other hand and started to climax. I knew he would throw his head back and close his eyes tight—as he always did. In that moment, as he climaxed inside me, I got my right hand around a glass shard from one of the smashed bottles on the kitchen island and drove it into the side of his neck. Matt roared and drew back. I freed myself and scampered away.

I raced to recover the crowbar from the lounge floor. Matt took a few seconds to react as he painfully extracted the shard. He turned to me and, realising I was armed and advancing towards him, he backed away behind the kitchen island. I speared his right arm, smashing it against the refrigerator door. He yowled and stumbled away, clutching his arm. I ran around the island towards him. The tables had turned. I was now the hunter.

"Fucking bitch," he yelled, as he tried to flee. He made it to the front door and grasped at the doorknob, trying desperately to open it with his good arm, muttering under his breath, "C'mon, open up. Fuck."

I was hot on his heels. I swung the crowbar, shattering his left wrist and thumb. He screamed again. "It's a nice house, Matt. Too bad your neighbours are so far away."

Now both his right arm and left hand were out of commission. Matt ran past me, away from the door, leaving a trail of blood as he bolted for the stairs. I chased him, trying to stab him anywhere I could. I managed to skewer the back of his left knee with the crowbar and he fell forwards, halfway up the stairs.

As I grabbed his good ankle, I jeered menacingly. "You are going nowhere."

With gravity working in my favour, I dragged him back down to the polished wooden floorboards of his lounge.

Even with a shattered wrist, a broken elbow and a busted knee, Matt still strained to get away. As he crawled, I took my time to walk with him around the lounge. "How much did you sell me for?" I asked.

Panting with effort, he begged. "It wasn't like that Denise, I swear."

"Sure, Matt. What did you owe the bikies?"

He sighed, resigned. "When I set up the restaurant, I needed to borrow more than the bank would lend me to finish the interiors. The restaurant was not doing well in winter, but the first year is always the hardest. I had maxed out on my credit cards for the ring and then added to my problems by gambling, but that had nothing to do with what happened."

I asked him the question that had plagued my mind, "Then why, Matt? Why? I would have shared it with you." My voice was choked and broken. "Over Carine?" I asked.

His silence said it all. He really had been sleeping with her behind my back.

"Carine told me that you said no, but then Sam went with you to the cool room and you changed your mind."

"Samantha threatened to tell you she was carrying my baby." I reeled back, horrified; I'd expected there were other affairs, but not this. Matt continued like he hadn't just thrown my life upside down, yet again. "She knew that if both of them came clean, you would dump me. I went along with their plan because I didn't want to lose you."

"Excuse me?" I blurted.

Matt explained. Samantha had called Simon to pick her up

and then deliberately staged a fight with him. Matt had then asked Simon to take me home. In a surprisingly sombre tone, Matt added that it was the last time he'd spoken to Simon.

My mood switched again and the anger returned as I recalled he had shown no remorse at all after the event. I found an iron poker by the fireplace and rested it on the back of his neck, chuckling darkly. "I think I will leave you crippled just like you did me. Wouldn't that be fun?"

"Denise, no! It was Sam. It was all her idea. She wanted to leave Simon."

"Matt, my darling fiancé. I do believe it was you who impaled me with a crowbar and threw me off a cliff. I don't think petite and pregnant Sammy could have done that. Do you?" I spoke childishly, my hand to my cheek.

Matt contested weakly, "Carine was freaking out and kept saying that we would go to prison for life and Samantha was saying that we had no choice but to kill you. It was you or us." Matt breathed heavily, tears of exertion and pain dropped from his eyes. "That night was fucked up, Denise. It took us all where we never wanted to go."

"And yet, you went there. We were engaged. To be *married*. When two men had raped me, all you'd been able to think of was saving your own skin."

The truth of that hit me like a freight train. I broke down crying. I had always seen Matt as my knight in shining armour.

"I guess it would seem that way to you. Being afraid of going to prison combined with my claustrophobia makes it sound even more likely. I want you to know that attempt to kill you was not about saving my own skin. Neither was it about saving Carine, or Sam—even though she encouraged me to do it."

I took the bait, "Then why?"

"I felt compelled to."

I was outraged. "Compelled?"

Matt said softly, "At the time, I believed it was what I had to do. I can never explain it."

I had finally stumbled on why I could never thread it all together. Matt's actions that night, him presenting me with the diamanté watch just weeks after an engagement ring, just didn't match with the idea that it was a crime of passion, motivated by his intent to move on with Carine. There was even some perverse logic that made sense why Matt would agree to conspire with Carine and Samantha, just to save his relationship with me.

The theft, which had escalated to multiple rape, though inexcusable, I could understand. Fifteen million dollars was a lot of money.

The theft had been inspired by greed and the rape catalysed by opportunistic lust believing the drug they gave me would erase my memory of the night's events and protect them with a cloak of invisibility.

It was the attempted murder that defied all logic of what I knew my friends to be capable of. Until that moment, I was unaware of Matt's claustrophobia. It may have weighted his decision to select a restaurant so open to the elements on the beach and his house with large acreage. It strengthened the motive that an upcoming jail sentence could promote a panic stabbing. Yet here was Matt saying he felt *compelled* to do it and could not explain it.

The wind had been taken out of my sails. But I still had a few unanswered questions, so I soldiered on. "Why did you tell my mother to have me euthanised?"

Matt lowered his head. "I couldn't bear to see you like

that. You were a constant reminder of my betrayal." He responded weakly, "Once the car had crashed, there was no going back."

The last gasp of the romantic in me confessed. "Matt, I loved you. I loved you with all my heart and soul."

Matt looked me straight in the eye. "I loved you too, Denise," he implored remorsefully. But that remorse was ten months too late.

I snapped and screeched in rage. What I once believed as the love of my life had now been painted in the blackest black.

I ignored Matt's continued cries and pleas, took the crowbar with both hands and speared down as hard as I could into his chest—into his heart.

This was the night I had feigned love to escape death, and then killed someone in rage because he claimed to love me. My romantic soul had died months ago, but tonight I laid it to rest.

Late the next morning, when changing my sheets, Edith noticed the wounds I had received from my encounter with Matt.

Edith called in Inspector Jones who viewed the wounds suspiciously. I could sense it as he carefully checked each fresh injury. I had met Inspector Jones when he took up my case. I am sure he would have trawled through my life history and been aware of my career as a newscaster. It would have been very hard for him to suspect I could ever be capable of these brutal murders, even if I was the perfect fit. Nevertheless, he tapped just below my kneecaps a couple of times trying to elicit an involuntary reflex action. But the sun was up, and I couldn't and didn't move.

It had been a warm night, and Edith had left the windows open. If someone had wanted to enter, they could do it as easily as I had re-entered from the bedroom window at the crack of dawn.

Jones scoured the room for clues or evidence of a break-in. He left the room and I could hear him checking outside my window for footprints or any signs an intruder may have left behind. The hard wooden decking, which surrounded the house, had been religiously swept and swabbed clean by Edith as she did each Tuesday morning. I wondered if the inspector would check the Gemini when I heard a car door open and, after a pause, close. My heart sank.

Thankfully, he returned carrying a manila folder. It must have been his car he had gone to. He checked the room again.

"I was with Matt until past midnight discussing Carine's murder," he told Edith. "The three people murdered so far were all at Denise's birthday party."

"Could it be something to do with Vince? He knew both Davo and Carine," Edith asked.

"That doesn't explain why someone would try to harm Denise in her bedroom," Jones replied. He reached into his file and pulled out a photograph. "We retrieved this from Carine's camera. It was taken on Denise's birthday." He pointed to the picture and showed it to Edith. "We have a new suspect. Do you know this person?"

Edith peered harder. "Yes he looks very familiar but I just can't place him." She brought the photo closer to share it with me. In the corner behind Samantha, through the window, was the distinct face of a man. I recognised him immediately.

I looked up and in that instant, Edith's face lit up.

"Yes. Yes I remember him. That's the man who saved Siobhan's life. I had no idea Denise was still in touch with him."

Edith hadn't known what to make of that, as she had never seen or heard from that man since the day you nearly drowned. She asked to keep the photograph, and Jones gave her a copy. It's the one I left for you. From my past nocturnal meetings with the Devil, I knew he was there that night. I pondered on Matt's final confession about feeling compelled to impale me and wondered if the Devil had any part to play in it.

When asked about Samantha, Jones said he had been to see her earlier that morning. He added, "Bringing up a child alone is never easy." Apparently Samantha had moved to a beautiful little townhouse, in a secure complex in Palm Beach, right next to the Swagman's Pub. Silently, I thanked the inspector for giving this knowledge away.

I wondered if Samantha, once financially independent, had told Simon she was carrying Matt's baby to break it off after all.

The Ferrari now made more sense to me—a sports convertible was a single man's car. I couldn't help thinking of Matt's comment about that night being the last time he'd spoken to Simon.

As Edith walked Inspector Jones to the door, he promised to place someone on patrol in our street that night. Standing near the bedroom door, Edith mused, "You know Inspector, Carine, Samantha and Matt all seemed to be doing really well financially."

"Yes, apparently they were all in a syndicate and won a lottery jackpot. They didn't check the ticket for months."

Edith, perhaps taken aback by their lack of generosity to

my bills, commented, "They could have given a little to help pay for their friend's recovery."

Jones was surprised. "I'm sorry to hear that," he said. He then added dryly, "Money changes people." As he left, she asked, "Do you think the money has something to do with these murders?"

Later that night, as advised by Jones, Edith double checked all the windows and doors before she turned out my light and went to bed.

CHAPTER 18

HER TICKET TO FREEDOM

I crept out and checked the street, waiting in the shadows for the police car to do its rounds. At 11:00 pm the cruiser glided down the street and paused a little while before driving away again. Once the car disappeared, I got into my Gemini and drove to the pub near Samantha's townhouse.

I parked in the car park of the busy local pub and found Samantha's complex located diagonally opposite. I scanned down the list of names next to the buzzer by the front entrance and came to S. Lennox—townhouse nine.

The headlights of a car swept along the dark paths inside the complex and stopped at the gate briefly. It swung open and the car drove out, giving me enough time to scurry inside before the gate closed.

I walked briskly along a beautiful boulevard lined with manicured hedges. The townhouses faced each other around a beautiful pool and children's playground. I soon reached Samantha's.

The lights were all on and a black limousine was parked out the front. I darted across the lawn and over to the side of the house. Through the lounge windows I could see a sinewy man dressed in a black suit, who appeared to be waiting for someone.

Looking up, I saw Samantha pacing around the bedroom

on the first floor. I walked further to the back of the house to look inside the bedroom; I could hear the periodic crashing of waves behind me.

I did a bit of snooping and saw that the bedroom had large French doors that opened out to a balcony, overlooking the beach. The balcony was held up by two ornate pillars and the sides were covered with a trellis that had vines crawling their way upwards from the grassed patch below. A low wall that ran the length of the rear of the complex, beyond which was a narrow road along the beach.

I climbed the trellis and onto the balcony. The glass doors were open, letting in the gentle sea breeze. Samantha was busy in the adjoining bedroom packing her suitcases. I hid behind the balcony wall, armed only with a sharp knife I had carried with me into the complex. I heard Samantha call out to the man waiting downstairs. "Peter, come here."

I figured that the man must have been a hired security guard or chauffeur. Although it was night, he wore tinted glasses and a chauffeur's hat pulled down tightly. I heard his heavy steps on the stairs get louder, signalling his arrival, and just behind him came another set of footsteps, these ones lighter. I dared to look through the doors and saw a nanny, holding Samantha's baby. I watched Samantha take the baby girl, give her a cuddle, and hand her back to the nanny.

"Can you please take my suitcases down to the car?" Samantha asked Peter.

The man lifted the cases and made to leave. She put a hand to his arm, stopping him. I ducked away from the French doors and hid behind the adjacent wall. From my hiding place, I could hear her trying to convince Peter to go with her to London.

In a very strong Eastern European accent he declined,

"No Madam, I cannot leave." He paused. "I promise you have nothing to fear." He went on to say that airport security was the best with cameras everywhere. They had even organised someone to collect Samantha, her baby and the nanny from Heathrow airport. Peter headed down the stairs with her suitcases and the nanny followed him with the baby.

Samantha stepped into her wardrobe—a walk-in—and then went into the attached bathroom, shutting and locking the door behind her. I started to panic. She was about to fly the coop. I needed to kill her and get out as quickly as possible.

I saw Samantha's handbag and rummaged around inside. I found her passport and removed it. I heard Peter lumbering up the stairs. I hid under the bed just as he reached the top. He stopped outside the door. "Madam, we must go."

Samantha shouted back, "Just a minute, I will be down soon."

She returned to the bedroom and pushed the sliding balcony doors shut, and I heard the lock click into place. She picked up her handbag off the bed, switched off all the lights, and headed towards the stairs. A minute or two later, I heard the car drive away.

Once I heard the sound of the engine fade, I wandered around. The townhouse was immaculate; everything was new. The upper level consisted of two bedrooms and a modest study, which had been converted into the baby's room.

Downstairs, in the attached double garage, Samantha had a new Mercedes convertible. Among the tools in the corner I found an axe sitting beside some firewood. On one of the shelves I found a rope—I took it too—then headed back up the stairs with my booty. I opened each section of her walk-in wardrobe, marvelling at the amount of shopping she had done in such a short time.

It was all expensive and it was all new. There were shoe boxes on top of shoe boxes, each full of the most expensive brands, many of which had never been worn. I then stumbled across a box towards the bottom of the stack. It contained some of Samantha's adult toys, among which were two sets of fluffy handcuffs. These could come in handy.

All international flights departed from Brisbane airport and it would take her an hour and a half to get there. As I waited, I wondered when Samantha would realise she didn't have her passport. Two hours later, a little after half past one, the black car returned.

As Peter waited impatiently by the car, Samantha ran into the house and upstairs to her bedroom. I hid inside her walk-in wardrobe. I figured she may ask her chauffeur to help and it would be the least likely place she would allow him to look in.

With the wardrobe door cracked open a little, I could hear as she overturned the bed covers, pulled out the drawers of her bedside table, and ran through the wardrobe, into the bathroom. She was swearing furiously while she continued her search. She slid open the first mirrored door of her wardrobe and rapidly opened the drawers inside, spilling everything onto the floor.

She opened the second door. There I was, standing with the axe. I didn't have much leverage, but I hit her flush on the centre of her head with the blunt end. I'm not sure if she fainted from the shock of seeing me or from the blow, but it had the desired effect. I secured her hands behind her back with the handcuffs and then her legs too with the second set of cuffs. I gagged her with a pair of frilly panties and black fishnet stockings that had fallen to the floor in her frenzy.

I tried my best to keep the sound of my heavy breathing

and inadvertent grunting to a minimum as I dragged her out through the bedroom. I opened the balcony door and pushed her out.

"Everything all right, Madam?" I heard Peter's voice coming from the base of the stairs. Not getting any response, he raised his voice. It would only be a matter of time before he came up to the bedroom. I ran back and locked the bedroom door from the inside.

I pushed Samantha down onto the grass behind her townhouse, then tossed down the axe. I clambered halfway down the trellis, then leapt to the ground. I half-rolled half-dragged her to the wall. With some difficulty, I tumbled Samantha over the back wall of the complex, then dropped the axe over as well before I jumped over it.

Over the wall was a nature strip covered in thick bushes, edging along a small access road. I'd expected it to be empty, but there were four people smoking and chatting on a park bench facing the beach, some twenty metres away.

All I had to do was kill Samantha, but something inside me didn't want it to be quick and easy. Though logic was against me, I left her there, hid the axe, and went to get my car. I walked briskly past the happy crowd on the park bench.

As I got in the Gemini and drove out of the now almost empty car park, I could hear police sirens approaching in the distance. I drove sharply into the side street and to the back of the complex. Samantha was still there, and the four revellers had left. I lifted her into the back seat, retrieved the axe and put it in the tiny boot of the Gemini. As I drove off, I could see the red and blue lights of the police car reflected on the windows of the townhouses. I headed southwest, away from the beach and towards the hills.

I left the main road and turned onto a deserted section of Cougal Mountain Road. Not so deserted, it seemed. Red and blue lights flashed in my rear-view mirror. I looked at the dashboard and realised I had been speeding. I swore, then pulled the car over to the side of the road, knowing well that the undersized 1.6-litre Gemini had no chance of outrunning a 5.7-litre V8 Commodore police car. I saw Samantha begin to stir in the back and I swore again.

Through the rear window, I saw the policeman step out of the car and make his way towards me. It was Constable Dave Smith, who I had gotten to know over the years. Currumbin was like a small town back then and everyone knew everyone. As he got closer, I hit the accelerator. I would put some distance between us in the time it would take him to get back into his car.

I pushed the Gemini as hard as I could. I switched off the lights, but in only a few short minutes the lights of the police car were back in my rear-view mirror. I veered off-road onto a dusty lane that led up to the old abandoned Cougal quarry. The car kicked up dust behind me and the flashing lights disappeared in the dirty cloud. I snaked the Gemini up Mount Cougal, along the one-way road leading to the quarry entrance near the top.

By now, Samantha was wide-awake and trying hard to break free, but I couldn't focus on her. Before the road went back to being sealed near the quarry and my dust cloud cleared, I swung off the verge and sped across a flat paddock. A short while later, I slowed down and turned the car to straddle an old rail track leading into the cave-like opening. I turned on the headlights, but they didn't do much to help with the darkness of the quarry. I stopped the car a few metres into the entrance.

I dragged Samantha out from the back. She was twisting and turning in resistance. I took some rope from the boot of the car and secured her neck in a slipknot, which tightened as she struggled. I tied the other end to an iron shackle at the top of an old, rusted wooden box trolley. I then then heaved her up and managed to dump her unceremoniously inside.

I used the car to push the trolley up the incline along the track. The wheels squealed as the trolley moved, probably for the first time in years.

We reached the crest of the gentle incline. Some twenty metres inside the cave, the track descended into the heart of the stone mine. The trolley started to roll away from the car and into the darkness. I parked and got out, taking with me a box of matches, a can of petrol, and the axe. I found a small piece of wood from a broken pallet, doused it in petrol and lit it to use as a torch.

Guided by its dim light, I headed into the dark abyss of the mine, the walls occasionally dripping with water and I heard rats scurrying along the sides of the track. They could come in handy—Samantha was petrified of rats.

Walking down this dark tunnel, devoid of any light and optical stimuli, I knew all I had to do was kill Samantha. Unlike with the others, I now had all the information I needed, but I just could not get myself to let her go so easily. I realised then how much I had changed.

The trolley had stopped at the base of the track, near a small loading station. The makeshift torch I had used to guide me was now almost burnt to a stub. I looked around the loading station and spotted some old wooden crates. I put some petrol over one and lit it. It ignited slowly, but as it dried out it burned brighter and hotter. I could see Samantha's eyes, and she could see mine—for the first time that night. Her beautiful dress was tattered and bloodstained.

As I perched myself on the ledge of the trolley, I could see and hear her struggling inside. With her wrists and ankles cuffed, she was stuck in a kneeling position with her neck tied to the shackle. She was going nowhere.

She had a big cut on the centre of her forehead from the whack I'd given her with the axe. I couldn't help but smirk at the damage I had done.

I took the makeshift gag out of her mouth and Samantha shrieked and screamed, her voice echoing in the cavernous mine. I whacked her hard with the butt of the axe. "Shut it or I'll hit you again."

Samantha whimpered, but didn't scream. "I have a baby! You can't leave a little girl without her mother," she pleaded, crying.

"You didn't think of that when you attacked me," I reminded her darkly. I loaded another empty wooden crate onto the dying fire, and doused it with petrol once more.

I broke off a piece of wood from another of the crates and lit it. The scar and smell of the cigarette scorching the flesh of my thigh still lingered with me. I held the burning wood above her and asked, "Samantha, do you remember what you did with your cigarette the last time you visited me?"

Samantha said nothing. She was shivering, and I was seeing a side of myself I didn't know I had.

With the others I had justified the torture because I needed information. With Samantha, it was pure, sadistic revenge. I poked her thighs with the burning wood, searing her pale skin. She screamed again.

A few rats scurried by. I grabbed one and dangled it above her.

"Shall I leave a few rats to spend the night with you?"

"No Denise, no. What do you want? Please."

"Why did you do it?" I asked, anger lacing my tone.

"Because I hated you," she said with venom. "I hated your success, I hated your fame, I hated the fact that Simon still loved you and always compared our relationship with the one he had with you. I hated the way Matt and everyone doted on you—their little princess," she spat. "And when I thought it couldn't get any worse, I watched as you won fifteen million dollars and my ticket came up with nothing. Of course, it had to happen, you had everything and then you won the fucking lottery." Her sarcasm dripped from her words and I was taken by surprise at the acrimony that spewed from her mouth.

"Matt never 'doted' on me," I argued. "He'd bloody well slept with Carine and you behind my back."

"Matt was just a slut. Sure he slept with Carine and me, and there were others, but that's only because he could. He still doted on you.

"You know, once Simon crashed that car, there was no turning back," she said.

It was like a stuck record, I thought, the same thing being repeated again and again. Like the others, she said it was a set of unfortunate events that escalated and escalated.

Yet it was Simon's betrayal, more than any of the others, that made me question my own judgement about who to trust. It had destroyed my ability to trust anyone, including myself. After what Davo had said, I'd believed in his guilt, and Vince only corroborated that. It was Matt's comment about that night being the last time he spoke to Simon that had made me less sure. The Ferrari was evidence that he had cashed in on the crime, but I would never have thought Simon could be bought. I'd never been truly able to believe he could be part of this—Ferrari or no Ferrari.

"If you claim Simon never stopped loving me, then why did he do it?"

Samantha's face scrunched up. "What are you talking about? Simon wasn't involved."

I took a step back. My shock had been clear on my face and Samantha realised she had something to bargain with. She knew something that I didn't.

"I'll tell you, but only if you let me go."

"I have been a fucking quadriplegic for ten months, I am not in the mood to make any deals."

"You being a cripple was never the plan. It would have been a lot better for all of us if you'd died." Her words were cold, unapologetic, and I shuddered at the truth of it.

I released a rat into the trolley, and Samantha squirmed, but with steely resolve said, "Do your worst, I will take this to my grave."

I picked up another rat and shoved it inside her dress. Samantha beat around furiously as well as she could, further wounding herself with the cuffs around her wrists and ankles. In only a few seconds she'd gone still, her control back in place. I realised she was going to hold out.

Samantha compromised on her previous offer, "All I am asking for is that you promise me that my little girl will never know what I did." There were tears in her eyes. I would have thought these were crocodile tears, but there was a sincerity in them I didn't expect. This was a side of Samantha I had never seen; perhaps motherhood had brought it out in her. "You're going to kill me anyway. Just make it quick."

Time was running out and I knew the police would eventually find us.

"Fine," I agreed. "Now spill."

"That night, I called Simon back to pick me up. When he finally arrived, he was drunk. Apparently his family farm had been sold to a coal mining company from India for a fortune."

I knew how long his family had been trying to find a good price for their farm. It was only a money pit.

I interjected, "If he was going to be rich, why did you—"

"It would've been years before we saw any money from his stingy family. And I told him so. I knew that'd make him mad. He took the hook and flared up demanding I be 'happy for him for once.'"

I scoffed at her sarcastic tone.

She went on to explain that she'd goaded him further, asking what he had achieved, other than expect a handout from his family. "Simon stormed off and that's when Matt asked him to take you home. You were already almost out cold from the roofies," she went on. "For a long time, I wanted Simon out of my life and your lotto win was my ticket to freedom," she paused. "If you came out alive, we would never be able to cash in the ticket and we would all burn for it, each and every one of us. Simon left the party early that night. Don't you remember? He never even knew you won the lottery."

I shook my head in disbelief. "Are you saying Simon…?"

"Simon would never be party to any of this. Not for all the money in the world—you of all people should know that."

A voice in the distance called out. "Hello, is there anybody there? It's the police!"

Samantha screamed for help. I rushed to put the gag back on her, but the damage had been done. I heard the police call out in acknowledgement. I turned the lever of the railway tracks and started to push the trolley again, taking it deeper into the bowels of the quarry.

Groaning and squeaking loudly, it picked up speed on the descent. I could now hear loud footsteps and the police shouting, not far from where we were. I pushed the trolley with all my strength and was running almost full tilt. I saw the light of distant torches bouncing on the walls beside me and jumped into the trolley, alongside Samantha, desperate to get away. The trolley picked up more momentum, but the lights were getting closer. Samantha was pounding her hands and legs on the side of the trolley, trying to make as much noise as possible, but the screeching wheels drowned her out.

Finally, we broke away from the torch lights. But, just as I thought we were home free, the trolley started to slow as it went up an incline. The police were catching up. Two sets of fast-moving stomping boots echoed in the tunnel, louder and closer.

The tunnel seemed to turn from black to grey, the texture of the walls becoming visible. Then the wheels stopped squeaking and the trolley stopped rattling altogether. The cavern opened up, unveiling a magnificent night sky with beautiful stars shining overhead—and we were falling.

We had rolled off a cliff and fell about twenty metres before plunging into the small tributary of Tallebudgera Creek. The trolley rapidly filled with water then quickly sank to the creek bed, taking the shackled Samantha to the bottom with it. I broke the surface of the water and looked up. I could see two police officers staring down from the hole in the cliff face where the tracks abruptly ended.

I swam downstream to the banks of the creek and then ran through the state forest all the way home. I had barely got home, changed out of my wet clothes, and dried myself when I heard a police siren break the silence of dawn. I hurriedly slipped back into my nightgown and buried my wet clothes deep inside my cupboard under the neat piles of winter jumpers.

As someone rang the bell and then impatiently knocked loudly on the front door, I jumped back into bed and closed my eyes.

CHAPTER 19

THE PERFECT ALIBI

I shut my eyes momentarily and only a few minutes later, I heard Edith shuffle to the door to let Inspector Jones in. He rushed to my bedroom and flung the door open. He looked around the bed, lifted the sheet, examining my limp body. He lifted and dropped each arm, watching carefully as they flopped back awkwardly.

"What on earth is going on?" Edith intervened.

Inspector Jones ignored her. Shortly after there was a knock on the door and he was joined by a Dr Cooper. Dr Cooper then started a detailed analysis, taking out his hammer and checking my knees for reflexes.

"Tell me now, what is going on? What are you doing with my daughter?"

"This is a murder investigation. This morning we fished out Samantha Lennox's body from Tallebudgera Creek. Denise's car was found abandoned nearby in the Cougal quarry. The weapons discovered inside the car were likely to have caused the deaths of Carine Sanderson, Rakesh Dev and Vince Batista."

Edith was aghast. It was at this moment that two people barged into the room: Constable Dave Smith and another constable named Lisa Delahunty.

"Is this the woman you saw at the quarry?" Jones asked them sternly.

"This is absolutely ridiculous," Edith interjected. "She's a quadriplegic."

"She's right, Inspector," Dr Cooper confirmed. "There is certainly no possibility that this woman could have got out of bed, let alone drive a car, push a heavy mining trolley, swim or jump."

Jones was unconvinced, and looked at his staff to back him up.

Constable Smith answered, "Well, it was dark, and I never really got a good look. I've known Denise Russo for years; even if she could move, she isn't the sort who would harm anybody, let alone become a serial killer."

The inspector turned to Constable Delahunty. She responded, "I joined the chase in the dark, and I did not get a close enough look to identify the killer."

Still, Jones was sceptical. He turned to the doctor. "Is it possible to override a reflex action?"

"Sure, it's possible, but highly unlikely in this case," the doctor admitted.

Jones persisted. "Is there any way to eliminate Ms Russo's involvement beyond any doubt?"

"Well, this woman's spinal cord was almost completely severed in the incident last year. We could perform a plethora of x-rays, CT scans and MRI scans to prove this to be true. If you need, Inspector, further investigations can be undertaken in the form of electromyography tests, which can gauge the electrical activity of Ms Russo's muscles."

Edith was beside herself. She contested furiously, "Inspector Jones, my daughter cannot move an inch. The Cougal quarry is nearly five kilometres away. This is utterly preposterous!"

Inspector Jones was firm, "Then you should have no problems with me getting a complete check-up done on her."

"What motive could she possibly have?" Edith asked Jones.

He concluded, "At this stage, all the evidence implicates Denise as the prime suspect. I'm just doing my job, Ma'am."

Within an hour, I was checked into the neighbouring John Flynn hospital for a day of tests. I was put on an x-ray machine, followed by MRI scans and CT scans, then wired up to test the electrical impulses of each muscle. After the scans came blood tests and spinal cord fluid tests. By early evening, I had probably been on every machine the hospital owned.

That evening when Inspector Jones visited the hospital, he studied the x-rays, the scans, and the electromyography tests. The doctors had concluded beyond all doubt that I could not possibly move. Jones came in and checked in on me and announced that the tests proved it couldn't have been me. He left in a rush when he received a call that the house of Matt Chambers had caught fire.

With the tests all done, I returned home. Inspector Jones visited our home late that evening with Constable Lisa Delahunty. Matt's house had burned to the ground and a charred corpse, positively identified as that of Matt Chambers was found.

It was apparent from the broken bones that Matt had been tortured before he died, but the fire had destroyed all DNA evidence.

I was in hospital when the house caught fire, so now there was evidence that someone else was out there wreaking havoc, and it was not me.

Delahunty was placed on guard at the door of my room for the night. Jones had reassured Edith, saying that it was for my own safety. Edith recited her nightly rosary by my bed and then tucked me in, as Delahunty, almost embarrassed to be there, watched me. She brought in a cup of coffee for Delahunty, kissed me on my forehead and left. The constable got up, walked to the locked bedroom window and then paced up and down the floor. It was like guarding a statue in a locked museum.

As I lay in bed under constant watch, I wondered how I was going to complete my mission. A mission I no longer wanted to complete. Was this the Devil's plan? Set me an impossible task and take away my motivation as well?

Simon was innocent. Farmers in Queensland had affectionately dubbed the large payouts from coal mining companies as Coal Lotto.

The payout explained the Ferrari, but not why he had never visited. Perhaps Edith had held him responsible for driving the car drunk and he felt the same way. Perhaps he could not bear to see me as a quadriplegic.

It was what it was. I knew now he was innocent and if he chose not to see me, it was a choice he was entitled to.

This night, even after Edith had long left my room and perhaps fallen asleep, with Delahunty watching over me, I remained paralysed. I started to crave my mobility and freedom. The longer I remained a quadriplegic, the more anxious I got that this could be it. The end of the road. I didn't want to kill Simon, but I had wagered your soul with the Devil. The consequence of that was the fear of the unknown for I did not know what it meant.

Yet it was the fear of the known that was even more frightening. I would be helpless to stop my father from being named your guardian, should something happen to Edith.

I watched the clock intently, becoming more and more certain I was left with an impossible task as Delahunty progressively slouched further back in her chair at the door. It was 1:15 am when I felt a breeze and saw the Devil walk down the corridor towards the room. He flicked his right hand towards Delahunty and she slumped into a deep sleep. He looked at me and hurried me along. "You have three hours before she wakes up."

I was furious. "Simon is innocent! I can't do it."

The Devil shrugged. "You know the deal. You don't kill him and you will pay with Siobhan's soul."

I offered him an alternative, "Could I could take my own life instead?"

The Devil conceded, "You could, but it wouldn't make a difference. I will still take your daughter's soul."

I shook my head in disgust, "You tricked me!"

He laughed and in utter disbelief repeated my accusation. "I tricked you! Hello? I *am* the Devil."

I disregarded the irony and made my case.

He reminded me that all he'd said was that they had to get me out of Matt's restaurant and who better to take me home than the person who had done it a million times. He had never said Simon was a part of it. "As for the Ferrari, I only compared it to Simon's beat-up Magna and commented on what a nice car it was. It was you who made the connection that Simon had used his share of the lottery winnings to buy it."

He was right. It was I who condemned Simon as guilty.

The Devil left.

I stood by my window with my head in my hands

wondering what to do. As I looked up, I saw Simon pull up and park in the driveway before he went inside.

I had no choice.

If I stayed in bed, I would lose your soul and remain bedridden for the rest of my wretched life. There was also a part of me that wanted to see Simon more than anyone else.

With my decision made for me, I took a sharp cutting knife with me from the kitchen. It would be my only weapon.

I walked to the porch and lifted the loose tile where he always kept a spare key. I nudged open the door and crept through the lounge, treading as lightly as I could towards his bedroom.

The bedroom door creaked as I gently pushed it open. And there was Simon. Half asleep, he turned towards the door and saw me standing in the doorway. "Denise, is that really you?" he asked in disbelief, voice full of hope.

I nodded. "Yes, it's me."

He jumped out of bed, his face glowing with happiness. "It *is* you."

I hid my delight, as I did the knife, concealing it behind my back.

Simon apologised profusely, "I never forgave myself for what happened to you that night." He blamed himself for not being able to protect me. Then he added, "I could not bring myself to see you like that." His eyes had lost their spark. It was as though the events of the recent past had ripped out his soul. He commented on the recent spate of murders, but he made no mention of any involvement of Samantha, Matt and the others in what had happened to me. Just like me he believed the best in all people. He would never have suspected they would ever be party to such a heinous betrayal.

I stood with my back to the dresser and carefully lowered the knife down behind me. I wasn't ready yet.

I confided sadly, "I want you to know that no matter what happens tonight, I love you." As I lowered my eyes, he lifted my chin, looking straight into my eyes.

"It has always been you, Denise. Only you."

He moved in to kiss me and I found myself responding. I knew where this was going and I let myself pretend it was fine, still knowing this would only make my mission harder.

A natural magnetism kept drawing Simon towards the knife and I weaved to keep him away from it. He manoeuvred me towards the bed, undressing me and I responded, trying to keep the knife concealed. As we moved from the dresser to the bed, I held my weapon behind me, responding one-handed. Simon moved to caress my knife arm, but I danced away so he was now facing me and I had my back to the bed. It was a dance of death.

As he lowered me onto the bed still locked in embrace, I hid the knife under the sheets. I was attempting to keep it out of sight, but still within reach. Eventually, I decided to move Simon and myself away from it while we kissed passionately. Going with the flow, we soon started to make love.

"I never stopped loving you," Simon confessed.

"I wish I never left." And that was the truth.

After we finished, Simon fell asleep, more contented than I had ever seen him. I was both exhilarated and racked with guilt. Simon was the love of my life—this I now knew—and I had to kill him.

I turned to look at his sleeping, smiling face, the knife in my left hand. Time passed. When the clock struck four, I knew I had to choose between Simon and you, Siobhan. And I knew who I could not give up.

I kneeled across Simon's body, the knife above my head. His fluttered open his eyes, still half-asleep.

I choked on my tears. "Please forgive me," I pleaded. Simon smiled harmlessly and closed his eyes. The cold steel came down with deadly force and pierced deep into his chest. The lights in his eyes went out. His pale skin was stained as blood leaked out from the corners of his mouth.

I could hardly see through my tears, as I removed the knife from his chest and cut his throat to be sure. Wanting to be as far away from it as possible, I threw the knife out of the bedroom window onto the grass.

I didn't look back. I dressed quickly and left. I deadlocked the front door and placed the key back under the loose tile.

I'd had to make a decision between my soulmate and my only child. I never wanted to do it, but I knew I had to. I felt an incredible vacuum in my heart.

As for Davo, Vince, Carine, Matt and Samantha, I felt no remorse. I still believe—to this day—that each and every one of them deserved to die.

Once back in my bedroom, I dressed in my nightgown and lay down. As I fell into the numbness of quadriplegia, I wondered if the Devil had tricked me into killing Simon and would not keep to his word.

I heard Delahunty stir and I drifted into a deep sleep.

I felt myself flying above a rock formation that had the red-orange colour of Uluru. It was flat and notched, as though cracked by the endless cycle of heating and cooling, and ascended upwards at about a thirty-degree angle. The most similar thing I can think of is the red, iron ore laden rocks of the Kimberley, in Western Australia.

The rocks stretched out forever with great step-like formations without a hint of green, with geoglyphs like the Nazca lines. The sky was an eerie dark blue without a cloud. I floated upwards along this incredible vast empty orange landscape.

Suddenly I was on a beach. To my left was a wooden portico and to the right were two turtles, each at least the length of my Gemini, and with skin so green it almost glowed. It wasn't their size or colour that surprised me the most though, it was their shells that were shaped like hourglasses. Then, standing next to the turtles on the beach, dwarfing them with its size, was a green dragon, which looked a lot like a Tyrannosaurus Rex.

I heard your voice calling me; I turned and saw you standing with another young girl right behind me. "Come quickly Mummy, there's a dragon on the airstrip."

I didn't think to question you, I ran to the airstrip, where a small turbo prop plane, probably something built in the 1950s, was moving on a thin bitumen runway. I waved it down, but it had already seen the dragon and stopped.

A large black blob of saliva fell on my shoulder and dripped down my back. I was back on the beach, but I had now disturbed the dragon. A voice shouted, "Don't move. Just look in its eyes and pray for forgiveness."

The dragon lumbered its way towards me. It looked at me keenly and any hopes I'd had that it was a herbivore were fading. The dragon opened its mouth and I could see its teeth, like fine off-white toothpicks, each the size of my body. I could hear a voice—Edith's. She shouted, "She cannot move, but she is moving."

I expected the dragon to have an odour, but there was no smell. I was trying hard not to move. I held my hands together, crossing my palms, as though praying. As the dragon's face drew closer, the sharp teeth with it, it sniffed. The dragon's nostrils twitched, inhaling, and I cowered.

I heard Edith's animated voice again, this time more excited, repeating her words, "She cannot move, but she is moving."

I opened my eyes.

Edith was standing over my bed with Delahunty. I was crouched in a foetal position in my bed, something I should have been incapable of.

My eyes were wide as Edith spoke. "Honey, you've been moving in your sleep." Her voice was joyous, astounded at the miracle I presented.

I sat up and Edith fainted. Delahunty caught her as she fell. The Devil had kept his word.

It was a frantic morning. Edith fell to her knees in prayer and asked me to join her. I flatly declined. I knew who had helped me. It was not God.

Delahunty notified Jones and he rushed over. Immediately, I was escorted out and driven in the police car to the hospital. I walked into Dr Cooper's office with Jones. The doctor was in complete shock.

I was back on every machine the hospital owned. After MRI scans, CT scans, electromyography, and every test I took the previous day, the consensus was unanimous. My spinal cord was perfectly intact. Every bone was perfectly intact, every muscle was working, and every scar on my body had disappeared. It was as though it had never happened.

The entire medical staff of the hospital was dumbfounded. The hospital was soon visited by every specialist on the Gold Coast as the news spread like wildfire. The TV crews came, but Inspector Jones kept them at bay and ensured my privacy was protected.

Inspector Jones asked me what I remembered of the night of my attempted murder and I said I could not recall anything. I did have something I wanted to show him. I had one regret, which was that I had killed Simon. Killing an innocent person was the hardest thing to do and living with it was even harder.

We arrived back home and I led Jones, Edith and Delahunty to Simon's house. I took the key from under the loose tile and opened the front door. They followed me through the lounge, which, strangely in the light of day, had sheets covering all the furniture. I hadn't noticed them the previous night, but perhaps I had been so focused on entering the bedroom quietly in the darkness.

I pushed open the door to the bedroom. The furniture, including the dresser, was covered with sheets. The bed itself was, however, unmade, as though someone had slept in it. But there was no trace of Simon, and there was no trace of blood.

I was hysterical, "Where is he? He was here last night and I murdered him. There was blood everywhere. This is not possible."

Delahunty tried to pacify me. "Ma'am, you've been through a very traumatic experience. I watched you sleep all night."

I ran out to the garden to find the knife. It was obvious no-one had been in the yard in months—the grass was long—there was no knife to be found.

I ran back home to the kitchen where I had taken the knife off the block. The knife was there, sitting silent in its place beside the scissors.

"Why is it here?" I screamed.

Edith interjected, "Denise honey, calm down. You have been through an ordeal and been taking a cocktail of medication every day for months now. You must have dreamed it."

I screamed, "No, Mum! It wasn't a dream, where is Simon's body?"

Jones spoke up, "Denise, the night you were abducted, Simon Carter died in that car crash."

That couldn't be. "I saw him last night and I *killed* him!" I insisted.

Inspector Jones was quiet and sombre, "I removed his corpse from his car myself."

I tossed and turned in bed that night. I recalled Matt's remorseful words before he died. *That was the last time I spoke to Simon.*

I thought they hadn't spoken because Samantha told him who the baby's real father was. It was then I recalled Samantha's words, *Once Simon crashed that car, there was no turning back.* They'd known Simon was dead; whoever had stolen my ticket had been responsible for the crash and his death. The theft had already resulted in a murder. There was no turning back. They were already guilty.

I struggled to believe, but the proof was beyond doubt. Knowing that I hadn't killed Simon made it easier. I would be a better mother out of jail than inside it. I wondered, had the Devil tricked me by conjuring up a Ferrari? Was killing

Simon a test? Like how Abraham was tested when he was asked to sacrifice his son Isaac? There were no answers. I had none.

Over the months that followed, I collected cuttings from newspapers and magazines. I have attached these and I am sure you will be able to find more if you look. I have included these because I need you to believe what I am saying is true, as is the rest of my story. I have no hope of redemption, for God will never forgive my pact with the Devil.

Religious groups from around the world claimed it as their own miracle and scientists and neurologists came up with new theories. I shunned away from engaging in talk shows or publicity, but my miraculous recovery had launched me into the limelight on a national and international level. It did wonders for my career as a newscaster.

Jones never believed my miraculous recovery, but there was little he could do to prove his theories.

Matt's house, the only one where my DNA should have been found, had mysteriously burned down, the fire starting while I was under observation in hospital.

Carine's crime scene had also burned down and Samantha's rail trolley was so badly damaged by water and the impact that, when it was fished out from the bottom of the creek, there was nothing to tie it to anyone.

The newspapers and international journals had printed my 'before and after' x-rays and scans. By insisting on taking me to the hospital and getting me tested, Jones had inadvertently provided me with an irrefutable defence. Even if I confessed to the crimes, nobody would ever believe me anyway.

The Devil had kept his word, he had given me the perfect alibi. The case of the five murders that occurred in the first week of June 1996 would remain unsolved.

It was in early August that I realised I was pregnant. Even though Matt had raped me, I could never abort a baby.

When I got pregnant with you, your father wanted me to have an abortion and I'd refused. He wanted nothing to do with raising a child. He thought I insisted on having you so I could extract child support payments or so he would be forced to marry me. It was neither.

Young and broke as I was, I could not face abortion, and having you was the best decision of my life. I'm sorry I lied to you. Your father was not a war hero who died serving our country in Iraq. He was a drug addict who died of a heroin overdose about three months before you were born.

On the 9th of March 1997, your sister was born. She was soon to overtake me as your favourite person in the world. I could never name Matt as her father as that would have placed me at the scene of the crime. To Edith's horror, I said I was uncertain who Jess' father was and never named Matt. In time, people stopped asking.

The eleven years that followed were the best years of my life.

CHAPTER 20

RENDEZVOUS IN PARIS

Siobhan turned the page and saw that folded newspaper clippings had been glued inside the book. The first article was from the front page of the local *Currumbin Times*, dated the 9th of August 1995, about the death of Council officer Simon Carter. It also mentioned that TV reporter Denise Russo was missing.

A different article—this one from *The Australian Gazette* —reported the discovery of TV personality Denise Russo in a critical condition on a ledge at Mount Tomewin, a crowbar lodged in her back. The police had confirmed that Ms Russo had been sexually assaulted before the attempted homicide.

Siobhan turned the page and found a clipping from the *Gold Coast Chronicle*, dated the 24th of April 1996. The headline was '$15 million lotto winners found'. It had a picture of Vince, Carine, Matt and Samantha smiling with a large cheque.

Siobhan opened the next article from the *Gold Coast Times*, dated the 3rd of June 1996—'Two men found castrated and murdered'. The following write-up was from the day after and covered Carine's murder, just as Denise had described it. Next was an article on the murders of football hero Matt Chambers and his friend Samantha Lennox. The last was the front page of *Life* from July 1996, titled 'Miracle recovery—

did prayers beat medical science?', with a picture of Denise.

Siobhan sighed as she read through them all, matching the details with her mother's diary.

She leaned her head against the cool glass of the train window and closed her eyes, letting the sun warm her face.

Siobhan vaguely remembered Simon, she was only four when he'd died. The newspaper articles substantiated her mother's memoir, that indeed all six friends who attended her twenty-eighth birthday were dead and the validity of the lotto ticket story. The magazine clippings and newspaper cuttings also gave credibility to her mother's tale of miraculous recovery, which had baffled the doctors.

She had just learned that her father was not who she thought he was and her darling sister's father was a rapist. She deduced from her mother's fears that her grandfather, who she never got to see, was at best an alcoholic and a sadist. Siobhan shut her mother's memoir. Sister Margaret was right. A book written in anguish would only bring anguish to the one who read it.

Her thoughts drifted to the red monks, Father Jakub, the nuns and the Mother Superior. What was the legacy her mother had left behind? Was it her confession of the murders? Why did a few murders in a small suburb in Australia nearly eighteen years ago mean so much to people in Europe?

Reading her mother's story was to live it, and Siobhan was bone-tired. Without really noticing, she drifted into sleep, fluffy clouds casting shadows over her eyes. Siobhan was woken by a hand gently shaking her awake. The train conductor queried, "*Soeur, nous sommes arrivés à la Gare de l'Est. Descendez-vous ici?*"

Siobhan sat up quickly, gathered her things and said, "*Merci,*" to the conductor. She took her bag and left the train.

Gare de l'Est was buzzing with a throng of people. Siobhan walked to the head of the platform, towards the arches under a huge semi-circular window that marked the exit of the station.

"Siobhan!"

She turned and standing in the arch to her right was Father Jakub.

Siobhan hurried towards him. After all she had been through, it was a relief to see a familiar face. But as she got closer, she saw he wasn't smiling. Something was wrong. Two red monks stepped out from the pillars behind him. She turned around, but there were two more red monks closing in directly behind her. She had walked into a trap.

Jakub held his hand out. "Give me your backpack, quickly." Siobhan didn't respond. She looked around, hoping the crowd would notice. It was peak hour, and the Parisians were more interested in going home than caring about four monks, a priest and a nun.

Something sharp poked into her side. She didn't look to see what it was, she had a pretty good guess.

He demanded again, "Siobhan, nobody knows you are here in Paris. If you don't give me your backpack, these men will kill you."

She had no choice. She handed over it over to Jakub, and gave him a contemptuous glare.

He signalled to the two monks flanking Siobhan. They shuffled her along as they moved into a quiet corner just outside the main entrance. Jakub opened the backpack and extracted Denise's Bible. He then pulled at the ribbon and showed the monks the key attached. The monks nodded, then produced Siobhan's suitcase.

Jakub whistled loudly and a white Vito van drove into

the courtyard in front of the station. Jakub gave Siobhan her backpack and told her to get in. Once she was safely settled in the back, he signalled to the monks to load her suitcase in with her.

"You may check your passport is inside," said Jakub. Siobhan rummaged through it quickly and confirmed it was present. He shouted to Siobhan to lock the door of the van from the inside. Once she did, he gave the Bible and the key to the red monks. The monks were unhappy, but begrudgingly let him go. Jakub jumped into the passenger seat in the front and the van sped out onto the motorway.

"What is going on?" Siobhan demanded.

Jakub tapped the driver, and the van pulled over to the side of the motorway. He ran around, entered the back of the van with Siobhan, and drew the curtain shut on the driver.

"There must be a mole in the convent," he whispered. "Sister Catherine had only told the red monks of the key and the Bible before she was killed. I called you to Paris so we have some more time to get you on a plane back home before the Amalrican monks find that your mother's vault is empty."

Realisation dawned quickly on Siobhan. "You made a deal to save me."

Jakub smiled and added, "And *The Devil's Prayer*." For the first time Siobhan realised the red monks—or the Amalrican monks as Jakub had called them—were after the sealed section in the back of her mother's confession. The section her mother had begged her not to open until she had read her confession in its entirety.

A confused Siobhan asked who the red monks were. Jakub explained that the red monks belonged to a religious sect founded around the beginning of the thirteenth century by the first Inquisitor of the Papal Inquisition, the Butcher of Beziers, Arnaud Amalric. The Amalrican monks were once the equivalent of the papal Gestapo.

Siobhan interjected, "If these are religious men, then why are they killing people?"

Jakub shook his head sadly. "More people have died in the name of religion than any other disease."

The van stopped at Charles de Gaulle airport and Jakub hurried Siobhan towards the terminal. The next flight out to Brisbane was via Singapore. He bought her a ticket and rushed her to the check-in counter.

Saying goodbye, Father Jakub gave her his Bible. It had kept him safe and he wished it would do the same for her. Siobhan asked where she could find him. He answered, "The Book of Revelation holds all the answers." With those last cryptic words, he left.

Homeward bound, Siobhan settled into her seat on the Singapore-bound aeroplane. The flight would take over twelve hours. She anxiously waited for the plane to take off, aware that the Amalricans would be rushing back to the Moreruela convent at that very moment. Once the jet lifted from the tarmac, Siobhan opened *The Confession* once more.

Part 3:
The Quest

CHAPTER 21

THE SIGNS

MARCH 1997

On the 9th of March 1997, Jess was born. When I came home from the hospital with her, our new neighbours, the Perrys, had moved into Simon's house next door. Back then, Talitha Perry was in her forties and her partner, Peter Perry, a sinewy body builder, was considerably younger, in his late twenties. They had a one-year-old daughter, Amanda. The Perrys had traces of an Eastern European accent, but they tried heavily to disguise it with an acquired Australian one. I'd once asked Talitha where they were from, but she stared at me so coldly, I figured I must have offended her. I never asked again.

Talitha seemed forever busy looking after her daughter, scratching in the yard, taking out garbage, going to the shops. Eerily, Peter always stood in the same spot on the balcony that Simon did. And, like Simon, he was there each evening as I got home. Peter just stared and stared, but he never waved or acknowledged me.

The Perrys were always around. I constantly felt eyes on the house, even in the dark when I looked out of my bedroom window. I sensed them peering from behind the glass watching me. It was just bizarre. I never did know what they did for work.

There was one routine they never missed. Edith was the one who first recognised it after they had been our neighbours for about three years—by then it was July, 2000. Every evening at seven o'clock, irrespective of the day, they would climb over the back fence and disappear into the Nicoll Scrub Forest. They would return the same way at exactly eight-thirty.

Times were changing. The Gold Coast was developing fast from the sleepy, hippy surfer town into a bustling commuter city for Brisbane. The high rises of Burleigh Heads stretched further south, swallowing sleepy Currumbin into the vibrant tourist Mecca of the holiday town.

Jess, too, was growing up quickly. She was very reserved, a stark contrast to the gregarious soul you were. I often wondered if the changes in my values had a bearing on her personality. When you were born, my world was full of trust and hope—ingredients of life I would never know again. I had Jess at a time when the eclipse in my life had just started to clear.

For all the Perrys' strangeness, Jess and Amanda grew to become best friends. Jess loved the Perrys and the Perrys loved her. They often offered to babysit her and it was hard to refuse them when Jess clung tight to their knees with that look in her eyes.

Four years after the Perrys moved in next door, in 2001, I saw the first sign. I was in Calamvale, near Brisbane, back at work covering the opening of a new community centre. Calamvale had a a predominantly Chinese migrant population; it's an area known as lucky and dubbed by many real estate agents as the 'eye of the dragon'. Among the festivities, the Chinese, who believe strongly in Feng Shui, had invited an expert, David Chu, to approve the layout and interior design of the centre. He was accompanied by an old monk called Zeng, reputed to be a psychic.

The camera crew and my co-host, Kevin, were speaking with Zeng, asking him for advice about everything: from the next horse to win the Melbourne cup, to whether the person they had met was the love of their life. Zeng played along, speaking in riddles, citing signs and delivering cryptic messages to answer each of their queries. It was hard to judge whether or not he was having them on.

As a bit of fun, Kevin invited me over to see him. I refused. I had moved away from connecting with anything spiritual since my ordeal. I had no faith in any God or man. I had resolved to keep my head down and make the most of my second chance, to give Jess and you the best future I could afford.

The rest of the crew egged me on and practically dragged me over to say hello to Zeng. He was dressed in purple, with a bald head and a pair of rimless glasses. I bowed politely and met his eyes—deep brown pools that sucked you in. I had an uneasy feeling, as though he would be able to read my mind. If I told you not to think about a nun doing cartwheels wearing a clown's mask, you will find it impossible not to. I tried hard to shut out everything, but, by trying to close my mind off, I was only thinking about what my mind was trying to hide.

Zeng's eyes rolled backward, as though he was falling into a trance. He started to shiver. The happy crowd stopped its chatter and the silence spread through the hall in seconds. There was a hush in the room as Zeng collapsed to the floor and began to shake violently. I panicked, thinking he was having a seizure, and others in the crowd called for an ambulance. I put my hand out and held his shoulder, but withdrew quickly. I'd felt a strong shock when I touched him.

Finally, he stopped shaking and came back to us. The crowd waited eagerly for him to say something and prove he was okay. Zeng got up and then, without uttering a word, shuffled across the room. Everyone was silent as they watched the old monk head towards the door. His disciple, David Chu, rushed after him, calling out in some Chinese dialect. Zeng just raised his hand for David to leave him alone as he walked out.

About half an hour later, we were packing up to leave. We were all a little thrown by the incident, yet nobody really knew what to say. In the uncomfortable silence that lingered, I wondered if Zeng had seen something so terrible that he could not speak about it.

As we were leaving, David returned. He caught my eye and beckoned me to join him away from my colleagues. I asked him what the monk had said and why he had left in such a huff. David remained silent and offered me a small piece of paper with both hands, like he was handing out a business card. I took it and he explained that it was the fifty-fourth poem and a sketch from an ancient Chinese prophecy book called the *Tui bei tu*. Zeng believed that it related to me.

I looked at the poem and was surprised when I saw the sketch associated with it. The drawing showed five people with sticks herding a bull.

The poem went like this:

Messy, a deadly result, a peaceful ending.
People laugh but cry. They don't think logically.
Shave the hair, peel the skin, and still act tough.
Out of this incident a real dragon is born.
The 9 Curves Yellow River's water is not yellow.

The next morning before work, I visited a library to find out what this could possibly mean. It was a time before internet searches had the answers to everything. The *Tui bei tu* was from the seventh century and contained sixty surreal drawings, each accompanied by a cryptic poem. The poems are meant to signify events that occur in chronological order. Some scribes believed this fifty-fourth poem related to the Tiananmen Square Massacre that occurred in June 1989, which placed this seventh century prophecy in a time frame that could relate to me.

I intuitively came to associate the five people in the sketch with Davo, Vince, Carine, Matt and Samantha—the five people I had killed. Something in my gut told me that the bull was being herded to the slaughter and that the bull represented me.

I studied the poem. Did *shave the hair, peel the skin and still act tough* refer to my predicament when I was found in a coma?

It played on my mind for a while, but the rest of the poem made no sense to me. The verses related to the future of China, which had nothing to do with me. That gave me some cold comfort; perhaps Zeng had not seen right through me.

Still, I wanted to see Zeng and David again. Maybe they could explain.

When I read the morning's newspaper later that day, I discovered an article about a car accident on the road to Brisbane airport. A large truck had fishtailed on the wet freeway, swiping a small car into the sheer rock wall lining the road, killing both driver and passenger. The driver was David Chu and the passenger was Zeng.

A year later, I saw the second sign.

It was a warm November evening; I was sitting on the porch with Edith. You and Jess, who was now five years old, were playing with Amanda in the front garden. Peter was standing on his balcony watching over you playing as he always did. At around 6:30 pm, when the sun had almost set, Edith asked me if I could hear it. I didn't know what she was talking about, but I listened and could hear nothing. I shook my head. She asked me to listen again, carefully. Still nothing.

I asked Edith what it was. She pointed to the forest over our back fence and commented that even though we had a forest on our back doorstep, you couldn't hear a single bird or cricket or frog or insect. There were no mosquitoes or flies buzzing around our heads. Edith added that she couldn't remember the last time she had seen a cockroach or a spider in the house. Then I did notice it and the silence was deafening.

"What do you think it is, Mum?"

Edith shook her head. "Something's not right."

We went on with our lives, but the silence always raised the hairs on the back of my neck.

In the following year, 2003, on a beautiful autumn day in early April, Jess and Amanda were invited for a birthday party at the local Currumbin Wildlife Sanctuary. It was a perfect day and I was looking forward to seeing Jess' reaction when she got to feed the beautiful rainbow lorikeets—you know how they dominate the entrance to the park, Siobhan. The park had recently opened up the butterfly garden for the first time as well.

Once we entered the sanctuary, Talitha left me with the girls' bags and bottles as she took them for a toilet break. I watched the other children from Jess' kindergarten, also invited to the party, excitedly squealing as the lorikeets dropped down from the trees to sit on their shoulders, expecting some of the special grain the kids held in their hands. In their excitement, some dropped the grain and ran away, only to come back a little braver to try to befriend the birds again. Suddenly, from behind me I heard a strong gust of wind blow through the trees on what was until now a perfectly still day. I had goosebumps as the birds went still, turning their heads towards the breeze. They stopped squawking. Then, as one, in complete silence, the entire flock lifted off and flew away from the sanctuary. I turned around and saw Talitha and the girls watching the birds fly away. Talitha was smiling coldly. I didn't know how, but I felt she had something to do with it.

It did not end there. As we walked through the butterfly

garden, the butterflies crowded in the top corners of the nets, unable to escape. Jess and Amanda, not knowing better, were still fascinated, but I did, and I was disturbed.

Our group continued on through the sanctuary, past the koalas, the wombats, the Tasmanian Devils, the birds. The kids were growing disappointed. It was as though all the animals chose to hide, running away into tree hollows, holes and behind branches. A breeze rustled through the trees as we walked along, as though whispering a secret.

To break up the journey, we got onto the little train that slowly chugged its way through the beautiful park. I longed to hear the sound of a kookaburra, or any of the thousands of birds who lived in this little forest, but all was silent.

We stopped at the snake pit, got off the little locomotive and entered to see the show. We sat at the back of the amphitheatre as two rangers brought out boxes that held a few varieties of Australian snakes. I began to fear that the snakes would break loose, but I comforted myself with the knowledge that even if they did, they only used harmless snakes in the show. In the end, the demonstration was a non-event. The snakes refused to get out of their boxes and, when pulled out and held, struggled furiously until they were put back in.

Finally, we headed over towards the kangaroos that were basking lazily in the shade. The other children were playing and running around the docile animals, petting them. As we walked towards them, I heard the wind whistle past us in the trees above. The kangaroos pricked up their ears and hopped off into the bush together. I looked at Talitha, but she had that cold stare with her icy, all-knowing smile. I did not think it was worth asking if she had noticed it. I got the sense she was proudly acknowledging what was happening.

After much thought, I decided not to share my observations with Edith when we got home that day. She would only have dragged me to church, and that was no longer an option to me after I made my deal with the Devil.

Strange occurrences were happening all around the world. At the end of 2004, the Boxing Day Tsunami had occurred. It was the August of 2005, when Hurricane Katrina inflicted havoc in the United States. That 2005 Atlantic hurricane season was the most active in recorded history.

In November that year, my show did a recap on extreme weather events around the globe. It soon became apparent that catastrophic events were occurring worldwide at an alarmingly increasing frequency and intensity. There were biblical floods in parts of the world accompanied by extreme drought in others.

Everywhere we looked, something furious was happening. Deadly bushfires, record-breaking blizzards, extreme storms dropping golf ball-sized hail, crippling snowstorms and devastating tornadoes. Many freak weather events were occurring in some places for the first time in recorded history.

Something was bubbling, the events on the surface like the lid on a boiling kettle, bouncing up and down, threatening to blow off.

CHAPTER 22

ENCOUNTER

April 2006

One night I awoke around 2:00 am to get a glass of water. I walked towards the kitchen and saw Jess, who was only nine at the time, silhouetted by the moonlight, standing still by the bay window in the lounge. She was staring out into the night. I called to her, but she did not acknowledge me. She just stood there like a statue, not blinking, with her eyes transfixed wide open. I thought she might have been sleepwalking, so I gently held her shoulders. She did not break her stare, but very deliberately raised her hands and took mine off her shoulders, while maintaining her intense stare.

I looked out the window to see what she was staring at. Standing there on the balcony next door was Peter Perry, staring straight back at Jess, as though they were somehow communicating with each other. It made my skin crawl.

"Jess, stop this right now! Get back to bed," I demanded.

Then, without turning or blinking, she said firmly, "The first person who blinks loses. Go to bed."

And without knowing why, I backed down. I left Jess in the lounge and went back to my bedroom. I stood there, terrified and worried, wondering what to do. A few minutes later, I heard her footsteps on the wooden floor. I stepped out of my bedroom and saw her padding to her room. Quietly, the door clicked shut behind her, and I got the feeling she knew I was watching her.

I tiptoed back to the spot where Jess had been standing, afraid of making any noise. Peter was no longer on his balcony. I ducked my head into Jess' bedroom and saw she was sound asleep.

The next morning, I dropped in to see Inspector Jones. Strangely, I thought I could trust him, since he was the only person who still suspected my guilt.

I always respected him as a straight shooter, and I spoke to him about Jess and Peter Perry staring at each other. He said it was creepy, but there was very little he could do as there was nothing illegal about what had happened. I asked him if he knew who the Perrys were. We had now been neighbours for nine years and I still didn't know what they did for a living or where they had come from. Jones had no answers, but he promised to do a background check for me.

A couple of weeks later, Inspector Jones called the studio where I worked and asked if we could catch up for coffee. It was early afternoon when we sat at a nearby café, which overlooked a lake. He was fidgety and anxious.

He revealed that Amanda was the child of Simon (or as I knew, Matt) and Samantha. Talitha Perry was the nanny who had taken Amanda on a plane to London on the night her mother was murdered. Peter Perry was the driver who had taken Samantha to the airport and raised the alarm when she was found missing. The nanny was on the plane to London and Peter was with the police during the entire search for Samantha, so they were both presumed innocent.

I did not get a good glimpse of the nanny that night, and

I recalled that Peter wore dark glasses and his chauffeur cap pulled down hiding his face.

After Samantha's untimely demise, Talitha and the child stayed on in London with Samantha's mother. Within a couple of months, the older woman, a widow, was diagnosed with dementia and hospitalised. Even though there was no one remaining in the Lennox family, it's possible that Simon's family presumed the child would be taken care of by the Lennoxes. In any event, nobody contested the Perrys' guardianship request.

In his will, Simon had left his house to his then partner Samantha, who in turn had left everything to her daughter Amanda.

Talitha came back to Australia with Amanda, and moved into the house with her brother, Peter. "Peter is her *brother?*" I repeated in shock.

Jones just raised his eyebrows.

I bluntly asked Jones who the Perrys really were. He had no real answer. The Perrys had come to Australia from Romania on a business visa, having invested a quarter of a million dollars in a nanny and security business.

They were in Australia for only two weeks when they secured their only client, the now deceased Samantha Lennox. It begged the question as to how she found them. Indeed, it appeared as though they knew she would need them.

What was more curious was that Talitha was still paid to look after the child under an undated and open-ended contract signed by Samantha. She drew a salary and boarding from the money left to the child in accordance with this contract and paid her taxes accordingly. Nobody complained about the arrangement, which had been going on now for ten years.

Jones added, "Neither Talitha nor Peter had a criminal history in Romania. It's very strange, but I really do not know what I can do."

I was about to get up to leave when Jones held my hand on the table, urging me to stay. I looked at him and could see he was very uncomfortable. His shoulders were stiff and with his free hand he scrunched at his napkin. I wondered if he was finally going to ask me about the five murders. I slumped silently, not knowing what to say, awaiting the accusation. Jones asked me, "Denise, have you ever been inside the Perrys' house?"

I took a moment to respond. "Now that you mention it, no. I have peeked my head inside the front door a few times, to pick up Jess, but they have never invited me in."

Jones continued, "Once this strange arrangement came to light, I decided to drop in on the Perrys on the pretext of following up on the murder of Samantha Lennox. The Perrys were reluctantly co-operative. They guardedly answered all my questions, saying as little as possible. When I asked them to provide some evidence of the contract with Samantha, they left me alone in the lounge. It was then I noticed a small altar on their mantlepiece. I had a feeling that if I asked them about it, I would never see it again, so I discreetly took a photo of it."

Jones handed me an envelope. In it was a close-up of a two-picture solid gold frame, like the ones used to house photos of a married couple. In the left frame I saw a picture of Jess as a baby with her birthday date and the exact time. In the right frame was a photograph of a comet in the sky, visible during the day due to a total solar eclipse. There was a an etched gold tag at the base of the picture: *Comet Hale-Bopp, Burkhan Khaldun, Ikh Khorig, Mongolia 8:49 am on the 9th of March 1997.* Based on the time zones of Mongolia and Australia, the times were identical.

Jones and I agreed something was very odd.

FEBRUARY 2008

There are two defining moments in most people's lives: the first is when the parents hand over the reins of the future to their offspring. It usually happens in a time of crisis, and in my life it was the day you drowned. Before then, Edith had been my mother and guardian, but after that incident, I became the one she would seek advice from, and not vice versa.

The second moment is when you must make a choice between the two loves of your life. Everyone has to at one stage, and it is always between your two greatest loves. In my life, I'd had to make a choice between Simon and you.

It was 2008 and Jess was about to turn eleven. She had grown into a beautiful young girl. She looked more mature than her age and many people mistook her for being around fourteen.

On this particular warm summer evening, I parked the car outside the gates and waited for her. The kids streamed out, and after a while, the number of students tapered off, until no-one came out anymore. There was no sign of Jess.

I walked through the gates into the school quadrangle, becoming concerned that the school compound was almost empty. I strode through the narrow corridor surrounding the centre courtyard looking for her. There were a couple of older students still hanging around, but the classrooms had been locked shut. I hurried out of the gate, looking up and down the now deserted street. I dialled Edith from my

239

mobile phone. Jess wasn't home. Edith checked with the Perrys; she was not there either.

Starting to panic, I got into my car and looked everywhere, driving slowly through the neighbouring streets. I spotted a girl standing by a park bench, next to a duck pond. In hope, I stumbled out of the car and ran towards her. As I got closer, I realised it was Jess. She was talking to a man wearing a hat, seated with his back to me.

I called out her name, more anger in my voice than relief. She looked at me and waved, then continued talking to the man as if she didn't have a care in the world. I stopped and caught my breath. Walking towards her, furious, I yelled, "Jess. Come here right now!"

She walked towards me with an expression of utter disdain on her face. I scolded her, reminding her of my warning never to talk to strangers. She took a step back, asking me what I was on about. I pointed to the man sitting on the park bench. Jess looked at me completely confused and responded, "Mum, I was just talking to Dad."

I didn't realise what she was saying at first, but then saw a red Ferrari parked on the other side of the park. It clicked into place. I walked gingerly towards the man, my heart racing. I was so sure he was dead. I called out tentatively. "Simon?"

The man stood, turned around and smiled. It was the Devil. I saw his deep piercing eyes in the daylight for the first time. Pupils extinguished by soulless black holes. The same black holes I'd seen in Simon's eyes after I plunged the knife into his chest. The same eyes I saw in Jess' face.

Siobhan shut *The Confession*, unsure what to make of what she had just read. Her mother's confession had moved from unbelievable to delusional. Had her mother completely lost her mind? Siobhan rubbed her tired eyes; she could feel a headache coming on. Jess was her sister, whom she adored with all her heart. Yes, she was reserved, secretive and calculating, but could also be charming and delightful.

Jess had to cope with their mother's disappearance when she was just eleven years old. She had already grown into an exceedingly attractive young girl by seventeen, and had a wicked sense of humour to boot. Despite what she thought, Siobhan couldn't help but find Edith's innocuous words, that Jess was born with the charm of the Devil, suddenly eerie.

She'd never once felt jealous when her younger sister upstaged everyone as she swept into any crowded room, exuding a magnetising force without even trying. Her mother's story had gone from seemingly ridiculous to completely insane. She was asking Siobhan now to choose between the two loves of her life: the reverence she had for her dead mother, or her love for Jess, who she had brought up like a daughter.

Preposterous as it was, she knew she had to read on. With great strain, she opened the book. Her mother continued as though she knew Siobhan would read on despite the ludicrous revelation.

CHAPTER 23
THE EXORCIST VISITS

MARCH 2008

Jess had never wronged me. In her own private way, I believed she cared for me. It was very different from the overt loving mother-daughter relationship you and I shared. Jess was the centre of attention everywhere she went, but, somehow she never seemed to need anyone. For all her extroverted behaviour, Jess was a very solitary person. I felt responsible for this, as Jess was conceived during a time of trauma. I worried that my cynicism with life may have had something to do with her almost distant behaviour towards me.

Nevertheless, I loved her as much as I loved you, Siobhan. Now that I knew Jess was the daughter of the Devil, I needed to know what it meant.

With nowhere else to turn, and after twelve years of absence, I entered the blue-stone chapel of Currumbin's church. I was greeted by old Father Antonio, forever busy pottering around in his sacristy. He joked about the return of the prodigal daughter, reminding me that I was considered by many in his church as a living miracle. He hoped to see me back in his flock. I smiled politely and spoke to him under the pretext that I was researching a documentary on exorcisms. Although disappointed, he obliged me with ten minutes of his time.

"Have you seen God?" I asked Father Antonio.

"I see God in every creation, in the staggering beauty of this fragile world. I see God everyday in the kind acts of humans, in the gift of love, and in prayer."

"And have you seen the Devil? For if God is in all creation, then is the Devil restricted to only the unkind acts and dastardly deeds of mankind?"

Father Antonio considered his answer. "To believe in God, one must believe in the existence of the Devil. Without the Devil, religion has nothing to offer. Salvation means nothing if there are no repercussions to evil."

I posed my question again. "Have you *seen* him?"

Father Antonio thought for a while and finally responded, uneasily, "In the clergy house of Saint Stephen's Cathedral in Brisbane lives an old priest, Father Shem—he was once a practicing exorcist. Father Shem is a very private man and unlikely to be interested in any publicity. He considered his gift for exorcism a burden he was forced to bear."

I thanked Father Antonio and turned to leave. He left me with a caution: "Denise, prayers revolve around protecting us from evil. Do not stir the hornet's nest. The realm of the Devil is best left alone."

It was too late for that.

The next evening after work, I drove to the clergy home of Saint Stephen's to meet with Father Shem. I found him deep in prayer, alone in a quiet corner of the cathedral. He was old and balding, with a big, thick grey beard. His mottled, wrinkled hands shook as he prayed fervently. I kneeled down next to him and waited. It was an uneasy silence, as I felt it would be hypocritical to pray. It was a long hour, waiting in the pews, before the sacristan walked past to tell us that the chapel was about to close.

Once outside, I introduced myself, saying that I had spoken to Father Antonio. "I'm looking to find out something about exorcism."

Father Shem smiled gently and brushed me off. "Sorry, Denise was it?" I nodded. "I'm retired. I simply wait for the Lord to call me home. I don't wish to speak about exorcism. Ever again."

I was desperate to know if he was qualified to do something about the Devil, or if this were just another panacea for emotional and spiritual ills. I wanted someone to recognise what I knew with no prompting, hints or clues. Perhaps he could then let me know what it meant.

"I understand, but please, allow me to walk you home," I offered.

He nodded, albeit reluctantly, and as we walked slowly in silence to the clergy home, I wondered how to convince him to talk to me.

At the door I turned to him, "Please Father, would you have dinner with my family? My mother is a devout Catholic and would appreciate meeting you."

"No I—"

"Please, Father?"

"I'm sorry, Denise, I cannot." And with that he shut the door to the clergy house in my face.

For three more evenings, I kneeled next to Father Shem, followed by the routine eviction by the sacristan and the walk back to his quarters. Finally, on the fourth evening, he reluctantly accepted my invitation. I knew it was more out of a desire to be left in peace than out of politeness. He stressed that the visit to my home would be all. No exorcisms and no questions on his past work. I agreed, believing that if he was who he claimed he was, I would get the reaction I wanted as soon as he stepped into Jess' presence.

That weekend, I picked up Father Shem and brought him home for a family dinner. As we drove towards the Gold Coast, the priest opened up, perhaps sensing my fascination with the macabre. What he told me gave me chills:

"What most people don't know about exorcisms is that they are quiet and drawn out. Hollywood has created the image of exorcism to be spinning heads, green vomit, screaming, gravity defying levitation, and bloody graffiti on walls. These are nothing more than special effects designed to scare people.

"Real demons don't want to scare people. In fact, that is the last thing they want. They want to comfort people, caress them, give them confidence, draw them closer. Victims become reliant on demons, empowered by them.

"Sure, it can get violent sometimes, just like it can be when taking a needle from a junkie. But, the worst times are when they don't struggle; they don't scream or fight. They sit and stare, unmoving, basking in their arrogance and confidence. We are playthings to them. We wrestle, cajole, threaten, but that means nothing to them. They play by different rules.

"It's the eyes. They always stare, unblinking, unflinching. Hollywood portrays demons getting scared by words or holy water? By a few pieces of paper or a wooden cross? An exorcism isn't a battle of mortal objects. These demons were present in the Nazi gas chambers. They were present in the furnaces of the Carthaginians. They were present in the deepest dungeons of the Inquisition, always quiet, always there. They do not speak, they do not reason. Nothing you can say to them will make them fear, or flee."

My mind drifted to the unflinching stares shared by Peter Perry and Jess.

"It's a battle of faith. You call on God, not with your voice, but with your heart, with your soul. That is what they fear; not your voice, or your fists, but your faith. Unfortunately, most people do not have the faith, the conviction, or the willingness to do this. That's why the Devil wins.

"But," Shem continued, "the forces of nature usually accompany an exorcism. Sometimes the wind would rustle the trees, or the skies would darken, breaking in thunder.

"On rare occasions, exorcisms can be visual and aggressive. The spitting, the abuse, the sexual temptation of women throwing themselves in erotic positions, eyes rolling back in their heads. But more often than not, this is the exception rather than the rule. The only common thread is the demons attacking your deepest and darkest secrets, creating self-doubt. Which makes most people retract, defeated, and leave them alone."

I wondered if the wind would whip up and if the skies would rumble when Shem arrived at our home. Whether the house would shake and if indeed there would be a showdown, he had all bases covered. It could be Hollywood or bust, and in both cases it would mean the same. I listened quietly and politely.

As we sat there at the dinner table, I could tell Edith was extremely happy about my association with a priest and the church again. I had been surprised when Father Shem shook hands with Jess, his demeanour not faltering for an instant. Perhaps he wasn't what he claimed.

Father Shem was delightful and charming, asking both

Jess and you about your lives, peppering his dialogue with beautiful parables he had picked up along the way. His wit and sense of humour were contemporary and he brought out a lively conversation on love and life with both you girls. From birthdays to horoscopes, Father Shem was a wealth of knowledge, and the evening rapidly turned to night. At around 9:00 pm, he said a small prayer of thanksgiving, then asked to be taken home.

As we drove back, Father Shem was silent.

Wonderful as the evening was, I was shattered. I was so sure he was the only person who could help me. But he had shaken Jess' hand as if she were just another child, not the seed of the Devil.

As the last throw of the dice, I ventured a question to see if there was anything he may have noticed. I asked him, "Is there any religious significance of a comet being seen during the day due to a solar eclipse?"

Father Shem looked at me suspiciously for a moment before he said, "Total solar eclipses occur about twice a year, but they can only be seen from a very small area of the earth's surface. Comets bright enough to be seen by the naked eye in the sky are even more rare.

"There have been a few instances in history when a solar eclipse has revealed a bright comet during the day."

I sensed there was something he knew and was holding out. "Is there something you want to tell me?"

He paused for a second and then cautiously probed for more information, "Which comet?"

I replied, "The Comet Hale-Bopp. It was seen at Ikh Khorig, the place where Genghis Khan was born."

He looked at me quizzically. He read in my expression that I knew more than I had disclosed.

"I thought you may have feared your daughter was possessed. I am not sure there is anything I can do about the progeny of the Devil himself."

I was shocked into silence. I realised I had taken a pocketknife to a nuclear war.

Father Shem shook his head solemnly, defeated. "We were blind," he said. "It was written in the quatrains of Nostradamus in the 1550s." I had heard of Nostradamus before, a renowned and reputed French seer who had predicted major world events.

Shem continued, "The printing of the most famous of his quatrains, Century 10, Quatrain 72, was deliberately tampered with. The misprint circulated to the masses read as, 'In the year 1999, in the seventh month, from the sky there comes a great king of terror, to bring back the great king of the Mongols, Mars rules triumphantly before and after.'"

However, the original read, 'In the year 1997, on the ninth day when Mars rules triumphantly, from the sky there comes a great king of terror, to bring back the great king of the Mongols.'

"The 9th of March 1997, when the Comet Hale-Bopp was seen during the total solar eclipse over Ikh Khorig, the purported birthplace and lost tomb of the great king of the Mongols, Genghis Khan, we knew the child of the Devil was born." He buried his head in his hands, gutted. "We searched for a male child." Shem paused, reflecting. Eventually he turned to me and spoke. "I know today that this meeting was why I was kept alive, against my will. Is there any possibility you could arrange a time for me to meet with Jess alone?"

I thought for a while. Perhaps the brave exorcist would try to wean Jess away from her father and the Perrys. I agreed to arrange a time when you and Edith would be out for the evening.

Shem pressed further, "Are there any people around her who look out for her? The Devil's minions?" I thought immediately of the Perrys.

"Our neighbours," I said, "but they are never around between seven and eight-thirty at night."

By now we had reached the gates of Saint Stephen's, the wind had whipped up and the sky had broken into a wild thunderstorm. I watched as Father Shem looked up at the rumbling skies, almost in resignation.

Before he stepped out of the car, he said, "If anything should happen to me, you must seek out Reverend Zachary of the Sacred Monastery of the God Trodden, at Mount Sinai."

Shem stepped out of the car. He stared at the sky and raised his fists angrily. Drenched by the pelting rain, he stopped, looked up and roared at the dark clouds above, "Begone!"

Immediately, the winds dropped and the rain eased to a trickle. But then the sky rumbled once again and began to pelt down hailstones. I drove off to seek shelter as Father Shem buried his head in his coat, making his way towards the priests' quarters.

CHAPTER 24

THE SACRIFICIAL LAMB

A week later, I organised for Edith to take you out to the movies after school. I picked up Father Shem and brought him home. On the dot at 7:00 pm, the Perrys jumped the fence and headed into the forest. I set out dinner for Shem, Jess and myself. I had hoped he could talk to Jess and convince her to stop seeing her 'father'. Maybe, just maybe, he could influence her to be a normal person.

I sat Shem and Jess down to eat while I started to serve the meal out from the kitchen. I hoped it would give Shem a chance to break the ice. It was then that Jess said, "Thanks Mum. You do know I love you." I was stunned. This was a phrase you were so generous with, but one she had never expressed before. The hairs on the back of my neck stood up. It was as though she knew the priest was there to talk her out of her association with her father, Satan.

Sensing this, Shem pulled me aside and asked if he could spend some time alone with Jess.

We walked back to the dining room and I said to Jess, "I need to get something for Father Shem from the pharmacy. He will look after you until I get back."

"Can I go with you? Please?" Jess asked, pleading in her eyes.

"Sorry honey, you stay here and keep Father Shem company," I told her.

It would have been half an hour later when I returned. The table had food half-eaten, but the dining room was empty. A large roll of cling wrap had been taken out of the pantry and was lying on the kitchen bench. I searched the house and soon realised the lights were on outside on the pool deck. Concerned, I ran out and saw Shem kneeling by the pool, praying fervently.

"Where's Jess?" I demanded. He pointed to the water, his eyes transfixed on the sky.

There at the bottom of the pool was Jess, face down. Her body was held down by bricks tied to her hands and legs. It was déjà vu.

I leapt into the water, screaming to Shem for help, but he did not move, continuing to pray. I swam downwards, and, with considerable difficulty, managed to untie Jess from her bonds. I kicked off from the pool floor and brought her back to the surface. Her face was covered in cling wrap. The priest had suffocated her before sinking her body.

"What have you done?" I screamed at Father Shem, trying to get air back into my own lungs. "She is just a child!"

Shem turned to me, and in an icy voice he said, "Even Jesus did very little as a child. If she ever came of age, it would be the dawn of Armageddon."

Frantically, I pulled off the cling wrap, but her body was cold, the life drained from her. I furiously tried to revive her, my wet hair slapping me as I did compressions.

"Call an ambulance! Call the police!" I shouted at Shem, but he ignored me. "Do *something*!" I screeched.

The priest remained unmoved from his position of

prayer. He looked at me briefly, "My time has come to meet my maker."

I ran indoors to find my mobile phone. I pulled it out of my bag, which was lying on the dining room floor where I had dropped it, and dialled triple zero for help, calling for the police and an ambulance. In panic, I also called Inspector Jones, asking him to come urgently. As I was about to return to the pool to try to revive Jess, a voice called from behind me.

"The food's cold, Mum."

There, sitting on the dining chair, was Jess, dripping wet, her face still covered in cling wrap. I was frozen as I watched her slowly peel it off and place it on the table beside her plate. She picked up her knife and fork and started eating, as if water were not pooling at her feet.

Something in the corner behind me caught her attention. She smiled. I turned slowly. *He* was standing in the corner.

The Devil mockingly misquoted the Bible: "This is my beloved daughter, with whom I am well pleased." He then turned on me. "You left my daughter in the hands of someone who tried to kill her. You chose the only time each day I have reserved for my minions to update me on the progress of my daughter. The only time when my people who protect her would be away."

Although I had no idea the priest would try to kill her, I had placed Jess in his care. Afraid as I was, I answered boldly, "I only hoped he could convince her to stop seeing you."

Satan laughed. "Why do you think they were looking for my child in the first place? Did you think they would bring her gifts of gold, frankincense and myrrh?" he scoffed.

It was so obvious. Shem was a pious priest and it never

crossed my mind there could only be one reason they were looking for the child.

"After all I have done for you," said the Devil, "you tried to turn my own daughter against me." He turned to Jess. "Go to your room. I would like to have a word with your mother in private."

Jess put down her cutlery and hopped up from her seat, smiled at the Devil and trotted down the hall to her room.

The Devil watched her go until her door shut behind her. "Within a week, this will all die down," he said. "You will see this incident out and protect the identity of my daughter. After a week and before the fortnight is out, you will leave. You will disappear without a trace. You will not say goodbye. From that time on, you are never to see my daughter ever again. If you don't leave, or if you ever return, my minions will destroy what you love most." I knew the Devil was referring to you.

By now, the wailing sirens were just outside. The police were speaking with Father Shem, who confessed to suffocating the girl and then drowning her claiming the child was the spawn of Evil, the Dreadful One, the Dragon. He was speaking gibberish, feverishly praying all the time, stopping only momentarily to catch his breath.

The police handcuffed him and put him into the back of the van. The paramedics lifted a body onto a stretcher and covered it with a sheet. I was shocked. Someone squeezed my hand. I turned, it was Jess. She stood there stoic, staring blankly at me.

Inspector Jones waved me over. I looked at the stretcher as he removed the sheet, uncovering the face. For a moment, my heart stopped, thinking it may have been you, but it wasn't. It was the lifeless body of the twelve year-old girl from next door: Samantha's daughter, Amanda.

Jones asked me what happened and I said nothing. I was too afraid to say anything, lest some harm befall you.

Jones' attention turned to Jess. She was staring blankly at Peter Perry, who was standing beside the corpse. Jones and I watched as they stared without blinking. It was as though they were communicating telepathically.

Perry then turned to Jones and me. "I asked Denise to bring the priest to spend time with our child," he told Jones. "I did not think he would harm her." I wondered why he was lying, but then I realised that the Devil didn't want any attention brought to Jess. If there was any grief in Peter Perry, I couldn't see it.

That night, Father Shem was found dead in his holding cell, upright and kneeling in prayer, clutching tightly to a cross with both hands. He had bravely faced many a demon as an exorcist, yet his face was frozen in an expression of extreme fear, eyes staring up.

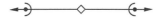

Siobhan shut *The Confession*. She had been seventeen when Amanda had died. She remembered the chaos and confusion that reigned for days after that terrible tragedy. She shuddered when she thought of Peter and Talitha Perry. They were both strange and had given her the creeps. She knew how fond Jess was of both of them and never understood it.

Her mother now claimed that she had been banished

from their home and forced to disappear without a word.

Unbelievable as her mother's story was to this point, there was nothing she could fault to disprove it. That is, all except her claims about Jess. Her mother was trying to convince her with signs and prophecies that her sister was the daughter of the Devil.

But Siobhan found that, in all this madness lay some element of truth, for her journey home had been a great escape, fleeing from mysterious religious figures. Sister Catherine had died; Siobhan herself had been hunted out of Spain; and Father Jakub had lured her to Paris. This could have nothing to do with the murder of some five people or a fifteen-million-dollar lottery, which happened eighteen years ago on the Gold Coast, of all places. The book had dragged her through places she never wanted to go and somehow she knew this was just the beginning of her nightmare.

Hesitantly, she opened the book again, and found it was as though her mother had read her mind.

CHAPTER 25
THE PROPHECIES OF NOW

March 2008

I still had no idea what it meant that Jess was the child of the Devil. I had been given two weeks to disappear. I considered committing suicide, but it would serve no purpose. Even though my soul was forever damned, I could not take my secret to my grave with me. Someone needed to know I had made a pact with the Devil and that I had borne him a child. The question was, who?

Every generation aims to leave the world a better place for their children than the one they inherited from their parents. I wondered if it was still possible for me to do that, given what I had done, and who I had brought into this world. Father Shem had left me with two leads. The first was the name of Reverend Zachary of the Sacred Monastery of the God Trodden in Mount Sinai. The second was his final statement that if the child of the Devil comes of age, it would be the dawn of Armageddon.

I turned to Father Antonio. I sought out a meeting with him, hoping he may know of Reverend Zachary. He confessed he didn't. I asked him about the church's views on an imminent end of the world. Father Antonio was slightly fearful and measured in his response: "From the beginning of time, all religions have spoken of the Day of

Judgement. Without the fear of Judgement Day or some terrible consequence or reward, the oldest business in the world collapses. The business of religion. If there were no Judgement Day, religion would forfeit its mortgage on time."

I persisted, "Are there any Doomsday prophecies that say the end is nigh?" Father Antonio spoke of the *Prophecy of the Popes* by Saint Malachy of Ireland, who lived from 1094 until 1148, and was the founder of the Cistercian Order in Ireland.

Saint Malachy wrote a collection of 112 short, cryptic phrases in Latin predicting the future Roman Catholic popes (and a few antipopes), beginning with Pope Celestine II. The accuracy of this prophecy was quite incredible, but more incredible is the fact that, back in 2008, Pope Benedict XVI was the 111th pope—or second last pope ever according to Malachy.

Above the grave of Saint Paul the Apostle, located just outside Rome, the Emperor Constantine built the Basilica of Saint Paul, around the year 324 A.D. Saint Paul's Basilica became the home to a long series of medallions, which, to this day, depict each pope throughout history. Antonio explained that the walls of Saint Paul's have room for only one more portrait, after that of Pope Benedict XVI.

The grotto of Saint Peter's Basilica, also known as the Basilica's crypt, is often referred to as the *Tombe dei Papi*, or Tomb of the Popes. It is rumoured that the crypt has room for only two more popes to be laid to rest, including Pope Benedict XVI.

Father Antonio then warned me, "Denise, I knew Father Shem for many years. He was a very pious and holy man. Whatever possessed him to murder that young girl must have been a terrible demon. You are stirring up the wrath of hell itself. Please for God's sake, leave it alone."

With that, he turned and retreated into the safety of his sacristy.

During the next few days, I lived in the library, reading up on the occult, prophecies and history, trying hard to justify to myself why I had been the unlucky soul who held the parcel when the music stopped. I also needed to know what it meant to have borne the child of the Devil. Had this happened before? Was it really the end of the world?

I read the ramblings of Saint John in the Book of Revelation, with its signs for identifying the Antichrist.

Rev 13:18—*This calls for wisdom: let anyone with understanding calculate the number of the beast, for it is the number of a person. Its number is six hundred sixty-six.*

But I was not looking for signs to identify the Devil. I alone already knew him. It was my belief that, on the night of the 6th of June 1996, I had slept with Simon, but before I killed him, I had seen the soulless eyes of the Devil.

My mind wandered to my meeting with Zeng, to the poem and sketch of the *Tui bei tu*. Although I had known intuitively that the five people in the sketch were the five I had killed, I was now convinced that the bull being led to the slaughter represented me. Armed with the knowledge that Jess was the Devil's child, the last two lines now made sense.

Out of this incident a real dragon is born.

The 9 Curves Yellow River's water is not yellow.

In 1997, the real Yellow River in China experienced its worst drought in history and stopped flowing for more than two-thirds of the year. In 1997, the real dragon, Jess, the daughter of the Devil, was born.

It is hard to find something when you don't know what you're looking for, but like a hungry child trapped in a sewer, I kept trawling through, hoping for a manhole to shed some light onto my dirty, damp, dark world. I searched for prophecies referring to comets, and I came across the works of Saint Hildegard of Bingen (1098–1197) and Mother Shipton (1488–1561). Most comets have two tails that can be seen by the naked eye; however, in March 1997, scientists discovered a narrow *third* tail on Hale-Bopp, located near the ion tail. This sodium tail was about 600,000 kilometres wide and about 50 million kilometres long. Mother Shipton's prophecy spoke of the dragon's tail cracking. Was it referring to the third tail of the Comet Hale-Bopp?

As for prophecies, there was also the Austrian monk Johann Friede (1204–1257), who foretold the impacts of climate change. He presented a warning that the current order of civilisation is about to end.

What concerned me most about these crazy ramblings was that some prophecies could be interpreted to represent the date when Jess was born.

Though there was enough doubt and murkiness with the obscurity of the writings, all doomsday prophecies pointed to some catastrophic event due to happen sometime in the near future.

Siobhan, out of fear that some harm would befall you if I inadvertently disclosed Jess' true identity, I tried my best to act out a normal life. To keep up appearances, I continued to work.

It was nine days after Shem had tried to kill Jess. Late in the evening, as I paced the floors of my office, I contemplated returning to the church I had turned my back on. I had nowhere to go and no-one to speak to. My spinning mind was disrupted by a loud knock on the door.

It was Jones.

"I need to show you something," he said. "Can we sit down?"

Curious, I led him inside. Seated, he pushed a folder of photographs across my desk.

"What are these?" I asked.

"Just look," he said.

And so I did. I recognised the room in the first photograph to be Simon's old bedroom. It looked just like it had that night twelve years ago, when I had slept with the Devil in disguise. Everything was in place as it was, the bed, the furniture, even the untidy bed sheets.

The walls, however, were covered with black pieces of paper. The next photograph was a close-up of the walls. The black pieces of paper formed a mosaic of photos of Jess, ranging from the time she was a baby, all the way to the present. I was speechless. The next few showed different sections of the wall: more and more pictures of Jess. There were thousands. The obsession with Jess had wallpapered the room from floor to ceiling. I was repulsed, but knew there was nothing I could do. There was nothing Jones could do either, and I knew I needed to get him off the case, lest he come to harm as well.

"I will speak to Jess when I get home," I said to him neutrally.

The inspector made to argue, but he must have seen something in my face because he left without a word. Just a single nod and the door closed behind him.

After Jones left, I took the scrapbook I had created with all the newspaper clippings of the murders, the photograph taken at my birthday party, as well as my investigations into prophecies and the occult, and went to my car in preparation to come home.

It was late and the car park was deserted except for two cars: mine and one I did not recognise beside it. Standing next to my car was a priest. He had a long flowing beard and wore the black cassock of a Greek or Russian Orthodox church. He introduced himself as Father Jakub and his accent revealed he was eastern European. He claimed Father Shem had sent him a message before he died, telling Jakub to find me and help me with passage to the Sacred Monastery of the God Trodden.

"If you want to go, we have to leave now," Jakub said. "You will not need any of your belongings where you are going." He flipped through the pages of my scrapbook. "You can bring this with you."

I knew I had to disappear without a trace, but I had still not considered the pangs of my heart for leaving without saying goodbye to my family. My frenzied mind reeled through a myriad of thoughts, from practicalities such as whether I needed my passport, to the promise I made to Edith to pick up milk on the way home.

I knew I had to go. I had a set of spare clothes I always kept in the car and I put these into a small bag before joining Father Jakub. We drove silently through the night. We stopped once for a break at a petrol station in the middle of the outback where Jakub purchased some toiletries and basics and handed them to me. At dawn we arrived at our destination, some eight hundred kilometres north. A solitary bulk coal carrier called *Vilis Capri* was docked at a desolate berth in the port of Rockhampton. I boarded the ship and learnt it was heading to Alexandria, Egypt.

Siobhan paused for a moment and took a deep breath. Irrespective of how fanciful and extravagant the tale, she had finally found some justification to her mother's prolonged and deliberate silence. Siobhan was compelled to continue reading. Was she starting to believe the unbelievable? Through this memoir, she had begun to find a semblance of recognition to the caring, thoughtful mother she once knew.

CHAPTER 26
THE CANON OF THE DAMNED

April 2008

I was a stowaway, given refuge by the ship's chief engineer, a Filipino man named José. I was housed in a tiny cabin connected to his own, with a small shower and toilet. The cabin had no portholes to see the passing world, and the door was locked from the outside. Each day José would bring me food and take away the empty dishes. He never spoke a word, locking the cabin each time he left. I had no access to a phone, the internet or other humans, excluding José. The trip to Alexandria was scheduled to take forty-four days.

It was nearly forty days later when the ship stopped. José came in and spoke to me in broken English at length. I learned that we were anchored for the night, waiting for dawn. At first light, a caravan of ships would head north through the Great Bitter Lake and wind its way through the Suez Canal into the Mediterranean Sea.

"I will call crew for meeting at 1:00 am and deck will be empty," José told me. "Go to the main deck and turn right till you reach the stern. Near the winch station, you must climb down the pilot rope ladder to a dhow waiting for you."

At 12:45 am, he unlocked the door to my cabin and popped his head in, saying, "Fifteen minutes." He shook my hand. "Good luck. If you are caught, never mention my ship or me."

"Of course," I replied. "Thank you."

At exactly 1:00 am, I left the cabin and worked my way quickly down the steep steel stairs to the lower decks, then to the aft of the ship. After my virtual imprisonment, the fresh sea breeze on my face was exhilarating, but I had no time to pause and enjoy it. I quickly moved to the rear of the ship. The rope ladder swayed in the wind. The ship pitched gently in the relatively still waters of the Red Sea. The dark of night and the wind made climbing down the flimsy rope ladder difficult, but below me were the billowing sails of a wooden boat (an Arab dhow), tethered by a rope left hanging from the back of the ship. The rope was held taut. The dhow was banked quietly alongside the rudder of the ship.

Once aboard the dhow, I realised not one of the four unsmiling crew spoke any English. I was quickly hustled down, out of sight into the lower deck of the boat. Here, I was in a land unknown, with total strangers and the knowledge that no-one in the world who cared about me had any idea where I was. I could have been sold into slavery and none would be the wiser. I had broken my ties with God and I was here to fight the Devil, so if ever I was alone, this was it. But there was something that gave me a strange sense of calm. If the intent was for me to disappear without a trace, I could have been tossed overboard anytime during the past forty days at sea and by now, I would have been somewhere at the bottom of the ocean.

The boat bobbed silently along the warm waters of the Red Sea. So far offshore, with no light pollution, on a night lit just by a sliver of a new moon, the blue stars twinkled more numerous than I had ever seen. I momentarily forgot my fears and remembered the words of Father Antonio: *I see God in every creation, in the staggering beauty of this fragile world.*

The captain took out a map and pointed to a route. We were going along the Gulf of Suez, to some sand banks called the Sharatib Shoals. I became less anxious and the blackness of the night enveloped me into sleep.

The sound of sand scraping the bottom of the dhow awoke me, accompanied by the gently lapping waves.

The boat soon beached a short distance from the shore. I saw from the deck that three of the sailors were already waist deep in water, walking towards land. The captain shooed me away to join them. I jumped into the water and trudged along to the coast.

The sun had yet to rise and one of the sailors beckoned me over, pointing to the horizon. Over the sand dunes, far southwest, a set of headlights flashed twice. We trudged up the sand together and a solitary VW Kombi van took shape in the darkness. Standing beside the van was a middle-aged priest with a flowing black beard, dressed in a black habit and black hat of the Greek or Russian Orthodox church.

I walked towards the priest and when I got close, I recognised him as Father Jakub. I had wondered if I would ever see him again, and to say I was surprised to see him here in the middle of the desert would be an understatement.

After a quick exchange of pleasantries, my escort left. Now alone, Father Jakub asked me with a grave look, "Do you want to continue on this journey of your own free will?"

"I don't have a choice."

Jakub looked puzzled. "You always have a choice."

I responded quietly, "Yes, but I have nowhere else to go."

He paused before saying, "You can have absolutely no contact with your family or anybody you know for a very long time." He solemnly added, "Maybe never."

The realisation that I was knowingly committing to

possibly never contacting my family finally hit home. For forty days, I was homesick, depressed and anxious, knowing the trauma my disappearance would have caused. The solitary confinement of being locked up in a ship's cabin with no access to any means of communication had been a blessing in disguise. When I was banished by the Devil and told to disappear without a trace, I had assumed I had no choice but to stay away from my family. Yet Jakub's question made me hope, I still had a choice.

Noticing my expression of indecision, Jakub said, "Your silence is the only way we can be sure you are working for us and against the Devil."

It had never crossed my mind until then. There was no way for him to know if I had chosen to infiltrate the inner sanctum of the Good, to promote the cause of Evil. If I was, in fact, still in thrall to the Devil, and working for him.

Thus far, I had only thought of trying to understand what it meant to have borne the child of the Devil. Now everything I loved was being withheld from me, perhaps forever. The soul has only one mirror and that is love, in search of its reflection is the journey of life. If I was never to see this reflection again, what reason did I have to live?

I was lost in thought. Jakub added, "This is your last chance to turn back."

Until now the Devil had always kept his word and I was sure he would steal your life back or worse. I replied sadly, "I cannot turn back."

There was no threat or ultimatum; he simply stated that if ever I contacted my family, it would be the end of the road. I was uncertain whether this meant the end of the road for me, or for the working relationship we were about to enter.

I made the choice and it was the saddest moment in my

life. I hope someday you will forgive me for it. I knew in my soul that I had to agree. I put my hand out and we shook on it. "I will not make contact with my family."

Jakub asked for my wallet. I handed it over, still full of credit cards, my license and cash. He stored it away and gave me a brown paper bag. In it was a nun's habit, also brown. He said, "From now on, you are *Sister Benedictine.*" He pointed to the back of the van for me to change. When I came out dressed as the nun I was about to become, he waved me to the passenger seat and took the driver's seat himself.

I vowed at that moment to beat the Devil at his own game, in the hope I would see you again one day. I needed to find an anchor for my lost soul.

We raced northwards along the desolate Ras Sedr-El Tor highway, bounded by the Red Sea on the left and the endless desert on the right. The occasional mud hamlets, outliers from the small towns and villages dotting the shores, were mere silhouettes, obscuring the endless waves reflecting the new moon and the stars. The sea breeze from the west battled with the dry desert wind from the east, alternating between humid and the dry. The road wound its way along the contours of the coast. It was a sparsely populated landscape. The spectacular night sky started to tire of its splendid show. The black turned to blue in anticipation of dawn and the endless stars began to fade.

During the journey, I told Father Jakub my sordid story.

After about half an hour of driving north, we turned onto a road heading due east. The black mountains ahead glowed with a dark orange halo, backlit as they were by the rising sun. While the coast road was dotted with small villages, the road to Mount Sinai was as dry as the air. The van was speeding, well above 150 km/h. The occasional car or truck travelling in the opposite direction sped by in the blink of an eye. I sporadically saw Bedouin nomads in caravan trails walking along the side of the road and in the never-ending desert that dominated the landscape on all sides except for the distant easterly mountains. The road was soon dwarfed by breathtaking rock faces riddled with caves. Jakub pointed out the four peaks of Mount Sinai, Mount Serbel, Mount Episteme and Mount Catherine.

I told him about how Father Shem had tried to kill Jess and he replied. "We had to find her before she turned nine. Shem knew that, yet he sacrificed his life, hoping we were wrong." The Devil had not shown his hand until Jess was eleven.

As we neared our destination, I asked him something that had troubled me all along, "Why me? Why was I dealt this horrible hand of cards?"

"If Jesus was destined for crucifixion, and Judas was destined to betray him, surely he was just fulfilling God's will?" Jakub answered. "In the words of Matthew 26:24: 'Yet woe is upon him, and he would have been better unborn.'" He went on, "The Vatican only proclaims individuals' eternal salvation through the Canon of Saints. There is no 'Canon of the Damned', or any official proclamation of the damnation of Judas. Yet the role of good and evil are intertwined and the actions of the damned, like those of Judas were also needed to turn the wheels of the world. Your destiny was written to fulfil a prophecy of damnation."

Like Judas, I belonged to the Canon of the Damned.

CHAPTER 27

THE MONASTERY OF THE GOD TRODDEN

The desert gave way to an oasis surrounded by palm trees and vines. There were crop fields, date plantations and a few small brick houses. An old wooden sign identified we were at Wadi Feiran. According to legend, near this oasis is the rock that Moses struck with his staff to bring forth a spring, creating the Oasis of Feiran, the largest in all of Sinai.

Jakub told me that one of the nuns' rooms had been made vacant at the Monastery of the Seven Sisters, at Wadi Feiran. The Mother Superior had been informed that I had taken a vow of silence and nobody was to speak to me. I wished to pray and study the scriptures in solitude. Each day, food and water would be supplied to my room through a small hatch and I was to place the empty dishes in the same hatch.

Father Jakub reiterated the rules: "No contact with your home and no contact with anyone else. You will maintain a vow of silence with everyone else but me. If you break your vow of silence, our deal is all over."

The nuns had two set times a day for an hour's communal prayer in the convent chapel. The chapel bell would toll six times to mark the time and call for prayer. I was to wait until I heard the nuns singing before I ventured out to the front of the convent where Father Jakub would pick me up. He then added, "When you get to your room, get some sleep. We will be working through the night."

"Doing what?" I asked, but he didn't answer.

The Monastery of the Seven Sisters was built in the fourth century and was now under the authority of the Monastery of Saint Catherine. It was modest, made from slate and sandstone, and very quiet.

Father Jakub knocked on the heavy, old door. An elderly, nun with kind Grecian features and a plethora of wrinkles, opened it. Jakub spoke fluently to her in a foreign language that sounded like Greek and pointed to me. I heard him say 'Sister Benedictine' a couple of times. He then pointed to the old nun and introduced her as Mother Superior Agnes. The nun smiled at him. Then she clasped my right hand with both of hers and led me into the ancient monastery. I looked back at Jakub, whose face disappeared as he shut the heavy monastery door. I entered the courtyard, which backed onto the seven rooms of the nuns' quarters. All the doors and windows were shut, I noticed, as I was led to the last door in the row.

Mother Superior Agnes opened the window, which had one wooden shutter on the outside and another on the inside. She spoke very slowly in the same Greek sounding language in the hope I would understand her instructions. She lifted a plate with some bread scraps and dates and placed it on the sill. She then closed the outside shutter and rapped on it three times. It would be the signal for me to open the window for my food.

She handed me a metal ring from which two ancient keys dangled. I tried the smaller key on the door and Agnes smiled as it opened. She walked into the dark, meagre room with me and switched on the single bulb in the ceiling. I was surprised that the place had electricity.

In the centre of the room was a small, ancient scriptorium desk with a wooden stool. There were holes for candles and an inkpot. Agnes opened the desktop, revealed a compartment housing a Bible, a collection of inks and quills, a large sheaf of paper and a bundle of candles with a box of matches. A study lamp had been clipped to the corner of the desk. Agnes proudly flicked on the switch to illuminate the desk. I assumed that the candles were there for emergencies.

In the corner was a copper tap above a stone bowl, a thin towel draped over the side, all beside a thoroughly worn toilet. What passed for a bed was a bedraggled coir mat on the floor with a blanket that seemed more loose thread than weave. Next to the bed was a folded nun's habit. The only decoration to speak of was a wooden Greek Orthodox cross that adorned the wall above the coir mat. There were some fine slats open in the roof on either side of the room by virtue of some clever masonry that allowed some sunlight to filter inside. You could not see in or out of the room, but the slats kept it aired and cooled.

Agnes turned to leave. I almost thanked her but stopped myself, remembering at the last moment that 'Sister Benedictine' had taken a vow of silence. Instead I only nodded in acknowledgement. Agnes shut the door behind her and I could hear her soft footsteps fading away.

I had a quick wash and then settled on the coir mat to sleep. It was hard and uncomfortable, but I was so tired that I soon drifted into a deep sleep. I woke up after what seemed like days to the sound of three sharp raps on my window.

The room was in complete darkness, but my eyes managed to make out the shapes around me. I walked to the door and flicked on the light, then opened the inner window. I sat on my bed with the quarter plate of bread, dates and other fruits that had appeared and greedily devoured it all.

The chapel bells tolled six times and I quickly got ready to leave. Soon, the quiet desert air was filled with the divine sound of nuns singing in harmony. I left my room and rushed through the courtyard, out to the wooden door of the monastery. It was locked. I tried the second, larger key on the ring and it creaked open. Father Jakub was waiting out front. After a drive that lasted about half an hour, we arrived at the base of Mount Sinai.

At the mouth of a gorge, at the foot of Mount Sinai, lies the Sacred Monastery of the God Trodden. Its ancient walls imposingly dominate the landscape. It was at this site that the holy relics of Saint Catherine were enshrined and is better known today as Saint Catherine's Monastery. It is believed that a bush held in the Chapel of Saint Helen, within its walls is the original burning bush seen by Moses.

Jakub parked the van, unlocked the massive iron gate and pushed it open. To me it looked more like a fortress than a place of worship.

That night, I learned this was the oldest continuously inhabited Christian monastery on Earth, with a history that can be traced back to its construction around the year 550 A.D. It is held sacred to all the Abrahamic faiths: Christianity, Islam and Judaism.

Jakub told me, "The Christian monks who live here claim that the Prophet Muhammad frequently visited and shared a great relationship with the monks in residence at the time. The '*Ashtiname* of Muhammad' is the Holy Testament of the Prophet Muhammad—a charter granting protection and other privileges to the Christian monks of Saint Catherine's, sealed with an imprint representing Muhammad's hand. In 1517, the original '*Ashtiname* of Muhammad' was taken to the Ottoman Treasury in Istanbul by Caliph Selim I, and replaced with a certified copy witnessed by the judges of Islam to affirm historical authenticity. The original is currently housed in the Topkapi Museum in Istanbul. If only the world could learn from this..." Jakub wistfully added, "This is a beacon of hope."

I was told that the monastics had lived in harmony with all religions for nearly 1500 years. It is inspiring that, in a world where religious differences are often ugly, this place has seen centuries of faithful worship, coexisting in peace.

The monastery has never been destroyed in all its history, with its Greek and Roman heritage preserved intact. It holds the second largest ancient library in the world, second only to the Vatican. In fact, a third of all the books in existence today written before the year 1000 A.D. are held in the library at Saint Catherine's.

Jakub ended the tour in the scriptorium. Alone there, we stood near the lit fireplace. He handed me another brown paper bag, this time with my civilian clothes.

"I urge you to burn them," he said.

I threw the dirty clothes into the fire without hesitation and we both watched as the flames caught and made the fabric smoke.

Jakub placed my wallet on the table. He removed my driver's license and the only bit of cash I had. "May I keep this?"

I nodded that he could, and then Jakub threw the wallet into the fire as well. As I watched my clothes and wallet burn, I knew that should I doubt my decision to stay, my routes of any contemplated escape had been taken away from me.

He put out two sheets of parchment on adjacent desks,

dipped a quill in ink and started to write the Greek alphabet on one. "Copy what I do," he told me.

We spent the next four hours painstakingly transcribing Greek letters and numerals.

At 5:00 am, the birds started to chirp and Jakub packed up our work. He handed me the parchment I was working on. "You must practice what you have learned during the day."

On the drive back, I asked him about the priest mentioned by Shem. "When will I meet Reverend Zachary?"

"When the time is right," he answered simply. We arrived outside the Monastery of Seven Sisters at dawn and waited until the singing voices of nuns filled the air again. Father Jakub then motioned to me to leave, and said, "See you here, the same time tonight."

And so it came to be. I soon settled into the rhythm of this daily routine with my days spent in sleep and practice at the Seven Sisters. Each evening, Jakub would pick me up and take me to the scriptorium at the Monastery of the God Trodden where I studied through the night. I learned to scribe the alphabets of numerous ancient languages: Koine Greek, Hebrew, Aramaic, Arabic, Coptic, Latin, even Mongolian. The focus was on being able to accurately identify the script and then reproduce it. There was limited tuition in the actual words, numbers or phrases, or what they meant.

An hour or two each night was spent on learning to identify the saints and demons from their symbols, to recognise each from their customary depictions, to be able to decipher that a large figure with a staff, carrying a child on his shoulder was Saint Christopher, or that Saint Mark held a quill in his right hand and the Gospel in his left.

The interpretation was often tricky or misleading. A man with a sword killing a dragon could be Saint George or the archangel Michael, pinning down Lucifer. The church has numerous saints and each has his or her established symbolism. A saint being cooked on a gridiron would be Saint Lawrence, whereas the man pierced by arrows would be Saint Sebastian. It was challenging enough to learn to recognise symbolically the hundreds of saints, yet the greater challenge was to learn to reproduce illustrations without error, using the small ink pots and quilled feather pens, in the same way as the monks had done in this scriptorium for centuries.

Twice a week, Jakub brought in a collection of printed articles on various natural catastrophes that had occurred each year since 1997. Just as I had discovered at the end of 2005, when I was researching a documentary, the magnitude and frequency of these events were progressively increasing. Paradoxically called Acts of God, these events were causing unprecedented loss of life and property.

I did not understand the reason for this esoteric training, but I knew better than to ask. I was diligent, working quietly, learning new skills each night and practicing my new-found art in the sanctity of my little cell in the Seven Sisters. I buried myself in work to mask the grief of leaving home which haunted me.

My skills soon progressed to deciphering and transcribing real ancient texts. The first was an attempt to replicate and then decode a photograph of the mysterious carvings found in the ancient Royston Cave of Hertfordshire, England. Jakub beamed as I tried to duplicate the Dragon of Saint George and the Wheel of Saint Catherine.

He made me work on reproducing the Book of Revelation, as written in Koine Greek. I soon realised that the act of transcription was a form of meditation and prayer, not just a mere replication of letters. I came to intimately know and experience the text. I also understood from my discussions with my tutor that the Book of Revelation, the only apocalyptic document in the New Testament, had something to do with my quest.

The hallucinatory imagery makes this 'Book of the Apocalypse' the most debated one in the Bible. While there is universal agreement that this is the only book of prophecies in the New Testament, it is the only book in the Bible that describes the war between the angels of God led by the archangel Michael, and the army led by the Dragon, or the Devil. In its pages are mentioned the birth of the Antichrist, the reign of the Devil and the struggle between good and evil.

Jakub explained, "The Gospels were written by four evangelists. It is certain that two of the evangelists, Mark and Luke, had never met Jesus during their lives. There is also debate as to whether the other two authors, Matthew and John, were apostles or whether their Gospels were written on their behalf around the end of the first century A.D.

"Indeed, Christ had the twelve apostles, each of whom walked in his footsteps and had their stories to tell. Yet, the decision to choose these four gospels to tell the story of Christ was made by men, albeit with divine intervention, some two hundred years after the writing of the four gospels. Their decisions now dictate what we accept and understand as the New Testament.

"The Gospels was written for people looking to live

their lives in the footsteps of Christ. You need to know what is in it, so you may find the answers you seek outside it."

Jakub was right. I was not looking to live my life in the footsteps of Christ. I had slept with the Devil and the answers to my quest lay somewhere outside the Bible.

CHAPTER 28

THE NAG HAMMADI CODICES

The days rolled into weeks, weeks into months. My training continued with a strong emphasis on improving the speed at which I could reproduce text and illustrations accurately.

Some time in October 2008, after months of nocturnal transcription and illustration, Father Jakub informed me that my time at the convent had come to an end. I was to burn all the paper on which I had practiced my calligraphy, and bring all my belongings with me. Packing was easy, I didn't have much. The nun's habit I wore, a spare habit, an identity card as Sister Benedictine, which had been made for me, and the little scrapbook of newspaper articles I had with me when I'd abruptly left home. That was it. I was to leave the key in the keyhole of the main convent door when I left that night. I knew it served no purpose in asking Jakub where we were going. I had learned to go with the flow and let life unfold itself as it was presented to me.

That night, Jakub picked me up and we drove back down the road to the coast. From there we turned north and drove another four hours. After a short break at the city of Suez, we took the road to Cairo and drove another three hours.

At about 4:00 am, we parked outside the impressive doorway of the Convent of Saint George. Jakub took out his mobile phone and dialled someone. When I saw the phone, I had to stifle a chuckle. It was, for some reason, the last thing I thought I would see in his company. However, I had to remind myself that, as much as its adherents hate to admit it, religion didn't exist in a technology vacuum.

Jakub spoke briefly in English into the phone and moments later, the door was opened by a Greek Coptic nun. Father Jakub reminded me of my vow of silence as we got out of the car. He briefly spoke to the nun, informing her that he would pick me up later that day. Jakub left me there without so much as a goodbye. The nun led me into the convent and up the stairs to a modest-sized, clean room with a bed and a window overlooking the distinctive round building that was the Monastery of Saint George.

After lunch, around 1:00 pm, Jakub collected me from the convent. During the short walk to the Coptic Museum, he said that we were going to study the Nag Hammadi codices. Apparently, in 1945, thirteen leather-bound papyrus codices, buried in a large earthenware jar, were found by two brothers while digging around the Jabal al-Ṭārif caves near Nag Hammadi, in upper Egypt. Neither originally reported the find, as they sought to make money from the manuscripts by selling them individually at intervals. Fortunately, most of these texts were retained within Egypt and handed to the Coptic Museum after the revolution in 1952.

When we reached the museum, it seemed the curator was expecting us. He led us deep into the restricted section of the museum, into an archive called the Nag Hammadi room. The curator proudly lectured, "This room holds twelve hundred of the original manuscripts found at Nag Hammadi, a collection of Gnostic texts, dating from the third and fourth centuries."

He moved alongside the walls quickly to a section brightly lit under a spotlight and pointed excitedly to one of the books. "The *Apocryphon*, or *Secret Book of James*." Shuffling along the book-lined walls, he stopped briefly from time to time, to point to other titles: "The *Apocalypse of Paul*, the *First and Second Apocalypse of James*, the *Gnostic Apocalypse of Peter*. The Nag Hammadi codices contain many forgotten versions of the Gospel such as the only complete version of the Gospel of Saint Thomas, which made this find so famous."

The curator then excused himself and left us alone with the ancient library. I looked at the vast collection of documents.

"This might take a while," I said dryly.

Jakub smiled. "At first I was unsure of your intentions, but now I am certain you are trying to unbirth what you have done." I nodded, agreeing.

"The Nag Hammadi codices also contain three texts," said Jakub, "namely the *Allogenes*, the *Gospel of the Egyptians* and the *Thirteenth Codex,* all of which have information relevant to your quest."

Jakub turned his attention to two of the Nag Hammadi texts he had named. The one called *Allogenes* was the sole surviving copy of the incomplete Gnostic tractate. The *Allogenes* dealt with the birth of the 'Dreadful One'.

The second text, called the *Gospel of the Egyptians,* identified a mountain called Charaxio where a redemptive document to deal with the coming of the Dreadful One would be hidden to ensure that it was there for use at the end of time.

It was described in the *Gospel of the Egyptians III*, 68: 1–5, as a 'high mountain on which the sun does not rise, nor is it possible.'

Jakub explained, "The sentence once ended with 'nor is it possible to access. An eclipse of the sun will reveal a comet with the Devil's trident by day,' but unfortunately, the papyrus fragments have been lost. Charaxio, we believe, is Burkhan Khaldun in Mongolia."

I would learn that Burkhan Khaldun is considered the most sacred mountain in Mongolia and was first designated as such by Genghis Khan. The area is almost inaccessible, as it lies in mountainous terrain covered in thick forests.

It is located within a region called *Ikh Khorig*, also known as Great Taboo, or the Forbidden Zone. Ikh Khorig is a 240-square kilometre area, protected by a tribal group called the Black Darkhads. Only the Black Darkhads, a group of elite warriors entrusted with the task of ensuring that no-one entered the area, were allowed within.

The Darkhads and their descendants have guarded the area faithfully with their lives from the time of Genghis Khan's death in 1227. The penalty for trespassing is death.

In 1924, the USSR established the Mongolian People's Republic as a satellite state. In fear that if the region were made publicly accessible, memories of Genghis Khan could possibly encourage Mongolian nationalism, the Soviets declared it a highly restricted area and cordoned off 10,400 square kilometres of surrounding land.

Ikh Khorig is not only near the birthplace of Genghis Khan, it was also rumoured to be where his tomb is located.

Before he died, Genghis Khan asked to be buried in a secret grave. His descendants and followers went to great lengths to ensure his wishes were honoured. According to legend, in order to keep the location of the great Khan's tomb secret, the funeral escort killed anyone who crossed the funeral path. Many horses were then used to trample over the site and trees were grown there to further obscure the location. Finally, after the tomb was completed and hidden, the slaves who built the tomb were murdered. To further remove any remote possibility of the location of the grave being disclosed, the soldiers who killed the slaves were then also massacred.

In 1989, a group of Japanese and Mongolian archaeologists combed the Burkhan Khaldun area and detected 1380 ancient tombs. It was one of the great finds of the century. Three years later, the ongoing work was stopped under intense local pressure.

Then, in 1992, the Mongolian government demarcated the area surrounding Burkhan Khaldun, approximately 12,240 square kilometres, as Khan Khentii, the birthplace of Genghis Khan, and named it a strictly protected area. Access to the wider Khan Khentii area is controlled by the Mongolian government and is forbidden to tourists and locals alike—with only rare exceptions.

The tomb of Genghis Khan, the man who rose from complete obscurity to become one of the greatest conquerors in history, has never been found, and to date its location is a mystery.

I opened my book and showed Jakub the photo that Inspector Jones had given me. The one with the image of Jess in one frame and the image of Hale-Bopp in the other.

He nodded. "The phrase 'the sun does not rise' was a

reference to the end of time—the Apocalypse. When the eclipse occurred with the comet Hale-Bopp in view, the observatories of the Vatican were certain the stars had aligned and the son of the Devil was born. Most comets have two tails, Hale-Bopp like the Devil's trident had three. We scoured the earth looking for a male child and we failed to consider that many ancient texts were scribed in now dead languages that used gender interchangeably." Jakub concluded, "We believe that at least one of the texts we need is somewhere in Burkhan Khaldun, probably in the lost grave of the great Genghis Khan."

He then spoke of the third text relevant to my quest, the *Thirteenth Codex*. This text was reported as burned by the mother of the brothers who made the Nag Hammadi discovery. She was apparently worried that the papers might have 'dangerous effects'.

I was deflated. Just as I started to make some headway, we had hit a dead end. Jakub, sensing my despair, said, "Worry not. We have the *Thirteenth Codex*, the *Hieroglyphs of Herod*, in our possession."

In hindsight, the trip to Cairo was more for my benefit, to let me know that I was now accepted as being on the side of good. I was given a chance to touch and feel the Nag Hammadi codices and to know they were real. I saw the Gospel of the Egyptians and learned that it was foretold that a comet with three tails revealed by a solar eclipse at Burkhan Khaldun would mark the birth of the Dreadful One. It would be the first sign of the Apocalypse.

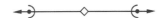

Siobhan turned the page and studied the photograph stapled to the next page. As her mother had described, it was a picture of two photos in a tandem frame. The left frame had a picture of Jess in it, while the other showed a solar eclipse and a strange whitish blip that must have been the comet. An etched gold tag identified the place as Ikh Khorig and the date was the 9th of March 1997.

CHAPTER 29

THE THIRTEENTH NAG HAMMADI CODEX

A couple of days later, we left Cairo and drove east through Suez and Nekhel to the town of Taba, just across the border in Israel. Jakub was on a first name basis with the border guards on both sides, suggesting he had been here many times before. After a short break in Taba, we drove north along the Israel-Jordan border, to Jerusalem. Our destination was the Shrine of the Book, which was famous for its collection of the Dead Sea Scrolls discovered between 1947 and 1956 in caves near Qumran.

Written in the 'War Scroll' discovered in Qumran Cave #1, is the apocalyptic prophecy of the war between the Sons of Light and the Sons of Darkness. The Shrine of the Book was built to symbolise the War Scroll, the white dome representing the Sons of Light and the black basalt wall representing the Sons of Darkness.

The Shrine of the Book houses over fifteen thousand fragments of the Dead Sea Scrolls. In the heavily guarded, monitored and climate controlled rooms containing these fragile texts was a nondescript library with large bookshelves. Moshe, our guide, showed us to the room and left. Jakub locked the door and then pushed a small lever on one of the bookshelves. The shelf moved slowly, revealing a trapdoor underneath. We went down a flight of rock cut stairs, dimly lit by the light filtering from the open trapdoor. The stairs ended in front of a large steel slab that was embedded in a thick reinforced concrete wall, at least half a metre thick. Jakub stood with me in front of the door and pointed to a camera above. As we both looked up, the steel door quietly slid open.

We stepped into a bunker lit by electric lamps in the ceiling. The room resembled a bomb shelter with no windows or doors except for two small vents in the floor and ceiling. There were six pages of illustrations, each roughly the size of an A4 sheet of paper, each encased in glass and mounted on stands, encircling the room.

Jakub pointed to the disturbing drawings. "While all other Nag Hammadi codices are predominantly text, this *Thirteenth Codex* is a collection of illustrations detailing the time of the coming of the 'Dreadful One'. The mother of the farmers who found the codices could not understand the script of the other books, but she could comprehend these drawings. She knew they were wretched. These despairing illustrations perhaps prompted her to want this particular codex out of her hut."

The Hieroglyphs of Herod was the name given to the six sketches drawn from descriptions by King Herod of his nightmares. The sketches were considered apocalyptic prophecies of the environment's demise, a world in which all evil was justified in the name of survival.

The first of the drawings depicted numerous men cutting down the last remaining trees in a felled forest, men killing and quartering the last remaining animals, and boats floating above a single fish, pierced with spears, in a sea devoid of marine life. Beside the boats was an overcrowded island of hungry humans screaming to the hunters and fishermen for

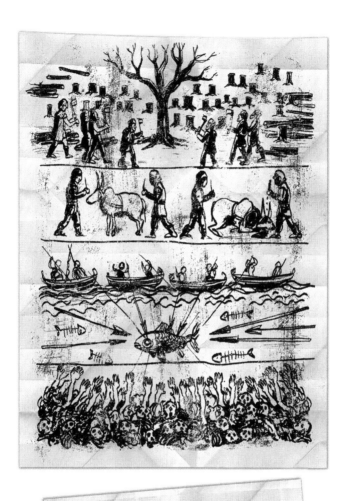

"The Arrogance of Humans—
When human life is more important
than all of God's creations."

food. The caption in Koine Greek read, *The Arrogance of Humans—When human life is more important than all of God's creations.*

I realised that this first sketch detailed the extermination of other species for the preservation of the human race. Each year, we were wiping out hundreds, if not thousands of species from our planet. Unlike the mass extinction events of geological history, the current extinction challenge is one for which a single species, namely ours, is wholly responsible.

Jakub explained that it was the parable of Noah's Ark. "Earth is the ark and the human race is Noah. There is enough place on this ark for each and every one of God's creations, but if Noah chose to carry four elephants instead of two, he would have to leave behind the giraffes or the zebras to die. If Noah chose to carry a thousand humans on his ark, he would have had to dedicate a large section for crops and cattle specifically to feed his passengers.

"The ever-expanding human population stretches its tentacles, claiming forests for cattle ranches, natural land for cropping, housing developments, rail and roads. Large sections of the ark have been modified and renovated to meet the demands of one species, evicting others that can't hold on, forcing them into extinction.

"These are all God's creatures, and it was Noah's task to save each and every one of them. It was Noah's mandate to protect the food chains of each species, to give them an ecosystem and allow them to procreate and live in balance with the environment they inhabited."

I understood then that it was the height of arrogance for us to believe that we had a greater right to live on this planet than all the rest of God's creations combined. It was as though Noah decided to fill the ark with humans and shut

"The Greed of Humans—
When few will have more than they need, and yet
continue wanting from the many who have not.
Yet the rest shall worship them."

the doors on all of God's other creations.

We turned towards the second sketch. It was of a well-dressed family sitting around a plentiful table. The family was surrounded by a large fence and were guarded by soldiers with spears. Hundreds of starving men, women and children were clamouring at the fence, begging or trying to climb in. The guards had killed some of the beggars to keep them out.

The caption read, *The Greed of Humans—When few will have more than they need, and yet continue wanting from the many who have not. Yet the rest shall worship them.*

I looked to Jakub and he said, "We have grown into a race that idolises the few who claim to have inherited the earth itself. We believe we have created wealth and progress for everyone, but all we have done is learn how to consume the resources of the planet faster. We have fooled ourselves into believing we own these resources and then sell them on to others at an ever-increasing rate, to be consumed or wasted.

"In our myopic world, we have failed to see that we are capable only of modification and incapable of creation itself. At the end of the day, what is on this planet is constant. The water we drink, the air we breathe, the arable land we till are all finite resources.

"We have learned to grow more crops on the same land by doping it with fertilisers and we have learned to extract water from the seas and purify our sewerage wastes, but in its wake we have sterilised more land each year and polluted more clean waters. What do you think this means?"

Pondering for a moment, I replied, "In time, the choice of survival will no longer be between the human race and all other species, but between the human race itself and the hoarding of food and water to ensure the survival of a few?"

"Yes," agreed Jakub, "Unlike other species that have accepted their inevitable fate without a whisper of complaint, the unfortunate humans who are excluded will have nothing to lose if they turn to violence, crime and war to survive."

I shuddered, knowing in my gut that this was true.

The third sketch was about poisoning the air we breathe and consuming it in our quest to fuel human greed. It showed the black depths of the earth burning and spewing out smoke. The sun was a misty black haze, barely breaking through the thick smoke. Men were displayed with cloth tied around their mouths, their eyes watering from the smoke, gasping for air and suffocating babies so they could get another gasp of air.

It was titled *Death of Air—Burning the air which their children could breathe.*

Jakub didn't need to explain this one for me. The fires emanating from the earth were a depiction of the burning of hydrocarbons from deep underground reservoirs, converting the oxygen in the air to an asphyxiating carbon dioxide.

Today we measure carbon dioxide levels in parts per million, but these levels are ever increasing. We have acknowledged that we have a problem and we have promised to solve it with innovation, such as replacing fossil fuels with renewable energy and energy efficient devices.

Siobhan, each day we claim to use less power and chemicals to create and use the air conditioning units, the refrigerators, the washing machines and all manner of other modern gadgets. Nevertheless, more than two-thirds of the human population have no access to these gadgets, and we want to bring these onto the already overloaded ark. Indeed,

"Death of Air—
Burning the air which their
children could breathe."

at the bottom of it all, one-third of the human race has no access to electricity at all, bobbing about at sea, trying to climb aboard.

This third sketch also depicted men suffocating their babies. I believed this signified—and Jakub confirmed—that we were robbing future generations of the tools to survive. To meet the greed of our current world, we were rapidly stripping the earth's assets. Rather than preserve and bequeath intergenerational equity to help future generations survive, we chose to borrow it, gamble it away and leave them in debt.

The fourth sketch showed oceans bubbling and dead fish floating. The waters had risen and were flooding cropped land. Men, women and children stood on rooftops, while thousands were washed away. A monkey sat afloat on an iceberg. The sketch was titled, *Death of the Oceans.*

"The oceans have sustained life on earth since the beginning of time," began Jakub, gesturing to the drawing. "The seas have provided food, a sink for carbon dioxide, and milder climates due to ocean currents.

"Today we have bigger trawlers, electro-netting, dynamite and incredible radar technology to hunt down fish in their millions. We understand the breeding and spawning cycles of fish and marine life better than ever before, but we continue to deplete the seas, removing vital parts of the food chain and poison the waters with our chemical wastes."

I looked at the drawing carefully. Jakub was right. We had broken all the rules to meet our selfish greed—if we didn't take it, someone else would. We have learned to sail faster, trawl deeper and continually improve our efficiency to hunt down and depopulate the seas of all the life they hold.

The gases escaping from the seas in the sketch were the

"Death of the Oceans"

oceans giving up the ghost, releasing the carbon dioxide they held into the atmosphere. The monkey sitting atop an iceberg represented the melting of the ice caps.

We moved to the next drawing.

The fifth sketch flowed on from the fourth. It showed a world with more severe climatic events—tornadoes, floods, storms, hailstones and blizzards. A solitary swing was flying almost perpendicular to the ground in a gale-force wind, a terrified young girl clutching onto it. Houses were flattened, the bricks and beams flying, killing all in their path. The windows, doors, and roofs designed to keep us safe from the elements were being ripped out or blown in, becoming deadly projectiles. Uprooted trees and debris soared in the wind, men and women smashed like overripe fruit on a wall. A few people lay dying on the ground, pockmarked with disease, gnawed by rats and vultures. The sketch was titled, *Vengeance of Nature*.

"Denise," said Jakub, referring to our bi-weekly study on 'Acts of God', "by now you know super storms, hurricanes and tornadoes are occurring more frequently and with far greater intensity. Our world was designed to withstand the events of the past, but, as these events get more intense, the power of the storms turns the protective shelters we have built against us: windows blow in, roofs blow off, becoming projectiles of death. We need stronger designs and materials to protect us from the ever-increasing fury of nature."

Jakub then pointed to the image of the terrified child, flying horizontally, grabbing the end of a swing and trying not to be blown away in a hurricane and asked, "What do you make of this?"

I responded intuitively, "I think the swing represents the planet earth and the child the human race. The storms,

"Vengeance of Nature."

hurricanes, hailstones and floods are getting more ferocious each day, pushing the swing higher and higher. The gentle swinging had been replaced by the nightmarish struggle to hang on and survive."

Jakub smiled. "I never saw it before, but you are right. That is exactly what it is meant to be." These were his first words of encouragement and I felt heartened.

As we moved to the last drawing, he added, "It is in these floods and disasters that pestilence and disease prevail. This is the recipe for crime. This is the recipe for war."

He gestured us forwards to look at the last sketch.

The sixth drawing was of deserts, dust storms, arid land and drought-cracked earth with dead leafless trees. The rich man and his family from the second picture were now skeletons seated around the same table. The decadent food that covered the table was replaced by piles of gold and precious stones. The caption read, *Death of Land*. It was clear that some of his family were victims of the *Vengeance of Nature*. The soldiers that had protected their lands were dead, their skeletons strewn across the perimeter fence. The crowds outside their lands were all gone.

"No food, no potable water and only polluted air. This is an Earth that has died," said Jakub, as I took in the details carefully. He sighed. "We are not killing the planet. It is our arrogance that makes us believe that we are capable of such destruction. The earth will be here at the end of it all, long after we're gone. The only thing the human race is destroying is our ability to inhabit it."

"As depressing as it is that our world is headed towards these apocalyptic outcomes," I said, "there is nothing supernatural about any of these sketches. What does this have to do with Jess being the daughter of the Devil?"

"Death of Land"

Jakub looked at the drawings once more and then turned to me. "These sketches are neither natural nor supernatural, but rather anthropogenic. It is in this systematic fuelling of excesses that we humans progressively exterminate every support mechanism. The earth progressively degenerates towards a form of quadriplegia, completely impotent to protect all it sustains. In this state, the options to survive become more and more limited, until none other remains but to survive at *any* cost.

"The human race will have no choice but to turn on itself in a fight to secure the morsels that remain. The ark has become a game of musical chairs. Every time the music stops, more people have to fight for fewer remaining seats. It is the perfect environment in which the Devil is blameless, and can reign supreme.

"In this situation, all evil can be justified in the name of survival. If there has been one consistent message in *The Hieroglyphs of Herod*, it is that Armageddon is upon us and the time is now."

Our quest was now to seek the book that dealt with what we could do to fight Armageddon. The answers and tools were chartered in *The Devil's Prayer*.

CHAPTER 30

THE DEVIL'S BIBLE

In search of The Devil's Prayer, we went from Jerusalem to Ben Gurion airport, Tel Aviv. On the way to the airport, we stopped briefly at a department store and picked up some warm winter gear. I was given a British passport—Lisa James, forty years old—with the same photograph as my identity card as Sister Benedictine. Getting through airport security as a nun and priest from the Holy Land was simpler than I'd imagined.

Father Jakub explained to passport control that I had taken a vow of silence. The airport staff was almost apologetic in their hurry to assist us on our way. With no luggage other than a small bag containing my warm clothes, spare nun's habit and a book with my collection of news clippings and my notes, we were whisked through.

From Tel Aviv we flew to Stockholm. We were going to see the *Codex Gigas*, or the Devil's Bible, which had been with the *Kungliga Biblioteket*, or the National Library of Sweden, since 1649. The *Codex Gigas* was taken as booty by the Swedes from Prague during the Thirty Years War and has belonged to the library's collection ever since.

As we travelled, Jakub told me about the *Codex Gigas*, which translated to 'Giant Book'. It is bound in a wooden folder covered with leather and ornate metal. The book measures ninety-two centimetres by fifty, and weighs about seventy-five kilograms. It is the largest medieval manuscript known in existence. Composed of 310 leaves of vellum allegedly made from the skins of 160 donkeys and calves, the Codex contains the entire Bible, except for the Acts of the Apostles and the Book of Revelation, which details the fight between good and evil, God and the Devil. The entire document is written in Latin, with additional Hebrew, Greek and Slavic alphabets.

According to legend, a Benedictine monk—Herman the Recluse—from the Podlažice Monastery in today's Czech Republic was condemned to death. He offered to write a book containing all the knowledge in the world in one night to escape his sentence. Realising his task was impossible, at midnight, he made a pact with the Devil to finish the gargantuan book in exchange for his soul. The Devil completed the manuscript and the monk added the Devil's picture on the 209th page out of gratitude for his aid.

Through analysing the handwriting and style, experts concurred that the Devil's Bible was written and illustrated by the same person and that it would have taken approximately twenty years working all day every day to complete the task. Experts concluded that, mysteriously, the writing and illustrations showed no signs of the author ageing and that there were no mistakes in the entire book. No other work of this author had been identified and where he was trained was unknown.

The Benedictine monastery of Podlažice was modest and obscure. It still remains a mystery as to how such a small monastery could have garnered the resources for the creation of such a massive book.

I stood there a long time looking at the large manuscript

in its glass box at the National Library. I then browsed the library's digitised version of every elaborate page.

The Devil's Bible initially contained three hundred and twenty-two sheets, though today twelve sheets are missing. It is unknown as to who removed the pages or for what purpose.

Once I had absorbed all of this, I commented to Jakub, "I could have read all of this on the internet. Why come all this way?"

Jakub replied, "You needed to see the original. The twelve missing pages of the Devil's Bible contain *The Devil's Prayer*, the object of our quest. You will have to recognise the handwriting, if you unearth the missing pages."

On the Singapore-bound plane, Siobhan was disturbed from her study by a gentle hand nudging her. Sitting on what had been the empty seat next to her was a woman dressed in a dark grey burkha; her face was completely covered save for her striking green eyes.

The woman spoke quickly and softly. "My name is Yasmin, I am a friend of Father Jakub. The Amalrican monks will know by now that you are on this plane. They will be waiting for you at Singapore airport."

Reading *The Confession*, Siobhan had almost forgotten about being hunted. Yasmin handed Siobhan her passport, her ticket stub and a large paper bag containing a dark blue burkha and a matching niqab. She added, "Wear this. You must sit with my family and leave the plane and airport with my husband Yusuf and my two children."

Siobhan hesitated, searching for some validation in

the woman's imploring eyes. The woman whispered beseechingly, "Please, you must go!"

Siobhan knew she had no choice. She had been rushed onto a plane at the last minute, and if someone else knew she was on this plane, the odds were in her favour that it was someone sent by Father Jakub. Siobhan took her book and bag, nodded her thanks to the woman, and made her way to the back of the plane. She changed into the blue burkha, and covered her face with the niqab, keeping *The Confession* tucked inside her shirt, then joined Yusuf. She was briefly acquainted with Salil, a skinny seven-year-old, and his sister Ayesha, a beautiful five-year-old with her mother's green eyes.

The plane touched down at Changi airport and Siobhan disembarked. Her heart raced as she headed out holding the hands of two very confused children. Ayesha looked back worriedly at her mother, who was now dressed in western clothes, sitting in Siobhan's seat letting the other passengers get off the aircraft.

Siobhan kept her head down as she followed Yusuf quietly, hustling the hand luggage they had. As they passed the entrance, a couple of men in suits were searching the queue of passengers, clearly looking for someone.

Siobhan had been saved—for now.

They headed straight to the immigration desk with four passports. The bored customs officer asked Siobhan to uncover her face and she barely glanced up to check. Their passports were stamped and they were let through without any trouble.

Yusuf had a hire car waiting and, minutes later, Siobhan found herself sitting in the front seat of a Toyota Corolla heading to Kuala Lumpur. Yusuf took back his wife's passport and gave Siobhan a spare white immigration card to fill out. The detailed escape was wasted on the Malaysian border security at the checkpoint, who didn't think twice about the car entering their country from Singapore. Siobhan's passport was stamped and, a few hours later, she was at Kuala Lumpur airport. Yusuf purchased a ticket on the next flight to Brisbane and sent her on her way.

She had barely spoken a word to Yusuf or the children the entire four-hour journey. She didn't know if she would see Yusuf, Yasmin, Salil or Ayesha again to thank them. Probably not. Just before she boarded her flight, she made a call home. She informed a very surprised Edith that she would shortly be boarding the last leg of her flight home. Not wanting to answer questions, Siobhan excused herself on the pretext that the flight was boarding and hung up the phone.

Once on the flight to Brisbane, Siobhan opened her mother's journal again, anxious to learn more about the missing pages of the *Codex Gigas: The Devil's Prayer.*

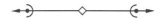

CHAPTER 31
OF DEALS WITH THE DEVIL

OCTOBER 2008

We drove from Stockholm some two hundred and fifty kilometres southwest to the Vadstena Abbey. On the long drive, I asked Father Jakub a question that had bothered me: "There are many religions, each having its own gods. So which god is the Devil fighting?"

Jakub answered softly. "You are confusing God with religion. It is like water. Water is water, whether you drink it from the tap, or you get it from a bottle sparkling or still, it is always water, irrespective of the brand or packaging. God is like water and religion is the brand or packaging."

"What are your thoughts on the hundreds of thousands of innocents killed over the ages in the name of God? As a priest, how do you still believe in God?"

Jakub replied, "The problem is neither with religion nor with God. The problem is with man and what he does in the name of God. Religion is like a knife: in the hands of a surgeon, it heals, but in the hands of a murderer, it kills.

"Every religion encourages you to have a regular dose of God in your life in the form of daily prayer and meditation. In the words of Renaissance physicist and occultist Paracelsus, *'Sola dosis facit venenum'*, which means *the dose makes the poison*. Even oxygen and water, which are essential to all living creatures, are toxic if the dose is too high. And so it is with religion, too."

He went on, "The Devil's advocate would ask, 'Why have you chosen to fight against your youngest daughter? A fight that can only be won if she is killed. Has she done you any wrong?'"

It was a moment of truth I never wanted to face. His question was valid. Until I found out Jess was the child of the Devil, I loved her unconditionally. Why did that change anything? I was now well aware that the aim of my quest was to stop Jess. That would almost certainly mean her death. Was this any different from any other murder carried out in the name of God?

I pondered his words. The reference to the Devil's advocate triggered fears deep down inside me. Perhaps I had never come to terms with trusting another person after the betrayal of my friends and fiancé, but it took this one seemingly innocuous question to spark the deep mistrust once again.

Was this man leading me to work for the Devil against my will again? I had met Jakub not knowing anything about him. He claimed the exorcist Father Shem had contacted him before he died. How could I really trust him?

Now suspicious, I asked Jakub about who had funded our whirlwind trip, which had taken us through Egypt, Israel and Sweden.

His response was pragmatic. "Religion is the oldest business in the world.

"We sell faith. Faith is being sure in what we cannot see and being certain in what we live for. The greatest fear of the human race is loneliness. Religion offers you God as your companion, to be with you all the time, wherever you go.

"Faith is instilled in the very young by wonderful myths

like Santa Claus that bring enormous happiness to children. Many come back to religion when death knocks at their door; for with religion you will not walk alone, and perhaps you will not walk alone when you leave this earth. Every day, in nearly every city and town in the world, some old man or lady dies, leaving behind something in their will—a house, some money, some land—all to the Church, their last friend who kept them company in their time of loneliness. Some hope it buys their way to heaven or makes amends for their sins in the past. Guilt is the currency of the Catholic faith."

Siobhan shut the book. Those last words were the same words Mother Superior Margaret had used in Spain. She had a terrible sinking feeling that she was being led across the globe by an elaborate lie. Jakub had told her that Reverend Zachary had requested him to take her mother to the Santa Teresa convent, and that her mother had taken a vow of silence, never speaking to him. He told her that she had broken her vow of silence only on her last day at the confessional. Yet it was now evident that he had lied to her. Was Jakub playing Siobhan as well?

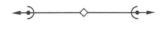

October 2008

Sensing my uneasiness and distrust, Jakub changed the topic to Saint Bridget. He quoted one of her prophecies verbatim:

"In the year 1980, the wicked shall prevail; they will profane and sacrilegiously defile the churches by erecting in them altars to idols and to the Antichrist, whom they will worship, and will attempt to force others to do the same."

I was now a sceptic. I didn't trust Father Jakub and his motives. I scoffed. "Nothing of note happened in 1980."

Jakub, as always, had an answer: the internet. "It was first made available to universities and the general public from around 1980. Today, it is the information highway of the world. It has replaced newspapers, TV and all other forms of media."

I considered his answer. Then I asked a question that had been plaguing my mind: "Have you heard of any other women who made a deal with the Devil and then gave birth?"

Jakub remained silent. I decided to wait him out and eventually he spoke.

"In the fifteenth century, there was a famous Franciscan nun and mystic. She was called Sister Magdalena of the Cross."

"What happened to her?" I asked, needing to know.

"At around the age of ten, Magdalena tried to crucify herself to her bedroom wall. She managed to nail her two feet and her left hand until she fainted from the pain. The nails, not strong enough to hold her body up, had torn her flesh away and she fell heavily on her chest, breaking several of her ribs. Her parents found her and a doctor bandaged her wounds, but Magdalena wanted to feel the pain and removed the bandages. She fell terribly ill from infection.

"Magdalena was dying from these wounds. But then, at midnight on Easter Saturday, she let out a great scream and she was miraculously healed. There were no signs of the self-inflicted stigmata."

This sounded eerily familiar, but I needed to know more. I motioned at the Father to hurry up.

With a concerned frown, he continued, "At seventeen, Magdalena joined the convent in Cordova. She was very public about her spiritual life, even carrying a cross everywhere she went. By the age of twenty-two, the church had announced that she was destined for Sainthood, and Magdalena was ordained with great pomp. During the ceremony, while reciting the Kyrie Eleison, a dove flew from the top of the church and landed on her shoulder, surely a sign from the Divine. From then on, she was known as Sister Magdalena of the Cross, honouring the self crucifixion in her youth.

"Even when confined to the convent, she seemed to be aware of events outside its walls and of neighbouring noble families. Over the years, her fame had spread well beyond the boundaries of Spain. Her prophecies—such as the revelation of the death of King Ferdinand a year before it happened—only fuelled the already raging fire.

"In March 1518, Magdalena discreetly informed the Abbess that she was with child, claiming that she had been impregnated by the Holy Spirit. Although the Abbess swore Magdalena to secrecy, it was only a matter of time before her state became obvious, and it was evident for all to see that the famous Magdalena of the Cross was expecting.

"Many doubted the miraculous conception, as this had never happened before, other than, of course, for the Blessed Virgin Mary. Furthermore, there was nothing in the scripture that spoke of the second birth of Christ.

"On Christmas Day 1518, Magdalena gave birth. She insisted that an angel visited her and told her she must be alone at the time of the birth. Three days later, the child disappeared.

"Twenty-five years later, a suspicious priest invited a well-known exorcist, believing Magdalena to be a tool of the Devil. During the exorcism, Magdalena, held aloft in the air by an unseen force, cried out that she had made a pact with the Devil.

"By then, Sister Magdalena of the Cross had been fasting for thirty years. She confessed that the Devil himself had fed her in secret and she had become pregnant by him.

"The Inquisition did not condemn her to the purifying flames as she wished, but rather forced her to live out her life in penance.

"Nothing is known about the purported child of the Devil who disappeared."

Magdalena's story sounded true to me. Indeed, I could not find it unthinkable that someone could make a pact with the Devil, be it Sister Magdalena or the Benedictine monk Herman the Recluse. After all, I had made one too. The miracles of writing a book in one night or healing of stigmata were just as believable as the miraculous cure of my almost severed spine.

I thought about this as Jakub reminded me, "You were not the first to make a deal with the Devil."

Jakub told me about the dozens of ancient bridges around the world that stand testimony to this. There are forty-nine in France alone that bear the name *The Devil's Bridge*. These bridges were all significant technological achievements for their times. Most of these bridges share the same legend: a pact made with the Devil to build a bridge overnight in exchange for the first soul to cross it. After delivering on his side of the deal, Satan would then be outwitted by the builders, by for example, getting some animal to cross the bridge first, denying the Devil a human soul.

"Ironically, the Devil has placed more honour in keeping his word than most men." Jakub then added with a wry smile, "But Satan always has the last laugh. Just as a junkie always needs another fix, once you have made a pact with the Devil, even if you cheat him out of his prize, there is no God to turn to in times of adversity, and eventually you will turn back to the Devil you have cheated. You can't blame him for feeding a double-crossing junkie a bad hit the second time around."

There was a sense of awe in Jakub's voice when he spoke of the honour the Devil placed on keeping his word and, now that I doubted his loyalties, I was even more unsure.

Finally, we reached our destination: the Vadstena Abbey—founded by Saint Bridget of Sweden. Jakub told me that she was one of the few saints who had abandoned her children to join the convent. Perhaps he believed it would give me some hope that I was not fighting for a completely lost cause. The abbey had languished since the Reformation of 1547 until its doors were closed in 1594 by King Charles IX of Sweden. Then, as recently as 1963, the abbey had once more been reclaimed as a convent by the Bridgettines, a monastic religious order that follows the rules of Saint Augustine.

I tossed and turned all night in my little room. All my life, I had never wished to hurt anybody. I had always paid lip service to religion to appease Edith and keep the peace in the house. It made her happy. I reassured myself, I was a good person.

I could not ask for forgiveness, for I was not sorry for having prayed for you to cheat death, neither was I sorry for doing the deal with the Devil to protect your future. Given the chance again, I would trade my soul for your life a second time. As for Jess, I knew now why I chose this path. I felt responsible for bringing her into this world. Every generation aims to leave their children a better world than the one they inherited from their parents. I knew now that my generation had failed. You would not inherit a better world.

My nocturnal musings eventually brought some clarity to my mind, and I knew that, through all the smoke and mirrors, I was still blind to what I was trying to achieve. I needed to find out who Jakub was working for. The next morning, we met at the car. As he loaded his small bag into the boot, I confronted Jakub. "What is in *The Devil's Prayer* that is so important?"

Jakub looked at me straight in the eyes. "I don't know. We don't know." I looked at him suspiciously. He added, "We don't know what's in *The Devil's Prayer*, but it's all we have."

"I don't need to travel to any more exotic places," I blurted. "I don't need to discover any more prophecies of the coming of the child of the Devil. I have no doubt she is here. I gave birth to her. I have met her father and I know exactly who he is."

Jakub was taken aback and unsure. He asked tentatively, "What do you want to do?"

I replied, "I want to make my confession to Reverend Zachary. I have left everything I love to meet with him."

Jakub said nothing. He walked to the car, got in the driver's seat and waited for me. Exasperated, I got in. Jakub drove silently, ignoring my glares and attempts to re-engage in a conversation.

He dropped the hire car back at Arlanda airport and started to walk towards the airport terminal.

Irritated with his indifferent response to my request, I demanded, "I must see Reverend Zachary. I am not interested in anymore sightseeing."

Jakub smiled mildly. "Reverend Zachary is in Kutna Hora, an hour east of Prague. That's where we are going."

CHAPTER 32

THE KUTNA HORA CONVOCATION

By the time we arrived in Kutna Hora, it was late evening. We drove through the sparsely populated streets and parked in the empty car park of the impressive Church of Saint Barbara, built in the style of a cathedral. It was now past the visiting hours posted on the large church entrance. Jakub went to the side entrance and opened a time-worn locked door. Upon entering, I saw that the church was dimly lit by the light of dusk—and completely empty. He led me to a staircase, which rose up to the roof.

From our vantage point on the roof, Jakub pointed to an intricate carving of the Devil sitting watch over the cathedral roof door. He commented dryly, "God and the Devil—one does not exist without the other."

He unlocked a wrought-iron gate, grafted into one of the ornately carved stone pillars, to reveal a very narrow, stone spiral staircase hidden inside. He signalled for me to descend the stairs, barely wide enough for a single person. I took a few steps down and he followed, locking the gate behind him.

We climbed down in pitch darkness. The descent trailed through the hollow interior of one of the cathedral's pillars. It felt like an eternity, continually going around and around, descending into inky blackness. By the time the staircase ended I was calf deep in water.

Jakub encouraged me on. "It's only knee deep." He switched on a torch. He added, "We are in a disused shaft of the ancient Osel Mine, once the largest silver mine in the world. The tunnels of this mine descend almost six hundred metres into the depths of the earth, dug out entirely by hand over a period of five hundred years. Only a fraction of the tunnels and shafts are known or have been explored since the fifteenth century."

Father Jakub led the way expertly through the underground maze of interconnected mine shafts, many strewn with ancient mining tools. As we passed a section of cave, I recoiled. There along the walls were human skeletons, their chests impaled by rusted swords.

I looked at the Father in fear, my eyes wide from the horror of it all.

"During the Hussite wars of the fifteenth century, some two thousand Hussites killed by the Crusaders of Pope Martin V were thrown down the mine shafts, their bodies left to rot."

I was growing increasingly anxious as we moved deeper into this labyrinth.

"Stay very close to me," Jakub said. "If you get lost here, nobody will ever find you. Some tunnels don't even have breathable air."

Had Jakub been sent by the Devil to ensure I did not disclose the true identity of my daughter? Had he made me take that vow of silence to guarantee just that? Now concerned I might identify Jess to the public; was he going to get rid of me where nobody would ever find me?

My fears were heightened even more when Jakub stopped next to a large piece of rope coiled on the ground. He lifted it up and asked me to hold the torch as he wrapped one end of it securely around his waist and asked me to do the same with the other end. He took the torch back from me and switched it off. It was a pure darkness, as though this was where light came to die. I struggled to stop myself from hyperventilating.

"Take small steps and follow me," Jakub said. I held the rope in one hand and followed him as he twisted and turned expertly through the maze of tunnels. It was better than any blindfold. In the darkness, I could not see the rope tied to my waist or Jakub walking less than two paces in front of me.

"Where are we going?" I asked.

"To Reverend Zachary's cave," Jakub said without preamble.

After about fifteen minutes of walking, he switched on the torch again. We had arrived at an ancient, studded iron door. Jakub knocked loudly three times and waited. There was no response. He then pulled out an almost comically over-sized key and opened the door, which groaned loudly in protest. It revealed another cavern. Jakub undid the rope tied around his waist and encouraged me to do the same. He then lit a few kerosene lamps placed around the room, and I saw that we were in a very large underground library, its walls lined with ancient books. He turned to me. "He's not here. Wait here, I'll go and find him."

Before I could answer, he left and shut the heavy door behind him. I tried to open it, but it was locked.

My heart sank. I wondered if I had been betrayed for the second time. It had been the perfect ruse. Nobody knew I was here. Had Jakub panicked when I'd asked to meet Reverend Zachary? Had he decided to bring me somewhere to die where nobody would ever find me? Was he just going to hand me back to the Devil?

I lifted a kerosene lamp and looked around at the bookshelves. Each and every book was about the occult: the Devil, grimoires, spells. If ever there was a Devil's library, this was it.

I walked through the library and found six containers of almonds and dried cashews placed in a row in one corner. Beside them, a trickling stream of water flowed out of the rock and into a narrow short channel along the base of the wall before it drained into a hole. Two glasses placed on the lip of the channel indicated that the water was drinkable. Next to the corner were two openings. The first opened to a small enclave with a bucket and soap. The second led to a cramped cave, on the floor of which was a small coir mat and, folded neatly next to it, a red cassock.

A voice came over the airplane PA system: "Ladies and gentlemen, we have started our descent into Brisbane. Please check that your seatbelts are fastened, your seats are in an upright position and your tray tables are stowed away."

Her mother's discovery of the red cassock sounded warning bells to Siobhan. Even now she relived her escape from the Amalrican monks. She shared the sinking feeling her mother must have had. Siobhan was now certain that Father Jakub had played her too. There was nothing she could do for now, as she would be in Brisbane in less than an hour. Suddenly a realisation came over her: Siobhan now identified with her mother being in jeopardy. It was the first time she had actually considered her mother was not insane or delusional, but may be telling the truth. She reopened *The Confession* and continued reading.

October 2008

I returned to the entrance of the library and decided to settle in for the night next to the door and await my fate. A few hours later, I heard the key in the lock of the door. Jakub had returned, alone. He beckoned to me, "Let's go."

We headed back through the tunnels, the same way we had come, tethered to each other by a rope and in complete darkness. We reached a point deep inside the tunnel network when Jakub switched on the torch again, undid the rope and returned it, coiled, to its original place. From there, we retraced our steps back to the car, climbing to the top of the roof of the church and then back through the main hall. Night had fallen.

Jakub drove through the town of Kutna Hora and then parked in a deserted street. We walked a short distance alongside the high walls that partly obscured the lower half of a church. Jakub turned the handle of a large wooden gate that extended to the top of the walls. I followed him on a short cobblestoned path leading to the door of a church. He opened the door and it groaned slightly. He ushered me in and said, "He is in there." Jakub stayed outside, pulling the door shut behind me.

The room was lit by thousands of candles. A small set of steps led down to a larger room below. The walls and arch around and above the entrance to the stairs were lined with human bones and skulls. As I descended into the main chamber below, I found to my left and right were two cages with hundreds of skulls arranged in a pyramid, one atop the other. Ahead of me in the chamber were nine concentric circles of candles laid out. Four pillars, adorned with skulls of diminishing sizes and crowned by eerie looking cherubs, intercepted the fourth circle from the centre. Above the centre was a large chandelier-like structure, made entirely of bones and skulls. I shuddered.

In the sixth row of candles from the centre, a white bearded man was walking on his knees, dressed in a red habit. I watched, spellbound, as the priest slowly and methodically shuffled around the circle, chanting. The nine circles of suffering was Dante Alighieri's depiction of Hell.

Finally, the priest stood up and headed towards me.

Judging by the way his eyes were sunk deeply into their sockets, he looked as though he had not slept for at least a decade. His long white beard was unkempt and his teeth yellow, but his smile was warm. I felt instantly I had come to the right place.

He noticed my gaze wander around the macabre location. He smiled. "This is the Ossuary of Sedlec, a suburb of Kutna Hora," he said. "In the year 1278, the abbot of the adjoining Cistercian monastery was sent to the Holy Land by the King of Bohemia. He returned with a piece of earth removed from Golgotha, the site where Jesus was crucified, and sprinkled it on the grounds adjoining the monastery. This made Sedlec one of the most desired burial grounds in all of Central Europe.

"Years later, the graveyard was dug up and around the year 1870, a local woodcarver, Frantisek Rint, was given the task of adorning the chapel with the bones. The skulls and bones of more than forty thousand people were rearranged to form these chandeliers, furniture and other decorations in this chapel."

I was dumbfounded by the macabre ornamentations, and was awed at the care and detail with which they had been arranged.

Reverend Zachary continued, "Shall we leave?"

I nodded in agreement. He turned and led me out of the church. As we exited the Sedlec Ossuary, Jakub appeared from the shadows. He had been waiting patiently.

After a two-minute walk, we arrived at the Cathedral of the Assumption of Our Lady of Sedlec. Zachary pointed to the large structure adjoining the cathedral. "The Cistercian monastery of Sedlec. In the thirteenth century, the Devil's Bible was held either in this monastery or in the Ossuary we just left."

Once inside the cathedral, Reverend Zachary disappeared into the sacristy.

Jakub spoke, "There is no confessional in the Sedlec Ossuary."

I had almost forgotten my request for a confession, the one I thought would smoke out Jakub's true master. Now though, after seeing the trust Zachary placed in Jakub, I knew my fears were unfounded.

Zachary returned with a purple stole around his neck. I kneeled inside the confessional.

I had not prayed in a church since before my twenty-eighth birthday, when I won the lottery—now more than thirteen years ago. Without thinking, from the depths of my soul, I said, "I am the handmaiden of the Devil. I am here to unbirth what I have done."

PART 4:
THE UNHOLY ALLIANCE

CHAPTER 33
REVEREND ZACHARY'S CALLING

November 2008

In time, Reverend Zachary told me his story. In some ways, I came to believe his calling to God and more particularly his quest to find *The Devil's Prayer* was ordained from above. I have transcribed it for you below.

July 1971

In 1971, a young Spanish priest, Zachary, was documenting libraries in the ancient churches of rural Spain. In the small dust-covered library of the Santa Maria del Morel church, Villafáfila, he came across two parchments.

The first, a letter in Latin, dated 1221, from the apostolic judge, deputy of Pope Honorius III, to the Church of Villafáfila in response to its requests for funds. The second was a Papal Bull, a sealed charter from Pope Honorius III, dated August 1222, dispatching the Papal Legate Arnaud Amalric to urge King Georgi IV of Georgia to join his Crusade.

Excited by his find, Zachary wrote to his supervising Reverend, Monseigneur Ignatius, in the Parish of Zamora, but received no reply. In the weeks that followed, he meticulously scoured every corner of the library in the hope of finding more documents, but his search was in vain. At the end of his stay, the young Zachary decided to 'borrow' the two documents and continued on his way to the neighbouring parishes in the Zamora Archdiocese.

Three months later, having finished his cataloguing task, he returned to Zamora and persisted with the Monseigneur about the strange Latin papal documents. Monseigneur Ignatius replied that he had forwarded his pupil's request to the Vatican. The response from the Vatican was that the first document, their reply to a plea for money from the monastery, was genuine; however, there was no record of the Papal Bull assigning the Papal Legate to Georgia. Ignatius comforted his zealous protégé, and said that impoverished monasteries appealing to the Holy See for help was unfortunately a very common occurrence. It only made one thing certain: that around the year 1221, the church, which lived off the manufacture of salt, was struggling financially.

A determined Zachary embarked on a mission, scouring Spain's oldest library, which was in the neighbouring university city of Salamanca.

Zachary soon found records from the time. He learned that Arnaud Amalric was the seventeenth abbot of Citeaux, the supreme head of the powerful Cistercian order, from 1200 A.D. In 1204, he was endowed with the full powers of the Papal Legate by Pope Innocent III. He soon rose to be the Grand Inquisitor and, for a time, the military leader of the Crusades, and later the chief political advisor to the Papacy.

According to the writings of Caesarius of Heisterbach, during the sacking of Beziers in 1209, when Almaric was asked by a Crusader how to distinguish the Cathars from the

Catholics, he responded, *"Kill them all. For the Lord knoweth them that are His."* And with that he condemned thousands of innocents to their death.

In his letter to Pope Innocent III, he proudly claimed, *"Our men spared no-one, irrespective of rank, sex or age, and put to the sword almost twenty thousand people."*

With his star on the rise, Amalric was appointed Archbishop of Narbonne in March of 1212. He moved south shortly after and was present at the great battle of Las Navas de Tolosa, Spain, on the 16th of July 1212, where the allied forces of Castille, Aragon and Navarre defeated the Moors. If Amalric's own accounts were to be believed, he made a significant contribution to this historic victory.

So powerful was Amalric that, when he fell out with the powerful Crusader King Peter II of Aragon, one of the victors over the Moors of Spain, he threatened the king publicly with excommunication. A year later, in 1213, in the Battle of Muret in which Peter II was slain, Amalric joined Simon de Montfort in his victory march into the valley of the Rhone.

In 1215, at a council convened and presided over by Amalric, all the territories conquered by the Crusaders were conferred on Simon de Montfort. Amalric was quickly becoming known as a kingmaker.

A couple of years later in 1217, when retreating from the siege of Toulouse against Raymond VI, in a fit of rage, he burned more than eighty people under his protection as heretics. A grim reminder that, even as a kingmaker, he prized his reputation as the 'Butcher'.

It was at this juncture that the extraordinary alliance between Amalric and Simon de Montfort started to deteriorate. By early 1218, the once inseparable friendship had degenerated to passionate enmity. On the 25th of June 1218, less than five months later, Simon de Montfort shared the same fate as King Peter II of Aragon. He was killed in the siege of Toulouse, his head smashed by a wayward stone that was hurled by a mangonel operated by the ladies of Toulouse. After this event, many feared Amalric as the 'Cardinal of Death'. All those who crossed him met with a horrible end.

Arnaud Amalric was a mobile morgue; to follow his journey through life, all you had to do was follow the trail of dead bodies he left in his wake. His life story could also be traced from his bloody footprints in the biographies of others. That was until around the year 1222.

While much was documented about Amalric up until this date, he faded into obscurity soon after—the years that corresponded with the issue of Zachary's mysterious papal documents. History justified his absence by noting that, contrary to expectations, he took no part in the ongoing quarrels between the sons of Montfort and Raymond.

Undeterred by the lack of records from Amalric's last years, Zachary took his investigations to the Royal Library of El Escorial in Madrid, but found information neither to validate the document nor dispute it. On the 29th of September 1225, Arnaud Amalric, the Butcher of Beziers, died in Fontfroide, France, the last three years of his life shrouded in mystery. His death failed to gain more than a passing mention in the historical ledgers of the time.

To the young Zachary, it made no sense. Arnaud Amalric, Georgi IV and Pope Honorius III were all alive in 1222. Why would anyone so painstakingly forge a fake parchment just for it to collect dust in a small church in a remote Spanish village?

In desperation, he approached his mentor Monseigneur Ignatius again, presenting his case, asking him permission to visit the libraries of the Vatican to further his investigations. The usually placid Monseigneur, who had listened patiently in the past, took Zachary's diary, with all his findings, and threw it into the fireplace. The Monseigneur was shaking with rage as he watched the diary burn to a cinder.

He reprimanded Zachary, saying he was stirring up a story of a Papal Legate who had allegedly massacred thousands of innocents in the name of the Catholic Church. Zachary remained silent, suspicious that his superior was so well versed in the history of Amalric, who had lived seven hundred and fifty years ago.

Without any further justification, the Monseigneur labelled the Papal Bull as a fake and banned Zachary from any further investigations into the matter. Zachary left in shock; his mentor, who had always encouraged his disciple to question everything in the past, had shut the door in his face.

Back in his small room in the seminary, he sat at his desk and stared at the two papal documents he'd borrowed from the library, contemplating what next to do. He decided to learn the art of the scribe, in order to make a copy for himself.

After three months, with the documents meticulously and painstakingly reproduced in secrecy, Zachary made the trip to return the papal documents to the ancient Church of Villafáfila. The old parish priest, Father Giuseppe, greeted him warmly with his toothless grin, but Zachary could sense a sadness in his heavily wrinkled brow. The old priest showed Zachary to the room that once held the library. It was empty. The walls were black and the ceiling charred.

The library, which had survived for more than eight hundred years, had burned down just weeks after Zachary's visit.

Giuseppe invited Zachary into the quiet sacristy. He explained that he needed someone to tend to his flock here at Villafáfila, for he knew his journey was nearing its end. The pastor saw something of his younger self in Zachary, and asked if he could encourage this strange city slicker to move to this small and remote part of the world. To Giuseppe's surprise, the young Zachary grabbed the opportunity with both hands, but on one condition: the old priest was to place the customary job advertisement in the *Zamora Catholic Bulletin*, and no-one was to know of their meeting here today. Zachary promised he would apply anonymously for the position, leaving it in the hands of God. A couple of months later, in February of 1972, Reverend Zachary got the job and was transferred to the parish of Santa Maria del Morel in Villafáfila.

FEBRUARY 1972

Villafáfila lay about forty kilometres to the north of Zamora. The small, tight-knit community was affable and delighted to welcome the young priest. The ancient Iglesia Santa Maria del Morel was a quaint church; a mix of Gothic, Romanesque and Moorish architecture built around the middle of the twelfth century. The interiors of the church were decorated with sixteenth century Baroque altars and sculptures.

Zachary started searching for information on how a seven hundred and fifty-year-old Papal Bull reached this remote parish. The church records from the early years of the 1170s were all intact, but they were mostly faded and illegible. The papal letter in response to their request for help was noted, but none of the entries related to the Papal Legate Arnaud Amalric or the Papal Bull. In the months that followed, Zachary slowly got into a regular routine at the church, helping out the farmers and the new wildlife industry developing in the area in his spare time.

MARCH 1972

In the last week of March of the first year Zachary lived at the parish, the locals held their traditional Palm Sunday auction. It was here he learned that the one hundred and fifty-year-old auction had started when the neighbouring Moreruela Abbey had been closed down in 1820.

As a result of the War of Independence and the Confiscation, the Cistercian monks, who had inhabited the monastery since the year 1170, were evicted. The long-standing feud over the rights to the neighbouring salt mines and pastoral lands between the Monasterio de Santa Maria de Moreruela and the Iglesia Santa Maria del Morel finally came to an end when the parish of Villafáfila granted a home to the last remaining monks.

That year, on Palm Sunday, the Cistercian monks held an auction of the goods from the closed-down monastery, transferring some of the altars and images to the church. Although the monks returned to their monastery in 1823, they were evicted again in 1835 and the Moreruela Abbey fell to ruins. It was believed that many of the monks left assets of the abbey to the families who housed them in their last years in their wills.

In 1841, the last Prior of Moreruela, Father Manuel Lebo, died in the Iglesia Santa Maria del Morel, and with his death the abbey formally went into extinction.

Zachary finally had a clue as to how the Papal Bull may have made its way to the library of this obscure church. Once the busy *Semana Santa* celebrations were over, he got on his motorbike and made his way to the ruins of the Monasterio de Santa Maria de Moreruela, fifteen kilometres to the west of Villafáfila.

The ruins were impressive, but completely run down. The monastery had been completely stripped of any decoration over the last one and a half centuries. In time, even the stone had been stolen for use in construction in neighbouring towns. At the head of the church, carved into the wall, sat an inscription: 'ERA:MCC.' *The year 1200*— the year Arnaud Amalric had taken over as the supreme head of the Cistercian Order.

In the many weeks that followed, Zachary spent much of his time studying the history of this ancient and once powerful abbey. He was now convinced that Arnaud Amalric must have spent his last couple of years here, in an abbey that he had probably funded himself.

However, that was 1225, seven hundred and fifty years ago. Zachary thought it unlikely he would find any hints

after such a long time. The walls remained silent and there were no secrets to be uncovered. There was, however, one strange carving hidden away on one wall. It appeared to be a carving of an Alquerque, the old Moorish board game. The carving was even more unusual as it had twenty-eight squares instead of the usual sixteen. This alquerque had four rows of five squares and above the centre top square was a box forming the twenty-first square. Beneath these twenty-one squares was a row of seven smaller squares making it a total of 28 squares. All except one were etched with a diagonal line. The solitary square without the diagonal was located in the top row, second from the right hand corner and etched with a maker's mark. This mark was dissimilar to any other stone mason's marks found throughout the abbey.

It was a puzzle that would remain unsolved for the next five years.

December 1977

In 1977, the old parish priest, Father Giuseppe died. In preparation for the funeral mass, Zachary decided to clean Giuseppe's church from top to bottom. It was the only way he knew to deal with the grief of losing the closest friend he had made in the five years he'd been in this little rural village.

On the night before the mass, Zachary held a candlelight vigil and placed a candle in every crevice of this ancient church, lighting every level of the altar.

After he placed the last candle, Zachary looked down the centre aisle towards the altar where he had placed a portrait of Father Giuseppe on top of his coffin. From this position further back, he noticed something strange.

The altar's design had the twenty-one boxes of the alquerque with the seven smaller boxes below—exactly the same as what he had seen at Moreruela. The light from the candles showed the diagonal lines of the strange alquerque from a fold in the wall behind each square shelf, except for one. And there, in the one box without the diagonal, atop the altar, the candles lit the mason's mark on the wall behind.

Zachary fetched an old wooden ladder and climbed up to the top of the altar. With a torch, he peered at a small statue of Santiago, or Saint James, riding a horse, trampling a Moor. Other than the ancient statue of Santiago riding a horse, the solitary top shelf was empty. Zachary tried to lift the statue from its base, but found it was attached firmly and would not move. Looking around the shelf, he noticed the same mason's mark etched in the back of the wall. It was in the shape of the letter 'A'. He traced the mason's mark with his finger and found the two curved, ornate ends of the mark were slightly raised. He pressed them and heard a click.

He tried to lift the statue again and found it now came up easily, revealing a thin, vertical plate from the base of the statue that locked into a slot at the base of the shelf.

But the statue revealed nothing; the shelf was still empty. Disappointed, Zachary climbed down the ladder and placed the statue gently on the altar. His heart had been racing when he recognised that the carving at the Abbey represented the church altar, but it was another dead end.

He stared at the statue of Santiago under the light of his torch. There seemed to be nothing attached or hidden in it. The statue and its base were carved of stone and had been painted over. It was definitely all one piece. The vertical metal slot was sheathed into the stone. He tried to pull it out, but it was locked in solid.

He noticed the gold brooch, holding the red cape of Saint James, was not made of stone, as it glinted in the torchlight.

He pressed it, but nothing happened. He then tried to turn it and it twisted easily, releasing the iron plate from the bottom. Carefully, he removed the plate, discovering a cylindrical pin engraved with strange notches attached to the topside.

His heart pumping even harder than before, and with his hands sweating slightly, Zachary took the strange metal piece and climbed up the ladder again. He reinserted it into its sheath in the altar, this time with the cylindrical metal pin reversed, slotting it into the base of the shelf. The ceiling of the shelf dropped about eight inches, revealing a large book. Now trembling with anticipation, he extracted the book from its secret compartment. Still perched on the ladder, he opened it and all the candles in the church simultaneously snuffed out.

CHAPTER 34

AMALRIC'S ALMANAC

Clutching the book tightly, Zachary raced back to his quarters. Once inside, he turned on the lights and locked the windows and doors. He placed the book on his desk and stared at it for a while before opening it. He began to read, discovering a chronicle of the last few years of Arnaud Amalric's life.

Sometime around the year 1221, much of Europe was abuzz with rumours that the 'Christian King of the East' had been moving west to attack the Muslims in the Holy Land, under the command of the legendary King David or the mythical Prester John. Unknown to people at the time, this was no host of a Christian King of the East. In fact, the great Mongol hordes of Genghis Khan, under the command of his two generals Subutai and Jebe Noyan, were heading towards Europe.

In 1222, Pope Honorius III sent the Papal Legate Arnaud Amalric to Georgia with a mission to convince King Georgi IV to commit more firmly to the Fifth Crusade. The Georgian army was considered one of the most sophisticated in Europe at the time. With the Mongols knocking on their door, King Georgi IV took seventy thousand troops to the banks of the Kura River to face the combined forces of two *tumen*, or twenty thousand Mongols, led by Subutai and Jebe. Arnaud Amalric accompanied the Georgian troops as an observer.

The hidden city of Vardzia was built into the mountains along the banks of the Kura River. The city consisted entirely of caves chiselled into the cliff side. Carved around the year 1180 A.D., these caves stretched along the cliff for about five hundred metres and had up to nineteen tiers. Vardzia initially had around six thousand apartments, a church, a throne room, a complex irrigation system watering terraced farmlands, six chapels, a hearth for iron making, fortifications and was effectively hidden from the outside world. The only access to the complex was through well-hidden tunnels near the Kura River.

Zachary read that Amalric had stood at the cliff face to watch the assured demolition of the outnumbered Mongolian army. Indeed, the Georgian forces so heavily outnumbered the Mongols, the battle was expected to be a show of force demonstrating the might of the Georgian war machine.

Below, on the river plains of the Kura, the two armies collided. It became clear immediately that the Mongols had far superior weapons and armour. Arrows that could pierce steel, bows that horse riders could fire at full pace (even backwards), gunpowder, catapults, and the dark alchemical substance of tar and pitch. The Georgian army was routed and Georgi IV was seriously wounded during battle. He took flight, and Arnaud Amalric left with him through the secret entrance near the Kura River to the hidden city of Vardzia, following secret passages all the way to the royal palaces at Tbilisi.

These were not Crusaders from the east coming to rescue the Holy Land. The Mongols had slaughtered all in their wake, Muslim and Christian alike. They had bribed enemy armies to leave their rulers, only to hunt them down, slaughter the deserters and reclaim their gold. The Mongols were merchants of death.

During the Mongol campaign against the mighty Shah of the Khwarazmian, even soldiers who had surrendered at Samarkand were executed. At the wealthy city of Urgench, each of the fifty thousand Mongol soldiers was given a task to hunt down and execute twenty-four citizens. According to legend, over a million people were massacred over this edict.

Arnaud Amalric knew that his deeds at Beziers were just a faint shadow in comparison to what the Mongols had done. Now he had seen with his own eyes the coming holocaust, more devastating than any that had preceded it. It was only a matter of time before they would all be slaughtered. And, when the Mongols had finished with them, they would ravage Europe like a horde of locusts.

Amalric had seen the Devil's Horsemen in action at the battle of Kura River.

On reaching the fortified walls of Tbilisi, Amalric decided to go back and meet with the leader of the Mongol forces. As the representative of the Holy See, he first met with the Nestor Christians, who were part of the Mongol horde. Then, in December 1222, he was granted an audience with the two generals, Jebe Noyan and Subutai.

On behalf of Pope Honorius III, he spoke of the Crusades and his journey to Georgia to muster up the support of the good King Georgi IV. If the Catholic nation of Georgia were to fall by Mongol swords, the Crusaders would descend on the Horde in full, merciless force. It was a huge bluff. In his heart, Amalric knew the Crusade depended heavily on the union of the Georgian army with that of Emperor Frederick II of Germany. The German Emperor was only paying lip service to appease the Pope to avoid excommunication and the Mongol forces had effortlessly decimated the powerful Georgian army.

However, unknown to Amalric, the Mongol forces were purely on a reconnaissance mission in search of a specific prize. They would need to call on the Great Khan to send reinforcements.

Jebe was certain that if anyone would know the location of the prize they were seeking, it would be this man, who had killed so many in the name of God. The Mongols requested a private audience with King Georgi, knowing that Amalric would attend on behalf of the Pope.

However, the brave King Georgi was still wounded from the battle. To hide the King's condition and to limit the audience to a select few, the cunning Papal Legate offered to organise the meeting, but only if it could be held at the Katskhi Pillar.

This pillar lay deep inside Georgia, two hundred kilometres west of Tbilisi. It was an impregnable limestone monolith rising forty metres straight into the sky.

The sheer cliff faces of the Katskhi Pillar were almost impossible to climb, except by the most skilled of mountaineers, yet perched on its top was a mysterious monastery, which defied explanation as to how it came to be.

Amalric's reason for choosing the Katskhi Pillar was that it was a location that could only be entered by four men at a time, apart from the monks who resided there.

Away from the Mongol army who lay in wait outside Tbilisi, the four men: Jebe, King Georgi, Amalric and Hotula Khan—a Mongol interpreter and bodyguard—were hauled up by rope by the monks who lived at the top. A small Mongol troop and King Georgi's personal bodyguards waited at the base of the Pillar.

Once settled in a meeting chamber, Jebe laid out the terms. "Hand over *The Devil's Prayer*. We will turn around and go home."

King Georgi was at a loss, ignorant of what the Mongol was referring to.

However, Jebe was familiar with the twelve pages at the back of the mythical Devil's Bible—*The Devil's Prayer*. He insisted that the Papal Legate, Amalric, must certainly know the location of the Devil's Bible, the largest and most ornate manuscript in existence.

Arnaud Amalric had searched the libraries of the Cathars and the Waldensians, but there was no sign of the elusive book. Burning with frustration and fury, Amalric torched the libraries, destroying them entirely. He conveyed his honest ignorance of its location. It was Jebe's next statement that made Amalric recoil in surprise.

"The Pope is writing a Grimoire, a thesis on the occult, presumably using the Codex for reference. It must be somewhere in the Vatican Libraries."

The fascination of Pope Honorius III with the Devil was a closely guarded secret. The Mongol spy network must have penetrated the inner sanctum of the Vatican itself. Amalric wondered if the Dominican monks had gained favour with the Pope by finding and delivering this elusive text.

He immediately saw an opening in which he could finally get a hold of it. Yet, handing over *The Devil's Prayer* to the Mongols would have been the equivalent of handing over a nuclear warhead to terrorists. Amalric refused outright, saying he would never be able to convince the Pope. However, he added, he could possibly arrange for a copy to be made.

Jebe, now believing that Amalric knew where *The Devil's Prayer* was, had no intention of letting him out of his sight. He agreed to wait outside Georgia, giving Amalric six months to get him the original, allowing Amalric to keep the copy. In all that time, Amalric would wear Jebe's own bodyguard and interpreter Hotula like a shadow. The negotiations continued back and forth and finally the parties arrived at an agreement known as the 'Deed of Mistrust'.

The terms of the Deed stated that Arnaud Amalric would have nine months to bring the entirety of the Devil's Bible to Asen's Fortress in Bulgaria. He would be accompanied by Hotula Khan wherever he went.

A truce would exist until the end of September 1223, and continue if Amalric produced the Devil's Bible by that time.

Under the supervision of Jebe and Amalric alone, *The Devil's Prayer* would be extracted from the Devil's Bible at Asen's Fortress.

The Devil's Prayer would be divided into two equal portions, one half of the original to be held by the papal library and the other half to be held by the Mongols.

A contingent of six scribes, three from the Mongol side and three from the Papacy, would copy the original half to be held by the other side. The location of transcription would be the Bachkovo monastery near Asen's Fortress.

The Mongols would take a complete version of *The Devil's Prayer*, half in original and half as a copy; and Amalric would take the other half in original and the remaining half as a copy, for the papal library.

Should all the above be honoured, the Mongols would leave Europe, never to return.

The Deed of Mistrust was signed by Jebe and Amalric with Georgi IV and Hotula Khan as witnesses.

Shortly after, while arranging the marriage of his sister to the Shah of Shirvan in Bagavan, King Georgi IV succumbed to his previous wounds and died. History recorded that in 1223, the victorious Mongols at the doorsteps of Tbilisi, did not enter the city and deferred their plans regarding Georgia.

Arnaud Amalric's mission to retrieve the Devil's Bible ran into a dead end. Pope Honorius III waved Amalric away and said the Devil's Bible was just a myth. The Pope was not convinced that a band of barbaric men from the east could ever hope to overcome the combined forces of his Crusade. Amalric was not sure whether the Pope was playing politics and intentionally keeping him in the dark, or whether he was just naïve. Amalric's star had long been on a steady decline from his heady days as a close associate of Pope Innocent III.

Nevertheless, he had seen with his own eyes the wake of destruction the Mongols had left behind them. He had no doubt of the havoc they would wreak if he did not deliver. With his reputation as the Butcher of Beziers, and accompanied now by the foreigner Hotula Khan wherever he went, he soon found most doors shutting in his face.

Amalric resorted to the oldest investigative practice in the world. He followed the money trail. If the Devil's Bible was indeed as magnificent and large as it was noted to be, and even if the Bible had been completed in one night, it would have cost a lot of money. Amalric trawled through the account books of the large monasteries. Finding nothing, he then searched through the ledgers of the smaller monasteries. After weeks of diving through dusty old tomes and ledgers, Amalric finally uncovered it. A secluded Benedictine monastery in Podlažice—in today's Czech Republic—had racked up an enormous debt, so much so that they had written to the Pope himself asking for help.

With time running out, on the 2nd of August 1223, Amalric and Hotula Khan knocked on the doors of the impoverished Podlažice monastery.

An unannounced visit from the Papal Legate was indeed a grave shock to the Podlažice abbot. The Butcher of Beziers offered him a clear ultimatum: with his guard waiting outside, Amalric would search the monastery for the Devil's Bible. If he found it, all the monks would be burned as heretics and the monastery destroyed. The other option he offered was to pack the Devil's Bible in a sealed box to be carried by four monks, who would join Amalric's caravan on its journey to Asen's Fortress, where it would be opened and checked.

The abbot hesitated and in that instant, Amalric knew he had found what he was looking for. Fearing the book may be destroyed, Amalric assured the abbot that the monks would not be harmed. The abbot caved in and called a monk to pack the Devil's Bible in a lockable chest and to take three of his peers with him to Asen's Fortress.

On the 29th of August 1223, Arnaud Amalric's caravan reached the base of Asen's Fortress.

Amalric went alone to the upper storey of the Church of the Holy Mother of God and invited the four monks in, where they proudly displayed the Devil's Bible. One of the monks was wrapped almost entirely in dirty bandages. Amalric assumed he was a leper.

Amalric removed a bag and laid one thousand crowns on the church altar, offering to pay off the debt of the monastery in exchange for the Bible. The monks feared the Devil more than they feared death. The Devil's Bible was not for sale and if the Butcher of Beziers chose to kill the monks and steal the Bible, he could do so at his own peril. The monks would defend it with their lives.

Jebe was standing in the aisle, watching the drama unfold. Amalric asked if he could study their prized possession in private. The monks agreed and left the book with Amalric and went into the next room. He quickly flicked through the Bible, then took out his bejewelled knife and removed the last twelve pages in the presence of Jebe Noyan. Jebe took six pages and Amalric carefully tucked the other six inside his cardinal's robes. He shut the Bible.

Amalric told the monks that, instead of selling him the Bible, perhaps the Benedictine order could borrow one thousand crowns in order to pay off their debts, the Devil's Bible to be held as collateral. The monks, knowing this to be the best opportunity they would ever have to pay off their debts, reluctantly agreed. The Bible was put back into its locked chest. Amalric kept the key and allowed the monks to carry the chest, containing their beloved script, to the Cistercian monastery in Sedlec, close to their own monastery in Podlažice. There it would be locked away as security until the Benedictines paid their debt to Amalric in full.

A group of sixteen men, including Jebe and Amalric, descended the steep slopes of Asen's Fortress to the nearby Bachkovo monastery. The hand-picked contingent included six scribes, three from Amalric and three from Jebe. The scribes were housed in six separate rooms and were given two pages each to copy.

The papal scribes' rooms were closely monitored by two Mongol guards. These corridor guards were further held hostage by two of Amalric's guards, who stood sentry by the main entry door. A similar arrangement was organised for the Mongol scribes, with two of Amalric's guards in the corridor and Jebe's guards protecting the entrance.

The only contact the scribes could have with the outside world, be it a request for food or supplies such as parchment and ink, would be through these sentries.

When the task of scribing *The Devil's Prayer* was complete, the originals and copies of *The Devil's Prayer* were collected by the guards and delivered to their leaders, Amalric and Jebe. Here, an exchange of copies occurred, so each person had twelve pages, with six of the original and six of the copy.

Under the orders of Amalric and Jebe, the corridor guards killed each of the scribes they held hostage. The gatekeepers then killed the inner guards and, when that was done, the gatekeepers themselves were executed, so nobody would know what had transpired in the makeshift scriptorium.

Amalric had secretly dispatched two guards to follow the four monks carrying the remainder of the Devil's Bible back to the Sedlec monastery, where it would remain under lock and key. When the two guards failed to report back, Amalric went to Sedlec, where he discovered that the Devil's Bible had arrived safely.

Amalric then went to the Podlažice monastery to enquire if the monks knew anything about the fate of his guards. He learned that only three of the monks had returned to the monastery.

The monks at Podlažice, who had delivered the Devil's Bible to Sedlec, said that the missing monk, who had covered his hands and face throughout the long trip, had at the onset confessed to having leprosy. Amalric remembered this particular monk well. He had wondered how the other monks had permitted a leper to continue to reside within their monastery.

This monk was Herman the Recluse.

Herman warned his companions that soldiers of the Papal Legate would track them down and kill them, recovering both the Devil's Bible and the thousand crowns they carried. He convinced the monks that it would be safer if they should return to Sedlec by first going south to Perperikon, and then taking the route back via Varna. That first night in Perperikon, Herman disappeared into the darkness. Just as the other three were about to set out to look for their brother, he returned with blood and dirt on his hands, face and tunic. Herman had discovered two soldiers who were stalking them and had killed and buried them to protect the Devil's Bible.

Herman urged the monks to carry on their journey without him. He would follow at a distance to see if anyone else was tracking them. The monks gladly agreed, as it meant they were no longer required to travel with a leper, a man they were afraid to oust from their group due to his known close alliance with the Devil himself. They never saw Herman again.

Upon hearing the monks recall this, Amalric knew he had been duped. On the day before the copying of *The Devil's Prayer* had started, the entire ink stock of the Bachkovo monastery had mysteriously run dry. A day later, out of the blue, a stranger appeared at the doors of the monastery with ink for sale.

There was only one person who knew beyond all doubt what the Legate of the Pope and the General of the Devil's Horsemen could possibly want from the Devil's Bible. That one person was Herman the Recluse, who had traded his soul for the book.

Now, over two months since the day he 'relieved' the Benedictine monks of *The Devil's Prayer*, Arnaud Amalric started his journey to track down Herman.

The ancient Thracian city of Perperikon was located just eighty kilometres southeast of Asen's Fortress. According to legend, this was the location of the famous Greek temple of Dionysius. Being the spot where Herman was last seen, Amalric began his search there. He thought tracking the reclusive monk was going to be difficult, but upon reaching Perperikon, Herman was waiting for him.

Herman warned Amalric that *The Devil's Prayer* had to remain sealed; it was written for the Chosen One. It was the guide for the child of darkness, containing a map of the evil phylactery and incantations to polarize the peoples of earth with mistrust and hatred, herding them to the Devil's bosom.

The Devil's Prayer was for the privilege of the damned—those who had wagered or done a deal with the Angel of Darkness himself. They were the only ones who could read and learn its contents. Anyone outside the damned who chose to chant or study *The Devil's Prayer* risked unleashing the worst plagues, pestilence and natural disasters, all of unprecedented frequency and magnitude, on the world.

Herman had chosen the path of the damned, for God had abandoned him. God's own agents, the pious Benedictine monks, had condemned him to a horrible slow death. Herman had chosen to take the secrets of *The Devil's Prayer* to his grave with him. Now, he feared even death would be denied him.

Herman warned Amalric that he was not just playing with fire; he was rousing the wrath of Hell itself.

Amalric paid no heed. He had no interest in the mad ranting of the fanatical monk. He killed Herman and hammered an iron rod through the monk's still heart, fixing him permanently to the ground in a shallow grave. To finish the ritual, Amalric sawed off Herman's left leg and placed it beside his head, giving him the proper burial for a vampire of the night, ensuring he would never wake from the dead.

Herman had left a legacy. The ink he'd sold to the Bachkovo monastery was an alchemist's concoction, laced with acid, mercury, arsenic and cyanide. Slowly, over time, it worked its way into the parchments of the copy texts, the toxin dissolving the pages into miniscule fragments, leaving a microscopic poisonous dust in the sweat of the reader's palm.

As Amalric tried to learn the secret of the six crumbling pages before they disappeared forever, he ingested the poison of *The Devil's Prayer* through his sweat and through the pores of his skin. In only two months, the once mighty Cistercian abbot was hiding in the shadows. He retreated far from the vicious whispers of Rome and Narbonne to the remote Cistercian monastery of Moreruela, near Zamora, Spain, which he had built. The poison had turned his skin scaly and his nose mottled. Later, it started to peel and fall off, like the decaying papyrus. His eyes grew dim and his nails and hair fell out. In two years, the copied parchment turned to dust, until all that remained were the original pages.

On the last page of his diary, Amalric left his final warning from the little he had gleaned from the disintegrating pages. The progeny of the Devil could only be stopped by one of the damned, a person who had made a pact with the Devil and only before the child turned nine. After that, any transgressor against the Devil's child would believe they were harming the Devil's spawn only to find they had been tricked into inflicting the same harm on an innocent undeserving bystander.

On the 29th of September 1225, Arnaud Amalric, the Butcher of Beziers, died in Fontfroide, France. On the same day, Jebe Noyan, the General of the Devil's Horsemen, died in Samarkand, Uzbekistan.

CHAPTER 35
DENISE'S LEGACY

NOVEMBER 2008

It was a chilling reminder that the Devil had not disclosed Jess' identity to me until after she had turned eleven. In my case, the Devil had given me a similar warning as Amalric and had nominated the innocent bystander: if I attempted to harm Jess, I would find that the Devil's minions would harm the person I loved the most—namely you.

It was said that were *The Devil's Prayer* to be read by anyone not damned, it would unleash on the world plague, pestilence and destructive weather. The plagues that followed in the annals of time, including the infamous Black Death of the mid-fourteenth century, were all believed to have originated from the Far East.

At the end of November 2008, I was sent to the Santa Teresa Convent in Moreruela. Sewn into the inside back cover of Arnaud Amalric's almanac was a key. It was the key Reverend Zachary gifted to me. The same key I sent to you.

The key opened a repository that had been sealed since 1225 in the Vault of Confessions. When I opened the vault in January of 2009, I found it contained a map detailing the secret passage from the abbot's residence in the Santa Maria Moreruela Abbey to a tunnel under the river Esla, which leads to the underground scriptorium of the red monks in the original Santiago Abbey.

Enclosed in the sealed section of this confession is this map. In the scriptorium there is a statue of Saint Peter; the key he holds in his hands can be removed. On the far wall is a large painting of Arnaud Amalric giving the Benedictine monks the thousand crowns and the Devil's Bible being placed in an ornate chest. The key fits into the keyhole in the painted casket and opens the door to the Vault of the Damned behind it.

The Vault of the Damned contains the remaining six pages of *The Devil's Prayer* held by Arnaud Amalric.

Next to the river Esla, the few caves of the original monastery were still occupied by an ancient sect of red monks—the Amalrican monks. The locals believed the old caves hid a complex labyrinth. They never ventured near any large holes in the ground, believing them to be openings to the netherworld. The most famous local legend was that all tunnels and underground passages in the area led to the bottomless pit they called the Gateway to Hell, over which the chapel of the Santa Teresa Convent was built.

The cloistered Amalricans, who chose to live in complete isolation, had remained almost invisible to even their closest neighbours for nearly eight hundred years. It was only at the *Semana Santa* each year, when hundreds of monks congregated for their annual parade outside the Santa Teresa Convent, that the strength of their numbers was evident. Their distinctive banner, *Novit enim Dominus qui sunt eius*—The Lord knoweth his own—was a memory of their founding father, Arnaud Amalric, and their red cassocks signified the rivers of blood he spilled.

While the red-clothed Amalricans attended the *Semana Santa* each year, I would make my way into their lair, to the scriptorium, and copy the pages of *The Devil's Prayer*. This was the only time safe enough to venture there.

Each year on Good Friday, I would meet Father Jakub in the confessional at midnight and deliver a copy of the scripture I had copied. In exchange, Reverend Zachary and Jakub would send me back a detailed update on your lives.

I set about my task to copy and transcribe the six pages over the years. I maintained a vow of silence with all, including Jakub, for fear that I may leak something about *The Devil's Prayer*, which might inadvertently be repeated by someone who was not one of the damned, who then would unwittingly unleash the miseries locked within. As neither Zachary nor Jakub had made a deal with the Devil in the past, Zachary held my copies of the ancient text in safekeeping but unread, in case something happened to me.

On the Good Friday of 2013, the second last time that I saw Jakub, Zachary sent a large envelope containing a comprehensive translation of the first four pages of *The Devil's Prayer* I had sent him. It had edits on my work and he was convinced that my translation skills were more than adequate.

Attached to it was a confession: The night when the candles went out in the Iglesia Santa Maria del Morel, Zachary stepped out of the church and found the Devil standing in the dust, greeting him. He knew that, in order to stop the Devil's child, he had to glean the secrets held in *The Devil's*

Prayer, which could only be read safely by those who had wagered with Satan. Zachary made a deal with the Prince of Darkness, vowing to deliver *The Devil's Prayer* to the Devil's progeny. He never intended to keep his promise, but he still became one of the damned. Zachary joined the Amalricans to infiltrate their inner sanctum. He soon learned that the monks never opened the Vault of the Damned and guarded it with their lives. Although their founding father Arnaud Amalric did not heed Herman's warning, he passed it on to his followers.

My journey from the time I left Queensland to the point when Zachary double-crossed the Devil was relatively free of jeopardy. Although I believed I was working against the Devil, I was playing right into his hands, extracting *The Devil's Prayer* at the behest of Zachary for his child.

Siobhan, if you have received this Confession, then I have met with the same fate as Reverend Zachary, and the red monks will be waiting for me this Good Friday when I go to retrieve the sixth and last page. At the end of this book is a sealed section that contains a copy of the original and the translation of the first five pages of *The Devil's Prayer*.

In my life, I have learned that on many occasions the most heinous acts in the world, like those of the Papal Legate Amalric, are done in the name of God, and the most honourable acts, like those of Reverend Zachary, committed in the name of the Devil. For the existence of God and the Devil are intertwined: one does not exist without the other.

In his last will and testament, Arnaud Amalric shared the knowledge he gleaned from one of the six pages which crumbled in his hands, the original of which is believed to lie in the long lost tomb of Genghis Khan. Once the child of the Devil reached the age of nine, there was only one person who could stop his child: the person whose soul was out of the Devil's reach, for it was wagered with and paid for in full. This person, although not damned, would need *The Devil's Prayer*, as would the spawn of Satan.

Siobhan, only one person can stop Jess and that is you. Your soul was wagered with the Devil and paid for. And in the process, I was cheated into bearing his child.

I implore you to find the remaining pages of *The Devil's Prayer*, including those taken by Jebe and the Mongols. I have given you everything I have collected to help you in this mission.

Only open it if you choose to take up the task.

MAY 2014

Siobhan shut *The Confession*. She looked out of the window of the plane as it landed in Brisbane. She walked out through the terminal, her mind blank, her face expressionless, and saw Edith waving madly, delighted to see her. Edith yelled out towards the far corner of the airport lounge to Jess, who was in deep conversation with a man.

Jess quickly pecked the man on his cheek, as she affectionately bid him goodbye. Then she turned and ran to Siobhan. As she absentmindedly hugged her sister back, Siobhan's eyes were fixed on the man Jess had been talking to. He turned around and locked eyes with her, holding her stare with black pupils that seemed to stare into her soul. He tipped his fedora to her. It was the man in the photo of her mother and her friends on the night it all started. It was the face that haunted her from her childhood.

It was the face of the Devil.

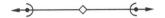

AUTHOR'S NOTE

The Codex Gigas was written somewhere between 1204 and 1220, around the time of the advent of the Mongols, who are reputed to have killed some thirty to fifty million people. From 1346–1353, the world was further ravaged by a plague called the Black Death, which claimed anywhere between seventy-five million to two hundred million people. Over half the world's population was wiped out in just over a century.

History is written by the survivors and victors. It often presents both the bravery of the oppressed and the greed and conquest of tyrants in the same light. Yet, it is in the facts that cannot be explained and fingerprints ignored when there is an inkling that all is not as it seems.

And so it was with the story of Genghis Khan, who lost his father when he was very young and lived much of his early life in captivity. It is an enigma as to how he rose to become one of the greatest generals in history or why his armies came knocking on the doorstep of Europe. Yet, after destroying the Georgian army in glorious victory, the Mongol armies of Jebe never entered Tbilisi or Europe at large. Instead, they turned around in 1224 and headed back home. History records that they were summoned by the Great Khan, who was dying. Yet the sophisticated messenger system of the Mongols would surely know that the Great Khan was still fighting fit. Genghis Khan lived for three more years before he died on the 18th of August 1227.

To date, the grave of the Great Khan is still unknown and the area it is believed to be in is one of the most restricted places on earth, guarded from outsiders by the Black Darkhads since the time of the Khan's death.

If the actions of the Mongols were not as one would have expected, the actions of Pope Honorius III are just as curious. In 1226, living in a time of Inquisition where people were tortured and burned at the stake for possessing any book that contradicted the modern day Bible, the Pope is rumoured to have written and then published a thesis on the occult. *The Grimoire of Pope Honorius* is today considered one of history's most notorious books on black magic.

History does not mention that two of the most prolific killers of the thirteenth century, Arnaud Amalric and Jebe, met at the Katskhi Pillar. Yet, if you look closer, the footprints of their journey can be found embedded in the monuments of their time.

The eighteenth-century Georgian scholar Prince Vakhushti reports in his geographic description of the kingdom of Georgia: *There is a rock within the ravine standing like a pillar, considerably high. There is a small church on the top of the rock, but nobody is able to ascend it; nor know they how to do that.*

Around the year 2007, the Katskhi Pillar was scaled and a small limestone plate, with the *asomtavruli*, Georgian inscriptions prevalent at the time of Queen Tamar and King Georgi IV, was found. They were palaeographically dated to the thirteenth century, revealing the name of a certain 'Georgi', who was responsible for the construction of three hermit cells. The inscription also makes mention of the Pillar of Life, a name the Katskhi Pillar is known by even today. The Deed of Mistrust was signed atop its peak and the Pillar of Life earned its name from the lives it saved when the Mongol war machine turned its back on Europe and went home.

Room II of the Vatican Museum houses the famous Stefaneschi Triptych, originally made to serve as an altarpiece for one of the altars of Old Saint Peter's Basilica in Rome by Giotto di Bondone. The Triptych is painted on both sides for a free standing altar, so that the congregation could see it from the front and the church fathers could see it from the back.

In the back painting, depicting the Crucifixion of Saint Peter (64 A.D.), are the portraits of a Mongol warrior and, riding next to him, a man dressed in the red garb of the Albigensian Crusade. The painting has four horsemen, a clear reference to the Four Horsemen of the Apocalypse mentioned in Chapter VI of the Book of Revelation (by Saint John) in the Bible.

The Albigensian Crusader identifies closely with Arnaud Amalric, the Butcher of Beziers, the Papal Legate and the first Grand Inquisitor of the Papal Inquisition. The Mongol warrior resembles Jebe Noyan, the general of the Devil's Horsemen. The third horseman, on the right of the image, wearing elaborate headgear, is thought to be King Georgi IV of Georgia. The fourth and last horseman is unknown, but could be Hotula Khan, Jebe's Nestorian bodyguard and translator.

The Bachkovo monastery, where the scribes of Jebe and Amalric used the poisoned ink to copy *The Devil's Prayer*, is still in operation in Bulgaria. The only part of the Bachkovo monastery from the thirteenth century standing today is the ossuary. From an architectural viewpoint, its plan looks foreign to local traditions. The doorway is painted with a Georgian cross. Depicted above the entrance is the only known painting of Ezekiel's apocalypse. The ground floor is intended for a crypt and has fourteen unknown burial niches. These were specifically constructed in advance, designed to house fourteen specific corpses under the floor pavement. This unique style is not found in other ossuaries anywhere else in the world. The murals of all these saints have their eyes blinded out, a punishment reserved during that era for conspiracy and treason.

The neighbouring Church of the Holy Mother of God, also built around the twelfth century at Asen's Fortress, is mysteriously the only structure to survive from the time. The entire fortress complex surrounding it was razed to the ground, yet the church remained untouched. It shares a similar architecture with the Bachkovo monastery and the eyes of all the saints in the upper chapel have also been blinded out.

The Basilica of Saint Francis of Assisi contains the Vault of the Doctors of the Church, the men considered influential in the selection of the Bible today. The painting by Giotto di Bondone, who lived around the time when the Devil's Bible was reclaimed by the Benedictines in 1295, shows one of the doctors of the church, Saint Jerome, dressed as a cardinal, a position which did not exist in his time. In his hands he holds a Bible written in Mongolian script.

In another fresco by Giotto at the same Basilica, of the Death and Ascension of Saint Francis, the face of the Devil is hidden in the clouds.

It is widely believed that Dante, the great Renaissance poet and friend of Giotto, was inspired by this depiction of Hell in Giotto's painting of the Last Judgement at the Arena

Chapel, Padua, when Dante wrote *Inferno*, a book describing his journey through Hell.

On the 13th of October 2014, a thirteenth century skeleton of a man believed to be in his late forties was found in Perperikon, Bulgaria. The man had an iron rod hammered through this heart and his left leg had been removed and placed beside his head. This was the first skeleton found given the burial rites reserved for vampires and the Damned.

ABOUT THE AUTHOR

Luke Gracias is an environmental specialist who has been working part time in the film industry since 2006. An avid photographer, Luke traveled through Europe during the development of the film script for *The Devil's Prayer* in 2014 and 2015, documenting a 13th Century conspiracy between the Mongols and the Papal Inquisition on which *The Devil's Prayer* is based.

See the amazing locations from The Devil's Prayer at
www.devilsprayer.com.au

Printed in Great Britain
by Amazon